D1577637

GIN & BITTERS

Gin and Bitters is a stirring novel of London during the years 1690-1720, one of the most calamitous periods in English history.

The gin was introduced through Dutch influence following William of Orange's attaining the monarchy in 1688; the bitters were the development of Money Power, the foundation of the National Debt and the introduction of Dutch methods of finance. How those developments intimately affected the "laborious" classes of London is revealed in this novel relating the fortunes of a small brewer and his family. With them the reader treads the streets of the City newly risen on the ashes of the Great Fire, visits the humble taverns and coffee-houses, shares the fun of St Bartholomew's Fair, gapes at the Crown Jewels in the Tower, watches a bull-baiting at Hockley-in-the-Fields, hurries to the draw of a State Lottery and follows in the wake of criminals trudging to Tyburn.

The predecessor of such fine historical novels as *Ember in the Ashes* and *A Wind through the Heather,* Jane Lane's story of the swift degeneration of cheery citizens to sodden degradation is achieved with Hogarthian vividness, and is as readable now as it was twenty years ago when it was first published and sold 50,000 copies.

By the same Author

FICTION

A WIND THROUGH THE HEATHER
A STATE OF MIND
FAREWELL TO THE WHITE
   COCKADE
THE CROWN FOR A LIE
SOW THE TEMPEST
EMBER IN THE ASHES
CAT AMONG THE PIGEONS
COMMAND PERFORMANCE
QUEEN OF THE CASTLE
CONIES IN THE HAY
THE PHOENIX AND THE LAUREL
THUNDER ON ST PAUL'S DAY
THE LADY OF THE HOUSE
THE SEALED KNOT
DARK CONSPIRACY
FORTRESS IN THE FORTH
PARCEL OF ROGUES
LONDON GOES TO HEAVEN
HIS FIGHT IS OURS
HE STOOPED TO CONQUER
YOU CAN'T RUN AWAY
SIR DEVIL-MAY-CARE
COME TO THE MARCH

PRELUDE TO KINGSHIP
KING'S CRITIC
BE VALIANT STILL
UNDAUNTED

HISTORY

THE REIGN OF KING COVENANT

BIOGRAPHY

PURITAN, RAKE, AND SQUIRE
TITUS OATES
KING JAMES THE LAST

FOR YOUNGER READERS

THE MARCH OF THE PRINCE
THE RETURN OF THE KING
THE TRIAL OF THE KING
THE ESCAPE OF THE PRINCESS
THE ESCAPE OF THE DUKE
THE ESCAPE OF THE QUEEN
THE ESCAPE OF THE PRINCE
THE ESCAPE OF THE KING
DESPERATE BATTLE

THE KINGSBURY EDITION

Jane Lane

GIN & BITTERS

FREDERICK MULLER

First published in Great Britain 1945 by
Andrew Dakers Limited

Reprinted 1945, 1947

Republished in Great Britain 1966 by
Frederick Muller Limited, Fleet Street, London, E.C.4.

Printed and bound by
The Garden City Press Limited
Letchworth, Hertfordshire

One

(i)

A YOUNG gentleman came through St Paul's Churchyard in the City of London on a December morning of the year sixteen hundred and ninety, and turning into Cheapside, stood for some minutes gazing curiously about him.

He had not the look of a countryman, and yet it was plain from his hesitating step and wondering glance that he was a stranger in this part of London. Indeed, ever since he had left Fleet Street behind him he had had the feeling of being in a new world. He knew that this noble and spacious street which stretched before him was the very heart of the mediaeval City, from which arteries branched to the great highway of the Thames upon the south, and to the gates in the City wall, north, east and west. The scars of the Great Fire still showed plainly, here an open space not yet filled with the new flat-fronted brick houses which had risen up on every hand since that mighty conflagration, there a survivor of Tudor London, with scorched timbers and out-of-date dormers rising from the walls. A few moments ago he had passed St Paul's, the piers of its unfinished dome surrounded by a nest of scaffolding, a wooden bridge leading to its great west door, and the busy figures of sawyers and masons perched precariously on planks or toiling along with hods of mortar. The ring of hammers punctuated the bustle of the Churchyard, where the crowds clamoured round the print-shops and mockingly applauded some dancing-master's 'prentices who were trying over the steps of a new minuet in a music-shop. And pricking up over the roofs on either hand he saw the distinctive three-tiered spires of some of those many churches designed during the last twenty years by the great hand of Wren.

Cheapside held his gaze, for it was his goal this morning and, if all went well at the interview for which he was bound, might become his permanent home. It seemed to him that this domain of commerce had an air, a smell, a look all its own. All the foot-passengers seemed to be in a hurry; housewives bustled along with baskets on their arms, servant-maids hurried towards the Little Conduit to fetch water, 'prentices stood at their masters' doors bawling "Buy! Buy! Buy!", porters with their packs pushed their way along with a very purposeful air, and every street-seller was surrounded by a little group of customers. In place of the gentlemen's coaches and the chairs which thronged Fleet Street, there were strings of pack-horses come up from the country, slow-moving processions of drays and wagons, and a few hackneys carrying merchants to 'Change. Everyone here was soberly dressed, many in the distinctive livery of a particular trade; nearly all the men wore their own hair, close-cropped, and on it the City flat-cap; the decent broadcloth of the merchant and the blue frock of the 'prentice predominated, and the women wore the warm and practical hooded cloak. High over the rumble of wheels and the busy footsteps and the strident voices there rang at intervals the bells of the many churches, chiming the quarters of the hour, and a multitude of kites, hovering over the refuse in the kennels, added their squawks to the general din.

The gentleman, crossing the open space where St Michael-le-Quern had stood before the Fire, began to walk down the south side of Cheapside, keeping to the footpath, which was divided from the street by posts. A gallery of signboards swung and creaked above him, a bravely painted picture-show, not the heraldic signs of great families, but the arms of the Livery Companies and the emblems of trade. He stared up, fascinated by this gallery, as he walked. There were lasts and gloves and coffee-cups, there were dolphins and half-moons and daggers and pigeons; there was a Naked Boy and Star, a Peg and Wassail, and, most curious of all, a Dog's Head in the Pot.

He was cogitating upon the meaning of this when somebody cannoned into him and an indignant voice exclaimed:

"Damme, sir, cannot you look where you are a-going?"

The gentleman made haste to apologise, and found himself confronting a tall, well-grown boy who was wearing the blue frock of an apprentice. The boy was hugging a canvas bag which gave forth a suggestive jingle, as of coin. He was handsome in a rather cheap way, but his eyes were set too close together and his look was insolent.

"I really beg your pardon," said the gentleman, lifting a hat which was braided with tarnished metal lace. "I was admiring the signboards, which indeed are very pretty and curious, and did not look where I stepped. But pray tell me, sir, can you direct me to the Cock-on-the-Hoop brewhouse of Mr Nathaniel Vance?"

The close-set eyes glanced sharply at him.

"Mr. Vance is my father. You have business with him?"

"I am appointed to call upon him at eleven of the clock, but I fear that my ignorance of the way has made me late."

Even as he spoke the City bells gave tongue, some deep, some shrill, some near at hand, some at a distance, making such a chorus that the bustle of Cheapside was quite drowned. The apprentice waited for the din to subside, then turned and pointed eastwards.

"Keep upon this side of the street and you will find it. It lies upon the near side of Bucklersbury."

"Bucklersbury?" repeated the gentleman vaguely.

"H'm," said the 'prentice with a sniff, "a foreigner, I take it." He sighed. "Go straight down Chepe, past Friday Street, Bread Street, Bow Lane and Queen Street; a little beyond the last-named you will come to Bird-in-Hand Court; two taverns, Le Bere Tombeth and the Lion, stand one on either side of it. My father's dwelling-house and his brewhouse occupy the south side of this court."

"I am mighty obliged to you, sir," said the gentleman, bowing.

Young Master Vance returned the salutation stiffly, his gaze wandering over the other's shabby black suit and walking-sword.

"You must excuse me now," said the 'prentice grandly, "for I am in haste. I am come from 'Change, where I have transacted some business for my master, Mr Maynard of the Angel, and must not stay."

"The Angel? That would be a tavern, I suppose?" murmured the gentleman, his eyes wandering over the creaking gallery above him.

"A tavern! " exclaimed the other, for some obscure reason very much affronted. "Mr Maynard is a topping goldsmith. Did you not know that this"—he made a large gesture towards the houses near him—"is Goldsmiths' Row?"

The gentleman humbly confessed his ignorance, bowed again, and walked on. He felt unreasonably depressed as a result of the recent encounter. The errand which had brought him into the City today was indeed a strange one and not very congenial, but it was necessary and he had schooled himself to face it with resolution. He had even pretended that his endeavour to hire himself as clerk to a City brewer was an amusing adventure, and in any case he was convinced that it would provide the right environment for his real work. But his encounter with Master Vance had made him as nervous as a boy going to his first school, and had served to bring home to him how utterly out of his own element he was in this community which circled round the Guildhall and the Exchange, and whose sole aim and business in life was trade. A "foreigner", Master Vance had dubbed him, and to the City all those born outside her sacred liberties were foreigners. Would the City ever accept him sufficiently to listen to what he had to say to her? And he, would he ever learn her language, her prejudices, her conventions, and her etiquette? He had lived on the fringe of the City for a year or two, in the stews and rookeries around Fleet Street, and before that he had lived for some time at Court; but as he walked up Cheapside on this December morning he knew that he was as ignorant of the real London as on that day when he had come riding up to Whitehall from his native Kent.

(ii)

He had passed the red lattices of many an ale-house before
he came to those which screened the customers of the tavern
curiously named Le Bere Tombeth. Bird-in-Hand Court lay in
cold shadow, hemmed in on all sides by the smoke-blackened
brick of tall houses; as he plunged into it the rumble of iron
wheels was deadened, and he heard instead the harsh rattle of
the chain of the well which stood in the centre. That was the
first sound to greet him, an ugly sound, ominously reminiscent
of the period he had spent in Newgate prison; but when it
ceased its place was taken by something very different: a
woman's voice singing in the house which stood upon the
southern side.

Late though he was for his appointment, he paused to
listen, curiously intent. Through the silence of the court the
words came out distinctly:

"All sorts of men when they do meet
   both trade and occupation,
With courtesy each other greet,
   and kind humiliation.
A good coal fire is their desire,
   whereby to sit and parley ;
They'll drink their ale and tell a tale
   and go home in the morning early."

A fitting song for a member of a brewer's household, reflected
the gentleman, and yet it seemed to him oddly incongruous,
for the voice which sang was frail and musical. He knew instinctively that the song accompanied some household task and
that the singer did not think upon the words she sang. With his
mind's eye he saw a pair of sensitive lips trilling like a bird and
dainty white hands busy with sewing. Then he called himself
a fool, and stepped briskly forward in the direction of the brewhouse of Master Nathaniel Vance.

The brewhouse lay behind a high wall, with an arched entry
in the middle. Above this entry stood a gilded cock upon a
hoop, and below the bird there was carved out in plaster a

9

coat-of-arms; the gentleman made out three kilderkins sable hooped silver between six barley sheaves saltre of the same, and the motto: "In God Is All My Trust." He guessed that these must be the arms and motto of the Brewers' Company. He entered through the wicket and his nostrils were immediately assailed by an all-pervading odour of new ale; he stood in a fairly spacious yard, paved with round cobble-stones, and surrounded on all sides by houses and high walls. In one corner of the yard some lads were busy washing out casks. Drawn up in the centre was a large dray, harnessed to a magnificent cart-horse, its brasses shining, its mane and tail neatly plaited with ribbons. A drayman in his red cap was assisting a couple of labourers to hoist mighty barrels from the dray through the open doorway of the brewhouse, from which issued clouds of pungent steam. The gentleman stepped aside as a brisk "By your leave" sounded from behind him, and two porters trotted past, carrying between them a cask slung upon a rope. The singing from the house was drowned in the clatter of the yard, and the gentleman felt diffident again; everyone seemed so busy and at home here and no one took the slightest notice of him. However, he stepped resolutely towards the group which was engaged in cask-washing, and asked for Mr Vance.

One lad immediately stepped forward, a raw-boned, sandy-haired boy of about fifteen, with wooden sabots on his feet and a canvas apron tied about his middle. He said civilly, speaking with a slight Scottish accent:

"The master's in his counting-house, and if you are Master Pennington, he looks for you. Will you please to follow me?"

Master Pennington followed the lad across the yard, noting with pleasure the air of independence and sturdy strength expressed in the broad shoulders and upright carriage of his guide. The boy tapped upon a door above two worn steps, and at a summons from within opened it, and ushered the gentleman through.

"Here's Mr Pennington, master," said he, inclined his head to the visitor, and bustled off to his work again.

The counting-house was a little box of a room with one tiny window beside the door, its panes filled with thin horn in place of glass. The place was dark and cold, but everything was as neat here as in the yard, and was pervaded by the same strong scent of ale. Perched upon a high stool before a desk was a portly little man in his early forties; he was in his shirt-sleeves, which were rolled up high on his muscular arms, and wore a pair of grogram breeches and a long waistcoat with metal-plated buttons. He, like the 'prentices, had clogs upon his feet, and tied round his armpits was a leathern apron, black from long service. His hair was close-cropped above a broad red face, and at the moment he balanced a pair of iron-rimmed spectacles upon his nose. His eyes peered over these at the visitor with a glance which obviously was intended to be searching, but which was, in fact, only rather apprehensive.

"Master Vance?" enquired the gentleman, taking off his hat.

"The same, sir, the same. And you, I take it, are Master Michael Pennington?" The brewer climbed down from his stool, breathing heavily, and waving his visitor towards the only chair, himself leant against the desk. Mr Vance cleared his throat and continued: "Now, Mr Pennington, I understand that you—ahem!—wish to engage yourself to me as my clerk to keep my books, and therefore must you understand that I must needs —ahem!—enquire into your qualifications."

"Sir Noel Tredennis," began Michael, smiling, but the other straightway held up a warning hand.

"Not that name here, sir, *if* you please. We will speak upon such—ahem!—such matters in a more private place. You understand me? All I desire to know here and now is your proficiency in clerkship, d'ye see?"

"Why, I can read and write and keep accounts, sir," said Michael, keeping a serious face.

"But have no knowledge of the mistery of brewing? Nay, I speak foolishly; I understand that your—ahem!—upbringing and circumstances would not have brought you into commerce with such ancient misteries."

"Why, sir, I do know somewhat of that mistery upon a small scale, for my father had his own brewhouse in the country where I was bred, and his butler brewed for our requirements and for those of the tenants."

Mr Vance sniffed, and his former nervousness gave way to an air of patronage.

"Ay, I understand you would be fain to depend upon such poor stuff in the country. But, setting craftsmanship aside for the moment, let me tell you, Master Pennington, that there is no liquor in the whole of England, and I do not except the famous Burton, which brews such good ale as the River Thames. Marry, sir, I say it," went on the brewer, waxing red and fierce, "I would not give a leather farthing token for your Medway ales and your Devon Whites, your Cumberland Morocco, your Yorkshire Stingo nor your Norfolk Nog neither; nay, even though the London liquor be defiled of late by all this stinking smoke of sea-coal, which some brewers (and I could name one, sir, that lives not a stone's throw from my door) burn in their furnaces, I do maintain that ale brewed from liquor taken from the Thames is the best in the world."

"Indeed, sir," said Michael soothingly, "I will admit I never did taste better beer than is served here in London."

He was alarmed to find that, far from being mollified, Mr Vance glared at him as though he had offered the most deadly insult, and that the face of the worthy man grew so alarmingly crimson that Michael feared he was about to suffer a fit.

"Beer, sir?" thundered Vance. "Did you say *beer*? Nay, Mr Pennington, if you do wish to engage yourself to a beer-brewer, you had best betake yourself to my neighbour, Master Bunch, at the sign of the Old Swan in Bucklersbury, for let me tell you, sir, you never will find a drop of that whip-belly vengeance in my brewhouse. Is't possible that you, a man of education, can be so ignorant that you know not the difference betwixt ale and beer?"

Mr Pennington could only murmur a humble confession that he was so ignorant.

"Ale, sir," said the brewer loftily, sticking his thumbs into the top of his apron, "has been the drink of Englishmen ever since there was an England. Beer, on the other hand, is an interloper and an alien; it was fetched over by the Flemings in the fifteenth century to poison men's bellies and rot their guts and seduce their minds. Malt and liquor, sir, properly compounded, has been in times past the drink of princes as of porters; but beer, which is but indifferent ale made more palatable by an infusion of that wicked weed, the hop, is an insult to the gullet of a louse."

"Why, sir," protested Michael, smiling, "you can scarce expect me to rail against hops, seeing that I come from Kent which is called the hop-yard of England."

"The hop, sir," conceded Mr Vance, "has its uses. From the fibres of the stem good rope is made, the hop-bine is excellent, they tell me, for fattening cattle, and the young shoots, eaten like sparrowgrass, serve as a purge. Moreover, the flowers are useful for the concoction of various juleps and balms, or so my wench tells me, and she is a very pretty housewife. Do you put your hops to such uses, Master Pennington, and I will say no word against the weed. But leave good ale alone." Having delivered himself of this advice, the brewer fetched his hand-kerchief from some recess about his person, blew his nose loudly, and continued in a milder tone: "But now, Mr Pennington, since it would seem that you are proficient in the duties of clerkship, let us adjourn to a more private place where we may discuss—ahem!—other matters."

So saying, Mr Vance rolled down his sleeves, took his coat from a nail upon the door, kicked off his sabots and put on a pair of shoes, clapped his flat-cap upon his cropped head, and ushered Michael out of the counting-house. Having taken care to lock the door behind him, he yelled "Alec!" in the direction of the brewhouse, and there came running from it the same lad who had been Michael's guide at his first coming.

"I am going to the Dagger for a whet, Alec," said his master, handing him the key, "so do you take charge of this while I am gone, and if the wardens of the Coopers' Company come hither, as I am expecting them any day now, ask 'em to be so good as to conduct their search in my absence, d'ye see? Ay," said Vance, with a hearty chuckle, "and bid 'em search diligently, for they know how many unmarked casks they may expect to find in my brewhouse."

He nudged Michael, who laughed dutifully (the nature of the jest being entirely lost upon him), and turning his back upon the main entry led the way down the yard to the mouth of a narrow alley which ran off in a southerly direction. Observing the brewer as they went in single file down this passage, Michael felt a warm affection for him rise up in his heart. There was something so perky and comfortable about the little man; he was like a plump London sparrow, drab indeed, but useful and independent. He rather trotted than walked, his short legs in their grey worsted stockings twinkling along beneath the long skirts of his sober coat. Rolls of fat lay neatly one over the other above his neck-cloth. From their brief conversation Michael had gauged something of his character: a craftsman wedded to his "mistery", full of absurd little prejudices, inclined to pomposity, simple enough to feel awkward and to show it in the presence of a "gentleman", but preserving his dignity, full of healthy self-respect, courteous and kindly. And Michael guessed then something he was to learn by experience later, that in all matters which were not connected with his craft, Nathaniel Vance was as simple and as gullible as a boy not out of the petticoats.

They passed the wall of a church anon, and came into a narrow street; this, Mr Vance informed him, was St Pancras Lane, and that was St Pancras Church, in which he and his family had a pew, "for we of Bird-in-Hand Court are of that parish, sir, and I may tell you, Chepe is a confusing place for the stranger, since it lies in many parishes and likewise many wards. On the north side there is the smallest parish in the City, I mean that of All Hallows, Honey Lane, which has but twenty houses in it and maybe less than that number since the Fire, for they are set upon all this widening of streets and making two great houses where a dozen small ones stood before, d'ye see, which is a sign of the times, sir, a sign of the times. They say we are a much more sanitary city than before we were, that the Plague and the black rat are disappeared with the old timber houses, and that large dwellings are more health-ful than small ones; it may be so, I cannot tell, but it sticks in my mind that many great men use it as an excuse for squeezing out their smaller neighbours, and as for sanitation, why, my Tiger catches a dozen of rats every week, some black, some brown, and moreover you are as like to have a chamber-pot emptied on your head by a busy housewife at her window as ever you were before sixteen sixty-six."

The Dagger tavern stood a little back from the lane, with a covered bowling-alley at the side of it and in front a courtyard, wherein were benches for the convenience of customers in the summer-time. Trotting along in front of him, Mr Vance led Michael into the house, where they were met by a tapster with one corner of his apron tucked into his waistband in the manner of his kind; this fellow greeted the brewer as an old acquaintance and asked him where he would please to sit today.

"A private room, Sim, a private room, for I have business to transact with this gentleman, d'ye see? And how relished the Worshipful Grocers my strong-ale, Sim?" continued Mr Vance as they climbed the narrow stair. "I'll warrant it gave 'em such a breakfast as'll make 'em forswear old Bunch's rot-gut for ever."

But when the tapster had ushered them into a little room above-stairs, and had gone to fetch the pottle of ale which Mr Vance had ordered, a strange nervousness seemed to descend upon the brewer; he paced up and down, blew his nose, cleared his throat, scratched his head, and stared hard at an abstract of the Acts of Parliament against Tippling and Swearing which hung upon the wall; lastly, taking out his pick-tooth case, he weighed it in his hand with a frown, as though it were of the first importance that he should discover the weight of that familiar article. When the tapster returned, Vance snatched the pottle and the drinking-cans from him, dismissed him with an air of mystery, and watched his retreat with a suspicious eye; not satisfied, it seemed, he tiptoed up and down the passage, craned left and right from the window before closing it, hastened to bolt the door as though such a precaution could safeguard him from eavesdroppers, and finally, sinking down into a chair with an air of resignation, thus addressed his companion:

"Master Pennington, hearken unto me. I enjoyed during the late—ahem!—I should say, the former King's reign—ahem!— you will understand, sir, that I mean King James II—the patronage of His Majesty's Lieutenant of the Gentlemen Pensioners, Sir Noel Tredennis. Sir Noel, after a banquet at the Guildhall, when he was in attendance upon His Majesty, did chance to—ahem!—to lose his way in the City, and found himself straying in my brewhouse, whereupon he was pleased to partake of a quart or two of my strong-ale, over which we had merry conversation, and so enamoured was he of my brew that he swore never afterwards to taste of claret, nor of sack, nor of any drink save pure malt and liquor. He was a merry gentleman, and often after this he would come to my door and call for my ale, and would sit down with me, for all the world as though he were a cit himself, and then we would quote Chaucer to each other, the Water Poet likewise, good Mr Herrick, and other such poets and learned men, for you must know, sir, that—ahem!—I have some knowledge of these great ones who sung so lustily in praise of English ale. And when the time came for Sir Noel to be—ahem!—gone overseas with his master, I was right sorry to lose his company, and vowed that if ever I could serve him I would do so with a glad heart, for old acquaintance' sake."

He paused, but the other made no comment. For Michael was seeing very vividly with his mind's eye at that moment the cheerful chaos of Sir Noel's lodging at Whitehall, the half-finished inventions, wild and various, the spinet with its litter of music, and Moll, with her hennaed hair and wicked eyes, sitting in the midst of it all, smelling strong of Eau d'Auge.

"Now Sir Noel hath writ to me," continued the brewer, shifting uneasily in his chair, "from overseas, desiring me to find employment—ahem!—I should say rather that he hath recommended to me very warmly a certain young gentleman (yourself, sir), who had place in the Band (for so I believe the company of Gentlemen Pensioners to be called), who enjoyed his particular friendship, and who now desires to live very private in the City, and needs must earn his bread. It hath so happened that my clerk, being last week in a tippling company, got himself impressed as a soldier for this war we are waging 'gainst France, and therefore, lacking someone to keep my books (and I will confess very frankly that I have no head for figures and accounts, especially since these new taxes are laid upon ale), I did send for you, sir, this very morning, in the hope that you might prove yourself worthy—that is to say, proficient—nay, sir," panted the poor man, cutting short the tangle into which his words had wound themselves, "I hoped you might fill the requirements, and that is all about it."

Still Michael said nothing; and Mr Vance, after giving his throat a most thorough clearing, plunged further.

"Mr Pennington, harkee; I am a simple citizen of London, d'ye see, and a man of few words. There be some matters that are hanging matters, and in them I will have no part. But for all that, sir, I have bowels which cannot but be moved by the misfortunes of those I love, as in truth I swear to you I love Sir Noel, and by the misfortunes of their friends." He paused a moment, then added in an undertone: "Mr Pennington, I understand that you are—ahem!—greatly attached to a certain Gentleman now overseas; and I do not mean Sir Noel Tredennis."

"As you say, sir, I am greatly attached to that certain Gentleman. He is my King and my master. Both my duty and my inclination impel me to serve him with my life, if need be."

"Mr Pennington," said the brewer in a low and hurried tone, "I must be plain with you, I really must. Candour is necessary betwixt us on this matter now this once, if we are to be master and man and live neighbourly. I know not what Sir Noel hath told you regarding my sentiments in public affairs, but I must tell you roundly, sir, that I for my part am resolved to live peaceable under the established Government, I mean King William's. I will confess, sir," continued the brewer, and Michael saw that his square hands trembled a little as he twisted them together in his lap, "that my head rather than my heart impels me to this decision. I will confess that I cherish a sincere affection for—ahem!—the Gentleman (not Sir Noel) of whom we spoke just now, that I pity his misfortunes, that I am aware that he was, save for his religion, as good and as honest a king and an Englishman as we have had upon the throne these many centuries. But I do not, sir, and I will not, meddle in politics, nor have part with those who intrigue to fetch him back."

Again the pause drew no response. He continued doggedly:

"I am a man with a family, d'ye see, and likewise am I a master-craftsman, with journeymen and 'prentices in my employ; to them, and to my family, I owe a duty, and as it seemeth to a plain man like me, a duty which must come before all others. I may regret what was done in 1688, because I am a fair-minded man and hate all underhand business and the fetching over of foreigners; but I must needs accept the fact that it was done, and must accept likewise the Government which now rules over us, if my family is to enjoy peace and my craft prosperity. You stare at me and utter not one word, but I can guess what you are thinking. Here is a sordid cit, think you, a cowardly sort of fellow. Well, sir, you are young, bred up in different sort of traditions and, as I believe, unmarried. Moreover, you did serve His—ahem!—that certain Gentleman in his own Household and, in the language of the waterside, you disdain to strike your colours. All honour to you, young gentleman, but do not expect the like of me, who have more to lose and maybe less to gain."

Then Michael smiled at him and said:

"It is true that I, for my part, have only my life to lose now in this cause, for I lost all else at the Revolution—my patrimony, my place at Court, my fortune, even my name. As for what I have to gain, sir, it is the peace of mine own conscience, and that is much; but much though it is, highly though I prize it, I must take the freedom to point out to you that there are gains not so inconsiderable which you forfeit by accepting the established Government. Your spiritual liberty, your independence, the safeguarding of your craft and your family, the protection which only a lawful king can give you; these you may be sure of only by the return of that—certain Gentleman." But as Vance would have spoken he held up a hand and went on rapidly: "But I'll not quibble with you now, sir, nor seek to win you to my side in these great matters. All I desire of you at this present, Master Vance, is that you will be pleased to engage me as your clerk at whatsoever wage you deem fit; no more than that. And I for my part swear that I will serve you faithfully in such employment; if my service prove insufficient, why, you may turn me out, and there will be an end of it."

"Not so fast, sir, prithee not so fast. You are plainly a gentleman of education. Why do you desire to engage yourself as clerk to a City brewer?"

"That I may earn my bread and live very private."

"But wherefore did you not go overseas with your master?"

Michael paused a moment before answering. Then, with a wry smile, he said:

"To answer that, I needs must make known to you my history, and certain matters which, as you say, are hanging matters. It is not necessary, sir, that you learn of these things, for I do assure you that, if you engage me, my clerkship and my private life shall be kept strictly separate."

"Yet am I resolved to hear all this once," said Vance doggedly, "that I may know what manner of man he is whom I think to engage."

"As you please, sir. My real name is Michael Montague. I am five-and-twenty years of age, the second son of Richard Hugh Montague, esquire, of Montague Court in the County of Kent. I was sent up to Court by my father in the year '87, to become a Gentleman Pensioner to King James, Sir Noel Tredennis being at that time Lieutenant of the Band and my father's old friend. I had no desire for such an honour; my wish was to live retired in the country and to pursue certain historical studies, particularly those concerned with the history and nature of Monarchy, and to undertake such writings upon the same as I had talent for. I had not been at Court many months ere Sir Noel, who condescended to give me his friendship and patronage for my father's sake, did disclose to me that there was a plot afoot against His Majesty's Government, whereby it was designed to fetch over the Prince of Orange, that the bribes of that prince had seduced from their loyalty many even of His Majesty's Privy Council, that the pretence was to be the safeguarding of the Protestant religion and the real object the destruction of kingly government, and that it was my bounden duty, considering my principles and my post, to discover all I could concerning this treason and to aid in frustrating it. I did not at first believe what Sir Noel told me concerning the plot; but investigation proved to me that he was in the right of it, and henceforth I did all that in me lay to warn His Majesty and to expose the traitors."

"You warned His Majesty?" came in awed tones from the brewer. "Sure you must have stood mighty familiar with him, sir, so to have gained his private ear."

Michael laughed shortly.

"I was not at all familiar with His Majesty. I was but a humble member of the Band. I burst in upon him most unmannerly; and—he never forgave me that discourtesy. Nay, I wrong him when I say that; he never forgave me for including the name of the Lord Churchill, now the Earl of Marlborough, and others whom he counted his dear friends, in the list of those corrupted by Orange's bribes. Well, sir, I will not weary you with all that followed; for the public events, you know them as well as I, and for my lowly part in them, it failed, and that is all about it. When His Majesty went overseas, I lived for some while retired in London, endeavouring to find a printer willing to undertake the publication of my Treatise on Monarchy, a work upon which I had been engaged for some years."

"Faith, sir," interposed the brewer, "you are then, it would seem, an author?"

"That is what I desired to be in my youth, but I am become since a mere pamphleteer. Well, there came anon the order for the general taking of the Oaths to William of Orange, and I hasted down to Kent to be with my father who, I was well aware, would refuse to take them, which indeed fell out as I thought. He was arrested and imprisoned in Maidstone jail, but ere he could be brought to his trial he died of a jail-fever. Meanwhile, one of the Deputy Lieutenants of Kent, a man who had long coveted our estates, got an order for seizing upon them, and so my patrimony was altogether lost. I returned very privately to London, adopted my mother's maiden name of Pennington, took up my abode in the stews, and lived for a while upon the sale of the few jewels and other articles of value my father had contrived to place in my hands before his arrest."

He shifted in his chair as though old sorrows troubled him. Then he continued more briskly:

"I had had much talk with Sir Noel ere he went overseas, and continued to correspond with him by means of a cipher. He never did cease to read me this lesson: that I should change my style of writing and endeavour to put forth tracts and pamphlets, writ in plain, sober language, which would appeal, said he, to laborious men, for with such, he was well assured, lay the only hope of bringing about a lasting restoration. Accordingly I put by all such high-flown treatises such as I had ever longed to write, and set about the making of such tracts as would appeal to the working people, and I was fortunate enough pretty soon to chance upon a printer who told me he was willing to publish and distribute all the broadsheets I would write. He has been as good as his word, too, and for a full year now my writings, perforce anonymous, have appeared upon the streets. But meantime the little money I had by me was all used up, frugal though my habits were become, and having applied to Sir Noel in this necessity, he bade me take up some trade, and, living quietly in the City under a name not mine own, to pursue my writings when my day's work was done, and thus to earn my bread and to serve my cause at the selfsame time. This is the reason, sir," concluded Michael, "why I am come hither today to crave from you employment as your clerk."

(iii)

There was a considerable pause. Vance had scarce taken his eyes from Michael's face during this recital; his can of ale stood neglected at his side and his mouth hung a little open. Now he passed his tongue over his dry lips, scratched his cropped head meditatively, exhaled a long breath, and murmured:

"Bless me, I never heard a stranger history; 'tis like a stage-play, it is indeed." Then he planted a hand on either of his knees, leaned forward, and said with a certain sternness: "Sithee, Master Pennington, you have been mighty plain with me and I thank you for it, yet are there certain questions I must put to you ere I can come to a decision. These writings of yours, sir; what is their nature? Are they—ahem!—seditious, inciting to revolt, dangerous to His Majesty's person—I mean of course King William's person, ahem!—or to the peace of the realm?"

"Why, sir, if you will please to glance through a specimen of them," said Michael, putting his hand into his coat, "you may judge for yourself."

But Vance shot out of his chair at that, and warded off the proffered paper as though it were infected with the pest.

"Not for the world, sir, not for the world!" He waited until Michael had secreted the dangerous paper in his breast again, then sank back in his chair with a sigh of relief. "But still, sir, I must know——"

"Mr Vance, since you will not see for yourself, you must take my word for it that my writings do not incite to revolt nor to murder nor to any such violence. I am come over to Sir Noel's way of thinking, and am convinced that the only restoration which can be just and permanent must come by way of the free invitation of the people to His Majesty to return to his kingdom. My task is to endeavour to convince the people that such a restoration is necessary to their interest, to show them what they have lost in losing their lawful Sovereign, to warn them of the practical evils they must expect under the kind of government which now rules over us, and to set forth, as well as I am able, the advantages they enjoyed under the ancient Monarchy. Yet such writings are counted treasonable at the present time, and the author of them, if caught, would certainly be punished as a traitor."

"I understand you, sir, I understand you. There's one thing I will take leave to say for you, here and now, upon such short acquaintance: you are an honest young gentleman, and if there is one virtue I prize more highly than the rest, it is plain honesty. Ahem! But harkee, Master Pennington, if you enter my service, will your presence in my counting-house endanger me or mine? Come, sir, give me an answer fair and square."

"Alack, sir," cried Michael, "how can I answer plainly? If it is within my power to prevent injury to you or yours, I will so prevent it, my word on that. But is it within my power? If by some accident I should be discovered as the author of these tracts, there is the chance that, if you and I live neighbourly as master and man, you may be involved in my ruin, innocent though you may be."

"You tell me this," said Vance shrewdly, "when instead you

might tell me that there is no risk at all. You see me for what I am, a plain and simple cit, easily bubbled; yet you will not bilk me with fair words, but will tell me the plain truth, fair and square. Ay, whatever else you are, you are an honest young gentleman, and 'ounds, I do dote upon honesty in a man." Then he shook himself and continued briskly: "But let us enquire a little further, sir, into the great risk you run, since involved in it there seems to be a certain threat to mine own household if I engage you. For example, your printer, can you depend on his discretion? I have heard that printers love above all things to turn informer against their authors in such cases."

"You must take my word for it, sir, that he is the very soul of discretion."

"Well, sir, I will take your word for it. But then, what of your old acquaintance about the Court and the Town?"

"I never did appear in print, sir, while I was at Court. My Treatise on Monarchy was writ, it is true, while I was a Pensioner, and I showed it openly to certain of my friends at Whitehall; in this strange world, sir, the loyalty of today becomes the rebellion of tomorrow, and in those days of which I speak the only treason a man could commit was against King James and his Government. Moreover, such a work could scarce be counted treasonable, even now, being a mere academic study, overloaded with quotations from the Ancients, crammed with obscure references and such-like stuff which, in one's youth, passes for learning. I am sure that these friends (who, by the way, believe I am gone overseas with others of my way of thinking) would never recognise my hand in the plain dull broadsheets which I write now. As for the Town, sir, there is but one therein who knows my secrets, and I can assure you there is nought to be feared from her." But at that pronoun Mr Vance's sympathy vanished, and a look of mingled disgust and alarm took its place.

"'Adsheart, sir, sure you are not so mad as to have entrusted such hanging secrets into the bosom of a female? By St George, I'd as soon trust an Irish milk-walker with my watch."

"I believe there must be some honest Irishmen, sir, as I am well assured there are some discreet women."

"Not upon this side the grave. A secret in a woman's breast

is like a purge in men's bellies; it soon wambles and will come out. Now marry come up, you have quite shaken my former opinion of you." He sprang to his feet and began to pace the room, deeply agitated. Presently he paused beside Michael, and said pleadingly: "Sithee, Mr Pennington, do you assure me that this—ahem!—female of whom you spoke is perchance your lady mother, or at least a kinswoman, or maybe some—ahem! —some virtuous damsel to whom in happier times you were betrothed."

"I never was betrothed, sir," said Michael shortly, "and as for my mother, she died in giving me birth. Yet albeit the woman who shares my secret is no kin of mine, and never will be my wife, nor is even, as the phrase goes, a woman of virtue, I tell you I have entrusted her with my life, and would again, and am so well assured it is safe in her hands that if an angel from heaven came to persuade me to the contrary I would give him the lie in his teeth." Then he glanced up into the anxious face of the man who stood beside him, and added smiling: "She is my friend, sir, and has shared all sorts of fortune with me, and if we may not trust such friends, we may as well cease to trust ourselves."

"I like it not," murmured Vance, shaking his head dolefully. "Yet I like you very well indeed, and I do believe you will live honest by me."

"I will, sir." Michael rose and faced the other squarely. "If you engage me, think of me but as your clerk, devoted to your interests, for so I vow I will be. As for how I employ myself in my leisure hours, you must be no more concerned with it than with the guzzling of a good drayman who, however he may booze of an evening, is stone sober when he comes into your yard next day."

Vance stared at him a moment; then the broad red face broke into a grin.

"I will engage you, marry will I. There is somewhat about you draws forth my trust, and makes me sure that whatever shall befall I never shall have cause to regret this day's transaction. Now come, sir, come, let's drink together, and cement our bargain in good English ale."

Two

(i)

THE City bells were chiming noon when the brewer, having foisted upon Michael a hastily invented "family" (he was to be the son of a notary in Covent Garden, brought up in every luxury, but upon the notary's untimely decease had found his patrimony eaten up in debts and himself forced to earn his bread), paid the reckoning and invited his new clerk home to dine with him. Upon their way back to Bird-in-Hand Court, Mr Vance gave Michael some account of his own household and business. It appeared that he enjoyed the distinction of being a "housekeeper", that is, one who rented or, as in Mr Vance's case, owned his house, inhabited a certain portion of it, and let off the spare rooms as lodgings. It seemed further that Mr Vance still followed the old customs of feeding his 'prentices at his own table and of housing those whose parents lived at a distance.

"In this way, sir," said the brewer, "I keep 'em from frequenting ale-houses, where they would be sure to get into bad company, and from that 'tis but a short step to Newgate and thence to the gallows. But alack, sir, nowadays half the masters hereabouts care not a fig what becomes of their 'prentices once the shutters are up, though the terms of indenture do make them responsible for the lads' welfare both of soul and body, and besides proper clothing and shelter ordain that the master must instruct his 'prentices in the Christian religion and in reading and writing, and contrive such innocent recreation for them as will keep them from discontent. Yet there is many a master-craftsman I could name who gives his lads money to be rid of them when work is done, and thus are young lads driven to the brothel and the gaming-house for their pleasures and join the mob to find them companions."

Mr Vance then went on to tell him that he had several journeymen in his employ, all of whom had served their full time with him as 'prentices, that he had six apprentices at present, besides draymen and labourers; he spoke of the latter contemptuously as of men trained to no particular craft, and forming, it seemed, part of that mysterious section of the City population termed "the mob". Michael learned that Vance both hated and feared the mob, was inclined to attribute to it all variety of mischiefs, and spent a great portion of his time preventing his 'prentices from forming "mobbish" habits.

"I take pains to instruct my lads in the King's English, sir, and I will not have the cant of thieves employed in my brewhouse. It is a small matter, think you, but I tell you, sir, that small things lead to great, and once a lad begins to ape such beastly speech he is half-way to apeing beastly habits."

It transpired that, contrary to the almost universal custom of the City, Mrs Vance did not pursue some trade of her own, though she often gave a hand in the brewhouse; from the little the brewer let fall regarding his wife, and much more from his manner when he spoke of her, Michael gathered that her husband cherished a deep affection for her, and also that she was permanently, but vaguely, unwell. Vance added that he had a daughter "who is a good little wench and does us much service", and then went on to speak of his only son, Nathaniel, whom he described as a "most promising youth, a thought too forward in his notions, maybe, but of an excellent understanding, and apprenticed to a topping goldsmith whose son loves Nat like a brother". Michael mentioned that he himself had encountered this promising youth on his way to the brewhouse that morning, and the mention of the encounter seemed mysteriously to advance him a prodigious way in the brewer's favour.

As Mr Vance and his new clerk came into the brewhouse yard, a bell began to ring in the entrance-arch, and immediately from the brewhouse there debouched a bevy of noisy 'prentices who, upon sight of their master, quieted and bowed to him, a salutation he returned in a very courteous and pleasing manner. The group closed in behind him as he led the way to the door of his dwelling-house, which portal being opened allowed a most savoury smell of roasting meat to greet their nostrils and a suggestive clatter of cans and dishes to increase their appetites. They trooped into the living-room, which was upon the left of the entry, and found therein Mrs Vance, to whom Michael was presented with all due ceremony.

Ann Vance was a handsome woman in her late thirties, but looked older because her face was very lined, whether from pain or from ill temper Michael could not at first decide. In manner she was fussy and irritable, she seldom smiled, and her eyes seemed perpetually on the watch for something or someone to criticise. Those eyes were heavily undershadowed, yet she seemed brisk and active enough and gave no clue to the nature of the malady at which Mr Vance had hinted. She greeted the newcomer somewhat curtly, and looked him up and down; it was plain she had heard from her husband that he was thinking of engaging a "foreigner" as clerk, and that she did not approve. But immediately after the introduction she turned to what was clearly the congenial task of bullying the apprentices, scolding one for coming indoors in his clogs, sending another to go and scrub his hands again, and demanding of a third whether he had mistaken his neckcloth for a halter that he wore it knotted under one ear. It was obvious that Ann Vance had a feud with 'prentices in general, and that while in the brewhouse she might exercise no authority over her husband's lads, she was determined to show them who was mistress in her own domain.

The company stood around the table while Vance murmured grace, then took their seats, the 'prentices below the salt and Michael, as a guest, above it. They were just sat down when there entered by another door a girl in her early teens; she was carrying a great dish of marrow-bones which she placed before the brewer, who smiled at her and said to Michael:

"This is my wench, Maralyn."

The girl, in return to Michael's salutation, bobbed a small curtsy and smiled a small smile; then she was off again to the kitchen, returning in a moment with a pile of plates. Michael

27

observed her frankly; he was sure that hers was the pretty frail voice he had heard singing the rollicking drinking song on his first coming into Bird-in-Hand Court. There was nothing frail about her person; she was sturdy, but with a promise of shapeliness when she matured; the face was childish and yet wise and serious; she wore a snowy "safeguard" over her plain gown and a mob covered her curly hair. She said little; all her movements were deft and unhurried; and, whenever you looked at her, her eyes were smiling. Those were the first impressions made on Michael by Maralyn Vance.

As the meal proceeded (a good, solid, well-cooked meal), Michael observed the room in which he sat. It was scrupulously clean and neat, yet comfortable and had a well-used look. The walls were hung with a cheap bright cotton material called pintado, and the floor was strewn with rushes over the well-scrubbed flagstones. There was a wide open fireplace opposite the door from the entrance-hall, and the high chimney-shelf was bright with pewter candlesticks and snuffers; before the hearth stood that species of fire-dog which had a cup-like top, useful for keeping spiced ale from growing chilled. There was also a most novel sort of toasting-dog, made of wood, gaily painted like a toy; his tail had been contrived into a handle, and from his forehead projected a kind of fork on which bread to be toasted was affixed. By the hearth stood a spinning-wheel, and in one corner was a sixteenth-century clavicytherium, the parent of the spinet, with some music-sheets arranged beside it.

The furniture of the living-room was plain and solid. Michael and the 'prentices sat on plain wooden chairs without arms, but Mrs Vance had one of the Tudor variety, with arms, back and legs shaped like horseshoes, while her husband presided in his own particular enclosed arm-chair, the seat of which, being lifted, disclosed a recess wherein he kept his tobacco-box, his pipes, and the Greybeard-jug from which he always drank, a curiosity which had come over from Holland in the previous century and which was adorned with a likeness of the great square-cut beard affected by Cardinal Bellarmine. There was a little court-cupboard hung up in one corner of the room, and Michael guessed that herein Mrs Vance, or perhaps her daughter, kept the precious spices beloved of every good housewife; but all this furniture centred round the great table, with its bulbous legs and snowy cloth, like an emblem of plentiful plain fare and hospitality.

Having observed the room, Michael turned his attention to the persons in it, and from among the half-dozen apprentices he picked out two who aroused his interest. One was the Scottish lad who had ushered him into the counting-house, and whose name, he had learnt, was Alexander Moray; the other was a thin boy with fanatical eyes, his dress untidy, his black hair ruffled as though he had a habit of combing his fingers through it, his manner something between sullenness and enthusiasm. It was quite obvious, even to the stranger, that this lad, who was addressed as Nick, was deep in love with his master's daughter, and Michael, who knew all about calf-love from painful experience, pitied him profoundly. The burning eyes followed Maralyn's every movement, and if she chanced to address him he flushed from forehead to chin. Whenever this happened, one or other of his fellow 'prentices would nudge his neighbour, and smirk, and whisper behind his hand (with a watchful eye on Mrs Vance); all save Alexander Moray, who continued to eat his food with a stolid, purposeful air, as though eating was a serious business and absorbed his whole attention.

Maralyn herself appeared to notice nothing of this by-play, but, seemingly without effort, stepped into uncomfortable pauses, acted as a kind of respectful umpire between her mother and the apprentices, saw that everyone's plate was kept filled, passed the ale about, and in some mysterious way managed to make everyone feel entirely easy and comfortable.

It was not until Mr Vance was escorting his guest to the door, to bid him farewell that Michael noticed an object which his previous observation of the room had overlooked. It was a little shelf of books. He paused before it in the way of all men who are fascinated by the written word, and ran his eye over the tiny collection; he noted instantly that the volumes, always sold unbound at this date, had been most carefully encased in canvas jackets, and that at the same time they had an air about them of being much used.

"My authors," said Mr Vance proudly, pausing at his elbow. "Dear friends of mine, sir, if I may take the freedom of calling 'em so, and every man-jack of them deep in love with English ale. There's Master Chaucer now; many's the evening I pass with him and his pilgrims. And let me tell you, sir, that not one of those good folk were acquaint with that interloper beer, but as for ale, it was their daily drink, as for instance the two Cambridge students and the miller their host:

> " 'They soupen and they speken of solace,
> And drinken ever strong-ale at the best.
> Abouten midnight wenten they to rest.' "

"Ay, sir," returned Michael, smiling, "but you must confess the miller proved but a troublesome bedfellow, for:

> " 'This miller hath so wisely bibbed ale,
> That as a hors he snorteth in his slepe.' "

Mr Vance stared at his new clerk in delighted astonishment for a moment, then gathered him in his arms and fairly hugged him.

"You are acquaint with Master Chaucer! 'Adsheart, I knew I was right when I engaged you. Oh, Master Pennington, what evenings will we have together; what readings, what quotings, what turn and turn about with recitations! And if we tire of these, I will fetch down my collected ballads in praise of ale, and Maralyn shall play for us, and we will roar 'em out till we drown the sound of the tippling companies at Le Bere Tombeth and the Lion. Master Pennington, your hand; give me your hand, I say, for I do swear I love you like a brother."

(ii)

Upon Mr Vance's suggestion, Michael lodged in the brewer's house, his board being deducted from his wages. He chose a garret that he might be private for his evening's work; it had one small window giving on to the leads and was bitterly cold as well as dark, but he had accustomed himself to work in all kinds of physical discomfort and asked only privacy and quiet.

His duties in the counting-house were simple enough, though the hours were long. Brewing began at four in the morning and there was always a great bustle to get the drays laden, for a law in the City forbade the appearance on the streets of drays and wagons after the hour of eleven, since such vehicles occupied too much of the road for the ordinary traffic to pass. At noon there was dinner, after which the journeymen and 'prentices scrubbed out the mash-tuns, coolers and fermenting-vats, collected the used grains, which were sold to the swine-tenders on the out-skirts of the City, washed and repaired casks, and prepared all things for next day's brewing. Their day finished earlier than most trades', for very few shopkeepers put up their shutters be-fore eight or nine o'clock, whereas Mr Vance and his 'prentices supped at seven and there was no more work after that hour.

After supper, until fatigue altogether overcame him, Michael applied himself to his writing, except on certain evenings when Mr Vance claimed his company in the living-room for songs and readings. Sunday was his own, and after putting about the story that Mr Pennington spent that day with his fictitious family in Covent Garden, the good brewer tactfully refrained from en-quiring how it was really spent, imagining that Mr Pennington employed the Sabbath either in conferring with his printer or indulging in those mysterious recreations proper to one born of the gentry. He would have been surprised could he have known that Michael really did spend his Sundays in the neighbourhood of Covent Garden, and horrified had he guessed that they were passed in the company of a young woman of easy virtue named Moll.

Michael was awakened at an early hour on his first Sunday morning in the City; he rose and went out on to the leads and looked down into Bird-in-Hand Court. Its Sabbath peace was disturbed by a bevy of 'prentices from the head-dresser's shop round the corner, who were knocking on the house doors to de-liver the Sunday wigs of their master's customers, such wigs being kept in the barber's custody during the week. The bells of the neighbouring churches began to ring for the first service of the day, and the pattering feet of some charity-children sounded from Cheapside, where they were being marshalled along by the beadle towards Bow Church. Michael yawned and returned to his bed. There could be no church-going for him: he was a Catholic and it was death to hear or to say Mass.

At ten o'clock he rose and dressed, thinking with pleasure of the day he would spend at the Crown with Moll; as he was passing a small window on his way downstairs he heard voices and footsteps in the court below, and craned out to see what was to do. And there was the brewer leading his household and family to St. Pancras Church, not by the short-cut through the yard, but in solemn procession into Cheapside and so down Queen Street. Michael stayed where he was, watching this spectacle.

Mr Vance was almost unrecognisable. In place of his week-day attire, he wore a hair-camlet coat and vest of a bright mustard-colour, the long skirts concealing his tight-fitting breeches, the ends of which were hidden in the rolls of a pair of snowy stockings. His shoes, which tapered towards the toes but had the ends cut square, were adorned with upper-spur leathers ascending up his shins and twinkling gilt buckles; and his cropped head was covered by one of those monstrous perukes which had now gone out of fashion. Perched upon this monstrosity was a hat cocked upon three sides, a species of headgear known among the vulgar as "Egham, Staines and Windsor", and under one arm he carried a cushion and a prayer-book of huge dimensions. His habitual gait was a trot, but today being the Sabbath he had made it a slow, ceremonious trot, exceedingly ludicrous to behold.

Beside him walked his wife, resplendent in a gown of petunia thread-velvet, the skirt caught back by ribbon bows to expose in front a portion of the petticoat. Her bosom was pushed well up by a tight stomacher which gave her the look of a pouter pigeon; over her shoulders hung an olive plush cape. She wore upon her head the fashionable *commode,* tiers of wired lawn rising bolt-upright from the forehead, and long lappets, like a spaniel's ears, hanging over either shoulder. She too carried a prayer-book, and in the other hand a fringed handkerchief. She kept looking back over her shoulder to reprimand the 'prentices.

Behind their parents walked the son and daughter, Nathaniel

32

dapper in a suit of grey broadcloth, and Maralyn very pretty indeed in the long cloak called a mantua, with a wide hood over her curls; she carried two cushions to assist the comfort of her mother's knees and back in church. Maralyn alone of the whole party looked easy and natural; all the others appeared self-conscious and walked as though their shoes hurt them. The 'prentices brought up the rear, two by two, their hands and faces red from scrubbing, their cropped heads covered by thrum-caps, and their bodies arrayed in cheap fustian coats and breeches; they had a meek, tamed appearance, though in church, sheltered by the high-backed pews, they would munch gingerbread and whisper bawdy stories.

Having watched this crocodile disappear into Cheapside, Michael came downstairs and set out westwards. It was a cold raw morning with some fog about, and he shivered in his shabby suit; despite the knowledge that he was to spend this day with Moll, he could not shake off a certain depression which had nothing to do with the weather. The year was nearly at an end, and looking back upon it he saw how the shadows had deepened over the cause he served.

In July, King James with a totally inadequate and ill-trained army had suffered the crushing defeat of the Boyne. By autumn, Ireland had been beaten to her knees; town after town had been taken by the Williamite forces and only Limerick still held out. In Scotland, lacking the inspiration of the dead Dundee, the Jacobite army had been routed at the Haughs of Cromdale. And in England there was nothing but intrigue and double treachery as the great lords who had betrayed King James now set themselves to betray King William in his turn. Michael's gorge rose as he thought upon the information contained in the letters he received from Sir Noel at St-Germain, of how Marlborough, Shrewsbury, Godolphin, and half a dozen others in the Ministry and Household were corresponding secretly with James, always, of course, through a third person whom they could throw to the wolves if their treachery was discovered, and of how Marlborough had gone so far as to promise to bring over the English Army to James if he might have a written pardon for his former betrayal and some great office in the restored Government.

There were, of course, the Jacobites, reflected Michael (now walking down Ludgate Hill, with the iron wheels of the hackneys, the trotting of chairmen's feet, and the peremptory summons of church bells making accompaniment to his thoughts), but he cherished no illusions now about the majority of his fellow-partisans. Most of them were infected with the fashionable disease of trimming, especially the great ones. There were a few lords who had not followed their master overseas and yet had taken no part in the fetching over of Orange, though after a fuss, and a multitude of prevarications, they had taken the Oaths to save their heads and their estates. These lords compromised; they went to Court and even accepted office, but they knew they were permanently out of favour with Dutch William and therefore sighed secretly for the return of James.

Then there were several Jacobite, or semi-Jacobite, societies; there was the Oak Club, for instance, which met for dinner at a Fleet Street tavern once a week, most solemnly passed their glasses over a water-bowl when they drank to the King, and indulged in mildly treasonable talk well concealed beneath cant names and cryptic allusions. The hall-mark of this kind of club was its obsession with the past; a man could not be hanged nowadays for professing a devotion to King Charles I, but he could be hanged for professing allegiance to King James II. Therefore did the Oak Club and the Anti-Revolution Club, and others of the same kidney, honour and almost worship the dead King Charles by name, but ignored the living King James, or referred to him in whispers as "Mr Goodman". They were like children playing at secret societies, only of course in a very genteel manner; they drank a multiplicity of cryptic toasts, squabbled over whose ancestor bore the proudest record of loyalty, grew white roses in their gardens, and called their sons Charles and James.

And lastly there was the ordinary, decent, average man, the shopkeepers and craftsmen and their families, the people who Sir Noel and Michael believed could bring about the only restoration that would be lasting. The average man of 1690 resented being ruled by a foreign King, particularly a Dutch one, because it was only twenty years since England had been at war with Holland; he resented also the hordes of Dutchmen whom William had brought over with him, and missed the pomp and pageantry which the morose Orange despised. But, for all that, he was resolved to "live peaceable under the established Government" and to shun politics, because he was absorbed in his trade and was tender of the security of his family. He was attached even yet to King James's person, but he hated and feared King James's religion. He deluded himself with the belief that all that had happened in 1688 was the substitution of a Protestant king for a Papist one, and meantime he had his bread to bake or his ale to brew or his cloth to weave, his City Company to protect his interests, his 'prentices to instruct, and half a dozen petty private feuds to pursue with his rival tradesmen. Unpromising material, reflected Michael drearily, as he came under Temple Bar; but it was not fair to judge yet, for the citizens were still to him a little-known quantity. And by and by, when they saw themselves taxed and preyed upon by the exploiter and the great, as inevitably they would be under the present Government, they might well rise up and demand "The King Again" (the favourite Jacobite slogan), and at least they were more honest and realistic than the Oak Club, less dangerous and fickle than the mob who, in a spasmodic fever of loyalty, would now and again disturb the peace by breaking Whig windows or pelting the coaches of Whig potentates.

He had come by now into Drury Lane, and presently turned up by Wills' Coffee House into Russell Street. It was a street of fashionable tradesmen, mercers, drapers, and head-dressers; the shutters were up today, and all Michael could see of these emporiums was "NO TRUST BY RETAIL" printed in gold capitals over the doors, and a neat notice offering "MONEY FOR LIVE HAIR" nailed on to the head-dressers' shutters. A chair trotted by him to ply for hire near the fashionable church of St Paul's, Covent Garden; a ragged man with a basket on his head slouched in the kennel, and Michael instinctively clapped a hand to his own head, because he knew that such a basket often concealed a small boy whose business it was to snatch a periwig in passing. Then he smiled to himself as he reflected that a snatcher would despise the old and ill-curled wig which was all he could afford nowadays; and a moment later he smiled more broadly, for there, stepping jauntily towards him in a walk that suggested a dance, came his friend and mistress, Moll.

(iii)

She was known to everyone as Moll, though when necessary she could clap on the surname of Stephens, for she had been married by a "copper-captain" in Alsatia to a broken lawyer at the age of fifteen, and had attended the lawyer's hanging a year later. She was in her middle twenties now, but in appearance had not changed since her teens, and with luck and care would look much the same when she was forty. For she was possessed of an extraordinary vitality; every inch of her was vividly alive. She had chosen her profession deliberately and thoroughly enjoyed it; she made no more of a secret about being a prostitute than of hennaing her hair and painting her face.

As she came along now, with her habitual lilting step, she was like some exotic flower in the drab London morning. Her clothes were cheap and daring, but she wore them with such an air that they perfectly became her. She looked ready for anything and anybody (as indeed she was), and the strong whiff of her favourite perfume, Eau d'Auge, was heady, robust and cheerfully vulgar. The painting of her face was a work of art, and she could wear the popular patches better than any woman Michael had ever seen. She was in a canary-coloured gown today and a bright green petticoat "regarded" with black velvet; over these, but negligently unfastened, was a black hooded cloak, the hood hanging on her shoulders lest it disarrange her unnaturally red hair, which was dressed high in front and with long corkscrew curls behind, one of which she had brought round to hang over her shoulder. She carried a mask on a long handle, and this she clapped before her face as she made Michael an ironically demure curtsy; her bright eyes twinkled through the slits in the faceguard, and, as she lowered it, one of them closed in a genial wink.

"Good morrow, sir," said Moll, fluttering her eyelids in mock modesty. "But that you lack a green brief-bag I would take you for a Gentleman of the Temple, and let me tell you that is a huge compliment, for there is scarce a punk in Town who does not claim to have been debauched by a member of that honourable fraternity. You seem out of spirits," she went on, taking his arm, "for you walk as stiff as a Scotch runt going to Smithfield Market. But come your ways and let me alone to put a little heart into you. A bowl of the Crown punch and a few hours in my company; there's not a topping physician in London could give you a better remedy for lowness of spirit."

Michael only smiled at her in answer, remembering vividly the first time she had taken him to this same tavern, the Crown in Russell Street, on that most evil day of his life when he had watched his King and master leave Whitehall for ever, and then had gone on to that horrible and final interview with Eve Barrowes, his first and only love. Moll had rescued him from unplumbed depths of misery on that occasion, appearing from nowhere to make him laugh and drink and talk and feel the warmth of her comradeship; and on so many occasions since she had proved a tonic and a friend in need.

Michael's affection for Moll was of a peculiar nature. He never could forget for a single moment that she had saved his life once when she had nursed him through a dangerous fever, nor that she had saved his reason many times during that strange period when he had lived in the stews, and when filth, abject poverty, the loss of everything he had, the shattering of his whole world, had threatened to overwhelm him; and Michael was of that nature wherein gratitude is strong, deep and enduring. He was attracted to her physically and was faithful to her in this respect (a fact which obviously amused her); he was enchanted by the complete lack of possessiveness in her, not only because he disliked possessiveness in her sex but, much more important, because the nature of the work on which he was engaged, and the risk which it entailed, prevented him from having a licit relationship with any woman. He had never pretended to be in love with her in any but the purely sexual sense of the word, nor she with him; he told her all his secrets, even those which concerned his writing, not because she sympathised with his ideals, or even understood them, but because it was necessary that he unburden himself to someone, and because Moll listened patiently, was his dear friend, and was, he was convinced, incapable of betraying him. He admired her immensely; her life had been a fight from the moment her unmarried mother had deposited her upon a convenient door step, and she had entered upon that fight with perky courage, a genuine zest, a ready wit, and unfailing adaptability. He was humble enough to realise that she possessed by nature qualities which he was acquiring only by the most painstaking effort; and taking her as he found her, knew that he had acquired a mistress, a friend, and a confidante all in one.

He paused for a moment now, before they entered the tavern, and smiled up at the sign; it was making that friendly, comic sound he knew so well, that anguished creak which was associated in his mind with so much comfort and refuge. It was altogether a comfortable, shabby sort of tavern, enjoying the reputation of compounding the best punch in London, yet not fashionable, known only to the local tradesmen and a few connoisseurs. Its sign had not been repainted for years, and was dim and faded, yet Michael never glanced up at it without a certain lifting of the heart, for through the dust and dirt the emblem of Monarchy showed plainly, defying neglect.

"By heaven!" cried Michael, bursting into a laugh, "I'm as hungry as liverymen at a hall-feast, for it is only this moment I have remembered that I neglected to break my fast this morning."

"Liverymen at a hall-feast," echoed Moll, chuckling; "how soon you learn the cant of the cits. But let me set an edge to that appetite, my friend, by rehearsing the bill of fare: a whet of old hock, a calf's head with onions, and a noble Cheshire cheese. That's the tune of it, Michael, and then we'll wring your news from you over a bowl of the famous punch."

An hour or so later they sat side by side on a high-backed settle in the warm kitchen, with the comfortable hum of talk around them and the click of dominoes from a far corner. Moll had one leg crossed over the other, exposing a generous display of shapely calf, while Michael held her hand in both of his and stared into the fire, replete and comfortably drowsy.

"Hang me," murmured Moll, kicking off one shoe that she might waggle her toes in sensuous enjoyment, "but how I'd love to see you in your counting-house, perked up on your arse like a bear, adding up figures and teasing your brains to remember the price of malt. I'll vow you look as complete a cit as ever wore the flat-cap."

"I hope I do. A conspirator should learn to wear his adopted role as easily as a glove."

"You are out in your metaphor; the cits don't wear gloves. Howsoever, I trust you wring some enjoyment from this droll of yours. This vast bombard of a brewer has a wife, say you?"

"He has a wife."

"Is she handsome?"

"Tolerably so."

"Then you must make haste to debauch her, for I assure you 'tis expected. Every husband of a handsome wife in the City looks to be cuckolded by a 'prentice or a journeyman or, failing these, a clerk, that he may appear neighbourly with the rest of his tribe at horn-fair. Now marry come up, my friend, have you lived a whole week in the City and yet know nought of the gentle art of cuckolding? This is bad. But stay! Perchance your brewer has a pretty daughter?"

"Now I think you must have been consulting some astrologer, Moll, else how come you to be so knowledgeable concerning my master's household?"

Moll snapped her fingers.

"Pish, what need have I of planet-readers when I have the play-house? There's not a comedy of the City that ever I saw which had not a handsome wife or a pretty jilt of a daughter. I tell you, 'tis the mode. But now, since you appear so ignorant, I will give you some advice. You must entertain your master's wife with sad talk of your fallen greatness (and maybe with a trifle of lip-lechery once in a while to add salt to the dish), and you must please your master with your modest demeanour, by your industry, and by a 'Yes, sir', 'No, sir', 'I'm just a-coming, sir'; and one fine day you will marry the jilt and inherit the brewhouse and be elected a Worshipful Brother of the Brewers' Company and grow a fat belly and live happy ever after—unless of course you are snabbled for your treasonable practices and make the poor wench an hempen widow. But now I have told you the way it should run, Michael, so set your mind to it and lift up your heart, for there is a modest fortune awaiting you."

"Why, now, Moll," said Michael, mock solemn, "that is all very fine, but I must tell you that I have a rival to contend with, one Nick Hammond, my master's 'prentice; he is mad in love with Miss, and for the matter of that, she is so pretty and modest that she cannot walk in Drapers' Gardens of an evening without the eyes of every City beau a-following her. So that I fear me your fairy-tale will lack its happy ending."

"Let's not turn the comedy into a tragedy," said Moll, reaching out for the punch-ladle. "Or else you will make me jealous of this brewer's wench."

And then she laughed, and he laughed; and no premonition clouded their foolish, trivial mirth.

Three

(i)

In the course of a few months Michael had come to be on friendly terms with every member of his master's household except two; one was young Nathaniel who, indeed, he scarcely saw, for Nat took his dinner at his goldsmith master's; the other was the brewhouse cat, Tiger, a vast tabby whose business it was to keep the rats at bay, and who treated with indifference and disdain the human world in general, excepting only, Miss Maralyn, in whose company Tiger would condescend to purr.

Mr Vance himself treated his new clerk with great kindness, and took a fatherly interest in his welfare, giving him sage advice on all sorts of matters, particularly as to which local taverns he should use and which he must be sure to shun. For instance, he was not on any account to frequent Le Bere Tombeth, which was famous for its cock-ale, "or so they call it, sir, but it is in truth but small-ale mixed with treacle," and as for the Mermaid in Bread Street, he was to avoid it like the pest, "for that knave of a landlord mires the ale with resin and salt, and if you heat a knife red-hot and quench it in the ale, so near the bottom of the pot as you can put it, you shall see the resin come forth hanging on the knife. As for the salt, that is an old trick, for the more the drinker tippleth the more he may, yet never shall quench his thirst. 'Ounds, sir, had I my way, such knavish landlords should stand in the stretch-neck or be whipped at the cart's tail for their crimes." In the same fatherly manner Mr Vance set Michael right on various minute points of etiquette and custom: most citizens spoke of Cheapside as "Chepe", but as Michael was a "foreigner" it would be resented if he used this diminutive; and with the most admirable restraint the brewer informed his clerk that water was never referred to as such in a brewhouse, but became "liquor" immediately it came into his yard.

Michael succeeded in winning the good graces of Mrs Vance in an entirely unlooked-for manner. The lady had continued to eye him with suspicion until one day when Michael, hearing her call her daughter from the kitchen, complimented her upon the choice of so charming a name for her offspring. Mrs Vance flushed up like a girl, bridled, beamed upon him, and exclaimed:

"Now bless me, Master Pennington, you do my heart good when you say that. I perceive you to be a man of birth and genteel breeding, and it takes such an one to perceive the prettiness of the name Maralyn. Fanciful I know it is, and maybe unfitting for the daughter of a cit, but it suits her, sir, I vow it does, and since you like it I will tell you how it came about I chose it for her. Vance took me to the May Fair, d'ye see, before we were wed, and there was a music-booth there into which we went, and a ballad-singer therein was trolling an air called 'Sweet Maralyn'. I had never heard the song before, and never have I heard it since, but it stuck in my mind for a sweet pretty ballad, and I swore to myself that if ever I was brought to bed of a daughter I would call her Maralyn."

Thereafter Mrs Vance treated Michael with a new respect, enlisting him on her side in any argument with her husband (to his extreme embarrassment), and quoting him freely and inaccurately in her gossiping with neighbours. He had become "that gentlemanly Master Pennington" instead of "that foreigner whom Vance would engage as his clerk though I was ever against it"; and Michael's birth and upbringing, which formerly had been the cause of the lady's grudge against him, now became his greatest assets in her eyes. Michael himself was sorry for Mrs Vance, for he had discovered by now the nature of her mysterious malady; it seemed that she was the victim of chronic insomnia, which was sufficient to account for her restlessness and irritability. Every evening Maralyn prepared a dish of lettuce for her, the best-known remedy for this evil, and every evening Mrs Vance patiently devoured it; but neither this nor a hop-pillow, nor all the prescriptions of apothecaries, nor the recipes contained in Culpeper's *Herbal*, seemed to have any effect, and the shadows under the handsome eyes continued to darken and the poor woman's temper to grow more and more uncertain.

Michael's acquaintanceship with Maralyn progressed but slowly, for she was always busy, and although not shy seemed somewhat reserved. Often when he was at work he would hear her singing about her household tasks, as he had heard her on that first day of his coming to the brewhouse, singing as though she could not help it, as though to lift her pretty frail voice in song was as natural with her as to breathe. She spoke very little, and then with a limited vocabulary and only about things she understood, household tasks and recipes and sicknesses and marketing. Her work was endless, yet she seemed to thrive on it; her pleasures were few and simple: a new mob or a yard or two of ribbon, a Sunday visit with her parents to one or other of the City tea-gardens, and a dinner at Brewers' Hall to which women were admitted on election-feasts; but she looked forward to these pleasures and enjoyed them with the zest of a young child. She was, indeed, but a child in years, but she did the work of a woman, and her natural grace and tact lent her a curious and rather pitiful maturity. Never once had Michael seen her out of temper, and never once had he known her, young as she was, unable to manage a task or cope with a situation.

From the very first Nick Hammond had taken every opportunity of cultivating the new clerk's acquaintance, though why this should be so Michael was for some while unable to imagine. Whenever Nick was sent to the counting-house on some errand of his master's he would linger to talk, and often at table Michael would catch the boy's fanatical eyes regarding him with a strange sort of eagerness. Then there came a day when, just as he was about to leave the counting-house after delivering some message from Mr Vance, Nick hesitated, closed the door carefully, tiptoed to the desk with a great air of mystery, and said in a hoarse whisper:

"You will have heard that Preston is reprieved again?"

"Preston?"

"Ay, my Lord Preston. Pish, Master Pennington, you need not fear to speak openly on such a matter with me."

Michael stared at him in silence. In the December of the previous year, Lord Preston had sailed for France with letters from various English Jacobites to the exiled Court; the captain of the ship had betrayed him, and he, his papers, and some associates, had been seized and brought to London. Two of his companions had been hanged, but Preston, though condemned to death, had been reprieved, with the obvious intention of persuading him to betray all his accomplices. All this Michael knew very well, but he wondered, rather anxiously, why Master Hammond should deem him interested in such an affair.

"You're a Papist," went on Nick, leaning himself against the desk and continuing to speak in a stage whisper. "You need not to deny it. Why else are you hiding down here in the City, you a gentleman of birth and education?"

"Why, my father left me no patrimony, and therefore I——"

"Pish, don't give me that stuff. I know better. You're a Papist, I say, and therefore are you likewise of the honest party."

"Meaning the Jacobites?"

"God rot you, not so loud. Ay, the Jacks. Come now, don't deny it. Why should you so with me? Harkee now, I'll tell you: I'm a member of a Jack club called the Lads of the Lion, and if you but say the word I'll carry you to a meeting, where you'll hear great talk. There's one of our company carries letters from my Lord Marlborough himself to St-Germain, and I'll tell you this: Marlborough's behind this demand of Parliament for the withdrawal of William's Dutch regiments from England, for my lord believes that, once the mercenaries are gone, he with the English Army at his back can play the part of Monck."

"Master Hammond," said Michael sternly, "that's mighty indiscreet. Do you go around publishing such hanging secrets to strangers?"

Nick's thin face flushed angrily.

"I know what I'm about, and I know a Papist when I see one. We should hold together, we of the honest party, and have no secrets from each other——"

44

"So that pretty soon you may have no secrets from your enemies." He turned his face away; he hated to hurt this boy who was so deadly in earnest but who was such a menace to himself and his cause. "Harkee, Master Hammond, I'm a clerk and you a 'prentice in Master Vance's brewhouse; let it stay so betwixt us."

"Now God damn you for a mealy-mouthed Whig!" cried Nick, crashing his fist on the desk beneath Michael's nose. "But let me tell you this, Master Pennington, I'll live to see you and your whiffling company riding up Holborn Hill in Jack Ketch's cart when the King comes into his own again." And with that he stamped out of the counting-house and slammed the door.

Michael was genuinely sorry for Nick Hammond and regretted that he had been compelled to make an enemy of the lad, but he could not afford to receive or give confidences to such an irresponsible firebrand. Nick was a pitiful creature in every way, for he was a parish child, and had been 'prenticed at the age of seven by parish officers, who were ever ready to part with such unwanted children at the earliest possible moment and so to rid themselves of a burden.

Nick had been fortunate indeed in finding Nathaniel Vance for a master, since the brewer was a man of sound principles and tender heart, and treated the poor little parish child with the same kindness and care as he bestowed upon the 'prentices whose parents had paid a high fee for their indentures, but he could not protect Nick from the sneers and ill-nature of the other lads, who took delight in tormenting the "parish brat" and in reminding him continually of his origins. Nick himself had given them an additional excuse for this cruel teasing by his inability to conceal the calf-love he had conceived for his master's daughter. Nick was of that nature which can never learn to be discreet in its affections, be the object of them an ideal or a girl, but to his honour it must be said that he endured the petty persecution of his fellows with patience, and even with a certain pitiful dignity, and that beneath the extravagant fire of his calf-love there did really burn, even now, a more steady warmth which might in time become noble.

(ii)

From the very first Michael had liked the Scots 'prentice, Alec Moray, and had been on pleasant terms with him. Yet for all that, he was very surprised when, one summer's day in '91, as they were returning to work after dinner, Alec came up to him and asked him to accompany him to the Rainbow coffee-house that evening. He was surprised because, although Alec was always courteous and civil, he had all the reserve of his race and seemed to stand apart, of his own choice, from his fellows; one could not imagine him frequenting coffee-houses or taverns, or unbending sufficiently to seek any man's company. However, it seemed that for some reason or other he desired Michael's company that evening, and the clerk readily agreed to sally forth with Alec after the brewhouse closed.

When the hour arrived, punctual to the minute Alec appeared at the door of the counting-house, his apron laid aside, his thrum-cap on his sandy head, and a book hugged under his arm. He nodded in greeting, for he was a lad who never spoke more than was strictly necessary, and in silence watched Michael draw down his shirt-sleeves and put on his coat. Side by side they emerged from the little office, crossed the court and turned into Cheapside, neither speaking a word, until they arrived at the Rainbow, which stood upon the north side of Chepe on the corner of Honey Lane. It was, Michael observed, a poor little place with an air of decay about it, and he remembered to have heard that it was one of the oldest of the City coffee-houses but had lost much of its trade when the more opulent Kiftells had been built after the Fire.

"If you will please to follow me, sir," said Alec shortly, "I will lead the way."

They went through a narrow entry which ended in a flight of steps so steep that a rope had been nailed to the wall to assist those who ascended. At the top was a door, which Alec opened without knocking, and ushered Michael into a small room in which sat an old woman mending a sheet. She peered at the visitors in a short-sighted way, nodded to Alec, rose, and took up an earthenware coffee-pot which was warming before the fire. Michael observed that the window had been mended with brown paper and that the fire was fed with bits of rag, which smelt very ill. The mildewed walls were hung with bills advertising liquid snuff, beautifying waters, dentrifices, and Doctor Somebody's cure for gonorrhea. There were no other customers present, though from the low talking and the shrill laughter of a woman which sounded from an upper room, Michael guessed that the coffee-house had its private apartment, probably set aside for debauchery.

The two sat down at a rickety table and were served with small wooden bowls containing a liquid which proved to be saloop, a cheap substitute for coffee. Michael made polite conversation for a while, but it elicited no response, and it was plain that Alec had something on his mind. Presently he spoke in a kind of burst, his large hands clasped around his bowl and his eyes carefully averted from the other's face:

"I'm a-trying to teach myself French, d'ye see, and as a kind of exercise I take any book I can find and endeavour to translate it into yon tongue. I have heard ye're a gentleman of education, and I thought maybe you could assist me, for I must confess I find it a wee bit teasing."

And, very red in the face, he took the book from beneath his arm and laid it upon the table. Michael took it up and glanced at the title. It was Gervase Markham's *English Housewife*, and when he saw that title he straightway forgot all about Alec Moray. It was not so very long ago, though it seemed to be in another life, that he had seen another copy of this same book in a very different setting when he had come into the dainty parlour of Eve Barrowes to tell her that he was a ruined man, that he had thrown up his post at Court, and that he could not ask her to marry a penniless outlaw. *The English Housewife, Containing the Inward and Outward Virtues which ought to be in a Compleat Woman.* She had been reading that book when he had come into her parlour, but had flung it aside and had run into his arms; he could see her face now and feel the touch of her soft fingers, and hear the very tone of her voice as she had begged him not to throw away their happiness for the sake of a lost cause, as she had pleaded with him to come away with her and live retired in the country and take no further part in politics. The pain of that memory was so sharp that he had to grit his teeth together lest he cry aloud: then, with a great effort, he mastered his emotion, and so became aware that he was staring down upon the fly-leaf of the book, and that there was inscribed upon it, in a laborious, childish hand:

"Maralyn Vance, her Book."

"Maralyn Vance," repeated Michael aloud. And then he looked at Alec, and saw that the 'prentice had grown very red in the face and that his eyes were defiant.

"Miss Maralyn was pleased to lend it to me, for that I had no other." A pause. Then, like a challenge: "I love her, d'ye see, and she returns my affection."

"You are a fortunate young man, Master Alec," murmured Michael, smiling, and feeling strangely grateful to these two children whose adolescent love affair had rescued him from memories of his own. "May I wish you joy?"

"It must not be known," said Alec solemnly. "I ken not why I told you. If her father kent——"

"I understand. I do assure you, your secret is safe with me. It is hard upon you both, for I suppose that you must wait for your happiness a long while yet."

Alec stared hard at his companion for a full minute, apparently sizing him up. Then, suddenly, he seemed to come to a decision, leaned forward and in disjointed sentences gave Michael his family history and his future hopes.

It was not a very distinguished history. Alec's father had been coachman to my Lord Stair in Edinburgh, and had married a servant-maid from a neighbouring tavern. When Alec was twelve years old his father had died, as a result of my lord's coach being overturned in a street brawl; his widow, an English lass, had made up her mind to return to her own country, though all her relations were dead, had walked to London with her son, and, with the gift of a few guineas my lord had bestowed upon her in compensation for the coachman's untimely death, had opened a green-cellar in Bedfordbury. For two years Alec had helped her in the shop, but at fourteen she had apprenticed him to Mr Vance; that was two years ago, and not until he was twenty-one would he be out of his indentures and able to earn a wage as a journeyman.

But it seemed that the lad's head was full of other plans. He was obsessed by the thought of the riches to be found in the Americas and by the prospects emigration offered to young men ready for work and hardship. Scotland was poor and had no colonies and no free trade with England, but some Scots whom he had met in London at this very coffee-house were talking of expeditions to the Indies, or to Africa, or to the New World, where they might settle and found a new Scotland, and assist the old one to grow great and prosperous with the wealth they should discover in these unknown lands. When such an expedition sailed, said Alec, he would go with it, and he would take Maralyn with him as his wife (though he had mentioned nothing of all this to her, because it would not be right to speak of such matters until his plans were formed and he had made his suit to her father). Meantime, he saved every penny of his pocket-money, and in the evenings, before he went home to his mother's humble lodging behind her green-cellar, he earned a little by doing odd jobs about the streets, turning link-boy and lighting fine gentlemen to the playhouse, or giving a hand to the Tom-turdmen in collecting excrement-tubs from the houses and carting them to the lay-stalls.

And at night he set himself to master the French tongue, that he might fit himself for his great venture, for he had heard that French was the most useful language for one destined to sail to the unknown world. He had some education, he said, adding, not without a touch of smugness, that it was not with the poor of Scotland as with those of England, for Master John Knox had given his countrymen the blessing of free education, and there was scarce a man in Scotland who could not read and write and add up simple sums. But the learning of foreign languages was a different matter, as indeed it should be; if an honest Scot could read the Scriptures in his own tongue that should suffice him without plaguing himself with foreign and Papist lingos. Yet since his, Alec's, situation required that he should so plague himself, he would be mighty obliged if Mr. Pennington could help him translate the *English Housewife* into French.

(iii)

Michael had scarcely recovered from the surprise of this encounter with Alec Moray when he found himself experiencing another of a somewhat similar nature, but even more unexpected, for this second invitation to spend an evening out was issued by no less a person than young Master Nathaniel. It was, indeed, rather a command than an invitation, for Nat followed Michael out from supper one evening, tapped him on the shoulder, acquainted him that he had a mission for him, and that he would make known its nature that very evening, nay, that very hour, at the Exchange tavern in the Poultry.

Michael had never quite made up his mind about Nat, for beneath the pertness and cheap snobbery he sensed a genuine hardness, a cunning which might or might not develop with maturity. The boy had been spoilt by both his parents, that was plain; he for his part maintained a surface respect towards them, but Michael guessed that he despised them in his heart. Nat lived his own life; all day long he was busy at his goldsmith master's, and as soon as supper was finished at his father's board he sallied forth upon his own mysterious pursuits. He never aped the beau, as did so many young citizens, and he was never seen the worse for drink; where and with whom he spent his evenings Michael did not know, and was pretty sure the lad's father did not know either. Nat was secretive; but whether this was a pose or not Michael could not quite decide, only he was quite sure he did not like the boy. As they walked along Cheapside this evening, Nat talked in a condescending tone to his companion, boasting of his master's wealth, of his own close friendship with his master's only son, of the amount of property owned by the goldsmiths in the City, and of how there was scarce a rich merchant on 'Change for whom Mr Maynard did not keep "running cashes". Michael noted that when the lad spoke of money, a genuine interest, even a kind of reverence, crept into his voice; but there was also something of familiarity, as though he, a poor 'prentice, the son of a small brewer, was perfectly acquainted with the intricacies of finance.

The Exchange tavern stood upon the north side of the Poultry, near Scalding Alley; it was evident that its name had been selected because the house commanded a view of the Royal Exchange, over the roofs of Stocks Market into which the Poultry opened. It was growing dark as Michael and Nat reached their destination; the hackney-coach stand was deserted, the fruit- and oyster-stalls which lined the Poultry had packed up, the link-boys were hurrying to the chandlers to fetch their links, prostitutes paraded outside the taverns and coffee-houses on the look-out for their prey, and the watch, newly set, came by with rattle and lanthorn, calling the hour. Intermingling with the footsteps of pedestrians was the smack of balls against a high wall, proclaiming that the prisoners in the Poultry Compter were still at their favourite game of rackets, and from some distance away there echoed a dull uproar and the cry of "All's fair, no body, no body!"—the customary challenge of the mob when in their pranks they had damaged the property of some peaceable citizen.

Nat led the way into the tavern, and ignoring the open door of the kitchen from which sounded the laughter and talk of the humbler customers, climbed the stairs and entered a room at the top. It was crowded with journeymen and the better sort of 'prentices and their women, and thick with tobacco-smoke; a party blockaded the fire and every table was occupied. Michael, glancing at Nat, saw that his gaze was fastened upon a girl who, from a certain air about her, Michael guessed to be the daughter of the house, and who was standing by a table at which sat a gentleman all alone. A rather curious expression came upon Nat's face as he looked at the girl, an expression Michael had never seen there before; there was determination in it, and a kind of fierceness, and even a hint of fanaticism. Then, without a word, Nat pushed his way through the throng, came up to that particular table, and accosted the gentleman who sat there.

"Why, how do, Frank?" said he.

The man addressed was about Michael's age; he was not at all handsome, for his shoulders were bent, his body too plump, and his nose comically upturned at the tip. But there was about him an undeniable charm which made itself felt the moment you met him; he had an easy, genial air and a ready smile. His dress was smart: a blue coat, red stockings, a silver-hilted sword, and an edged hat beneath which showed a fox-coloured wig with the long pole-locks so fashionable among the beaux. He had one plump hand in the pocket of his coat, a pocket set very low in the skirts after the new mode, and continually jingled some coins therein. The girl with whom he had been talking was dark and thin and handsome, very neat and trim in her person, with a hard red line of mouth and watchful, calculating eyes. From her manner and talk it was plain she had been given a fancy education, had been to the dancing-school, and had a very high opinion of herself and her worth.

The man addressed as Frank welcomed Nat with outstretched hands, and cocked an enquiring eye at his companion. Nat introduced them; this was Master Frank Maynard, son of Mr. Maynard the goldsmith, and this was Master Michael Pennington, "a friend of mine" (not a word about his being Mr Vance's clerk, Michael noted). Mr Maynard was charmed, and would Mr. Pennington take a whet with him? He could recommend the Exchange's ambrosia. Mr Pennington lifted his eyebrows in enquiry, and was informed that the Exchange's ambrosia consisted of half a pint of sack laced with gin. Michael smiled and said he would prefer some ale, at which Frank winked at Nat and said it was a pity Mr Vance senior was not with them, for it would have done his old heart good to find a gentleman preferring ale to ambrosia. Michael was then presented with some ceremony to the girl, who turned out indeed to be the daughter of the house, Miss Susan Pritchard. Miss Pritchard graciously consented to fetch him his modest dram and Nat his "usual"; Michael observed how Nat's eyes followed her as she went upon her errand.

"You are well met, Nat," said Mr. Maynard, clapping a hand

upon his shoulder in an affectionate manner, "for I had occasion to walk upon Cornhill today and called at the Lottery-office. Here is your ticket, my dear gossip, and may I be the first to wish it may turn out a benefit."

Nat took the proffered slip of paper, and Michael, still observing him, noted that he seemed to forget Susan Pritchard for an object even more absorbing, how he turned and turned the paper in his hands, his eyes seeming as though they devoured the print upon it. Looking over his shoulder, Michael saw that it was a ticket in the new State Lottery, the first of its kind to be seen in England, though private lotteries had been fairly common for some while. This was called the Million Lottery; the biggest prize or benefit was one thousand pounds, each ticket costing ten pounds, a very high price. Its object was to raise money for the war which King William was waging against France.

"You have a share in this ticket, Master Nat?" asked Michael; for he knew it was customary for the poorer sort to buy an eighth or even a sixteenth share in the tickets for private lotteries which cost far less than those for this new venture.

"A share in it!" exclaimed Nat, flushing. "Wounds, no, I have bought it outright."

Maynard winked at Michael over the other's shoulder.

"Why yes indeed, and he will win a benefit, if I know aught about him. He has an eye for money, has our young friend, and let me tell you, sir, that is not an idle expression; there are eyes which can see money in a scrap of paper or a parcel of barren land, and eyes which are so blind to it that they cannot see gold when it lies beneath their noses."

"Six-three-nine," murmured Nat, still staring at the ticket in his hand. "Three and nine are lucky numbers; moreover, the half of six is three, and six and three make nine, and the whole adds up to eighteen, which is but nine doubled and six times three. 'Adsbud, I do believe I shall win the biggest prize of all."

"And if you do," said Miss Pritchard, appearing with the drinks, "what will you please to do with it, Master Vance? Will you buy yourself out of your indentures, set up as a master brewer, and prove a rival to your father?"

"Nay, nay, Sue," chided Maynard with another of his winks;

"he'll set up as a topping goldsmith and ruin my poor father, I'll warrant him."

"Or maybe," chimed in Michael, "he'll spend the whole of it in a good tippling society on the Exchange's ambrosia, and straying through the streets when the City is in darkness, find himself taken up by a press-gang and receiving the King's shilling. Thus will he doubly assist His Majesty to wage his glorious wars."

"You like not this idea of a State Lottery, Mr. Pennington?" asked Maynard, with a shrewd look at him over his glass.

"I like it not, as you say, sir. In my opinion it demeans the kingdom and excites cupidity. If a nation desires a war, it will find the means to pay for it without the Government inviting the poor to squander their savings on a turn of fortune's wheel."

"Why how now, Master Puritan!" cried Maynard good-humouredly.

Michael laughed.

"I assure you, sir, I never was that kind of a man. Only I cannot help but think it is small benefit to ten thousand people who have struggled hard to make up between them the sum of one thousand pounds when one man gets the whole and he, belike, in no need of fortune's favours. But enough of this. I am in labour to know what Master Nat will do with his winnings if he gets them."

Nat glanced from one to the other, and there was a kind of cunning mirth in his eyes.

"Wait and see, my friends; just wait and see." And then his glance rested so meaningly upon Miss Pritchard that she blushed, tossed her head, and turned away.

"I have won already at the lottery," Nat told Michael later, after Maynard had bidden them a genial goodnight and had withdrawn. He set his glass upon the table and rested his elbows on either side of it, and he did not look at his companion save in sidelong, fleeting glances. His face seemed curiously to have sharpened, and his eyes strayed between the ticket which lay upon the table and the elegant figure of Susan serving customers near by. "Frank is right when he says I have an eye for money. I had a twelfth share in Neale's Monthly Chance last year and drew a benefit of ten pounds. It is this same ten pounds with which I have bought a ticket in the State Lottery."

Michael had nothing to say. He felt sickened and uneasy by this get-rich-quick craze which the Government was fostering among all classes.

"I shall win," went on Nat, biting his thumb. "Nine is my lucky number. I have dreamed of it, and an astrologer gave it to me, and I work in the ninth house in Goldsmiths' Row."

"So likewise, I take it, does Mr Frank Maynard."

Nat flashed a quick glance at him.

"Ay, he does, but what need has he of lottery tickets? His father is a topping goldsmith, and he will inherit a fortune. But not yet," he went on, speaking more to himself than to Michael. "Let me win my prize first, and there's a greater prize I'll snatch from him."

"Miss Susan Pritchard?"

"And why not?" cried Nat, whipping round on him. "And what is that to you?"

"Nothing in the world, Master Nat. I hazarded a guess, that was all. But since it seems that I have guessed correctly, I will take leave to ask you: Could you not win the second prize without the first?"

Nat laughed shortly, like a bark.

"As a poor 'prentice? You speak like a fool. She knows the value of money, does Sue, and I respect her for it. She has been brought up mighty genteel and could make a match with a master-craftsman if she chose. But she likes me, I know she does, and if I win the biggest prize in this lottery, ere Frank comes into his fortune, I'll snatch her from him, rot me if I don't, for it may be years ere Frank inherits and she knows that." Then he broke off, sipped his dram, and continued in a different tone: "I invited you hither this evening, Mr Pennington, because I understand you have enjoyed an expensive education, and therefore will be able to oblige me in a certain matter. There is a letter I desire to have writ, d'ye see, a—a love-letter, I suppose you would call it, but not a vulgar sort of letter, you understand; it must be vastly genteel and fanciful, for I desire to impress Miss with it. You will know, sir, that young jilts are apt to be flighty and value pretty compliments and high-flown phrases. You are to cram this letter full with such stuff, and write it as do the poets, with classical reference and so forth. She'll not understand the half of it, but it will tickle her vanity."

"More even than a thousand-pound benefit?" asked Michael dryly.

"I must retain her interest," snapped Nat, "until I have won. I am in labour lest Frank make formal request for her hand ere that happy day arrives, d'ye see? He is my good friend, but friendship does not prevent a man stealing a woman from his crony; all's fair, they say in love and war. She likes me better, I am persuaded of that, but his prospects are sufficient to tempt any wench. And his father has been sick of the stone and any day we may hear of his death; then Frank will inherit everything, and I shall lose her. But if God in His mercy spares Mr Maynard," pursued Nat with perfect seriousness, "and I can retain Sue's interest with a trifle of love-billets, and win this thousand-pound benefit (as I shall do), her liking for me will make her choose the immediate advantage rather than wait for dead men's shoes."

"I see," said Michael dryly.

"You need not fear, sir," continued Nat, reverting to his lordly manner, "that I seek to have this service from you for nothing. I am willing to pay you for your pains the fee customary for a news-letter writer, neither more nor less, you understand? And I should think that a man in your circumstances would consider himself well compensated."

Michael burst out laughing.

"Faith, Master Nat, I desire no payment for such service. I will write your letter for you and welcome; and if it please you, you shall carry it to Miss Susan; if it please you not, go you to your scriveners and get a better one."

Nat turned and stared at him, and there was frank contempt in his eyes.

"You desire no payment? By God, you're a bigger fool than I took you for, and it is no wonder to me now that you must earn your bread as a clerk. None but a fool gives something for nothing in this world."

Four

(i)

ALTHOUGH in his after-supper talks with Michael the brewer never referred to that gentleman's past, nor to his secret writing, there were times when of his own accord he would begin to speak of public affairs, and on these occasions Michael was deeply interested, for they served to help him understand the man's character and attitude, and he had discovered by this time that his employer was a very typical citizen, and that the point of view he adopted towards politics was almost identical with that of most of the trading class. Michael was often enough exasperated by the man's refusal to think for himself, by his gullibility especially where the printed word was concerned, and by his patient endurance of petty tyrannies, a patience that came perilously near to inertia, yet he was at the same time more and more enamoured of the brewer's strong sense of justice, his tolerance, his humour and his simplicity of heart.

One of the most comforting things to Michael was Vance's deep attachment to the Monarchy, though his comfort was pricked by exasperation when he found that Vance insisted upon believing that England was still ruled by a monarchical government. When Michael spoke of the oligarchy which had usurped the power of the Crown Mr Vance grew very indignant.

"'Ounds, Mr Pennington, I will not have such talk in my house. You speak, i' faith, as though the going of King James had robbed England of her ancient Constitution, which is, and ever has been, King, Lords and Commons. You err in this, hang me but you do, sir. We but exchanged one king for another. I grant you that King William, being a foreigner, has not the interest in his English dominions as was felt by the ancient House; yet he has accepted of the Crown with all its awful responsibilities, nor must we forget that his mother was a Stuart and that his wife and her sister, the Princess Anne, the Heir Presumptive, are likewise."

"William accepted of the Crown when it was offered him, sir —mark this—not by the nation, but by a faction. Leaving aside for the moment all question of the hereditary principle, it is a fact that he is and must remain the nominee of a small group of men, with behind them a much larger group composed of the landed classes and the greater merchants. He must, therefore, rule as this faction dictates, since he owes to them his throne. I ask you, then, are we still ruled by a king, or by a clique? It is the prime duty of a king to rule all for the good of all, to administer the laws impartially as the representative of the nation, to stand above parties and conflicting interests, to protect the poor from the rich and the weak from the strong. But how may he do this when he owes his throne, not to Divine appointment, not to hereditary right, but to a comparatively small section of his people?"

Vance was silent, puffing hard at his pipe, his homely face set in a frown of deep uneasiness.

"I tell you, sir," continued Michael earnestly, "the Monarchy itself is doomed unless the ancient and legitimate House returns. For a show of continuity, the wealthy men who drove out King James have set their creature on the throne, but they will see to it that his power grows less and less, until the king shall become but a meaningless symbol, a puppet dressed up in robes and crown to amuse the populate and trick them into believing that they still have a Sovereign to protect them from the greed of the exploiter and to administer their ancient laws."

"Now God forbid! " cried Vance. "The love of Monarchy is in an Englishman's very bones, and he is a fool and a knave who seeks to uproot it. As for what you say about King William being the tool of a faction, you do forget, sir, that his ministers are bound to confer with him, that he can dismiss them at his pleasure, and that he is still, and please God his successors ever shall remain, the supreme legislative and executive power in Government."

"Not the King any longer but the King in Council. A distinction the significance of which is missed. It is but a step from that to the Council only. And as for the love of Monarchy, is it in the bones of English lords and nobles? I think not. The civil disturbances which have racked this kingdom throughout the centuries have been caused by rich, powerful men who coveted the King his power."

"I have not the wit to argue with you," said Vance, after a deep draught of ale, "but I tell you that for my part I am content to see a king upon the throne, though he be a Dutchman, and shall take care to live peaceable under him while he administers the laws in the ancient fashion. I take no part in politics, as I have told you many a time. I know my place, and am content to leave great matters to great folk."

"Then must you leave small ones to them likewise. Already your trade is threatened by the hordes of foreigners William brought over in his train, by all these new taxes to aid a war which is William's, not England's, and by this recent Act for throwing open the distillery trade. What of that, Mr Vance? Is it not true that by this Act, the Royal Charter given to the Distillery Company by Charles I is overridden, and that any man may now distill without a licence so he gives ten days' notice to the authorities?"

"Pish, sir," cried Vance in genuine contempt, "know you so little of our tastes that you can believe Englishmen will choose to ruin their bellies with Dutch gin when they can have English ale?"

"I have not forgot you told me," said Michael softly, "that once upon a time they forsook English ale for Flemish beer and still continue so to do. And make no mistake about this business, sir; it will not be Dutch gin only, which because of its high price is beyond the reach of laborious men. Our English landlords are crazed with this new scheme of enclosing the common lands that they may grow vast fields of corn, and when they have a surplus, what will they do with it, think you? They will sell it to the distillers, who will distill cheap spirits and sell them cheaply to the poor."

"Pooh, you're raving!" scoffed Vance. "You're fit for Bedlam, sir. Only the mob is so abandoned that it will burn out its vitals with these hellish spirits."

"Well," said Michael, with a shrug, "we shall see, sir, we shall see."

(ii)

Mr Vance was accustomed to give his 'prentices a holiday for the annual fair of St Bartholomew's, and he informed his new clerk that he might share in this treat if he was so disposed.

"It is worth a visit, Mr Pennington," said he, "but do you keep a tight hand upon your money if you go thither, for it is the pocket-picker's paradise and every prig in the City will be there."

Michael went to the fair upon the second day and took Moll with him, or rather, since she was well acquainted with it, she took him. They entered by the Hospital Gate, pushed and jostled by a crowd of other merry-makers, and immediately were assailed by the most frightful cacophony. The squeaking of penny trumpets, the banging of drums, the cries of those who sold damsons, nuts and oranges, the shrill of fiddles from the music-booths, the savage roar from the bear-pit, and the incessant invitation from every stall to "Buy! Buy! Buy!" merged into a noise so deafening that the senses were bewildered, while uninitiated stomachs were sickened by the odour of roasting pork from Pie Corner, the stench of unwashed humanity, and the stink of the refuse with which the ground was littered.

Moll, perfectly at home, conducted her friend upon a tour round the fair, pointing out the waxwork-show and the rope-dancer's booth, the raffling-shops and gaming-houses, the puppet-shows, the bull-baiting ground and the cockpit, and the new gin-shops which were, she said, a novelty this year. They looked in at the cockpit for a while and watched a Welsh Main being fought between eight pairs: then went on to the various puppet-shows, where Moll, sucking an orange with relish, gazed enchanted at pigs forming letters into words with their feet, birds firing off pistols, and monkeys dressed up as men. Tiring at last of these simple amusements, she suggested that they should see a play, or rather, in the language of the fair, a droll, and said there was a mighty fine one to be seen at such-and-such a booth. It was called *The Devil of a Wife*, she informed Michael, adding that, as she believed it was all about a City cuckold, she was sure it would please him mightily.

Elbowing their way through the press, they came at length to the booth in question. There was a gallery outside it, upon which sat the actors dressed up in their costumes and paint, while a merry-andrew attracted the throng by some tumbling and similar antics. As Michael and Moll arrived he came to the edge of the gallery, and through a tin speaking-trumpet invited the ladies and gentlemen to "Walk in! Walk in! and take your places while you may have them. The candles are lighted and we are just a-going to begin." Paying their money to a man at the door, who sat beneath the customary notice proclaiming that this was the best show in the fair, the two friends were carried along with the stream into the stuffy interior, where a concert of fiddlers and oboes entertained the audience until the curtains should be withdrawn; but this music was drowned by the raucous voices of the fruit-sellers who, with their baskets on their heads, implored the company to "Buy oranges and citrons" and "Cherries in the rise". Even this discord was soon lost in the harsh clamour of the audience who, growing impatient, clapped their hands, stamped their feet, and yelled incessantly "Show! Show! Show!"

After an interval during which the curtains bulged and billowed, from the fevered last-minute preparations of those behind them, they were withdrawn, and the play began. It was punctuated by lewd remarks, pithy advice and cat-calls from the audience, yet it was plainly popular. The hero had venereal disease; the husband, a City merchant, had been cuckolded and could not discover by whom; and the heroine, the "devil of a wife" of the title, was equally unable to discover the identity of the father of her coming child. It was, in fact, the most drearily obscene stuff imaginable, and when the curtains were drawn at the end of the first act Moll voiced her opinion of it in no uncertain manner.

"The man who wrote this is a pumpkin; thrives best in filthy places. He should be whipped at the cart's arse for it, say I. Did you mark the hero's legs? They're so thin they would bid defiance to any parish stocks. But as for the lady, oh, I cry her mercy, for I'll warrant she's as honest a strumpet as ever earned a living at twopence a bout. The Lord confound the whole parcel of 'em for twat-scouring pimps, for as I hope to be saved they make a poor honest whore blush for her trade."

But Michael answered never a word. He sat taut and speechless, staring at a box in which sat a lady between two gentlemen. The lady was wearing a face-guard, but he had recognised her as Eve Barrowes.

(iii)

The tawdry surroundings vanished as he stared, and he saw only the dear beloved figure he had thought never to see again. The vile odour of the booth gave place to a smell of sweet herbs, and the raucous noise to a kind voice speaking. And he himself was no longer the serious young man dedicated to a cause, but merely a lover head over heels in love, afflicted even now, at twenty-six, with the reasonless, crazy, torturing, glorified, cloudy love of youth.

He knew that he had lost Eve for ever, indeed could scarcely be said ever to have found her; that Michael's persistence in ruining himself by adhering to King James had wrecked all their chances of mutual happiness. He had tried desperately, for nearly four years, to prevent the memory of her from interfering with his work; he knew that he could not, even had he wished, forget her, but he had hoped that he would never see her again, for the unhealed wound was bearable only if untouched. Now it was jabbed by the sight of her and he could have cried aloud with the pain of it. Yet, in a sort of frenzy of self-torture, he took in every detail of her dress, her gestures, her manner; she sat between her two escorts, holding her mask in one gloved hand, turning it with the turning of her head as she addressed one or other of her companions, quite composed in this strange environment, mildly curious perhaps, certainly contemptuous, a lady of quality viewing the unknown world of the vulgar, but a kind lady, a gracious lady, as much a victim of her upbringing as was Nathaniel Vance of his. . . .

After a timeless period he became aware that Moll had taken his arm and, without a word, was guiding him out of the booth. He did not question why she had taken him away nor whither they were bound, though he felt as if his heart were being torn from his body; Moll and everyone else save Eve had become dummy figures, unreal, meaningless. Presently he found himself sitting in a corner of one of the numerous drinking-booths, with talk and laughter flowing round him and a fog of tobacco-smoke enveloping him. Then at last Moll said gently, with a small, uncharacteristic sigh:

"Damn this for the most unlucky afternoon that ever I spent."

He tried to rouse himself.

"Your pardon, Moll. I'm a woundily dull companion."

"Did you mark who was with her?" asked Moll, ignoring this, and introducing the delicate subject without preliminaries.

He shook his head.

"One was my Lord Grey. He has some post at Court, Comptroller of the Privy, I shouldn't wonder, for they say William hates him for a true-blue Tory and brought him in only when he was compelled to make stronger his own insecure position by cosseting of both parties." A pause. Then, abruptly: "She is wed to my Lord Grey, Michael."

"Is she so?"

"Is she so! 'Adsheart, does it mean no more to you than that?"

"I knew that she would wed. I hope that she is happy."

"Why, there is my sweet little martyr," cried Moll. "Damme, were I in your shoes I'd be raging to pink as many eyelet-holes in his skin as he has buttonholes in his coat."

"You don't understand," said Michael dully. "I had nought to offer her and would be a knave indeed did I grudge her to one who perchance can make her great and—and happy."

There was a pause, during which Moll applied herself vigorously to repairing the paint on her face. Then she said shortly:

"It is a pity you did not mark the other gentleman, for he was your old acquaintance; none other, in truth, than Tom Fields, once your fellow-Pensioner, now Lieutenant of the Band in Noddy's place. But it is well that he did not mark you, my friend (and he did not, for I watched him closely); he is deep in love with Revolution principles, and might begin to suspect him what business you were at in London when your master is gone overseas."

"If Tom knew where I was and what I was at," said Michael tonelessly, "he would have me arrested in a trice; I know that."

"Ay, he's a rascally clip-nit and ever was, a cit by birth, mark you, but now as great a Tom-essence as ever was bred at Court, and stinks as strong of orangeflower-water, I'll be bound, as a Spanisher does of garlic. What a rage would he be in now if he knew he had been bilked of buying his old friend a halter."

"You wrong Tom grievously," snapped Michael. "He's as honest a man as ever I knew, and while he would clap me up right readily for his principles' sake, he would pity my undoing in his heart."

Moll said nothing. Had he looked at her then, he would have seen a curious expression on her face. At last she said deliberately:

"If you can tear your mind from the past for a space, you may buy me a dram. It is scarce mannerly to sit here and drink nothing, and likewise some liquor may serve to lighten our gloom."

At that, he did rouse himself, sat upright, passed his hand across his face, and smiled at her in an apologetic manner.

"On my life, I'm an unmannerly rogue, Moll, and presume upon your friendship." He beckoned to a passing tapster. "Come, what shall it be? A white-and-wormwood? I know that is your favourite whet."

"Nay, I am minded to taste this new spirit," answered Moll, quite pleasantly and yet with a certain constraint in her tone. "Every new vice should be experienced, and it is full time I made acquaintance with Madam Geneva."

"Nay, not that," said Michael quickly.

"And why not that?" demanded Moll, leaning her elbow on the table and looking provocative.

"It is an ill thing."

"I have a passion for ill things." A pause. "And if you will not stand treat for this one," added Moll, fishing for her purse, "I will even buy it for myself."

Michael caught her hand, and bade the tapster bring her what she desired. Neither said a word until the dram was brought; and it was not one of their companionable silences. When the tapster had gone again, Moll sipped her gin slowly, tasting it on her tongue.

"It is good for the melancholy, they say," she remarked, "and it warms the belly and it is cheap. Three excellent things in its favour, my friend."

"I hate it! " cried Michael, with sudden, strange fierceness.

"And shall I tell you why?" retorted Moll. "Because it came out of Holland, along with strong tobacco, deep pockets, he-whores, and a Dutch king."

"No," said Michael. "I cannot tell why I hate it, only I know that the very smell of it is somehow evil."

"So is that of a close-stool and a Tom-turdman, yet both benefit mankind."

He smiled abstractedly, stared at the colourless, sickly-odoured spirit, shivered, wondered at himself, and said with an effort:

"Let's go eat a pie or see the negro woman or listen to a music-concert."

"A music-concert! " Moll cried scornfully. "Two fiddlers scraping *Lillibulero* and a decayed soldier farting on a trumpet. You have low tastes, my friend."

(iv)

A black depression had settled on Michael by the time he had taken leave of Moll and was walking homeward. It was not only that he had seen Eve again, nor that he had offended Moll (he knew he had, and that she had reason to be irritated by him, though she had bidden him good night with her usual friendliness), nor even that the mention of his old friend and political opponent, Tom Fields, had brought very close to him the constant threat under which he lived, the threat of prison, perhaps of hanging. There was an odd, gnawing fear at his heart which had nothing to do with Eve or Moll or Tom, a fear vague and impersonal. The night was closing in around him and the watch were going their rounds, rapping on the doors of those housekeepers who had not yet hung out the lanthorn commanded by law to burn from dusk until eleven o'clock; and it seemed to him as though ghostly curtains were being drawn over London, and that the scene darkened like the stage at the close of a tragedy. He skirted a street brawl, satisfied a constable of the watch that he was a respectable citizen, and refused the invitation of a linkboy to light him home; but all the while he walked in a world of shadows, inhabited by the phantoms of his own premonitions.

A sense of failure weighed upon him. He had failed to convince King James of the treachery he had discovered in high places, and now that treachery was victorious and he, at six-and-twenty, was spending his days totting up figures in a brewer's counting-house and his nights writing anonymous tracts to an indifferent world which had decided to accept the established Government. He thought wistfully of poor Nick Hammond; he at least found excitement and romance in his wretched little Jacobite club, in his poor little treasons; in company with other fanatics in some back room he plotted the counter-revolution, and believed in miracles. But Michael had no companions in his work, nor was there a shred of romance about it, nor did he believe in counter-revolutions brought about by French troops or time-serving lords. He believed in a restoration brought about by the people, years, perhaps centuries, after he was dead; and he did not know the people, or at least did not yet believe in them, only he was afraid for them now as he walked through the London night; like a flock of busily feeding sheep, they were being driven by a hireling into the unknown menace of the wilderness.

He came down Cheapside and the signboards creaked and complained above him in the night wind, the signboards of trade. A hundred sturdy, independent little shopkeepers pursued their crafts beneath those signs, but for how long? The great ones who already had crushed out of existence a free peasantry must soon turn their attention to the small trader. Vance himself had spoken of great men squeezing out their smaller neighbours, but he could not follow the thought to its conclusion, had not the wit to see that this which he called a sign of the times was a writing on the wall for him and his like. Danger was in the air like a pestilence; Michael smelt it in the sweet sickly odour that came from a shop above which hung the sign of an old woman in a ruff and high-crowned hat: Madam Geneva, the patroness of gin. He saw it in the lottery-offices with their flaming, lying placards; he heard it in the clink of coin from behind the closed shutters in Goldsmiths' Row. But little men like Vance were blind and deaf to it, pursuing their petty feuds, intent upon their ancient "misteries", set in their absurd little snobberies; they would "leave great matters to great folk", they were "resolved to live peaceable", they persisted in believing that a king brought over by a wealthy faction had the power and the inclination to protect them and their sacred laws. And was it not the height of presumption and folly to imagine that he, a poor, anonymous pamphleteer, regarded by them as a "foreigner" because he had been born outside their City liberties, could ever convince them to the contrary?

The watch went by again, swinging their lanthorns and calling hoarsely "Eleven of the clock and a dark night!" And from the ale-houses and taverns the last customers came pouring, cheerful with songs and ale, hurrying home before the lights of London went out and plunged the City into that dangerous darkness wherein roamed the Roaring Boys and the footpads, the bullies and the housebreakers. Prostitutes scurried along with a wary eye for the watch, and from the direction of the Wood Street Compter came rattling a cart with two coffins in it, cheap deal coffins containing the remains of prisoners to be pitched into the nearest poor-hole. The curtains were being drawn over London, not to lift again until the raucous voices of the milk-walkers broke the silence with their cheerful "Any milk here?"; and the slattern with the tub upon her head came whining "Any kitchen-stuff have you, maids?"; and the wretched little chimney-boys, with their blackened faces and their emaciated limbs, trotted round to seek custom for their masters with their shrill "Chimneys to sweep, O!" Then would come the rumble of the loaded drays, the bleat of sheep and the lowing of cattle as the drovers herded their charges into Smithfield Market, the bang of shutters being taken down by yawning 'prentices, the bustle from the inn-yards, and the busy figures of housewives emptying chamber-pots and ashcans into the street. But that hour was far away, and meantime the curtain fell on London, as one by one the house-keepers put out the light before their door and the candles were snuffed in every tavern window and the street emptied of all save those who pursued unlawful business in the dark.

As Michael turned into Bird-in-Hand Court he paused and looked back along Chepe. Only the dim gleam of a watchman's lanthorn lightened the black gloom, feeble beacon for mariners in a world of pirates; the signboards creaked like the chains of a loaded gallows, and two dogs fought and snarled over the refuse in the gutter. But then above those sounds he heard a frail voice singing to itself, and turning saw a shadow flit across a lighted window, on the ledge of which stood well-tended pots of flowers; and a great sadness overwhelmed him for all the Maralyns of London City, and for all the Vances, for the little men and women, the too-patient men and women, who went about their business and reverenced authority, and took infinite pains to learn a craft and prided themselves on their responsibility and their skill and their independence, for this flock of human sheep who were too busy with their lawful business to hear the growl of the wolf or recognise the wilderness into which they were being driven, or turn to see whether it was the shepherd who drove them or a hireling.

This sadness lay heavy on his heart, and the gloom enveloped him; and the reek of gin was in his nostrils and the taste of bitterness was in his mouth, as he walked slowly to his master's door.

PART TWO

One

(i)

MR VANCE came into his yard with his brisk little trot, and paused under the lanthorn hanging in the entry to observe, with a searching eye, the unloading of a dray which had just come lumbering into the yard with barrels of "liquor" brought up from the Thames at Three Cranes Wharf, which lay at the foot of Queen Street. The dray horse was having his morning bucket of small-ale; from the counting-house there sounded already the squeaking of a busy quill; and through the open doorway of the brewhouse there issued a cloud of steam, the crackle of wood in a furnace, and an odour of malt. Mr Vance opened his lungs to inhale a deep breath of that glorious odour, and trotted into the brewhouse, taking off his coat as he went.

He loved this early morning hour, when the City was still asleep and the smoke of his brewhouse chimney ascended into the clear air. To him there was nothing under heaven so romantic, so deeply exciting, so all-absorbing as his craft. His hearty voice boomed forth to the tune of *Monday's Work*, which was his usual morning hymn:

> "Good morrow, neighbour Gamble,
> Come let you and I go ramble,
> Last night I was shot
> Through the brains with a pot,
> And now my stomach doth wamble.
> Your possets and your caudles
> Are fit for babes in cradles ;
> A piece of salt hog
> And a hair of the old dog,
> Will cure our drunken noddles."

He went first to inspect his sacks of malt, being always fearful lest some knave of a maltster's 'prentice had put good malt on the top and defective stuff beneath, or, in the language of brewing, had "capped it in the sack". Having satisfied himself that all was in order, he climbed the short ladder that led up to the copper in which the liquor was heated, and finding that the temperature was correct, called down to a 'prentice to stand by the hand-pump. Trotting down once more, he went to the wall and took down the wooden mash-stick and fork; he handled these implements lovingly, and spent a little while inspecting them to make sure that they were clean and had not been roughly handled in yesterday's brewing; they were black with age and frequent use, for they had come down to him from his father; such tools had a kind of magic in them for him, but 'prentices had no reverence for the implements of their craft, and only last week he had found with horror that improper handling had started a splinter in the stick. Alec and a journeyman were waiting beside the huge oak mash-tun into which the liquor was now being pumped, and solemnly handing the mash-stick to the journeyman, Vance gave the word for the sacks of malt to be tipped in. The master stayed a while to watch the initial stage of mashing, then passed on to inspect yesterday's ale which was cooling.

The open, shallow cooler was filled almost to the brim with new ale, and again the brewer opened his lungs to inhale that good odour. Light from the rising sun was stealing in through a window on the east, so he closed this and opened another on the west that the fresh breeze might assist the cooling. Then he went on to his fermenting-vats, standing a while by each as he used hand, nose and eyes to discover the stage of fermentation; he shouted to a 'prentice to begin skimming one of them, and seizing a wooden oar himself began vigorously to "rouse" another. One tun was being run off into a huge vat, where it would be kept until "old and stale", the correct state for strong-ale; it was casked only when required by the customer. Vance drew no more than five kilderkins from a quarter of malt for this strong-ale, which was his pride and joy, and for which the slang term was huff-cap.

He returned presently to the mash-tub, but paused by the way to contemplate, with a sigh, a certain antique chair with an oddly shaped seat, which stood against the wall. In the days when Vance had been apprenticed to his father there had been a ceremony connected with this chair and with the periodic visits of the ale-conner, an official employed by the Brewers' Company to test the goodness of all ale brewed within the City liberties. On such occasions the master brewer, with a solemnity proper to the occasion, poured a little ale into the saucer-like seat of this chair, and the ale-conner, who always wore leather breeches, then sat himself down in the fragrant puddle. He rose after an appropriate interval, and exhibited the seat of his breeches to his assistant; if ale adhered to them, all was well, but if not, it was judged that the brewer in question had adulterated his ale so that it was no longer thick and sticky as it should be, when it was the ale-conner's duty to "present" him to the Brewers' Company, who punished him as they thought fit. But times had changed, reflected Vance sadly, and all the ale-conner did now was to drink a measure of the ale and form his own judgment upon its goodness, and thus were the honest citizens of London very frequently cheated of their rightful beverage and were given adulterated ale. He sighed deeply again, and betook himself to the mash-tub, where he tested the gravity of the mash by dipping an expert finger into it. He called out immediately to have another sack of malt tipped in, for he at least believed in giving his customers good ale for their money.

With a short interval at nine o'clock for a tankard of ale and some bread and cheese, Mr Vance and his men worked vigorously all the morning; but the master left the brewhouse a little before the bell rang at noon on this particular day, because he was entertaining his friend and rival, John Bunch, to dinner.

Nathaniel Vance and John Bunch dined with each other alternately once a month, and had done so for many years. They had played together as children, and each cherished for the other a warm but secret affection; it was a time-honoured custom with them to quarrel violently, whenever they met, on the respective merits of ale and beer, for John Bunch was a beer-brewer. When they dined together, they drank wine, which both detested, but since Vance would not allow beer on his table and Bunch would not permit ale on his, and since it would have been discourteous to force upon a guest a beverage obnoxious to him, only wine remained. As Mr. Vance came trotting into his living-room this noontide he found that his wife, to whom he left the choosing and ordering of such "foreign" liquor, had placed a bottle of this new port upon the board; he peered at it and sniffed at it, and frowned; it smelt sweet and looked sickly, and it would infallibly give him a disordered belly. But since the commencement of this interminable war against France, the light French wines he had tolerated were forbidden to be brought over, so he supposed that this rich poison from Portugal must be endured. He was still sniffing at it when Mr John Bunch was ushered in.

Bunch was as tall and lean as Vance was short and plump. He was a childless widower and lived with his sister, a grey, gaunt woman of indeterminate age, whose sole joy, interest and aim in life was the occupation known as "knotting". Everything in Mr Bunch's house was "knotted", even to the wall-hangings and bed-curtains; the poor man appeared to live in a gigantic spider's web. He was, however, a genial sort of person, less irascible and pompous than his friend, yet without Vance's fundamental charity and honesty. Bunch prided himself on moving with the times, confessed frankly that he was not above adulterating his beer ("if I don't do it, the landlords will do it for me, and wherefore should they reap the harvest?"), burned the obnoxious sea-coal in his furnace, and since he agreed with Mrs Vance in deeming the whole breed of 'prentices arrant rascals, was gradually replacing these lads by labourers working under a foreman.

"I really must beg your pardon, Jack," said Mr Vance, after they were sat down and the host was busy carving up two leveets, "for offering you this newfangled poison called port, or indeed any juice of the spiteful grape, for I remember well what good John Taylor saith: 'Wine is but single broth, ale' "—he paused heavily on the word—" 'is meat, drink and cloth.' Ahem! "

The customary challenge being thus delivered, Bunch straightway took up the gauntlet, and by the time the dessert was put upon the table they were calling each other "John" and "Nathaniel", which changed to "Mr Bunch" and "Mr Vance" with the withdrawing of the cloth, and became a formal "Sir" as the wine got into them and the battle waged more fiercely. Mr Bunch, in a maddeningly superior manner, affirmed the antiquity of beer by a great show of learning.

"The Saxons, sir, knew all about hops, for there is reference to the hymele, or hop-plant, in the Anglo-Saxon version of the *Herbarium* of Aupleius. Moreover, the town called Himbleton in Worcestershire was originally Hymel-tun, which can signify nothing else but a hop-yard."

To this Mr Vance retorted by quoting the old distich:

> "Hops, Reformation, bays and beer
> Came into England all in one year."

Before Bunch could dispose of this, his rival began to roar out some verses from an early sixteenth-century song, accompanying himself by an impassioned banging on the table with his glass:

> "And in very deed, the hop's but a weed
> Brought over 'gainst law and here set for sale.
> Would the law were removed and no more beer brewed,
> But all men betake them to a pot of good Ale.
> But to speak of killing, that am I not willing,
> For that in a manner were but to rail,
> But Beer hath its name 'cause it brings to the Bier,
> Therefore, well fare, say I, to a pot of good Ale."

"My dear sir," said Bunch loftily, "such vulgar ballads prove nothing. Now I could quote you——"

"Vulgar, quotha, vulgar!" shouted Vance, springing up from the table. "Belike you would call Andrew Boorde vulgar, and the Water Poet, and Chaucer, and Will Shakespeare likewise; I defy you, sir, to find me one reference in the whole of Master Shakespeare's works to beer, but as for ale, he saith: 'A pot of good ale is a dish for a king.' And Boorde, sir, what saith he in his *Dietary*?—Here it is, sir, here is the very passage," cried Vance triumphantly, having by this time fetched a pile of printed allies from his shelf. " 'Beer is the natural drink for a Dutchman, but now of late days it is much used in England to the detriment of many English people; especially it killeth them the which be troubled with the stone, and the colick and the strangulion; for the drink is a cold drink; yet it doth make a man fat and doth inflate the belly'—what did you say, sir, what did you say? You are pleased to be amused, it seems. I beg you, sir, do not trouble to hide your mirth on my account. Prithee split your sides with laughing, since foolish mirth is all the defence you have to offer for the rot-gutting, liver-drying, gullet-shrinking pest-water which rightly is sold in hogsheads since it is fit only for swine.''

Pausing only to gulp a breath, Mr Vance roared out again:

"Ale is immortal, and be there no stops
    In honest lads' drinking, can live without hops."

He then sat down rather suddenly in his chair, and panting and glaring, silently dared Mr Bunch to argue further.

But Mr Bunch for once failed to take up the challenge. He seemed to have fallen into a meditative mood, and said mildly:

"It is the juniper-berry rather than the poor hop which should be censured nowadays, neighbour, for this guzzling of gin is spreading, not a doubt of that."

"Huh!" snorted Vance crossly, and obviously resentful of the change of subject, "you have been listening to the ravings of my clerk, who, though a good lad, hath a maggot in his brain and swears that gin will ruin half the City."

"I need not to listen to your clerk," retorted Bunch, sipping his port with distaste, "when it comes to talk of Madam Geneva. I have eyes and ears in my head, and both these organs tell me plain that she is a cunning strumpet and enlists new gamesters every day."

"Pooh, pooh! There are but two gin-shops in Chepe."

"Gin-shops, forsooth! Why, every tradesman is beginning to sell the stuff. You're acquaint with Borthwick of the Golden Sleeve? A year since his cloth was little better than is sold at Rag-fair, but now he has two topping grocers' sons bound to him, is carried to church in a hackney, and stands at his shop-door all day long advertising his goods upon his person. What think you has brought on to his shelves brocade at eight-and-twenty shillings the yard, and dimity and three-piled velvets and good Flanders serge? Why, it is the drams with which he seduces his customers to part with their money; and I tell you, all crafts are catching the same pest."

It was nonsense, said Vance; and he kept repeating to himself that it was nonsense as he went about his work that afternoon. Jack Bunch loved to exaggerate, to frighten and to tease. Yet he felt curiously uneasy as he superintended the scrubbing out of his oaken vats and the repairing and washing of casks, a feeling he resolutely attributed to that vile drink, port, and anon was pleased when a distant roll of thunder gave him an added excuse for so uncomfortable and foolish a lowering of spirits. He trotted out into the yard and looked anxiously up into the sky. Thunder was a notorious enemy to malt-liquor, and he had a pet tun of strong-ale maturing in his cellars against Christmas. He must cover the tun at once with solid pieces of iron kept specially for the purpose, but he could not for the moment recollect where they were stored. Maralyn would know; that good little wench knew everything. He stepped briskly into the house and approached the door of the kitchen; it stood open, and he stopped suddenly upon the threshold, peering in, arrested by what he saw.

Yet it was a very simple, innocent little tableau that kept him there, staring. Maralyn stood by the table, holding on it a deep bowl which gave forth a steam; and by her side, with his hands in the bowl, stood the Scots 'prentice, Alec Moray. So they stood, facing Vance, but not seeing him, for both their glances were turned downward into the bowl. Despite their unemotional attitudes, there was an air about each of them of simple, deep content, of intimacy even, the woman ministering to the need of man, but not of any man, rather of this one particular male creature. So much Vance sensed in a sudden flash of intuition which had passed almost before he knew that it had come. Then Maralyn looked up, noticed him standing there, and smiled with perfect naturalness.

"This late cold spell hath brought poor Alec's chilblains here already," she said mildly, "so I have boiled oats in water till

75

they be dry, and am causing him to steep his hands therein. It is an excellent remedy."

Then the pair of them stood silent, looking frankly, innocently, and without a trace of self-consciousness at Mr Vance, who, the vague depression in his mind unreasonably augmented, forgot what he had come about, and returned to the brewhouse without a word.

(ii)

In the weeks that followed, Mr Vance was given real and sufficient cause for uneasiness by a matter even more disquieting than a thunderstorm. For the draw of the Million Lottery was near, and the whole City seemed to have become temporarily insane. The news-sheets lay neglected in coffee-house and tavern, and only the ticket-catalogues were read; the talk was all of blank and benefit, and "My son has five pounds in it" or "My daughter was told by the astrologer that she would certainly draw the twenty-pound prize." Servants, 'prentices, labourers, even children, squandered their little bits of money, and sober house-wives, seduced by the "morocco-men" hired by the promoters to sell books of tickets, parted with the precious shillings with which they should have bought candles, meat and bread. For the past month even Nat seemed to have lost his senses, was for ever murmuring numbers to himself and rushing off to the astrologer, cast down one morning by an evil dream in which he had drawn a blank, feverishly elated the next evening because he had seen the number of his ticket written up in some "advice", that is, advertisement, on a wall. Vance could not understand the madness; what did any man want with unearned wealth which could be gained only by the ruin of thousands of his fellows?

The draw was announced to take place in December at Saddlers' Hall, which stood at the west end of Cheapside, between Gutter and Foster Lanes. To increase the excitement, the promoters had arranged that the drawing should last three weeks, despite the protest of the City Companies, who insisted that so long a period during which trade would be practically at

76

a standstill would ruin many small masters. Mr Vance himself acted with a high hand towards his own employees; he assembled his 'prentices and forbade them to attend the draw, asserting that any one among them disobeying this order would be considered by him to have broken the terms of his indentures and would be hauled before a magistrate. He would give no holiday, he said, for such an occasion; but to sweeten this bitter pill he announced that he had devised some treats for them on Sundays and for the evenings; he would take them to Gresham College to view the rarities there, to a coach-race in the Hyde Park (a great concession, this, for he seldom stirred outside the City liberties), to the baiting of a "green" bull at Hockley-in-the-Hole, and on every evening throughout the period of the draw he would entertain them in his parlour with strong-ale, minced pies, and songs. They would be ungrateful indeed, he concluded, if such entertainments did not compensate them for a sight of the wicked doings at Saddlers' Hall.

He awoke with a heavy heart on the first morning of the draw, and listened as he dressed to the shrill, excited laughter, and the pattering of feet, and the raucous cries of the street-sellers which already, at half past three of a December's morning, told of the migration of the City towards the scene of the draw. His craftsman's soul was revolted by this mad scramble for unearned gold, and he could not imagine why the Government had inaugurated such madness. Well, thank God it would soon be over, and a plain man could walk the streets again without having his self-respect insulted by a sight of the crowds feverishly jostling round the windows of the lottery-offices, drinking in the flaming circulars which promised wealth without labour, gloating over the piles of gold which, lied the placards, could be got for one guinea, and sober folk would cease to have their heads stuffed with numbers and turn them to honest craftsmanship again.

All that day the lottery intruded on him. His 'prentices were preoccupied, slack, and prone to whisper in corners when his back was turned; when he scolded them, they gave him sullen looks, and nothing he could say or do could make them attend to their business. One of his most trusted draymen had absented himself, as had all the labourers, over whom Mr Vance had no real control because they were not bound to him as were the 'prentices; and every hour, every minute, the normal sounds of the City and the dear familiar noises of the brewhouse were drowned by that ceaseless patter of feet all going in one direction, by the distant blasts of a trumpet which announced a prize or "welcome", and by the dull roar of voices, sometimes exultant, sometimes mocking, the voices of a people crazy with avarice and credulity.

That night when work was done he shepherded his sulky 'prentices into his living-room, closed the shutters and bolted the outer door, gave them an excellent feast of veal served with currants and some of Maralyn's famous marchpane, and afterwards gathered his flock around the blazing fire, beamed upon them as he mulled some ale, and informed them with forced jocularity that they were about to spend a most merry evening.

All the ingredients for merriment were here, he thought wistfully, glancing around the comfortable room. The toasting-dog had slices of bread upon his fork so that anon some good brown toast could float in the hot ale, the dishes of crisp minced pies were reminiscent of Christmas, the perfumes of his own nappy ale brewed from the finest malt and the best liquor in the world, filled the room with its aroma; here was he, a sufficiently prosperous craftsman, a master who exhibited a genuine care for his people, who instructed them daily in a "mistery" so ancient, so healthful, so beneficial to mankind that it might almost be termed sacred, and there were they, strapping lads upon the brink of manhood, being entertained without stint. Yet there they sat, as glum as schoolboys denied a holiday, gulping down his nappy as though it were physic, sullen and fidgety because they might not go and see a few men made rich without deserving it, and a multitude ruined by numbers drawn out of a wheel.

He set his teeth and resolved to make them contented even against their will. He called for his recorders and bade Maralyn sit down to her clavicytherium, and set them all singing *Philon the Shepherd*, a pretty madrigal by Will Byrde. Then Mr Pennington sang them Henry Purcell's *When I was Laid in Earth* to Maralyn's accompaniment, and afterwards played for her when she gave them *Now ponder well, you Parents dear*. The 'prentices munched and gulped in silence, and fidgeted, and cast furtive glances towards the window through which intruded the deadened echoes of a more entrancing music. Then Vance himself led a series of catches, and presently, sitting in the midst of the sullen circle, began to roar out his beloved ballads in praise of ale, *Sir John Barleycorn, Good Ale for my Money*, and then his prime favourite, *Jolly Good Ale and Old*:

> "I cannot eat but little meat,
>   my stomach is not good,
> But sure I think that I can drink
>   with him that wears a hood.
> Though I go bare, take ye no care,
>   I am nothing a-cold;
> I stuff my skin so full within
>   of jolly good ale and old."

"Now, lads, the chorus!" roared Vance. "Come on, you unmannerly, scowling young rascals!

> "Back and side go bare, go bare,
>   both foot and hand go cold;
> But belly, God send thee aye enough
>   OF JOLLY GOOD ALE AND OLD!"

But his lusty bellow was drowned during this chorus by an even greater din which came from without, which penetrated the closed shutters, and which seemed to draw nearer and nearer. There was a sudden silence in the living-room; Maralyn stood arrested in the act of handing the pies, Michael's hands paused on the strings of the clavicytherium, Vance sat with his mouth open, his Greybeard-jug flourished at shoulder-height, an incongruous statue.

"It is the mob," he muttered, his ruddy face paling, "bent on some mischief, I'll be bound. I'll fetch my pistols, marry will I, lest locked doors and closed shutters serve not to keep out the knaves."

But as he made to move, one of the 'prentices sprang from his seat and cried, his face working with excitement:

"Not so, master; it is the winning of the thousand-pound

prize, my soul on it. Hark! they are cheering as at some royal procession."

"They are cheering belike because they scent my ale," growled Vance. "I know them! This is a great night for such rascals since every constable will be gone to Saddlers' Hall and peaceful cits must needs defend themselves——"

His teeth grated on the word, for, loud and peremptory, there had come a thundering upon the outer door, and then a shout of "Open! Open! "

"Open, is it?" yelled Vance. "I'll open your guts, you bear-garden scum! I'll pump you full of lead——"

"Father! " cried Maralyn, seizing his arm. "Stay, for God's sake! That was Nat's voice. Belike he has won a benefit and brings company to celebrate his gains. I'll go to the door," she went on, quietly efficient as usual, "and will enquire through it the nature of this summons."

And before her father could protest she was gone; the uproar without had died to a confused murmur and shuffle of feet, so that they heard the unhurried patter of her slippers, and then her voice, pleasant but authoritative, enquiring who was there. A great clamour answered her, of voices mixed with laughter and cheering, and then they heard someone shout:

"It is the luckiest dog in London; let him in! "

After a moment there came the noise of bolts being with-drawn and the turning of a heavy key, and then there surged into the room a tide of human bodies, a confusion of shoving elbows, gesticulating hands, tramping feet, wildly working faces; in the forefront stalked Nat, his hands clasped together and holding something between them. He came straight up to his father, bowed with a touch of irony, and said, carefully matter-of-fact:

"I am come to beg your blessing, sir, and to make known to you that I have won the thousand-pound prize."

(iii)

For the next half-hour there was such a bustle, the 'prentices running to fetch in another kilderkin of the best ale, Maralyn stripping the larder of provisions wherewith to entertain the hungry throng, Mrs Vance, who had gone to bed some while before, appearing from upstairs in her bedgown, with her night-rail in disarray and her face bewildered, Michael pushing furniture about the better to accommodate so great a concourse, that there was no leisure to enquire the details of this apparent miracle. Meantime old Vance himself sat slumped in the chair into which he had fallen on the first receipt of the news, his eyes stupid, his face ashen, his plump belly rising and falling like a troubled sea.

Then at last Nat showed them the prize. He had it there in his hands, or rather he had a piece of paper which declared that the promoters of the Million Lottery would pay the sum of one thousand pounds sterling to the holder or holders of the ticket, six-three-nine. This promissory note was enlivened with a crude drawing of Fortune's wheel, the portrait of a gentleman supposed to be King Midas, and the true Protestant, pithy, but somewhat startling motto:

> "In God is my Hope,
> But a Fart for the Pope."

Then, seated in a place of honour by the hearth, Nat told them all about the draw. There was utter silence while he spoke, everyone hanging on his words. There was no sullenness or boredom on the 'prentices' faces now; they did not like the son of the house and when they had leisure to think about it they would grudge him his good fortune, but just at this moment they knew only that here sat a human being who really and truly had become rich in an hour, that they were actually seeing and hearing an acquaintance who had become possessed of fabulous wealth without doing a hand's turn to earn it. Their faces were awed as they stared at him, as though he were some being from another world.

Nat had arrived at Saddlers' Hall pretty early that morning, for his master had shut up his shop for the day, yet already the place was crowded and it was difficult to pass along any of the streets which gave access to it. He gave a very lively description of the crowd ("like cats round the horse-flesh barrow," he said), and recorded some of the conversation he had overheard, of how the women had bragged of the fine gowns they would buy, the flash cits of the handsome wigs they would purchase, the sots of what rare wines they would drink; and so on. Quite a number of the town gentry were there, said he, and Cheapside so thronged with chairs and coaches that all the ordinary traffic was at a standstill. By dint of patience and perseverance, he had managed by midday to get as far as the entry, where sat the booksellers' hacks selling the printed catalogues, with the crowd scrambling and fighting to buy. An hour later he had squeezed into the hall itself, but he could get no further for the solid wedge of people, some of whom had camped outside all night; he could see the wigs of the Trustees upon the platform, and that was all, except when a fellow appeared upon a rostrum to announce a benefit by a blast upon his trumpet. It was comic, he said, to see how a man or woman fought to get on the platform directly the benefit number was called out, shouting "That's mine!", defiantly waving a ticket, and attacking the people around with fist and voice, and how, often enough, when such a person had torn a passage through to the platform, he was proved to have mistaken his number, and would weep or curse or rave, the crowd hooting meanwhile with spiteful mirth.

It was not until late afternoon that there had run through the multitude a rumour that the biggest prize was about to be announced. How they had known, or whether they had only guessed, he could not tell; but as the rumour spread, a strange hush had fallen, and he himself had known that his fortune was about to be given into his hands.

"Tut, boy," murmured his father with an effort, "how could you have known any such thing?"

"'Twas the astrologer in Prescott Street told him," cried a voice from Nat's suddenly enlarged circle of friends. "The progressed Sun was trine to his Ruler in the fifth house and——"

"It was nothing of the kind," interrupted Nat easily. "I knew because I have an eye for money and attract it towards me as the magnet attracts iron. I tell you, I knew that I must win. Is that not so, Frank?" he added, turning to a round-shouldered gentleman in a fox-coloured wig who stood at his elbow, and who seemed to have assumed the rôle of protector or patron of the fortunate apprentice.

"Why indeed it is so," said Frank Maynard, smiling round upon the company. "Our young friend's eye is to him as the water-diviner's rod, though it perceives a more valuable commodity."

"And what will you do with such vast wealth?" cried a voice; and other voices echoed the burning question.

"I shall marry on it for a start," said Nat, with a swift, sidelong glance at Maynard. "And that, I warrant, is what a-many of you would do had you been lucky. Friend Alec here, for one," he added, turning to the young Scot who stood silent among the other 'prentices; and there was something faintly mocking in Nat's tone.

"I'd never have a thousand pounds by your way o' it, Master Nat," replied Alec, polite but cold. "I am content to earn my money by honest toil. It ever was the way o' my countrymen."

"And thus is Scotland the poorest nation in the world."

"And forbye the most honest. Nor is there aught to be ashamed of in being poor, or none that ever I kent. But if Master Nat can think of aught, I'd be obliged if he would tell me."

There was a slightly uncomfortable pause. Maralyn made an unconscious movement towards her boy-lover, who stood with fists clenched at his sides, his lips close-set, his eyes dangerous. Then Michael Pennington stepped into the breach.

"Gentlemen, ye have enjoyed Master Vance's right good ale, and I think we should drink a toast to him, and after it another to that most fortunate young citizen, his son. And then, say I, let us bid each other good night, for the hour grows late and we are laborious men who must be up betimes; ay, even Master Nat, until he has his fortune in his hands, must continue to take down his master's shutters at six of the clock."

He said the last few sentences with a smile and in a tone which robbed them of offence, and the crowd, forgetting the recent passage of arms, raised their cans in the toasts and presently began to drift away with much wringing of Nat's hand and wishing him joy in his good fortune. After a while there was no one left but Vance, Nat, Michael, Alec and Maralyn; for Mrs Vance and the other 'prentices had taken themselves to bed.

"Bless me," murmured the brewer, lying back in his enclosed arm-chair, stretching out his short legs, and drawing on a cold pipe, "I'm all amazed with this day's happenings and even yet can scarce credit that my Nat, at sixteen years of age, should be the owner of one thousand pounds. Let me have another look at that paper, boy, that I may assure myself there's no trick in it. I never did like these lotteries and would as soon trust an Irishman as I would a promoter."

"By your leave, sir, I will help Miss Maralyn redd up the room," said Alec; and the two young people began to clear away the tankards and dishes, not speaking, not even glancing at each other, yet giving an impression of harmony and intimacy as though the same brain and heart controlled two bodies. Michael, meanwhile, leaned against the chimney-breast, and Nat sat in his chair with his hands neatly folded in his lap, and his eyes looking steadily into the fire. Already he seemed subtly to have changed. There was about him a new, indefinable sense of power and a touch of that insolence which sudden wealth brings with it.

(iv)

"Money has a strange trick of causing jars and dissensions wheresoever it goes," mused Michael aloud, running his finger along the edge of the chimney-shelf, "whether in nations or in men. And yet I take it to be in itself but a neutral quantity, evil only when abused. Still I am not sure. It is not as other things in this world which are good until wrongly used; it seems in some strange way to corrupt whomsoever it touches."

"A very pretty sermon, Mr Pennington," sneered Nat.

Michael smiled down on him.

"I beg your pardon, sir, I really do. I was unmannerly enough to think aloud."

"You can scarce expect me to agree with your thoughts when I intend to devote the rest of my life to the pursuit of money."

"Pox on it, Nat!" exclaimed his father irritably. "What talk is this? Sure you cannot be so mad as to think you may live all your days upon what you may win in a lottery?"

"Ay, sir, in a manner of speaking I do, but it is not the kind of lottery which today has furnished me with a capital sum. To speak plain, I intend to buy myself out of my indentures straightway, and set up for a banker."

"A *banker*? And what strange creature may that be?"

"A banker is the new term for a goldsmith, sir, save that, unlike the old goldsmith, your modern banker needs no goods to sell."

"How now, prattle-box! Don't insult me with your riddles. Faith, Master Pennington, come to mine aid. Can you understand such mad talk?"

"I can, sir, but I must confess I am not at one with Master Nat in his favour of the idea. I believe the whole business of banking, as it is now coming to be practised, is an evil thing."

Nat looked up at him from beneath lowered lids and drawled:

"Bless me, nothing seems to please our Mr Pennington. I mind what a sweet sermon you did preach upon the evils of the lottery, and now here is another upon banking. Is it possible that you are disaffected towards the Government, Mr Pennington, and frown upon all things which came over from Holland with King William?"

"Banking originated in Venice," said Michael evenly, "if my memory fails me not. It was a native of that city, one Christopher Hagenbuck, who brought the idea to Queen Elizabeth when the English Crown was in need of extraordinary revenue. But the Queen would have none of it, and, saving your presence, it is not a trade which greatly commends itself to the English people."

"Nay," retorted Nat in high scorn, "we English have ever sat upon our arses and waited for the new ideas to grow stale ere we will adopt 'em. But now that we are fortunate enough to have gotten us a Dutchman for King, doubtless the English people will find themselves importing Dutch methods of finance likewise, whether they will or no."

"'Ounds!" cried poor Vance, utterly at sea, "will one of you be so good as to tell me what are these Dutch methods of finance?"

"Why, sir," condescended Nat, "I will tell you. From the time of the Union of the Crowns, the goldsmiths of London have received the moneys and valuables of those who desired to have such things in a place of security, and have charged a fee for the safe keeping of them."

He paused impressively, but his father snapped:

"So far you tell me nothing but stale news. Do I not deposit my moneys with Master Green of the Golden Mallet, as my father did before me, and pay him a just fee for securing it?"

"A just fee!" scoffed Nat. "That may be fine for you, but how does it advantage him and the trade of England? But let me take up my tale again. The exchange-banks overseas have learnt a different method. You must understand that these are not as banks of deposit, for the former need no capital of their own, but are established that they may turn the money with which they are entrusted into a currency which can readily be accepted by merchants, without need for testing the value of the coin, thus facilitating trade between nations. I hope I make myself plain?"

"A moment, Master Nat," said Michael, before Vance could reply. "The Bank of Amsterdam and other such exchange-banks are supposed to contain in their strong-rooms the whole amount of the bullion for which bank-money (I believe that is the term) is outstanding. But I believe you will not deny that this regulation is very indifferently observed. Moreover, it is a fact that the Bank of Amsterdam trades with the money entrusted to it, notably to the Dutch East India Company, and from what I can hear the practice is become general, and has been copied by the banks of deposit."

"I was about to explain this to my father," said Nat loftily, "when I was unmannerly interrupted."

86

"I ventured to offer the pill plain," said Michael, grinning, "and leave you to coat it as you may."

Vance rapped on the chair-arm with the stem of his pipe.

"Let me understand ye. The new banker, whether of exchange or deposit (and I confess I cannot distinguish betwixt 'em), not only trades with moneys entrusted to his care, not only pockets the interest he charges upon such loans, but actually issues bank-notes when he has not the bullion to back them. Pish, this is Bedllam talk."

"On the contrary, sir," said Nat, "'tis what the enlightened in our age term high finance."

"Is it so?" growled his father. "Well, I am a plain man, and I call it a beastly mixture of usury and cheating."

"My dear sir," said Nat wearily, "bankers are not in business as charitable institutions but to make a profit. The banker who sets himself up to live upon the trifling charges he receives for holding and letting lie idle other men's money, as do the out-moded goldsmiths, is a fool. Nay, I'll go further and quote Scripture to you; he is like to the man who wrapped his talent in a napkin and buried it in the ground. There's an excellent parable for you, and none but a Jew could have invented it."

"Hold your tongue, sauce-box!" roared his father. "I'll have no blasphemy in my house."

"Nay, sir, you mistake me; I have a profound admiration for the Jews, since they are the fathers of commerce and did, indeed, invent this banking system. Moreover, without them we never would have had the Revolution, for Suasso, of whom you may have heard, lent King William two million pounds for his expedition, and Sir Solomon Medina, his banker, did likewise. A bank begins to confer some real advantage on the realm only when it lends out the money it receives from this man to this other man who has need of it and will make it productive, and by creating money, by means of bank-notes and figures entered in a ledger, a bank quickens the nation's trade and keeps the circulation of cash flowing freely."

"The same might be said of coiners," murmured Michael, as the other paused for breath.

"Would you not be glad," continued Nat, ignoring this, "to

know, sir, that the moneys you entrust to the care of your gold-smith, instead of lying useless in his fettered trunks, were being employed by enterprising merchants, upon good and sufficient security, to enlarge the trade of the realm?"

"No, sir, I would not," flatly returned his father. "When I entrust my hard-earned money to a goldsmith, I do so only for safe keeping. He exacts from me a fee, which is right and proper since he does me a service. But he does not presume," cried the brewer, emphasising his words with his pipe-stem, "to trade with my money without consulting me, nor to pocket the interest from such ventures. If I please to adventure my money in some enterprise, I do so myself and expect return for it. And if, God help me, I should sink so low as to need cash upon whatever terms, I would hie me to the Jews and expect from that race who produced Judas Iscariot the beastliness of usury."

Nat sprang up. His face was flushed with a dull anger, and he looked suddenly younger and more like himself.

"Agad, I but waste my breath. Every new notion is viewed with horror by the men of its day."

"And sometimes likewise by the men of every day," slid in Michael quietly. "For I cannot call to mind that the methods of Iscariot, though they have been copied, have ever been generally approved."

"'Tis true," said Nat thinly, "that I myself have little liking for a man who struck a bargain and then repented of it."

Then Vance sprang up also.

"One word more like that in my presence, sir, and it will be the last time I call you son."

"You may call me what you please," snarled Nat, "but I'll warrant you'll change your tune anon, when I have made more money in a twelvemonth than you have earned since you were out of your indentures. I'm not too proud to learn from the Jews, or the Dutch, or any other, and though you'll never see me riding in my coach or apeing the beaux or buying a knight-hood, I swear you'll see me so hugely rich that the Lord Mayor will come a-begging of me to take charge of his moneys, and all the aldermen of every ward in London will make me the civility of their hats whensoever we meet."

They faced each other, the father and son, old Vance breathing heavily, his hands a-tremble, his face torn with anger, bewilderment, wounded love; Nat ugly in his youthful rage, his cunning eyes dangerous. And in that critical moment, when words might have been said which could not have been recalled, insults given which could not have been forgotten, it was Maralyn who drew the combatants from the precipice.

"Have you forgot, Father, that you have a meeting at Brewers' Hall to attend tomorrow morning? I'll warrant you'll nod over the wardens' speeches if you tarry here much longer. And you, Nat, you must away to bed and dream of your good fortune. Come, sirs, there's a last round left in the kilderkin, and we'll drink it in a last toast to Nat."

"Here's to banking and to all progress!" cried Nat defiantly, snatching the ale-can from her and draining it at a draught.

"Here's to honest trade," said Alec stolidly.

"Here's to Master Nat's health," said Michael, "which even he will own is more than wealth."

"And here's to his happiness," murmured Maralyn.

But Vance lifted his can in a solemn fashion, and with a new, unfamiliar note of sadness in his voice he said softly:

"Here's to my son."

Two

(i)

Mᴿs Vᴀɴᴄᴇ stood at the kitchen table, looking sulkily across it at her daughter Maralyn. The girl was in her mob and safe-guard, but her mother was dressed for going out, in a dove-coloured cloak and with a kerchief tied over her head.

"Now heaven defend us," cried she petulantly, "this is a fine thing when a chit of a girl begins to tell her mother what she must do. Will you set up for a female 'pothecary, Miss, that you profess to know the cure for every ailment?"

Maralyn went on busily kneading dough for bread, with a watchful eye upon the hourglass which hung upon the wall, for the moment was fast approaching when the red-hot faggots she had placed in the brick oven must be raked out, the inside hurriedly swabbed with a damp cloth, and the bread popped in. She said soothingly:

"I do but beg of you to give my remedy a fair trial, Mother. I say again that I am sure a walk and a gossip abroad on these fair spring mornings will induce sleep better than all your hop-pillows and 'pothecaries' mixtures. And since these remedies have done you no good, what harm is there in trying mine?"

"I have tried yours," snapped Mrs Vance, "and it hath done me no more good than the others. Moreover, I am no rich merchant's wife who can spend her mornings fingering laced nightcaps and scented gloves at the Exchange stalls."

"A few days longer, I beg of you, madam," pleaded Maralyn. "And besides," she added briskly, "we are in need of candles of both sorts, and I cannot leave the bread. It would be a kind-ness if you would but step over to the chandler's."

"Oh, very well," ungraciously consented her mother; and picking up a basket, she stalked out upon her errand.

It was indeed a fine spring morning; the air had a certain caress in it and the sun shone down from a sky of eggshell-blue; she remembered how, waking as usual that morning from a fitful sleep, she had heard the birds chirruping in the darkness. But she stood hesitant in the mouth of the court, scowling at sunlit Cheapside and nervous of that bustling thoroughfare. She had not gone out a-marketing since Maralyn had been old enough to run her errands for her, and she felt strangely awkward and shy, for her malady had made her neurotic, and she was, besides, approaching a difficult time of life. In a dim way the poor woman was aware of her constant irritability and regretted it; but a sort of fatefulness had come upon her, a melancholy resignation to her maladies of mind and body. She was fond of Vance in her way, but subconsciously she knew that he spoiled her, and therefore she felt towards him the faint contempt often to be found in the spoiled towards the spoiler. Maralyn she took for granted. Nat she had idolised because he was her only son, but she had begun to lose interest even in him since he had taken to a life of his own. Nor had she the consolation of the radically selfish; she was a very lonely, dissatisfied, helpless, rather stupid woman, who was losing her looks and knew it, whose health was really undermined by a disease for which there was apparently no remedy, who often glimpsed herself for what she was and hated what she glimpsed, a woman who had forgotten what it was to be happy and at ease.

She plunged into Cheapside, looking straight before her, nervously dreading an encounter with a neighbour, thankful that her errand would not take her as far as the Little Conduit, where she would have been sure to find acquaintances gossiping as they waited their turn to get water. The chandler's lay between Lawrence and Honey Lanes, and was not two hundred yards from her own door. She would hurry thither and buy her candles, then hurry back again. She had no faith whatsoever in Maralyn's simple remedy of fresh air and exercise, but lately it was too much trouble to defy even the gentle Maralyn.

Cheapside looked gay enough this morning. On the low pent-houses shading many of the shops stood pots of spring flowers, and the white posts that protected the side-walk from the street had been newly painted. It was still early, and the incessant procession of drays rumbled by with their loads, while high above this noise there sounded the sweet chimes of the Jesus Bells of Paul's School which stood in Milk Street. Some Children of Paul's, as the scholars were called, ran by in their blue frocks with books under their arms. The energy of spring and of early morning was abroad and the shrill voices of the street-sellers competed cheerfully: "White onions! New white St Thomas's onions!" "Green hasteds, ha!" "New mackerel, four for six-pence!" "Will you buy my radish and hard lettuce, mistress?" "Here are violets, a ha'penny a bunch." A Turk in a turban was selling rhubarb, a family of chair-menders was busy in the kennel; the bear-ward came along, heralded by drum and fife and followed by the dogs of several parishes; and the 'prentices standing at their masters' doors ogled the passing serving-maids and kept up a cheerful, incessant invitation to "Buy! Buy!"

She crossed the street, nervously dodging the traffic, and soon came to the tenement called the Cowface, in which was the chandler's shop. It was a humble but very useful sort of shop. The market-women and the street-sellers took their breakfast there, the link-boy called there nightly for his link, and servant-girls were sent thither at all hours of the day for half a peck of coals, a bag of sand, a besom, a quarter of cheese, or a penny-worth of firewood. Before entering the shop, Mrs Vance walked slowly past it, peering nervously through the bow-window. A butcher in his blue sleeves and woollen apron, with his bulldog at his heels, was gossiping with the proprietor, and she decided that she would dawdle outside until the shop was empty. She passed the time by staring into the tobacco-shop next door, wherein sat two or three Dutchmen, their hands in their breeches pockets as usual, their whiskered faces enigmatic, while they solemnly smoked a pipe before filling their boxes. After a while the butcher and his dog came out from the chandler's and Mrs Vance hurried in, deposited her basket upon the counter, and murmured that she required a pound each of waxes and tallows.

The chandler was an enormously fat person, with his linen stained brown from constant snuff-taking and a head as bald as an egg. He regarded Mrs Vance for a moment or two in silence, evidently trying to remember who she was; then, without moving, he said with satisfaction:

"Why, it is neighbour Vance's goodwife, so it is. Bless me, 'tis not often we see you abroad, Mistress Vance. Your daughter would be sick, perhaps?"

"No," replied Mrs Vance with a wan smile, "she does very well, but the morning being so fair I was tempted to take a walk."

The chandler digested this piece of information in silence, then reached under the counter and drew forth a long pipe, a box of tobacco, tinder and flint. Leisurely proceeding to fill and light the pipe, he observed:

"Some holds with beating the hoof, and some don't. Now me, I never take no exercise; never have and never will. Rouses up the bile, does walking, curdles the blood and tires the heart."

"Yes, yes, as you say," murmured Mrs Vance, nervously playing with the ends of her kerchief. "But I desire some candles, and if you——"

"Now I do call to mind," continued the chandler, taking no notice of the interruption, "that I've heard tell you don't sleep too well o' nights, neighbour. That's a pesty bad thing, that is, and I'll lay a wager the 'pothecaries can't do nothing for you."

Mrs Vance sighed and shook her head.

"Ah! I don't hold with 'pothecaries. Hand in glove with the upholders, most of 'em." Then he leaned a little forward over the counter, and continued slyly: "Now I could give you a little something that would make you sleep as sound o' nights as a malt-worm after a guzzle."

Mrs Vance's brittle temper flared.

"Now hang me, neighbour, I desire none of your remedies; all I desire from you is a pound of waxes and a pound of tallows, and I'll thank you to serve me and let me be gone about my business."

"Tilly vally," said the chandler, quite unmoved, "I did but hope to serve you in your affliction, and sure there's no offence in so neighbourly a wish. Methought you would be right glad to hear of something which would infallibly ease you, ay, and not only make you sleep sound, but warm your blood and please your belly and make you withal as merry as cobblers at a Crispin-feast."

"I have tried every remedy under the sun," wailed the poor woman, "and I tell you there is none which can cure me this side of the grave. Why, am I not now, this very morning, trudging about Chepe, a-burdened with a basket, all to please my young wench who hath got it into her noddle that there is nought like fresh air and exercise to induce a healthful sleep? A pox on her! Ay, and on you likewise. Give me my candles, I say, and let me go."

The chandler said nothing, but, slowly and appreciatively puffing at his pipe, moved off from the counter and disappeared into a back room. He was absent some few minutes, and when he returned he carried in his hand, not Mrs Vance's candles, but a small black bottle and a tiny measure. These he deposited, with an air of mystery, upon the counter in front of his peevish customer, leaned towards her, and with one elbow on the counter, and a large fore-finger wagged in her face, addressed her in a sibilant whisper:

"Now I'm a-going to give you a sample of my physic whether you will or no. Harkee, neighbour"—as Mrs Vance drew back— "I'll strike a bargain. You shall drink a measure of this and I will charge you not one ha'penny. While you drink it, I will fetch your candles, and if when you are ready to bid me goodday you still desire no further acquaintance with my remedy, why, then we will part neighbourly and honest, and no harm done. Come now, what say you to that?"

Mrs Vance hesitated, worn down by his importunity; besides, it was plain to her that the quickest way of getting her candles was to humour the man. Taking her silence for consent, the chandler uncorked the bottle and poured out a measure; this he placed carefully, as though it contained the most precious nectar, before Mrs Vance, recorked the bottle, put it under the counter, and with a significant wink, at last went off in search of the candles.

She took up the measure and looked into it critically. It was full of a colourless liquid which gave forth a strange smell, sweet and yet not sweet, repellant, and at the same time oddly enticing. After a while she ventured to take a sip; and immediately it was as though her mouth were ablaze and liquid fire ran through her body. In the shock of the moment she slammed the measure down upon the counter, gasping and choking and rolling anguished eyes towards the chandler; but he took no notice, tranquilly continuing his search for candles through the untidy shop. Then after a moment or two, the fire died down within her, leaving behind it a vivid, unnatural sort of warmth. Despite the spring weather, she had been cold all the morning; she was always cold whatever the weather, for she was always nervously fatigued; but now, from head to toe, there ran and spread this strange new warmth, so surprising and so grateful that she gave a tremulous, almost hysterical laugh.

"Now the pest take me," murmured Mrs Vance, scarce knowing what she said, "if this be not witchcraft."

Then she sipped again. This time she was ready for the fire, and her gasp was one of excitement rather than of shock. Again she sipped; and now she did not notice the fire, only the blessed warmth which was so penetrating that it seemed to have got into her mind as well as her body. She swallowed the remainder of the dram in one gulp; and straightway sat down upon a convenient stool, giggling foolishly, suddenly unself-conscious, oblivious alike to the fire and to the taste. It seemed to her very amusing that her vision had become blurred; the dusty, untidy shop, with its assortment of besoms and saucepans and lumps of cheese and jars of sweetmeats, was swimming in a most unaccountable way to and fro and up and down, but she felt no discomfort, only a kind of profound and surprised satisfaction, because she herself was hovering above it all, was the mistress of it all, was filled for the first time for many years with contentment and warmth and amusement and—yes, and the onset of a blessed drowsiness. Actually she found herself yawning; but the yawn ended in a foolish giggle as the large shining head of the chandler swam into her vision like a fish.

"Bless me, I took you for a chamber-pot. La, is that not a

sweet jest, neighbour? I took you for a chamber-pot hanging on a hook."

"Here are your candles, neighbour," said the chamber-pot, with a sly wink.

"Candles," repeated Mrs Vance profoundly. "Candles." And then, out of nowhere, a thought leapt into her mind, a thought so alarming that it stilled the swimming world and chilled the dear new warmth in her veins. "My husband," she faltered, tears starting to her eyes. "My hubsand will know that I have been—that is, he will infallibly smell it."

"Tilly vally," soothed the chandler, "d'ye take me for a green bull?" He pressed into her hand a little paper packet. "Sweet-meats, neighbour, sweetmeats flavoured strongly with mint. One sucked slowly in the mouth will drive all odour of Geneva from the breath, and likewise will serve to explain to your lord why you sleep this night as soft and quiet as a babe at the breast. Say to him you have discovered a magic sweetmeat which serves you better than all the remedies you have tried. He'll believe it; I know husbands, and in particular do I know your Master Vance."

At some later period of time she found herself standing outside the shop, and her legs began to carry her towards her home of their own accord. Everything was still very hazy, but pleasantly so; and she was warm in every part of her, glowing with it, smiling all over her face, because clutched in her heart was the knowledge that she was going to sleep tonight, sleep instantly, soundly, all night long, and tomorrow would not wake until it was time to rise, and when she did wake would feel rested and sweet-tempered, and would not snap at Vance nor grumble at Maralyn nor nag at the 'prentices. Meantime she was going home to dinner, and there was leg-of-mutton pie and a bean tansy afterwards, and this was a mighty fine street and the sun was shining, and tomorrow she would go to the chandler's again and buy another measure of this miraculous liquid, that she might sleep again tomorrow night, and so on every morning and every night; and no one but the chandler would be any the wiser. It was not even expensive, this elixir; the chandler had assured her that a dram cost only one ha'penny.

Dear Madam Geneva! Kind, cheap, warming, life-giving Madam Geneva! How great a benefit did she confer on mankind!

As though she sailed upon a calm sea, Mrs Vance drifted into Bird-in-Hand Court and up to her own door, slowly and luxuriantly sucking her mint sweetmeat and smiling foolishly at some children playing at club-kayles, a kind of ninepins, in the court. She even attempted to caress Tiger, who, with one hind-leg cocked in the air, was busy cleaning himself upon the door-step, but the animal, after a stare of cold resentment, arose and stalked away. In the kitchen she found Maralyn, mob pushed back from a heated brow, deft hands arranging a tray, nimble feet carrying her swiftly yet without flurry from the table to the oven. She paused when she saw her mother, opened her mouth to greet her, and then shut it again. A puzzled, slightly anxious expression came into her smiling eyes.

"Why, Mother—are you not well?"

"I am very well, sweetheart," said Mrs Vance, putting out a hand to steady herself against the table (she felt suddenly a little more drowsy than was comfortable). "I have had the most charming walk. And here are your candles and a chamber-pot. Nay, bless me, of course I remember now! it turned out to be the chandler after all, so I left him in his shop."

"Mother," cried Maralyn, now really alarmed, and running to Mrs Vance's side, "you must come to bed, and I will run to the 'pothecary——"

"A fart for 'pothecaries!" said Mrs Vance cheerfully, as she sank into the nearest chair. "But I will go to bed, for I cannot wait until night. Listen, sweetheart, come hither to me. *I have found that which will make me sleep.*"

Then, drawing Maralyn's hot face down to hers, she opened wide her mouth and puffed out a breath.

"Tell me, my angel, what do you smell?"

"Why, it is mint, I think. But, Mother——"

"Mint, saith she, and mint it is. Sweetmeats!" cried Mrs Vance, flourishing her paper packet under Maralyn's nose. "Magic sweetmeats such as would make Gog and Magog nod upon the pillars of the Guildhall." She gave a mighty yawn. "Nay, they and your fresh air together have quite overpowered me, and I will go to bed this very moment. Help me, sweet child."

Bewildered, incredulous, but ecstatic, her daughter helped her with a gentle arm to climb the stair, while Mrs Vance, swaying slightly, hummed her favourite air of *Sweet Maralyn* all out of tune.

(ii)

Moll opened the door of her hackney, which was crawling down crowded Thames Street, and yelled to the driver:

"What a-devil is ailing you? Can't you go faster than a Tyburn march, you stinking knave? I have told you already, I am late for an appointment."

"You'll be betimes at your own funeral, mistress," the coach-man shouted back, "if you open the door while I'm a-moving."

"What else can I open when in lieu of glasses you have a tin sash pinked for air like the backside of a colander? Mend your pace, I say, or you may whistle for your fare." And she banged the door shut again.

She must not be late today. All her life she had prided herself on being punctual for appointments; it was her one concession to the conventions. She had been late last Sunday, only a quarter of an hour, it is true, and Michael had taken it very well, indeed had not so much as mentioned it. But then Michael was always the gentleman. She had not told him the reason for that one lapse from punctuality, because she was ashamed of the reason even more than of the lapse. On the previous evening she had called for some gin. After that first taste of it at Bart's Fair, she had vowed she would never drink the stuff again, not only because of Michael's prejudice against it, but because she had disliked the taste. But last Saturday night she was tired, she had had some particularly tiresome clients, and she had gone for a drink by herself. And nothing she drank seemed to raise her spirits nor revive her. Ale was sweet and sickly, beer was cold, wine was only for fine ladies, and punch was pleasant only when drunk in company. And so on an impulse she had called for gin.

All the taverns seemed to sell it now, and Michael need never know, and she liked every new adventure.

Looking back on that evening, she experienced a wave of self-disgust. She had hated the stuff even while she had imbibed it, and yet she had gone on imbibing it until the tavern closed. And then she had gone home and been violently sick, and had awakened next morning with a foul taste in her mouth and the very devil of a headache, awakened, moreover, after a restless night, at a very late hour, and so had been late for her appointment with Michael. And furthermore she had known very well that all spirits were bad for one of her profession, and for that very reason had never taken them. . . . Well, she had learnt her lesson, that was one thing. No more gin for her as long as she lived. But meanwhile here was this confounded rogue of a hackney, who already had lost a precious ten minutes in Watling Street disputing for the road with another of his kind, and who now was deliberately crawling down Thames Street at the pace of a snail. The Lord damn all hackneys for rascally pimps!

But then her temper vanished as suddenly as it had appeared, and she gave a little chuckle. What a way of spending Sunday, dawdling round the Tower with a herd of country bumpkins who came to gape at the Menagerie and exclaim at the Crown Jewels! But what would you? The damned Puritanical law forbade the opening of theatres and bear-gardens on the Sabbath, and in this fine spring weather Michael was apt to grow restless if he sat in the Crown all day. One could scarcely blame him; cooped up in a counting-house every weekday and spending his evenings quill-driving in a garret. Sunday was his day, and like the Lord he rested on it, or rather he spent it watching archery in Tuttle-fields or playing bowls in a tavern alley or perambulating round the Tower. And strangely enough she enjoyed these excursions, she, Moll, who hitherto had spent her Sundays resting in bed after a week employed in a very different kind of sport from bowls or archery. Somehow or other she could always enjoy anything with Michael Montague.

Moll was not given to analyse her emotions, and she had not, therefore, the least idea that her affection for Michael had grown to be the strongest thing in her life. She did know, in a hazy kind of way, that she liked him better than any man she had ever met, better even than Noddy, otherwise Sir Noel Tredennis, who had taken her off the streets, had set her up in style as his mistress, and then gone off to France with his ruined master, King James. Noddy had done the right thing by her even then; he had offered to take her with him. But she had refused because, during all the time of her grandeur, she had retained a sneaking nostalgia for her old life, the hazardous, adventurous, up-and-down, devil-may-care life of a London whore; and while, as Noddy's mistress, she had felt it her duty to keep faithful to him and be accountable to him for her actions, she felt no such obligation towards his successor, Michael, nor did Michael expect it. They were free-lances, she and Michael; when they met it was in a world of their own, a narrow, impermanent, tiny world composed entirely of Sundays. Michael never asked questions about her weekday life, and she cared nothing for the details of his political life; each received such confidences as were freely given, and gave sympathy, not advice, in return. They met, they jested, they laughed, they loved, they ate and drank; and then they parted for another week; and that was all there was about it.

But as it happened, it was not all. If you had asked Moll why she trapesed round sight-seeing with Michael instead of resting in her bed, she would have answered that he was a dear good creature and that she pitied his loneliness. She was that kind of a person, she would have said, and never could see a stray, be it human or animal, without wanting to give it comfort. She was free to admit that she admired him, chiefly because of his courage, which in some ways resembled her own. She had a hearty contempt for what her world called courage, a showy, flamboyant bravado; but Michael's variety was of an entirely different kind. It was completely unspectacular; he was the kind of man who believed in something, and went on believing in it long after it was defeated, and not only believing, but serving, and not only serving, but serving inconspicuously, unrewarded, almost without hope of success. He had given up everything he had (and that was much) for a shadowy ideal, yet he took such sacrifice as a matter of course. He had embraced for the sake of a principle a most tedious, unnatural and exacting kind of life; he had accepted a real poverty after having been brought up in wealth; life had given him a knock-out blow at the Revolution; yet here he was still fighting and still getting the worst of it, and there were not even spectators to make his defeat romantic, just life and himself, with life always victorious. Privately Moll thought him a fool for sticking to a lost cause, but she could not but admire the way in which he accepted the consequences of this romantic folly, the zest with which he pursued the fight, the cheerfulness with which he took life's knocks, his quiet, persistent refusal to admit defeat.

But if you had told Moll that she depended on Michael, she would have laughed in your face. She was quite certain in her own mind that she was as free as a bird and always had been. She made this mistake because Michael was unpossessive; if he met her in the street with a stranger, he never enquired the name of her acquaintance, never wanted to know what she did nor where she had been. Because she was shallow, she mistook her outward liberty for freedom of the heart. Nor was this all. She *had* been free of heart during the early days of her relationship with Michael. She could never forget how really unaffected she had been by the knowledge that in those days Michael had been in the thick of his hopeless love for Eve Barrowes. Moll did not believe in that kind of love herself, certainly had never desired to be the object of it, but she had been very kind and sympathetic towards Michael, telling herself wisely that the poor young fool had but caught the disease inevitable to all young fools who have the ill-luck to be born of a romantic disposition, but that of course he would get over it, and that meantime she must do her best to humour him.

But then had come the day at Bart's Fair, when he had seen Eve again and she had tried to comfort him and had been met with something unexpected. Michael had behaved badly, or rather he had acted out of the character she had created for him. He ought to have raved, to have got drunk, to have turned to her for comfort; she ought to have had to restrain him from an attempt to explore my Lord Grey's vitals. Instead of that, he had remained calm, had gone off into some world of his own, had

101

snubbed her, had refused her comfort, not in despair but because he obviously had no use for it in this connection; and last but not least he had given her an intolerable suspicion that his love for Eve Barrowes was something which she really did not, and never could, understand. That had shocked Moll, and had made her call for gin. And the dangerous part of it all was that she did not comprehend the nature of the shock, nor the circumstances which had made it so violent. She did not realise that she was growing older, that she sometimes felt tired, that she had to make an effort to be kind to certain clients, and that in the mornings she did not like looking into her mirror before she had put on some paint. For Moll was of that nature which ignores all unpleasantness if it can; and usually, and rather unfortunately, it can. . . .

(iii)

Here was the Tower at last, and there was Michael. Moll forgot her anxiety about not being punctual, and ceased hating the hackney, and sprang out into her lover's arms, chattering like a magpie, commanding Michael to give the rascal driver his exact fare and no more, threatening that indignant personage with a rap from his own hammer if he grumbled, and even making a motion to search for that useful article beneath the hammer-cloth.

"And now what are you pleased to view first?" enquired Michael, after he had silenced the hackney's very voluble and original vituperation by a large tip. He took Moll's arm and began to escort her towards the gate-house. "The Regalia, the Armoury, the Church, the Menagerie, or maybe it is your ladyship's pleasure to inspect Traitors' Gate and have your dainty ears deafened by the cataracts hard by?"

Moll gave him a shrewd glance.

"Very pretty fooling, but you do not deceive me, my friend. Your spirits are low this morning, that is plain; you look as melancholy as a female wretch upon a Smithfield pile. What ails you, pray? It cannot be the news of King William's latest defeat at Neer—Neer Something or other; my English tongue trips over these heathenish place-names."

Michael said slowly:

"There is confirmation of the strange and horrid rumours we heard all last summer of a massacre in the Highlands of Scotland. The new Scots Parliament has demanded an inquiry, but it seems that William is vastly reluctant to accede to their demand, which fact seems to confirm the talk that this massacre had his blessing."

"And is that not what you would have looked for in your arch-enemy?" asked Moll dryly.

"Nay, I would have looked for it in none but an arch-fiend, Moll. For these MacDonalds of Glencoe were living peaceably, and their chief had taken the Oaths, though a trifle late; they were fallen upon, 'tis said, by a company of Argyll's regiment who had asked for and received their hospitality, and were butchered in cold blood. Murder under trust; it is as ugly a thing as ever I heard of."

"Nevertheless, you should take comfort," said Moll, yawning, "for it will serve to increase Dutch William's unpopularity."

"That could scarce be higher than at present, yet it brings us no nearer to a restoration. The great lords his masters dare not be rid of him, for King James would be back on the instant, and where would those traitors be then?" Then he glanced at Moll, and added: "Nay, we'll leave politics, sweetheart; this is our day and we will spend it merrily. Come, yonder is the Menagerie; let's go see the sights."

Now Moll had awakened that morning with a most unusual and unreasonable depression upon her, and finding Michael preoccupied with politics made her feel no better. She had always borne with his obsession, had listened patiently to his theories, and had taken care not to display any restlessness or boredom when he talked of these dull affairs of State, though on the other hand she had never pretended to share his ideals. But today she felt really irritated by his gloom and its cause; he had no right to be thinking about some petty little massacre hundreds of miles away in the barbarous North, when he was in her company, especially when she was wearing her new black silk petticoat with its red and white calico border, her cherry-coloured stays, and a pair of long lace mittens, the very latest mode. She had dressed her hair in a new style too, combing it up into twin peaks above her brow and arranging a lace kerchief over it in place of the *commode*. It had taken her hours to get the right effect this morning. And if all this were lost upon her tiresome swain, he really had no excuse for not noticing and admiring her latest thing in patches: the likeness of a sedan-chair, with bearers and all complete, which she had stuck daringly in the centre of her forehead.

The Menagerie, far from raising her spirits, distinctly lowered them. She had an affection for animals, and it was seldom her lodging was without a stray cat or a dog she had rescued from the bear-pit or a monkey she had bought because it was being ill-treated in a street-show. The sight of the mangy lions, the shabby tigers, and the despairing eagles made her angry; the two-headed lamb and the six-legged calf made her sick. But she was not the kind to let depression beat her without a fight for it, and all the while she kept up a running commentary, valiantly striving to rescue Michael and herself from this unreasonable dreariness of heart. She said, looking hard at an elderly spinster among the spectators, that the lions were roaring mighty loud today, and that it was a well-known fact they only roared in this manner when they saw a woman pregnant of a male child; she decided aloud that a particularly dejected-looking bear bore a distinct resemblance to the Earl of Marlborough (a remark which was received with applause by the crowd, for Marlborough's sun had set for the moment and he was in deep disgrace); and she persisted in interrupting in pithy asides the tale a keeper was trying to tell of how he had been trapped in the tiger's cage on one occasion, and of how the beast had actually fawned upon him.

"Two of a kind, brother, two of a kind," commented Moll. "By God," she added, in the midst of the malicious laughter, "let's away from this place, friend Michael, ere the stink slays us. I vow it smells as ill as a litter of piss-tailed children under the care of a parish nurse."

They drifted away in the direction of the Horse Armoury, the staircase which gave access to it having Grenadiers of painted wood arranged upon it as sentinels. Living warders, in old-fashioned laced doublets, petticoat breeches, and flat-caps hung round with ribbons ("Like a fool's hat on a holiday," remarked Moll), pestered them for tips; the crowd gaped, jostled, laughed and exclaimed; a cold wind blew off the river, disarranging Moll's coiffure, and from the cataracts on either side of Traitors' Gate there came a deep, continuous thunder. The press in the Horse Armoury was terrific, and the noise of their footsteps and voices quite drowned the monotonous tones of a warder who was showing a party round. Moll, who liked crowds, felt a little better, and coming to a suit of armour once worn by King Henry the Eighth, straddled before it, put her hands upon her hips, and went into mock raptures.

"Now heaven help all husbands! Will you please to look at that cod-piece. As big as a poop-lantern, I vow, and I have heard it said that if a married woman do but——"

"Hush, Moll!" said Michael, suddenly and peremptorily.

She turned upon him an indignant face.

"What a-devil is ailing you, pray? Are you turned Puritan? Or are you green with envy? Nay, I know what 'tis; you know too many cuckolds from living in the City, and——"

"Pray, Moll, lower your voice. My master is yonder, and all his household with him. Let us go see the marching-train of artillery."

"Oho! Ashamed to be seen with me, are you?" rallied Moll playfully, yet with a slight edge to her voice.

"You know that's not true. But it would mightily embarrass Mr Vance to encounter me here, since I am supposed to spend every Sunday with my pretended family in Covent Garden. Besides, how should I present you?"

"Why, as your maiden aunt," said Moll. "I'm sure I look the part. Nephew," she continued, raising her voice and putting on a mincing tone, "pray tell me, what is this strange round growth in the midst of this goodly suit of armour? I am most curious to——"

"Moll! Moll, for pity's sake." He took her by the arm and tried to draw her away. She came reluctantly, looking back over her shoulder at Mr Vance's party across the room; then she paused, and murmured: "Ha! the pretty daughter, eh?" Imitating Michael's voice, she continued: "She is so pretty and modest that she cannot walk in Drapers' Garden of an evening without the eyes of every City beau a-following her."

"She is a sweet pretty girl, do you not think so?" asked Michael frankly, looking back at the unconscious Maralyn with a smile.

Moll answered nothing, but she thought: Ay, a sweet pretty girl, no doubt of that. Unmodish in dress, naturally curling hair, a hood becomingly framing a smiling face, flowing skirts unstiffened, shoes with roses instead of buckles, and never a patch upon the fresh cheeks. Youth sat upon her like a crown, youth and innocence. She had hold of her father's arm, and often would look up into his face, sharing his enjoyment of this Sunday treat, listening intently to all he said, depending upon him and at the same time protecting him, guiding him by a slight pressure on his arm wherever the crowd was thinnest. Not handsome, merely pretty; she'd thicken soon, thought Moll; she worked too hard, did the brewer's daughter, took life too seriously, allowed herself to be imposed upon by those around her. She wore no gloves, and her hands, though scrupulously clean, were red, with slightly swollen fingers; you could tell she bent over the wash-tub and kneaded bread and scrubbed floors. A good daughter, and presently an excellent wife and mother; one of the raw 'prentice lads would be a lucky man one day.

"To the marching-train of artillery," said Moll with a certain abruptness; and she marshalled Michael out of the room.

(iv)

At a later hour she remarked:

"A good ale-house dinner and a bowl of the Crown punch afterwards. That is what we need, my friend."

Michael agreed very readily. Somehow the whole morning had been a failure, had gone from bad to worse. But Moll knew that her suggested remedy was not what she needed; deep inside her she craved for the quick, deceptive uplift of a quartern of gin. She knew it was deceptive, she knew that only a few hours previously she had sworn to herself that she would never touch the poison again, she knew that she would have to deceive Michael if she were to obtain it, she knew she would feel ashamed and sick and self-disgusted afterwards. But she had to have it; just this once. It was Michael's fault really; if he had only paid her one compliment, or ceased for a single moment to look abstracted, she would have resisted, she knew she would. And after all, what business was it of his if she chose to drink spirits? She had never interfered with his habits, and she was not accountable to him for her actions. And she was not a poor weak creature who did not know when to stop. She would buy herself one meausre, and that was all, so that she obtained the uplift and missed the nausea.

"My belly is too empty to endure the jolting of a hackney," said she, as they moved towards the gate-house. "By your leave, we'll go by wherry, and land at Temple Stairs, so do you engage a pair of oars, my friend, and I'll wait here out of this pesty wind."

He smiled at her and went to do her bidding; she watched him go, that shabby, gentlemanly figure so dear to her, suddenly so poignantly dear. A strange impulse seized her to run after him and confess that she must have a measure, just one measure, of the spirit he hated; but she resisted the impulse, and consumed with mingled shame and resentment, she flounced round an angle of one of the Tower buildings and dived into a small entry. A warder sat in a little box of a room, with a great bunch of keys at his side; he was smoking a foul pipe and scanning a news-sheet.

"A ha'porth of Parliament-waters," demanded Moll tersely, "and hasten."

The warder regarded her over his paper, looking her up and down in insolent appraisal.

"Parliament-waters, eh? That's an ill whet for one of your trade, mistress."

Moll went rather white beneath her paint, but she restrained her tongue.

"I will mind my business if you will mind yours. Give me what I ask for."

The warder shrugged, and reaching behind him drew from some recess a small black bottle and a measure. Before he could hand them over, Moll snatched them from him, poured herself out a dram with shaking fingers, gulped it down, slammed her ha'penny upon the table, and without another word flounced out again. Ah, that was better! She was warm once more, and she was herself, ready for anything, full of zest for life. It was amusing where before it had been horrid that she was deceiving Michael; she chuckled to herself as she imagined his disgust could he have heard her demanding "Parliament-waters", one of the many cant names for gin. But he ought to be thankful to gin, because it was going to make the rest of their day pleasant and merry, lift it out of the hateful gloom which had weighed upon them all the morning.

Michael was awaiting her at Tower Stairs, stamping up and down to keep himself warm, while the watermen, with the badge of their trade sewn on their canvas jackets and their heads thrust into the tops of old stockings, kept up their monotonous cry of "Sculls or oars?" around him. Michael smiled at her, and gave her his hand down the greasy stairs into the wherry which rocked at the foot. He also seemed to have recovered his spirits, and as the waterman rowed them upstream, pointed out to her the needle pinnacles of St Mary Overies on the southern bank, the domes of the theatres and bear-gardens in Southwark, the head of the Monument rearing up northwards, and presently the trees of Lambeth Gardens, already showing a misty promise of green amid the brown feathers of their branches. Moll, who had known all these things since babyhood and cared not a straw for any of them, nodded and smiled, and kept her head carefully turned away lest he should smell the gin on her breath.

They were nearing their destination when there came rowing towards them a large, six-oared craft, filled with men who obviously had been keeping the Sabbath at an ale-house. When this boatload came within ear-shot of the wherry, one of its occupants stood up and, cupping his mouth in his hands, greeted the waterman in what was called the "water dialect", very novel and obscene abuse, delivered, however, in the most good-humoured manner. The waterman, who up to now had seemed to be a silent, dour sort of individual, laid down his oars, stood up likewise, took a deep breath, and with every appearance of relish, replied in the same strain:

"You white-livered spawn of a night-walker, begot upon a chair at noonday by a Fleet Street bum-sitter, you cross-legged nit-cracker christened out of a chamber-pot, who gave you leave to sail this fair river and affright the King's swans with your bear-garden countenance?"

His acquaintance, nothing daunted, braced himself for a further effort, and was about to commence when Moll, whose eyes had brightened at the first exchange, sprang up in the stern, and standing with arms akimbo, and her elaborately dressed coiffure disarranged by the wind, uplifted a shrill voice and forestalled him.

"You cuckoldly company of salt-arsed ninny-hammers!" yelled she, her eyes twinkling madly. "You offspring of a dung-hill, can you find no better spokesman than yonder tame talker with his punch-bowl answers, who is scarce tall enough for a complete man nor short enough for a proper monkey? If you cannot, then hold your tongues, you nitty radish-mongers, lest I bid my friend here ram ye aboard, d'ye see?—and send ye down to poison the fishes."

The other immediately transferred his attentions from the waterman to this female fare.

"The Lord confound you for as arrant a strumpet as ever traded between Aldgate and Temple Bar! Have a care for your cheeks, you punk! We'll have you branded next Sessions. Or maybe you are lately come from the hemp and hammer, hey?" He put on a solemn tone, imitating the Bridewell judge: "All you who are willing this whore have present punishment pray hold up your hands. Yah! Is the flash bowman aft your twang, my buttock? He looks as though he has lately spoke with a gold piece or faked a cly. Yet have a care that ye be not knucks in quod come morning. Yah! Who was it tied her apron round her neck that she might boast she was kissed in a nightrail?" And so the strange sport went on.

It was obvious that Moll was thoroughly enjoying herself. But the waterman looked disgruntled at having his part in the game usurped, the boatload of men leered in ugly fashion and began to lose all decency of manners as well as tongue, and Michael sat silent, rather pale around the mouth. It ended at last, and each boat took its separate course, the combatants exchanging wordy broadsides as long as they were within earshot of each other. By and by the wherry bumped against the Temple Stairs, and Michael, without a single protest, paid the exorbitant fare demanded as a matter of habit by the waterman, piloted his companion up Ram Alley into Fleet Street, and thence, without a word, through Butchers' Row and Drury Lane into Russell Street.

But long before they came to the Crown, Moll had burst into a feverish monologue. She had enjoyed that encounter on the water, yes, by God she had! She had the water-dialect to perfection; did Michael not think so? Without waiting for a reply, she rattled on in a nervous spate of speech, repeating herself, enlarging on the wordy badinage, exhausting humour and growing more and more drearily obscene. Then all of a sudden she stopped dead, wrenched her arm from his, twisted round on him, and snarled:

"But you misliked it. You were ashamed of me. Oh, don't trouble to deny it; I know! I marked you as you sat there, prim as gossips at a christening before the wine gets into them, wishing to God I'd shut my mouth, comparing me with the Lady Eve, or maybe was it—the brewer's wench?"

"Moll—pray, Moll, let's have done with it." He stood drooping with fatigue, both mental and physical, running his hand along the lining of timber which ran, wheel-high, on the outside of the houses to protect the brickwork from contact with the iron wheels of the wagons and drays. He made an effort and continued: "We are both of us weary and out of spirits. It has been somehow an ill sort of day, and I am sure it is my fault because I could not tear my mind from this abomination in the Highlands."

"Don't tell me you failed to mark the brewer's wench and her pretty modesty," sneered Moll.

He ignored this remark and went on doggedly:

"Moll, once you said to me that those of your profession aged early. Do you remember? Well, so it is with mine. I grow fatigued very easily now, I have discovered. Each of us needs rest, rest and a little security."

"There is none of that for me, and forsooth I'd scorn to seek it." She was leaning back against the timber-facing, her head tilted back, her eyes defiant. "But you have it to your hand, my friend. A good little cit, comfortable as a house-cat in a warm brewery."

He watched a coach go by, his mind stumbling after the rumble of the wheels.

"I cannot make you understand what is in my breast. Words are dangerous things, yet what else have we? Moll, I have a trifle saved from the wreck of my fortunes; I had intended——'Tis but a trifle," he went on hurriedly, "but sufficient to set you up in tolerable comfort, and heaven knows you are welcome to it, as it is yours by right of our long friendship and of all you have done for me."

There was a long and horrid silence. He could have bitten out his tongue; what had possessed him to be so tactless? He had spoken on an impulse and from the depths of a strange, tearing pity; he had spoken his thoughts aloud, a habit of lonely men, but when spoken they were shorn of the kindness from which they had sprung. Three chairs went by at a trot, and a bevy of apprentices and their women ambled past with loud talk and silly laughter, before she answered, low and bitter like the hidden sharpening of a knife:

"By Christ's wounds, this is the first time you have insulted me in all the years I have known you. You have offered me money to be rid of me. You see the day coming when I shall be too old and stale for the streets, and you dread lest I should intrude upon your own pesty little plans."

"I am your age, Moll, neither more nor less," said Michael, shrunken into himself, despairing now of ever making her understand his thought.

Moll differentiated between the age of man and woman in a

few crisp, obscene sentences. And then, as Michael answered nothing, she continued in a brittle tone:

"Now I will tell you what I think, my little decayed country squire, my poor martyred zealot. I think you would have me settled snug as the mistress of a bawdy-house so that you may be free to pursue your suit to yonder pretty jilt, the brewer's daughter."

"Moll! You're jesting, Moll. Let's away to the Crown and eat and drink and forget what has passed between us."

"There are some things cannot be forgot. Oh, I see it all! So pretty and so modest quotha! Bakes a pie to perfection and is a wonder at bed-making. I'll warrant she has likewise a goodly portion of moneys hoarded in an old stocking, and old pewter and vats and pockets of hops for a dowry. 'Adsheart! a fit mate is she for a virtuous young gentleman so he can bury his past in a brothel."

"Leave her along, Moll!" He had turned on her suddenly, his lips sucked in, his dulled eyes glinting. "Leave Maralyn alone, I say."

"Maralyn! Oh, what a sweet pretty name! So I have pricked you, have I? Master Puritan is tender of his virginal mistress's honour and cannot abear to hear her name mentioned by a common whore."

"Moll, listen to me. Miss Maralyn is nought to me but a decent human being. She is a kind of symbol. I know that sounds silly; I cannot help it; truth often sounds silly, and I tell you, words are dangerous things. To me, she is the average woman, as her father is the average man. They are my business, almost my specimens, and as such I love them though I do not understand them. But I perceive a simple goodness in them, a love of craftsmanship, a frank honesty which draw forth my admiration and my reverence. And I tell you, I will not have them abused by you or any other."

"You move me even to tears with your picture of them," sneered Moll, glaring at a couple of pigeons which were pecking about at her feet. "Yet give me the freedom to remind you that simplicity in a woman has deceived many a goodly gentleman to his ruin. May I recall for you two excellent old proverbs? 'It is the still sow that drinks up all the draught.' 'Reserved in tongue, loose in thought.' "

Then Michael rounded on her, his self-reproach and depression swept away on a tide of anger.

"You have no sort of right to abuse this girl, and as for what you insinuate regarding my feelings for her, you are wrong from first to last. Her affections are deeply engaged with an honest lad, one of her father's 'prentices, and I have pledged myself to do all that in me lies to forward their happiness."

"I think I understand you," said Moll thinly. "The unripe fruit has proved sour in your belly, and therefore are you in haste to put it on another's platter."

For a moment his face flamed and he seemed as though he would strike her. Then he exhaled a trembling breath and muttered:

"Moll, I wish to God you would forswear this spirit-drinking. Oh, you have not deceived me; don't think it. And can't you see what it does? It has made us quarrel, and it has made you imagine follies which you would laugh at had you no acquaintance with Madam Geneva. For anything I have said amiss, I can only beg your pardon; you are very dear to me, Moll, and always will be, and I would not hurt you for the world."

She stared at him a moment; then her tautness broke and she burst into noisy sobs, covering her face with her mittened hands, rocking to and fro, abandoned. Passers-by stopped to stare at her, and a hackney-coachman shouted some jeering advice from his box as he drove by. Through her shielding hands, words came muffled, whining, unfamiliar words of self-pity. She was a poor lost girl. She had never had a chance. She was losing her looks and her youth. No one loved her. Her best friend turned from her in scorn because she took a dram now and then to keep her spirits up. She had taken such pains with her toilette this morning, and Michael had not noticed. She had hated the Menagerie with its poor captive beasts. She hated everyone and everything. She wished she were dead. She wished she had never been born. And so on; and so on.

Michael stood by helpless, wrung with pity, struggling with nausea. He had never heard her whine before; nor had he ever before been conscious of her origins, of her native crudity. He had seen a new Moll today, and the spectacle had shocked him; he had heard obscenity without wit and malice unsoftened by good humour. And now, in place of the jaunty courage that was so essential a part of her, there was this revolting self-pity, this weak and dreary whining. He could not now, in the thick of it all, follow up his first instinctive judgment, that he was hearing and seeing, not Moll, but Madam Geneva.

"Let's away to the Crown, Moll," he said presently, gently taking her arm, "and eat that ale-house dinner of which you spoke. It will make us ourselves again, and we will forget the whole sorry morning. Come."

She suffered herself to be led towards their old haunt; and as they went their minds held the same wistful hope, that maybe within the walls of the dear old Crown the former magic of their relationship would return, the comfortable comradeship so precious to them both. But the cheerful conversation Michael made over dinner was just a trifle forced, and the repentance Moll professed over a bowl of punch afterwards was just a little wearisome; and when, by mutual agreement, they walked towards Moll's lodging through the spring dusk, each was unconsciously admitting that the physical was the only secure bond left between them.

Three

(i)

NATHANIEL VANCE junior, his hat swathed in black crape, a torch in his right hand and a sprig of rosemary in his left, walked slowly and solemnly in the procession which, noisy with the sobs of paid "weepers", wound its way from Goldsmiths' Row towards the church of St Vedast. Ahead of him he could see the sinister shape of a coffin beneath a rich velvet pall, carried on the shoulders of six bearers, the coffin containing the earthly remains of his late employer, Mr Maynard, topping goldsmith.

Master Nat's thoughts were not entirely suited to the occasion. He was reflecting rather feverishly that he had won his benefit, and bought himself out of his indentures, and set himself up as a banker, and married Susan Pritchard, in the very nick of time. For shortly after he had done all these momentous things, Mr Maynard senior had been found dead in his bed one morning, and Mr Maynard junior had inherited the business and a very large fortune. A matter of a few months, and he would have been too late with Susan; she never could have resisted, no sensible woman could have resisted, the richest young goldsmith in the City. And Nat knew, and was ashamed of the knowledge, that his benefit and his banking would have meant very little to him without Susan; he was ashamed because he despised emotion and sentiment and all things which had nothing to do with cold hard cash and cold hard reason, yet a certain honesty compelled him to own to himself that his feelings for Susan were both sentimental and unreasonable. He had had to have her, and not only because she was a good business woman and had a considerable marriage settlement; she was the one weakness of his life, the one thing about which he could not coldly calculate.

Well, he had got her, and both she and Frank had taken the course of events very well. Frank had attended the wedding, had bestowed a handsome present, and with his usual charm had clapped Nat on the shoulder and declared that the better man had won. And Susan, on hearing of the death of Frank's father, had sent the bereaved a conventional note of sympathy and had made no comments to her husband. It was impossible to tell what she felt because she was not a woman who showed her feelings at any time, but she was certainly not one to indulge in the weakness of regret. She had taken Nat for better or for worse, and would make it her business to see that it was for the better.

The scents of rue and rosemary warred with those of an open poor-hole in the graveyard and a lay-stall at the foot of St Vedast's Lane. The torches made the summer night luminous with a savage glare, and casements were thrown open as the procession passed. There were many torches, signifying the wealth of the deceased, and Mr Grimes, the "upholder", had been very attentive, lavish with his rosemary and crape, generous with his "weepers", and now, walking with a proper melancholy at the head of the cortège, was obviously totting up a long bill. By and by, with discretion and respect, he would press into the hands of the mourners his funeral-cards which, tastefully decorated, set forth the exclusive style and moderate rates of his burials. Meantime, here was the Reverend Mr Peter Gimp, Vicar of St Vedast's, waiting at the graveyard gate with gown and bands blowing in the night wind, and in solemn tones welcoming the late Mr Maynard to his eternal rest by way of the handsome family vault. It was all most exquisitely genteel.

But at a later hour, and much more welcome to Nat, here was Mr Frank Maynard discreetly shepherding his friend into a private room of that house which was now his very own, leaving the other mourners to their baked meats and subdued gossiping; here was Mr Frank Maynard obviously about to impart some confidences to the young friend who was very curious to hear them. For Nat was very curious indeed to learn how Master

Frank intended to enjoy the fortune which was now his; and which so easily might have been Susan's also.

"Lord, what a crew!" exclaimed Master Frank, shutting-to the door of the little room and puffing out his cheeks. He looked odd, somehow, in his mourning, like a comedian dressed for a tragedy; his fox-coloured wig flamed against the black of his coat. He flung himself down in his father's elbow-chair, and bade Nat deal with a cobwebbed bottle which stood ready with glasses on a side-table. Nat fumbled clumsily with the bottle-screw, for he was unaccustomed to wine. While he manipulated the choice Canary, Frank indulged in a breezy commentary on the night's ceremony, declaring himself no hypocrite, deploring the prevalence of that vice among his acquaintances, and winding up with some compliments to Nat, who, said he, shared his own views on such matters and was, in fact, a man after his own heart.

"And because of it, Nat, I'm a-going to tell you a secret. Every man in the City is in labour to know what I'll do with my fortune, but I can be close if I choose. Let 'em guess, and let 'em speculate, and let 'em hope, say I. But you shall know because you have an eye for money, as I always said, and you'll appreciate my wisdom, that will you. Nay, Nat, I'm not for setting up as your rival in banking, and neither am I for plodding dully in my father's footsteps. I'm for putting every penny, every ha'penny, every farthing I possess, into the Debt."

He sipped his wine, twinkling over the glass at Nat, who was staring at him stolidly, though with a touch of bewilderment.

"You've heard of the Debt, Nat; ay, a keen business man like you must be sure to have heard of the Debt. And the pest take me if you don't second my vote that it's the best and richest venture of the age, and has in it more promise than the wealth of the Indies; safe besides."

"You mean my Lord Montague's scheme?" said Nat slowly.

"Ay," answered his friend, throwing one leg over the other and settling himself more comfortably in the chair so lately sacred to his father, "ay, Nat, I mean no other." He sipped his wine and smacked his lips. "Excellent stuff, i'faith. Henceforth I will drink no more ale, saving your presence, for wine is the liquor for gods and rich men, and though I be no god, I will be as rich as Crœsus, thanks to King William and his war."

"But this Debt of which you speak," said Nat, frowning, "is but one of many such debts contracted by the Crown in times past in the event of some national emergency, an abnormal, an ephemeral thing, which the Government has always been in haste to pay back as soon as possible."

"Aha! but in this instance the Government will give its creditor a very lengthy hold upon it, maybe even a permanent hold. For harkee, Nat, Montague's scheme is in the nature of a lottery, a lottery in annuities."

Nat stared at him, but said nothing. His friend uncrossed his legs and leaned forward; Frank Maynard's sly eyes gleamed oddly in the candlelight, and his upturned nose gave him the look of a sinister clown.

"Harkee, Nat," he said again, "you must know the precise nature of this scheme if you would understand its possibilities. King William is as usual in need of moneys for his precious war. He has taxed, and set up a State Lottery, and invented new duties, and even has been forced to the dangerous expedient of a poll-tax, but still he needs more. Wars, my dear Nat, may be ruinous to the nation, but they are mines of richness to clever men who understand money and have it to lend. William needs, at this precise moment, the sum of one million pounds, and it is with this million that my Lord Montague is concerned. He proposes that a number of wealthy private men shall subscribe the whole sum between them as a loan; that the interest upon this loan shall be at the rate of ten per cent (a good high rate, Nat); and that this interest shall be collected from the new Excise Duties which affect the whole population of the realm. Now the debt owed by the Government to each individual lender shall be extinguished with the lender's death, and as the number of the original creditors grows less and less, all that would have been due to those who have died shall accrue to the fortunate survivors, until these shall number no more than seven. After that limit is reached, with the death of each, his seventh share shall be extinguished. You will understand now what I said about this Debt's being in the nature of a lottery, for men will subscribe to such a loan in the hope of being themselves of the band of survivors; and you will understand likewise how excellent a chance I stand of being one of that lucky band, since I am but seven-and-twenty, in good health likewise, whereas many of those who subscribe will necessarily be in middle life, otherwise they would not yet have amassed sufficient wealth to enter such a scheme."

There was silence a moment, broken only by the ceaseless jingle of the coins in Frank's pocket as he stirred them with his hand. Nat was staring into his untasted wine, his face in shadow. From the living-room of the house came the sounds of discreet merriment, while from the staircase sounded the tiptoeing footsteps of those who went to offer their condolences to the widow in her crape-hung bedchamber.

"But this sum of one million pounds," said Nat at last, slowly, "can be repaid by the Government within a twelvemonth if they so choose. And I doubt not they will so choose, for they are not mad enough to desire a lengthy indebtedness to private moneylenders, nor the hold such indebtedness must needs give those moneylenders upon Government."

Frank chuckled.

"Doubtless they will desire to repay the Debt as soon as may be, but will such repayment be within their power? For consider: there is yet not one sign that we are nearing the end of the war 'gainst France; on the contrary, the struggle grows more bitter every year and our losses in material more huge. Take, for example, this recent disaster at sea; every ship of the great merchant fleet which Rooke was escorting has been either captured or sunk. Besides, my dear gossip, William's ambition is utterly to destroy the power of France, and that is not done in a day. Moreover, mark this: in entering upon this particular Debt, the Government has not to count the cost as heretofore, since the burden of the interest is to be borne by the entire population, and is in truth a sort of mortgage upon every member of society. Nay, Nat, far from paying back with expedition, I'll wager that the Government will be coming to us hat-in-hand again within a twelve-month, asking for more, and the next year 'twill be the same, until, my friend, this Debt will become a national institution; and meanwhile we, the lenders, will have got our grip upon the best of all securities: the Government's power of coercing its subjects to put their hands into their pockets whensoever they are bidden."

"And you are determined to put all your fortune into the Debt?"

"Every last ha'penny, Nat, every last ha'penny."

"But meantime, how will you employ yourself?"

Frank burst into a hearty laugh.

"How will I employ myself, forsooth? Why, I will tell you, friend. I will keep my brace of geldings, dine every day at a modish ordinary, go to the playhouse every night, stir nowhere without my coach, and have two or three of the quality waiting every forenoon in my parlour, as the King has his petitioners. And in a while I'll maybe buy myself a knighthood, if it pleases me, build a country-seat at Hackney or at Islington, and lay down pipes of good Canary wherewith to entertain my friends."

"But you will engage in no business?" asked Nat incredulously. As a citizen's son it appeared to him almost unbelievable that another of his kind should be able and inclined to spend his days like a town fop.

Frank shrugged his round shoulders.

"Oh, maybe I will walk upon 'Change now and then, between the hours of twelve and two, and give the fat merchants a sight of my Rhingrave breeches, my silver-buttoned coat and my amber cane. Ay, and when I tire of the walks, and am sickened with the stench of garlic from the Spanishers and the oronoco of the Dutchmen and the snuff-dyed lips of the Jews, I'll take a stroll around the stalls abovestairs, and from that merchants' seraglio will choose me a pretty bedfellow."

"But will engage in no sort of business?" cried Nat again.

"Now the pest take you, friend, why should I sweat myself into a decline with so wearisome thing as trade when the Government has engaged to pay me interest at ten per cent out of its subjects' pockets for the rest of my life?"

"The income will cease at your death."

"It is welcome so to do."

"Your sons and daughters will not think so."

"Sons and daughters quotha!" scoffed Frank, bending over to refill his glass, so that Nat could not see his expression at that moment. "The sons and daughters I shall beget may go upon the parish for aught I care, for I swear to you they shall all be bastards. I am fortune's darling, Nat; she gave me a rich father who has died at a time when I am young enough to enjoy the riches he so laboriously amassed, yet old enough to know how to spend 'em wisely, old enough likewise to have learned that a wise man can best avoid trouble and expense by living and dying a merry bachelor."

There was another silence; then Nat rose from his chair.

"I must go offer my condolences to your afflicted mother, Frank. The hour grows late."

"Ay, Sue will be waiting for you," said Frank, rising also and making rather a to-do about pushing his chair back against the wall. "By heaven, Nat, I must call upon you in Lombard Street during your hours of business, for I am in labour to see you manage your customers and fill in the amounts on your bank-notes. I'll warrant you turn a tight screw upon some of the merchants, Nat; ay, I'll vow they get no loan from you without good and sufficient security and a fat rate of interest besides."

"My customers appear to be satisfied," returned Nat rather stiffly. "I charge them what I consider fair, and if they do not like it they may go elsewhere for their loans; it is all one to me, for I have plenty of custom."

Frank clapped him on the shoulder; the sly eyes twinkled, whether mockingly or in real admiration it was impossible to tell.

"Why, that's my Nat, my Nat with an eye for money. Business is one thing and charity another, saith you; and you are right. Wealth was land in our fathers' time, but now it is gold, and he who hath gold and knows how to use it may soon command the world. But a word in your ear, my topping banker; there's a whisper I heard on 'Change t'other day concerning a Government bank. It may be but idle talk, I know not, but I heard the name of Paterson mentioned, and you know that's a name to be reckoned with in what the modish call high finance."

"Paterson? The Scot?" queried Nat, pausing at the door. He spoke the name and mentioned the nationality with the same slight scorn, for the man was supposed to have started his career as a pirate, and as for his nation, why, Nat supposed himself to know all about the Scots. His father had a Scots 'prentice, a stupid, plodding lad who never opened his mouth and who cherished a hopeless love for Maralyn, and all London was talking about Scotland just now, of savage barbarians who murdered each other because of some silly blood-feud in a heathenish wilderness called Glencoe.

"Ay, Paterson the Scot," answered his friend, shepherding Nat to the stair-foot. "I could get no details of what he would be at, but there is a parcel of wealthy foreigners in the scheme, Jews and Flemings and what-not, and I have a notion there is suggested an alternative scheme to the Debt. Nay, I'm not for distressing myself; we'll push our plan through ere Paterson can rid himself of the itch sufficiently to elbow his way into the King's presence, and then maybe we'll hob-nob with Paterson and his crew, for there's plenty of opportunity for any man with money-sense in this nation today, and we wish not to be selfish. And Paterson will persevere; not a doubt of that. Oh, I tell you, he's a man to reckon with, is Paterson the Scot."

(ii)

"Paterson," murmured Alec Moray, stirring his saloop with an abstracted air, "ay, he's a canny man right enough, and kens the world, both the Old and the New."

"He kens the Spanish Main right enough," observed Mr Walker, a hose-factor, dryly. "For rumour insists he started life as a buccaneer."

There was a burst of heated argument, some of the company defending Paterson, others as hotly criticising him. The little common-room of the Rainbow coffee-house was full this evening, and since it was a meeting-place for the poorer sort of Scots, everyone present joined in the argument.

"Och, you're prejudiced, Mr Walker," exclaimed Alec impatiently. "You've never liked the man and nothing he does gangs right with you. But you must own he's canny; 'twas he who set up this new Bank of England and collected the huge sum of one million, two hundred thousand pounds in ten days for the needs of the Government. You need to be a gey clever man to accomplish a thing like yon."

"A-ha," said Walker, puffing placidly at a very foul pipe. "I'll grant ye the man has done brawly for himsel', as forbye he did when he flew the Jolly Roger. But that's no' saying he's the kind of man I'd trust wi' my money."

"Brawly for himself, is it?" cried a fervent Patersonite indignantly. "Ye do him less than justice, Douglas. He's done brawly for this country in her hour of need."

"And no' so very badly for himsel' either," retorted Walker, "for in return for yon loan he has gained for himsel' and his friends the right to issue notes of credit under a State guarantee. Forbye he has gotten a monopoly, for I understand that no new bank may be established during the continuance of the Bank of England. With the custody of the Debt newly entrusted to it, and the Government with its powers of taxation as its guarantee, I've nae doubt it will prosper and be able to pay its salaries without breaking, though I understand these amount already to four thousand, three hundred and fifty pounds. It has a Fleming for Governor and the Jews are behind it, so I think we may count it a safe institution, though I would not go sae far as to call it a patriotic one."

"But what of this Scottish East India Company?" asked Alec eagerly, before anyone else could speak. "You're new come from Edinburgh, Mr Walker, and can tell us what talk you heard of it there."

Mr Walker, who was drinking usquebaugh, twirled his dram round in the measure for a few seconds before he replied. Then he said, more seriously than he had yet spoken:

"Why, Alec lad, they are saying many things in Edinburgh concerning the Scottish East India Company, but the canniest word I heard about that business came frae the mouth o' my friend Mr Watson, whom I met one evening in a change-house in the Canon-gait. 'It is a trick,' says he, 'to divert public attention from the business of Glencoe.'"

Again there came a clamour of voices, assenting and denying.

"Ay, he's in the right of it there. It is a way of soothing public fury because the murderers remain unpunished."

"Och away! I ken Watson, a hot Jacobite, a mischievous malcontent."

"He's no such thing. He's a decent Lowland body who cannot thole murder and treachery against whomsoever they be committed."

Alec rose abruptly in the midst of the argument, put down his reckoning on the table, and bowed briefly to the company.

"It grows late," he said. "I'll wish ye all good night."

"I'll walk a wee way with you," said Mr Walker, swallowing his dram, "since my road lies with yours as far as Paul's."

They walked in silence for a while when they reached Cheapside. It was scarce ten o'clock and the summer night was luminous; Cheapside was full of blue mystery and seemed as though it dreamed of a long past. A smell of the river came faintly to their nostrils, and above them the serried roof-tops were silhouetted sharply against the tender sky. Alec walked doggedly forward, oblivious of his surroundings, saying nothing, staring at the ground. Presently Walker laid a hand upon his arm.

"Ye've set your heart upon this settlement scheme of Paterson's, lad?"

"Ay, I have."

"But have you considered the public issues involved?"

"I ken the Scottish East India Act has received the Touch of the Sceptre which makes it law in our Parliament," said Alec stubbornly.

"Ay, and what has King William promised to do by yon Act? He has committed himself to the suspension of the Navigation Laws, to the chartering of a company which would set up for rivals of the English East India (a muckle rich and powerful company, yon, and vastly jealous of their privileges), he has promised to support those Scots who shall settle in lands where the rightfulness of the claims of several European Powers are to be estimated by the settlers themselves. The ships of this new Company are to return to Scotland only, and if any nation detains one of such ships, His Majesty promises to exercise his authority to have restitution."

"Ay," cried Alec, "and could anything be better?"

"Could anything be worse? Man, he's pledged himself to declare war on half the nations of Europe if he keeps his word to our folk."

"We have his word," persisted Alec, "the word of a king."

"So likewise," murmured Walker dryly, "had the people of Glencoe."

"Guid grief!" cried Alec, stopping dead and rounding on his companion, "that's perilously like treason, Mr Walker. You've been listening to the Jacks."

"I have listened to all men," said the hose-factor quietly, taking Alec's arm and walking him on again, "but my conclusions are ever my ain. For my politics, I care not a rush who sits upon the throne of England, yet care I mightily for the weal of my ain folk and would not see them ruined as the puir Hieland barbarians were ruined a while since. I like not this scheme, Alec, nor ever will. Aiblins Paterson is a gey canny man wi' the bawbees, and aiblins he was a terror to the Spanishers when he sailed the Main; but when he seeks to set up a rival to the English East India and relies on the word of a Dutchman and expects forbye that English ships will back him and English gold subscribe half his capital, why then I say that either he has lost his wits or else he is working for an interest which is not Scotland's. So this is my hope, friend Alec, and I care not who kens it: that, though Paterson be canny, Scotland will prove a wee bit cannier than he, and will think twice ere she ventures her precious gold in Mr Paterson's enterprise."

(iii)

On a November evening of the year 1697 Michael was sitting in his garret, his legs wrapped round in an old rug, his shoulders slooped with weariness, his frozen fingers driving the quill by the light of a farthing dip. He had been at it since dawn, for it was Lord Mayor's Day and a whole holiday, but now, hearing the opening and closing of a door far below him, he laid down his quill and rose. Mr Vance had come home, and he himself had earned a little relaxation. He knew he would be welcome down there in the snug living-room; he knew gratefully that his presence was always welcome to this simple craftsman and his family. He was no nearer converting them to his ideals, but unwittingly he had made a place for himself in their hearts.

Maralyn was assisting her father to take off his hood and gown, the livery of the Brewers. Mrs Vance, seated in her Tudor chair by the hearth, smiled blandly upon them with a certain set look which once or twice before had attracted Michael's attention. He hoped devoutly that his suspicions regarding her were unfounded; of one thing he was certain, and that was that neither her husband nor her daughter shared them. Mrs Vance's nights were restful; that was what mattered to her family. She slept so soundly that she had taken to lying in bed until the middle of the morning. Maralyn had mentioned this to him in triumph; the combination of fresh air, exercise, and this strange, almost miraculous sweetmeat which her mother bought at the chandler's had worked this wonderful cure. Michael was privately sceptical regarding the healing properties of mint sweetmeats, but he had come to know the citizens sufficiently well by now to realise that they were as credulous as country-folk, and it was possible that a blind faith in those healing properties had cured Mrs Vance's nervous disease. Yet he could not help remarking a curious and rather ominous change in Mrs Vance's manner and appearance; she, so passionately neat, had become almost slovenly in her dress, and her former peevishness had given place to a kind of silly vacancy. She would sit for hours without speaking; she stumbled and swayed sometimes when she walked; and although she slept at nights she appeared in the morning with a grey complexion and rings round her eyes. But he kept his suspicions to himself, for he could not bring himself to destroy the happy complacency of Maralyn and her father.

"Was it a good Show, sir?" asked Michael, after he had made his greetings.

Mr Vance sniffed. The brewer's stubbly hair had receded a little from his brow during the last few years, but his trot was as brisk as ever, his paunch as generous, his spirit as perky.

"Passable good, Mr Pennington, passable good. Truth to tell, sir," added Vance, sinking down into his enclosed arm-chair, "I saw but little of it."

"Indeed? Yet your seat must have been of the best. Surely the City Companies have places reserved for them in Cheapside on such occasions?"

"Only those they term the Twelve Great Companies, of which the Brewers is not one. Mind, sir"—Mr Vance held up an admonitory hand—"we care not a rush for such empty titles, but you must understand that our Brethren and the Common Council of the City have never been the best of friends, as our records show, and particularly have we fallen out with Lord Mayors. It was one such who contrived the uniting of the Ale Brewers and the Beer Brewers into one Company, a great insult to our ancient mistery, and all of that breed have been over-ready to put a finger in our pie, telling us how we must brew, and when and at what price, and I know not what else besides. Take Whittington, for example; he was the worst of all."

"The famous Whittington?"

"Ay, pretty Dick and his cat of the chap-books, but a hob-goblin was he to us, sir, a veritable nursery ogre, flung the Masters of our Company into the Wood Street Compter, he did, on some trumped-up charge of selling dear ale. But I will tell you the truth of that story, Mr Pennington," went on the brewer, mighty solemn. "Our Brethren had given him a dinner, d'ye see, whereat was a luscious swan-standard, and he, having a quarrelsome belly, d'ye see, was offended thereby next day, and instead of purging himself, like a sensible man, must needs pick a quarrel with the Brethren. Howsoever," concluded Mr Vance leaning back with an air of complacency, "his successor was a good man, and meek, and soft to speak with. The Brethren did present him with an ox and a boar at his swearing-in, and thereafter he did them no harm."

Michael began to laugh helplessly (he was limp with fatigue).

"You find that humorous, sir?" enquired Vance, prepared at all times to appreciate a jest so it were decent, but seeing none here.

"Ay, sir," said Michael, "I find that humorous. Indigestion

will excuse so much upon the Judgement Day, and an ox and a boar can settle so many quarrels in the City of London."

"They cost twenty-three-and-sixpence and thirty-shillings-and-ninepence respectively," Vance told him in faint reproach, "and were a mighty handsome present."

"And here is a dish of boiled oysters," said Maralyn, coming in at that moment from the kitchen with a rustle of her starched safeguard, "and a tankard of blackberry-ale, and these, though they cost but little, are very fine and comforting on a cold night after a huge great banquet at the Guildhall."

Vance beamed indulgently upon her.

"Blackberry-ale, forsooth! What other weeds and berries will you find, wench, wherewith to insult good malt and liquor?"

"It is just eight weeks since I gathered the fruit in the Moor Fields," said Maralyn, setting down the dishes and the tankard. "For six weeks it has been stopped up close in cask, and now is at its perfection for drinking. But if, sir," she added, with a twinkle in her eye, "your choice is still for a can of your pure ale, I will fetch it gladly."

"Nay, nay," said Vance, puffing a little as he dragged his chair up to the supper-table, "I'll humour you, wench, I'll humour you and your plaguey ale-cups."

Michael, watching this by-play, loved the two players all over again. Maralyn's ale-cups were famous, and she delighted to concoct such things, each for its special occasion, blackberry-ale for the cold nights of autumn, the wassail-bowl for Christmas, hum for a cold in the head, cock-ale for an invalid, cold-tankard for summer heats. Her father, while persistently declaring that ale was too sacred a brew ever to be used as the foundation for fancy drinks, always partook of his daughter's cups with great relish after a conventional protest, and if he did it, as he vowed, only to give the girl pleasure, certainly carried his unselfishness to considerable lengths.

They sat down to supper, the four of them, very cosy and content, with Mrs Vance in one of her most amiable moods and the roar of the festive mob in Chepe only emphasising the peace of this little room. The brass-faced clock ticked somnolently in its corner, and old Tiger deigned to purr in a deep bass upon the hearth-rug, and the fragrant tankard went round and the well-cooked food sent up a savoury odour.

"Well, thanks be to God," remarked Mr Vance, leaning sideways to spit a piece of oyster-shell into the fire, "we are like to have peace at last, and that means a revival of trade. They are bound to take off some of these horrid taxes, for I hear that young Mr Robert Harley has proposed a disbandment of the Army and that the motion was carried through both Houses, even the Whigs making no grumble though the measure was proposed by a Tory. Bless me, the whole realm is thankful to have peace abroad after so long and bloody a war."

"Except the King," said Michael dryly.

"Ay, I believe he will be sorry not to have the excuse of leaving us every summer for a campaign, for he doth not seem to have gotten him any great love for his English dominions. Poor soul, they say he hath grown mighty morose since Her Majesty's death. There's no day in a man's life more sorrowful, Mr Pennington, than that on which he loses a good wife," and the brewer threw a tender glance in the direction of his own spouse, who answered it with a vague sort of smile.

The talk then turned to young Nathaniel, who, it seemed, had weathered the storm which had submerged so many goldsmiths and small bankers on the establishment of the Bank of England and its monopoly, and was doing very well for himself. Mr Vance, who could never really grasp the meaning of these new methods of finance and retained a sneaking suspicion that they were dishonest, dwelt chiefly on Nat's industry and sobriety, praising his refusal to set up in grand style with the rise of his fortunes, and speaking respectfully of his daughter-in-law both as wife and business-partner, so that it was obvious that the old man dwelt in some awe of the masterful Susan. After a while, Mr Vance fetched down some of his favourite authors, and made the little gathering take parts in the reading of an old comedy called *The Arraigning and Indicting of Sir John Barley-corn, Knight*; Michael was the Judge, Mrs Vance was Mistress Hostess, Vance was Bull the Brewer, and Maralyn doubled the parts of Master Malt and Thomas the Ploughman. They grew very merry, and the tankard of blackberry-ale was refilled more than once; Mr Vance, becoming mellow, produced a slim volume and read them with great gusto Ale's argument for its own superiority in a dialogue entitled *Wine, Ale, Beer and Tobacco*.

"You, Wine and Beer, are fain to take up a corner anywhere, your ambition goes no farther than a cellar; the whole house where I am is called Ale House. Whoever heard of a Wine House or a Beer House? My Name, too, is of a stately Etymology; you must bring forth your Latin. Ale, so please you, is from *Alo*, which signifies Nourish; I am the choicest and most luscious of Potations. . . ."

And then, pushing his books aside, he leaned back in his chair and roared out somewhat huskily:

> "Come all that loves good company
> and hearken to my ditty,
> 'Tis of a lovely Hostess fine,
> that lives in London City.
> Who sells good Ale, nappy and stale,
> and always thus sings she,
> My Ale was tunn'd when I was young
> and a little above my knee."

Verse after verse he sang, drawing them out of the store of his memory, which was crammed with such simple, rollicking ballads, to the good old English tune of *Buffcoat has no Fellow*, and Michael and Maralyn came in lustily at the end of every verse—

> "My Ale was tunn'd when I was young
> and a little above my knee"—

while Mrs Vance nodded and smiled vaguely upon them all, and the clock ticked and the bright pewter winked upon the chimney-shelf and the solid furniture gleamed from much careful polishing, and the candlelight shone upon the bright hair of the girl whose presence seemed to hold all these familiar, homely things together, welding them into a little world of deep contentment and security.

And then there came the knock upon the outer door.

Vance's song was at its height, and the first time the summons came none but Michael heard it. He, hearing it, felt a strange coldness run through him, a queer shiver of foreboding, and instantly he was back in memory to that other night, the night of the draw of the Million Lottery, when upon the fortress of ale and good cheer and simple harmony there had beaten the summons of money, of how Maralyn had answered it, of all that had followed, the ill-feeling, the unconcealed insolence of the poor 'prentice suddenly rich, the quarrel between father and son, the smirch which wealth and all that it entailed had laid upon the brightness and innocence of this little household. That summons had been loud and peremptory; this was gentle and almost diffident, but somehow a thousand times more ominous in its hint of persistence.

Michael was a little drunk; he knew this, and tried to discount his premonitions accordingly. But he could not. He felt his heart beat with a sickening thunder and a wave of apprehension envelop his reason. As the second knocking sounded, and Maralyn's expression told him she had heard it, he reached forward and laid his hand tightly over hers where it lay upon the table, and said to her, low and urgent:

"Maralyn, do not answer."

It was the first time he had addressed her thus familiarly, but neither noticed it. She looked at him; and he was afraid the more because of the innocence of her eyes.

"What do you mean?" she asked—surprised, no more than that.

"Do not answer," he repeated (Vance, unconscious of anything except ale and its glories, went on roaring out his ballad, and Mrs Vance had fallen asleep). "Do not go."

She did not withdraw her hand from Michael's grip, but she rose, and stood for a moment looking down on him. Her eyes were bright as stars from the merriment of the evening, and her mob was just a little bit awry. She looked like a child fresh from a glorious game.

"Mr Pennington," she said gently, "there is someone knocking at my father's door, and needs must I answer the summons." There was a slight pause. He said nothing, but he felt himself as it were falling from a wave-crest into some dark trough, and fatefully he knew that a bright little world fell with him. "I must go," she said; and although he knew she spoke that sentence without significance, he shuddered to hear it spoken.

(iv)

Mr Vance, getting a little muddled towards the end of the fifteenth verse of his ballad, was rather annoyed when there broke upon his consciousness the fact that a person with horn buttons to his coat and a thrum-cap twisted in his hands stood beside his chair, and that upon the other side of him Maralyn was fussing about something.

"Tut, wench, you have made me forget," expostulated Mr Vance, brushing her away as though she were a fly.

> " 'The bonny Scot will lay a plot
>   to get a handsome tutch,
> And tumty, tumty, tumty, tum
>   so will the cunning Dutch.' "

"What a-devil is that line? Who's this you've brought in? Why now the Lord confound me, speak of Scotsmen and here one is! Why how now, Alec, what do you here? Sit down, lad, sit down, and pass the ale about. Now, Alec, tell me truly, know you this excellent song of the Merry Hostess? You must be sure to know it, and therefore can assist me—what a-devil ails you, sir, that you do not sit down?" Mr Vance roared out the last words in a very petulant manner, for he had just passed into that stage of intoxication when affability turns quickly into peevishness.

"I prefer to stand, sir," said Alec Moray in a queer jerky voice, "until I have said what I have come to say. I am——"

"You are drunk, lad," said Vance, amiable again. "I know very well what is the matter with you. Think nothing of it. Lord Mayor's Day——"

"Your pardon, master, I am stone sober. And I am come, sir, to ask you to release me from your service, and to tell you that I am sailing for the Americas."

Mr Vance stared at him, then burst into a shout of laughter.

"You are drunk, Alec, I say. Aye, you have been baiting the bombard, my lad. 'Ounds, you are but newly out of your indentures and are now a journeyman, ay, and a good one, and will prove in time the best in my service. Maralyn, fetch the poor lad a measure of small-ale, for he is clean fuddled and knows not what he says."

"Mr Vance," persisted Alec, in a low and hurried tone, "during all the time of my apprenticeship I scraped and saved my pocket-money and ran errands in the evening and held links and what-not that I might be ready against the day when a Scottish ship with Scotsmen aboard of her set off to found a new Scotland in undiscovered lands overseas. That day is coming very soon, and I am ready. My little hoard is sufficient for my passage. It grieves me that I must leave your service, for you have been a right good master to me and have shown me extraordinary kindness, but my mind is set upon this venture, and I cannot stay."

A kind of humming silence, deep as a well, met his words. Then, as though he dropped a stone into that well, he added:

"And I am come to ask you further that Miss Maralyn may come with me as my wife."

. . . Mr Vance's large red hand groped forward on the table, encountered his ale-can, knocked it over, and stayed where it was in a puddle of ale. He gave a kind of exasperated puff, closed his eyes for a moment, and began to murmur:

" 'The bonny Scot will lay a plot
to get a handsome tutch . . .'

"What said you, Alec? Pooh, you're drunk. I would to heaven someone would assist me with that missing line. Tumty, tumty, tumty, tum—— Come, wife, you know it well. Hush, she is asleep. Maralyn, wench, you know it as well as you know— Maralyn! " And his voice snapped and broke on the name; for he had looked at her and seen her face.

She dropped swiftly to her knees beside his chair, and clasped her hands loosely and caressingly round his arm.

"Yes, Father, I am here."

"Maralyn, what says yon silly fellow? I cannot understand . . .

I think that blackberry-ale of yours has o'erthrown me. Indeed I believe it has. Never meddle with good malt liquor, girl; leave it alone and it will leave you alone. The bonny Scot will lay a plot; the bonny Scot will lay a plot . . . but, by Jesus, not such a plot as this! " cried Vance suddenly, struggling out of his chair, knocking over the crockery and spilling ale over his precious books. His face was aflame, his lips trembling violently. "What, sirrah! Rob me of my only daughter, wouldst thou, and spirit her to the Americas. Over my dead corpse wilt thou do it then, thou shitten rogue, ay, and it will be fortunate for you if you have bones enough left whole to carry you to your Americas when I have chastised you as you deserve."

"Father," said Maralyn, not loud, and not stirring from his side, "I love Alec, and Alec loves me, and where he goes I would go also."

The brewer stood silent, only sniffing a little as though he had a cold; you could see the colour drain away from his ruddy face. He looked suddenly old and rather tired.

"What's that? Oh, ah, you love him and he loves you. I did not know. Ahem! That is——"

"And he has been a good servant to you for many years as your 'prentice and lately as your journeyman," continued the girl, steadily but with a very slight quaver in her voice. "Our affections have been engaged since the day Alec came to you, I think, but we would not trouble you with the matter while we were so young, and besides, Alec could not support me. But now, it seems, he is out to make his fortune overseas, and comes to ask you for my hand. I know no more of the matter than that, for you must know he is too honourable to speak to me upon such affairs until he had first made himself plain to you."

Vance sat down rather suddenly, groped for his handkerchief, and trumpeted upon his nose. The frost of a too-sudden sobriety had killed the mellowness of ale, and Maralyn's calm gentleness had shamed his rage.

"Ha, well, ahem, all this is news to me, and it is a great matter. I must bethink me, ay, I must bethink me. Mr Pennington," he added, brightening a little, "what say you to this business? Come, sir, you are as one of the family, and I should be obliged for your opinion."

"You honour me, sir, by seeking my opinion in so personal a matter," replied Michael with an effort, "but since you ask me, I will say that were Miss Maralyn my daughter there is not a man of my acquaintance I would sooner trust with her happiness than Master Alec Moray."

"Say you so? Why, Alec lad, you should be blushing to hear so huge a compliment. Well, well, sit down, and you too, wench, and let us have a glass of ale and talk a while in peace and quietness. Such matters as these are not to be settled in haste."

"Your pardon, sir, if I appear importunate," said Alec, sitting upright on the edge of his chair, "but I must plead with you to let me have your decision within the next few days. For I must needs set my affairs in order ere the expedition sails, and that, I hear, will be soon."

Mr Vance looked as though he were about to make a sharp retort, but catching Maralyn's eye said mildly:

"I know but little of this venture, and must require of you that you make all plain to me."

"You remember, sir," said Alec, leaning forward and speaking with a growing but restrained emotion, "that the books of the Scottish Company for Trading Overseas were opened in London as long ago as October '95, so that the capital for England might be subscribed first. There was alarm upon 'Change, for it was thought that England's commercial interests were threatened, and indeed English East India stock fell twenty points in a week. Both Lords and Commons addressed His Majesty against the Scottish Company, but the King replied evasively that he hoped all inconveniences might be remedied. There was then some panic, the Commons ordering the seizure of our Company's books and voting that the projectors should be impeached, but Paterson, Belhaven and the others were safe in Scotland, and when they found they could not look to England for subscriptions, they invited Scotland to subscribe the whole amount required, that is, four hundred thousand pounds."

He paused a moment, and a look of pride came upon his plain, honest face.

"Scotland responded brawly, sir. All over the country men plunged, both small men and great, though all this while there was no precise destination specified for the settlement, some saying it would be made in the Indies, others upon some island off the Africa coast. Towards the end of last year, the Company began to build themselves handsome offices near the Greyfriars in Edinburgh, and men were despatched to contract for weapons and supplies. Meantime, Mr Paterson went abroad to engage the aid of foreign merchants. By June of this year it was known where the settlement was to be made, a place neither in Africa nor in the Indies, but in the Central Americas, a place rich in gold and silver mines, the climate temperate, the food and fresh water abundant, the natives believed friendly, the territorial rights undisputed."

"A paradise," murmured Vance dryly. "A veritable paradise, or so it sounds. May one ask precisely where it is situated?"

Alec told him that it was upon the Isthmus of Panama, adding not without emotion:

"It will be known to all the world anon as New Caledonia, but at present men call it Darien."

Four

(i)

IN the course of the next few days Mr Vance gave his consent
to the marriage of his daughter with young Alec, for, after the
first shock, he could find nothing against the match. He liked
and respected his prospective son-in-law, it was obvious his
daughter knew her own mind, and as for the Darien business,
Mr Vance's attitude towards it was that of his century. The New
World was popularly supposed to contain fabulous wealth, and
although the brewer distrusted the modern tendency towards
speculation, and could not understand why any man should
wish to exchange England for "heathenish lands", he was
tolerant towards the pioneering spirit in the younger generation,
and he could not but applaud Alec's pertinacity and thrift. It
was plain that, both in physique and character, the lad was cut
out for the rôle of pioneer, and as for Maralyn, she would always
be equal to any situation.

But for all his approval of the match, Mr Vance suffered from
a certain depression. His daughter was busy with numberless and
mysterious preparations, and although she attended as assiduously as ever to the needs of her family, those preparations were
concentrated around a person not of her family. Always before,
when her father had seen her busy in the kitchen or the street
or the yard, he had known that she was working for the common
good of his own immediate circle and had taken her activities
for granted; now, as he watched her deft hands and listened to
her light, unhurried footsteps, he asked her with a persistent,
piteous curiosity what she was doing, where she was going, what
she was making, and when she would be home from shopping.

She was suddenly precious to him, and yet at the same time he resented her; she was upsetting his normal life, and like all simple men he hated the disruption of a smooth routine.

Michael watched her also, and with a certain uneasiness. He was disturbed by vague rumours he kept hearing in regard to Darien; the London merchants said confidently that the expedition would upset Spain, and added with malicious glee that the climate was unhealthy and the gold-mines non-existent. All this might be discounted because the commercial interests of England naturally resented poor Scotland's wresting a chance to make herself rich and found colonies; but it was nevertheless a fact that the English Council of Trade had examined the famous navigator, Dampier, as to the territorial rights of Darien, and had received the report that a Scottish settlement there would almost certainly conflict with the claims of Spain. This was common knowledge, and the Scots were not daunted by it; they retorted that they had William's promise to protect them, and that he had pledged the support of the English Navy if there was any conflict between the settlers and a foreign Power.

Maralyn's first care had been to engage a servant-girl; her mother must not be left with the cares of the household on her hands, and Maralyn would find some trustworthy lass and train her so that when she herself must depart she would leave behind her a competent substitute. So she went down to St Paul's to study the "advices" put up there in the nave by servants who desired situations, and after a careful selection, engaged a young girl named Nan Huggins, the daughter of a Spitalfields weaver. With her character vouched for in a somewhat perfunctory manner by the Presbyterian minister whose church her family attended, and with all her belongings tied up in a bundle under her arm, Nan duly arrived at the brewer's house and was installed in the kitchen.

In appearance, the girl had a curious resemblance to a cat, for her eyes slanted, her nose was flattened at the tip, and her large mouth wore upon it a perpetual smile. As though to accentuate this feline appearance, she dressed her hair in twin peaks above her brow in imitation of the latest style in wigs, and these peaks were very like two pricked ears. She said little, though she did not seem shy; she was meek, quick and obedient, and under Maralyn's patient tuition soon became proficient in housewifery. Mr Vance disliked her from the first, but only because she was a perpetual reminder to him of the change about to overtake his household; he would come into the living-room where Maralyn was instructing Nan in spinning, or laying the cloth, or cleaning the pewter, would grunt, mutter something and go out again. Mrs Vance said little to the girl and seemed to live in some slight awe of her, and the 'prentices ignored her as an inferior being, though it was not long before she had picked her favourite from among them in the person of Nick Hammond. Nick, who was in the lowest depths of misery since the news of Maralyn's betrothal, appeared oblivious of her attentions and luxuriated in aloof despair.

So Christmas came and went, and presently the street-sellers were calling snowdrops and violets, and Maralyn was busy stitching her wedding-gown, and Mr Vance was brewing a very special brew of strong-ale for the bride-stake, and Alec was hotly defending Paterson's reputation which had suffered from his being robbed of a part of the Company's funds by unscrupulous agents, and Nan was turning the spinning-wheel with such skill that it never once reversed action, and Mrs Vance, who still sallied forth every morning to "take the air" and returned smelling strongly of mint, alternated between fits of sentimentality when she would call Maralyn her own darling little daughter whom she could not bear to lose, and spasms of alarming temper when no one dared approach her. It might have been remarked by an acute observer, however, that Mrs Vance never railed at Nan in these otherwise universal storms, and that Nan, for her part, remained completely unaffected by them.

There came a fair May morning when the bells of St Pancras' church pealed out right merrily for the wedding of Alexander Moray and Maralyn Vance, and the little procession came slowly across Bird-in-Hand Court into Cheapside. First came the Morris-dancers, the fool with his bladder and fox's brush, Robin Hood, Maid Marian, a Queen of the May, and a piper (for Mr Vance was determined to give his only daughter a genteel wedding and to spare no reasonable expense). Next came the bridegroom, attended by young Nathaniel and the 'prentices, all with bride-laces intertwined with sprigs of green broom tied to their left arms. After them staggered two small boys, neighbours' sons, carrying between them a handsome bride-cup hung about with gay ribbons; of this cup, all would partake in church. Immediately behind walked Maralyn, on her father's arm; she looked unfamiliar yet composed in her finery, and her eyes were smiling more happily than ever. Mrs Vance and Mrs Moray, both weeping discreetly into clean handkerchiefs, followed after, and lastly came friends and neighbours and a "noise" of musicians hired for the occasion. Clutched tightly in his hand, Alec carried the ring on which he had squandered part of his precious savings; it was of silver in the form of two clasped hands holding between them a little shield on which was inscribed the motto: "In Good or Ill, I'll Love Thee Still."

After the service, the entire party returned to the house for the wedding-feast, and Maralyn, a little flushed but full of simple dignity, served out her bride-ale in the old fashion, each guest "paying" for a measure of it according to his means and thus forming a purse for the assistance of the newly married pair in their housekeeping. The wedding night was spent under the family roof, after the couple had been escorted to bed with the usual ceremonies of throwing the stocking, scrambling for favours, and drinking of possets. Next day, at a very early hour, the bride and groom attended by Mr and Mrs Vance, Mrs Moray, Nat and his wife, Michael Pennington and the 'prentices, set out for the Saracen's Head, which stood upon the west side of Friday Street, and from the yard of which there ran once a week the Edinburgh coach. For it was rumoured that the first of the Company's ships would sail for Darien within the next few weeks, and Alec was in a fever to reach Leith, lest it sail without him.

Two porters, hired for the occasion, carried the luggage of the young couple, very modest luggage, every article in it carefully selected during the preceding weeks; in Maralyn's trunk there were many home-made balms and remedies against fevers and salves for wounds, for despite Alec's assurances that the climate of Darien was paradisal and the natives friendly, Maralyn was nothing if not cautious and thorough. To make quite certain, she had brewed a kilderkin of mum, which was made from wheat-malt with the addition of various spices and had some new-laid eggs placed on top of the cask before it was closed, for not only was this drink said to be vastly improved by a sea-voyage, but it was believed to be a sure specific against every variety of disease.

It was not a very cheerful procession that made its way along Chepe in the clear May dawning. Mrs Vance was in a difficult mood, for she was not accustomed to rise at an early hour nowadays and was full of self-pity; Mr Vance, beneath a set smile, looked resigned and a little lost; Alec's thoughts were obsessed by highwaymen and other perils of the road; Nat and Susan were aloof and faintly contemptuous of everybody; Mrs Moray kept up a long weeping monologue in which she recited to the world at large her Alec's virtues; the 'prentices, not yet recovered from the festivities of yesterday, were inclined to be noisy and quarrelsome; and Michael was quiet and depressed. Only Maralyn was her usual self, easy and natural, not too much absorbed in her own happiness (which seemed to shine from her) that she could not be tenderly sorrowful at parting from her family, answering her father's forced jests and her mother's plaints with the same ready tact, walking briskly yet without haste, self-controlled without superiority, composed without sophistication. She had completed one task and was about to embark upon another, and she would bring to the new all that she had bestowed upon the old, the same pride in craftsmanship, the same devoted service.

The yard of the Saracen's Head was in a great stir, and the little procession paused as it came under the arch, instinctively drawing together for comfort in a strange and frightening world.

The yard was enclosed on three sides by the double galleries of the inn, galleries open to the air and communicating with the bedrooms. In this yard, in the days before theatres were known, had been acted plays and masques, the spectators ranging themselves along the galleries and the lower sort standing in a portion of the yard called the "pit". But now, here in the centre of the yard, there stood the coach, its body, of dull black leather studded with broad-headed nails, sloping steeply backwards, its four oval windows hung with red leather curtains, its immense basket, uncomfortable but cheap, hitched on behind, and a low railing round the roof for the security of the poorest sort of passengers who clung there at peril of their lives. The great iron-shod wheels, with their strong axle-trees, were bright and clean, though soon to be white with the dust of the rutty roads; on the doors were painted in huge characters the names of the towns at which the coach called and its ultimate destination: Edinburgh. Six huge Flanders mares were being fastened to the long traces with a great deal of shouting and jingle of harness; a little apart, sucking a straw in a nonchalent manner, and with his single spur jutting out from his boot, lounged the postilion who would ride the leader. The driver, with his long whip curled round its staff, stood in grave consultation with the landlord, and the passengers, gathered in groups, eyed each other suspiciously and fussed about their places, their luggage and their affairs generally. Meanwhile, porters, heavily laden, pushed their way through the throng with a strident "By your leave! ", servant-maids called across to each other from the galleries, vendors of fruit and pies and broadsheets pestered the passengers, and nondescript persons, probably thieves, slunk and mingled in the throng, as though waiting a chance to snatch a piece of luggage.

"Come," said Maralyn, smiling encouragingly upon her family. "We must find our places and dispose the baggage."

They followed in her wake as she walked resolutely forward, even Alec daunted by that most daunting scene: the first stage of a long journey. And in this case not only long but perilous; directly they left London they would be in danger of tobymen, of breaking an axle in a pot-hole, of the whole coach being over-turned by a large stone. And after Edinburgh, if and when it was reached, there was the long sea-voyage, and after the sea-voyage an unknown land. It would be years before they would see London again, if ever they did; and meantime here was the part-ing to be got through, the wrench of long if not final farewells, that moment of anguish when the roots of a life are torn up and familiar things disappear. So even Alec was silent and rather dazed, and it was Michael who found the places reserved inside the coach, introduced the pair to their fellow-passengers (a custom universally observed lest the unidentified be taken for highway robbers), and saw that the baggage was safely bestowed in the boot. It was Michael and Maralyn between them who managed the last horrible ten minutes, inventing a laboured jest or two, warding off the panic which threatens human creatures at such moments, by a flow of light conversation, striving desperately and with moderate success to establish for them all a memory of final cheerfulness. This mutual effort brought the pair of them into a sudden new comradeship, so that their eyes when they met were full of a mutual trust and gratitude, and each looked at the other with a new interest as though perceiving some quality or trait hitherto unrecognised.

She looked at him and saw a shabby but decently dressed clerk who yet carried with him always an indefinable air of breeding, a man losing his youth and gaining, at great cost, experience and knowledge and charity, fighting some inner battle of his own, continually, unwearyingly, a battle unknown to her, but fighting it with weapons familiar to her, courage, persistence and cheerfulness.

He looked at her and saw a craftsman's daughter, permeated with the traditions of a caste foreign to him, reared in an environment for ever strange to him, inbred with prejudices, loyalties, standards and tenets that meant nothing to him; a citizen's daughter neither clever nor especially intelligent, pretty but not beautiful, immersed in housewifery and in the common lot of women. But he saw also fundamental honesty in a pair of smiling eyes, resolution in an upturned chin, truth in a brow and fidelity in a look; he saw a person who never for one moment lost her human dignity and who was yet a stranger to pride, who faced life with zest and was equal to its problems, who was slow to grasp an idea outside her narrow little world, but who, having grasped it, would examine it with fairness and, if she found it to be true, would say so with honesty and courage.

The postilion was mounted, the driver was clambering on to his box, the yard echoed with the daunting word "Farewell!"

Out of the tumult and the confusion of voices and the final bustle, she leant forward and spoke to him, low and urgent:

"Stay with my father, Mr Pennington. He needs you. Promise me that you will stay with him."

"So long as he needs me, I will stay," said Michael steadily.

Her eyes, bright with unshed tears, thanked him with a glance. Then the glance strayed from him and swept over the little group which hitherto had been all her world, and overwhelmed by a tide of inarticulate pity she murmured:

"And pray be kind to poor Nick."

Then great wooden wheels broke an era into pieces, and the hooves of horses shattered a family life. There was dust, the creak of leather, the crack of a whip, a gloved hand waving, a last tender tearful chorus of goodbyes, and then all was merged into the receding thunder of the coach as it rumbled under the arch.

(ii)

In the months immediately following Maralyn's departure Michael had much to occupy his thoughts in the political sphere, and therefore he did not notice at first the subtle change that was descending on his master's household.

The anxious speculation that was shaking the larger world penetrated even into this little world of trade, and in the City coffee-houses and taverns men discussed in low agitated tones the question of the Succession. For, in France, King James was spitting blood, and in England King William was new-afflicted with the dropsy; two old antagonists were dying, and new combatants waited to take their place. When King James died, he would leave behind him as his heir a young lad of ten, his son, delicate but spirited, nicknamed the Little Blackbird because of his great black eyes, the lawful hereditary Heir of England. When King William died, he would leave behind him his sister-in-law, the Princess Anne, King James's daughter, a silent, dull-witted, obstinate woman in her early thirties, but prematurely aged by continual bearing of dead children, ruled entirely by her woman favourite, the masterful Countess of Marlborough, married to that stout nonentity, Prince George of Denmark, loathed by her brother-in-law, and yet, because of his childlessness, his Heir Presumptive. Here indeed then, was a situation to amuse the speculative and torture the time-server.

But Michael, adhering to his self-imposed task of studying the reactions of the common people, tried to ignore those of the politicians, and frequenting the City meeting-places, listened to the talk therein. It was wearyingly familiar, for it turned upon trade. How would trade benefit from a new regime? Queen Anne, because she was ruled by the Marlboroughs, would carry on William's feud with France; on the other hand, because she was native-born, she would seek to alleviate the burden of taxation and would most certainly see to it that the hordes of foreigners William had settled in England would no longer steal away her subjects' livelihood. The City, in its sentimental moments, sympathised with Anne's domestic misfortunes, approved of her staunch adherence to the Church of England and her hatred of Dissenters, and comforted itself with the knowledge that Anne had one son who had not yet followed his numerous brothers and sisters to an early grave, the eight-year-old Duke of Gloucester. If this sickly little boy managed to survive, and in due time succeeded his mother on the throne, England would be able to forget the rather unfortunate incident of William of Orange, and settle down under a genteelly Anglican and more or less hereditary regime again.

When Michael turned from studying the attitude of the City in general to that of its typical citizen, Nathaniel Vance, he found the same kind of opinions but mixed with a somewhat shamefaced hankering after a return of the direct line. Mr Vance no longer disguised his disapproval of King William, for that monarch had lately put a tax upon malt, a tax which was rising with alarming rapidity; Mr Vance had a great respect and even an affection for the Princess Anne, but he could not help feeling that it would be better if the rightful heir returned, for he had sense enough to perceive that only an hereditary title can guarantee stability. The poor lad in France, he said, was innocent of his father's mistakes, and it was not just that he should be deprived of his inheritance because of them. But of course, added Mr Vance hastily, he never would accept that young gentleman unless the latter were brought up a Protestant or changed his religion when he was old enough to form his own opinions, and although it was not his, Vance's, place to criticise his betters, he could not help deeming it too bad of King James to debar his son from the throne by insisting upon bringing him up in a faith so hateful to all Englishmen.

Mr Vance gave vent to these opinions with an abstracted air, and, watching him with affection, Michael perceived that he seemed to be listening for something. Often at table Mr Vance would lay down his knife, and sit silent, with a strained look upon his homely face, and sometimes he would wander out into the yard in the middle of his work and stand there, looking lost and wistful. Michael realised also that he himself, in intervals of his intense preoccupation with political affairs, had sensed a subtle change which was creeping upon his master's household, and now, as he and Vance sat silent over their evening ale, he began to cogitate upon the nature of that change.

For one thing, the company round the supper-table had lessened. Mrs Vance seldom appeared nowadays, but had a tray sent up to her room; Maralyn was overseas; Nick, now a journeyman, had taken up some wretched lodging of his own, and the new set of 'prentices aped the modern fashion of spending their evenings at the ale-house or the cockpit, resisting all their master's efforts to entertain them at home. So there were very few of those convivial evenings old Vance loved, very little singing of madrigals and catches, very little bawling out of ballads and passing round of tankards; Mr Bunch still visited his old crony and quarrelled with him in the fashion beloved of them both, but at other times Mr Vance had to content himself with the company of his favourite authors and of Michael.

But this was not all. The house itself seemed strangely to have altered. The food was adequately cooked, the covers were moderately clean, the rushes were changed punctually and there was no noticeable dust. But Michael remembered to have noticed that the flowers on the window-ledges were first drooping, then withered, then dead, and that nobody changed them;

that the atmosphere of the living-room had lost something of its old warm comfort; that stiff old Tiger never purred nowadays; and that the pewter on the chimney-shelf winked less brightly than of old. It was not, he reflected, that Nan Huggins was a less efficient housewife than Maralyn Vance; the difference was more subtle. With Maralyn's going had gone also the pride of craftsmanship, the eager service, the love which informs inanimate things and gives them a kind of life. In her place reigned a girl who worked for wages and for nothing but wages, who did her tasks for money and would not do them without money, who had no real interest in what she did, who cooked the meals and swept the floor and laid the cloth in order that at the end of the month she might be given money, and who had money in her mind all the while she worked.

And reflecting on these things, he knew at last what it was for which Nathaniel Vance listened so wistfully; it was for that undercurrent of joyous singing with which Maralyn had sweetened every task.

(iii)

Every day since Maralyn's departure her father had trotted down to the letter-office on Cornhill to see whether a letter in her handwriting lay there for him. It was not until the December of 1698, nearly eight months after her going, that his patience was rewarded.

One day towards Christmas he came bursting into the living-room, his face aflame, his eyes twinkling, his cap on the back of his head, and a paper flourished triumphantly in his hand. They had waited dinner for him, and everyone was assembled round the table; avid though he was for the treat of reading his letter aloud, he insisted that the meal be eaten first, lest it spoil. All through dinner (of which he made but a sorry pretence of eating) he kept up a spate of talk, repeating stories he had heard from time to time during the past six months concerning the Darien expedition, of the rich mines of gold and silver the settlers had discovered in their promised land, of the paradisal climate and scenery of the Central Americas, and of the splendid new town the settlers were building and which they had resolved to name New St Andrews. He even swore roundly that one fine day he would pay a visit to his daughter and son-in-law, ay, old as he was he would hazard the voyage, and of how he would carry a barrel of Thames liquor and a sack of malt with him and teach the natives the mystery of brewing ale. So he chattered away; and meanwhile Mrs Vance, her head wrapped up in an old shawl from which straggled untidy wisps of grey hair, picked at her food, stared vaguely at her excited spouse, and occasionally gave vent to a foolish giggle; the 'prentices munched stolidly and whispered to each other about their own affairs; Nan banged down dishes with an unnerving noise; and Nick Hammond's fanatical eyes burned sombrely with secret dreams.

The table was cleared at last, and a tankard of strong-ale placed upon the board, so that all might fill their cans as they pleased. Vance fished his iron-rimmed spectacles from a back pocket, placed them upon his nose with trembling fingers, spread out the precious letter before him on the table, gave his throat a tremendous clearing, and began:

" 'From on board the ship *Unicorn* in Caledonia Bay, November 1st, 1698.' "

Here Mr Vance paused, and glanced up from his reading to remark:

"You will note the date, friends, November 1st. This letter of my daughter's hath come hither to us in six weeks, most expeditious. They told me at the letter-office that an English sloop trading between London and Jamaica brought it with a cargo of tobacco, which is a proof how friendly the English merchants are towards the settlement, notwithstanding the silly rumours we have heard to the contrary. Ahem! "

No one answered him. The bored eyes of the 'prentices stared at him with the same expression with which they stared at the parson in St Pancras' church on Sundays; one had to listen to dull sermons when one might be playing football or baiting the mad folk at Bedlam, and one had to listen to the uninteresting affairs of one's master when one might be exchanging bawdy stories. That was life. The eyes of Nan Huggins were abstracted too, but they were not bored; they rested upon Nick Hammond, and there was a ruminative expression in them.

" 'Honoured Sir and Madam,' " continued Vance, after another pompous throat-clearing, " 'I hasten to write you a brief Account of our coming hither, because they say there is an English ship lies weather-bound off Golden Island, the which has promised to carry our Letters upon her Voyage to England, she being ready to set sail with the first favourable wind. You will have heard no news of us since the Letter I sent through the Public Post from Leith on the eve of our embarking, and since I do account myself so fortunate as to have always your Countenance and Favour, I embrace this opportunity of making thus grateful Acknowledgement of the same by sending you an Account of the welfare of my Husband, of our Friends, and of myself with all expedition.' "

Vance paused to draw breath, and this time his glance encountered Michael's. The other murmured politely:

"How excellently she writes, sir."

Vance made rather a to-do about reaching for his handkerchief and blowing his nose. His face was brick-red with pride and emotion.

"Oh, tolerably well, sir, for a citizen's wench, tolerably well, I do believe. Ahem! But to her news. 'At the commencement of our Voyage we had pretty blustering and troublesome weather until we passed the Northern Islands of Scotland, after which we had, by the Mercy of God, as fair and favourable a passage as we could desire, coming into Madera-road towards the end of August, the Governor of those parts being mighty civil to us. Upon the last day of October, we anchored in a fine sandy Bay about three leagues to the westward of the Gulf of Darien, and our Voyage was at an end.

" 'The women among us are not yet let go ashore, by reason we know not the temper of the Natives, nor the general wholesomeness of the place, but our colours are set up in a crabb'd hold which some of our Company are fortifying with digging of earthworks and building of palisades, and which we have named Fort St Andrews. The morning after we came hither, there came out to us several Canoes full of Indians, who were received by us with civility. We were mightily surprised to find that they spoke excellent Spanish, and that two of their Captains, viz., Pedro and Augustine, carried silver-headed staves such as Spanish captains carry, notwithstanding that we were given ample Accounts before our coming hither that all these People were at war with the Spanishers and would sure to be our fast friends. Howsoever, they declare they are very willing to go with us to plunder the Spanishers, and do not seem able to understand us when we say that we have no such intention. The chief among them are dressed up very sober and Christian-like in white drawers and red stuff coats; they are of very small stature and seem weakly. We gave them meat and drink, which they used freely, especially the last, for they got drunk and lay aboard all night, nor could we prevail upon them to depart, for they vowed they loved us well.

" 'When we came hither our food was run short, but those who are let go ashore bring us abundance of good wholesome water and likewise flesh of monkeys and baboon; the Natives assure us there is plenty and variety of choice fish, fowl and venison, likewise wild hog, but we have not seen any yet. The flesh of the baboon is not easy to dress, but I have experimented several ways and have chanced upon a good Method of serving it so that the darkness and strength of the meat is not offensive. These People tell us there is incredible quantity of straight, well-grown Timber, which is taken for a testimony of fertility wheresoever it is found. We have much rain here, and those of our Company who understand such matters say: That it is a wet climate, for the ground in many parts is swamp. However, they say likewise that when the ground can be cleared and regularly planted it will yield a vast Increase. There are several orange-groves, the which I long to see, and likewise excellent cedar-trees, mahogany, sugar-canes, and plantains in great abundance. We cannot tell yet what mines there are here, for the Natives are shy upon the matter and we have not yet had leisure to make proper search, only we found one silver-ore, which Mr Kylle, the refiner we brought with us, now says is but copper, upon trial. There is much gold-dust at our watering-place, in and about the water, which is in itself but poor and slimy stuff, yet gives us hope that we shall discover true gold beneath it.

" 'Yesterday there did come aboard the Commodore a Lieutenant of a French ship in her long-boat; he had much talk with our Council, and did assure them there are no gold-mines in this Country save those worked by the Spanishers; but we pay little credit to what he says, for we believe him to be jealous of us. He said likewise that he was lately come from Carthagena, where, says he, the news of our Arrival is known, the President of Panama having given an Account of it to the Governors of Carthagena and Porto Bello, but that, albeit the Spanishers are in great Consternation at the news, yet they lie quiet, investigating the territorial Rights and awaiting orders from Spain. This makes the Council hurry on the building of the Battery upon the Fort, and they have given order likewise that our Ships lie in order of battle in the mouth of the Harbour. Howsoever, they look for no interference from the Spanishers, since they have stated publicly they intend to give not the least offence to any other Nation, being set down and settled here solely for the advancement and encouragement of Trade.

" 'I must not stay for more, but to beg you to present my Service to all of your Household, you and they being always in the thoughts and Affections of her who will be ever,

" 'Sir and Madam,

" 'Your loving, dutiful Daughter and Servant,

" 'MARALYN MORAY.' "

Mr Vance slowly lowered the letter, and stared before him with an expression of childish wonderment.

"To think of it," he murmured, "only to think of my daughter living neighbourly with heathen savages and dressing the flesh of the baboon."

Before anyone else could speak, and without the slightest warning, Mrs Vance burst into a passion of tears.

(iv)

There was something so unexpected and disconcerting about this outburst that for a while no one offered her comfort. The tears ran down her cheeks in a continuous stream, the sobs poured from her throat in noisy abandonment, her fists thumped the table in wild despair, and jerky, half-finished sentences of complaint made themselves audible through her sobs. Her only daughter had been snatched from her bosom by an unworthy 'prentice who had carried off this prop and stay of her age into a savage wilderness where, if she were not devoured by cannibals or torn in pieces by wild beasts, she would inevitably be poisoned by tropical vegetation. And meanwhile the bereaved mother would never see her beloved child again and was left uncared for and unloved, no one remembering to use the warming-pan in her bed nor to enquire after her health nor to make her a hot posset nor read to her when she felt dull. She was a poor, forsaken, sick and abandoned old woman, and the sooner she was put into her coffin the better for herself and everyone else. So the hysterical tirade continued.

Vance sat speechless, his mouth agape, his face pale, his poor eyes staring stupidly at this stranger who was his wife. The 'prentices sniggered and nudged one another, Nick paid no attention whatsoever, and Michael, embarrassed and apprehensive, tried in vain to think of some means of quietening the woman. It was Nan Huggins who grappled with the situation. She rose with her customary clatter, came round to her mistress's side, gave the heaving shoulder a little pat, and said calmly:

"Come to bed, mistress."

Mrs Vance glanced up in the middle of a sob, and there was an odd mixture of pleading and defiance in that glance. But she said nothing, only wriggled her shoulder away from Nan's hand, and continued her paroxysm of self-pity. Nan said again, still perfectly matter-of-fact:

"Come to bed, mistress. You are unwell. I will give you your physic and you will grow better apace."

Again the glance, but now the pleading was uppermost. Perhaps because he sensed that pleading, without in the least understanding it, Vance snapped at the girl:

"What physic is this you give your mistress, wench?"

The slanting eyes met his, indifferent, with a tinge of insolence:

"It is good physic, master, got from a topping 'pothecary. It cures all distempers and humours."

Before Vance could question Nan further, his wife ceased her sobs abruptly, staggered to her feet, and clutched the girl's arm.

"Ay," she said vaguely, "it is good physic, and this is a good wench. Lead me abovestairs, Nan my girl; I do but distress the company."

Vance sprang up at that, trotted round to her, and offered his arm with tender solicitude, but she pushed him aside and clung to Nan, and so the pair of them went slowly from the room. Vance stood looking after them for a space, then returned to his chair and sank into it; there was such a look of hurt bewilderment upon his homely face that Michael felt the tears start to his own eyes. The younger man signed to the 'prentices and Nick to return to the brewhouse, and was about to follow when Mr Vance called to him, and he turned back.

"Mr Pennington," said the brewer, swilling the ale round in his can and staring into it, "think you my wife is ailing?"

Michael hesitated in an agony of doubt. Should he voice his suspicions at a moment when his master was all bewildered and hurt by his wife's strange behaviour and must be troubled likewise by certain ominous hints in his daughter's letter? And suppose those suspicions were unfounded? He had no proof that they were correct, and until he had such proof it surely would be brutal to pass them on to the devoted husband. So presently he licked his lips and said quietly:

"I think, maybe, sir, Mrs Vance is but naturally upset by the departure of Miss Maralyn but has not shown it until now. A hidden wound when touched makes the strongest of us cry out."

"She is strangely altered," said Vance, almost as though he had not heard, and staring hard into his can. "I rejoiced at the time her sleeplessness seemed to be cured by these mint sweetmeats of which she talks so much and partakes of so freely, but now I do bethink me that it is from her first resorting to them that she has become changed in spirits and in habit. And now there is the wench's talk of some 'pothecary's jolloping. I would Maralyn were here; she would know what to do. My wife is apt to talk very strange at times, so that I begin to fear me she is wandering in her mind, and she is full of whims. Likewise is there an air about her——" He stopped abruptly and drained his can as though to hide his face from his companion.

Michael felt the sweat break out on his body. He cursed himself for what he knew was a weakness, and yet he could not for the life of him frame the fatal words: I suspect she is a victim of gin. He could not bring himself to deal this troubled, simple man so dreadful a blow at such a moment, a blow which, moreover, could not remedy the situation, for, if his suspicions were indeed correct, Mrs Vance was long past curing of her secret vice. So instead he murmured, hating himself all the while for his prevarication, that Mrs Vance was at a difficult time of life; then, trying to make some sort of amends for his lack of moral courage, added that he considered the girl Nan unsuitable as a nurse, and that maybe it would be better to engage an older woman. Vance looked at him with an abstracted air, and then said mildly:

"Nan is a good girl, Mr Pennington; it is true I have no liking for her, but that is nought to the point. While she does her duty, and obeys her mistress, she is under my care and I am responsible for her welfare, as I am for any 'prentice's. I am bound, as she is, by the terms of the indentures, and will abide by my bargain. Likewise is it plain that my wife is attached to her; you saw how it passed just now."

Michael said nothing, for there was nothing to say. Presently Vance gave a great sigh, and took up his daughter's letter again and skimmed through it in silence; then he began to smile a little, and murmured:

"That is a marvellous thing, 'odsme it is, that my little wench should be eating monkeys and meeting barbarians dressed up in Christian drawers." And then, as Michael made no comment, he glanced up and asked eagerly: "Do you not think it an excellent letter for a cit's wench to have writ, Mr Pennington?"

154

"Indeed, sir, most excellent. But I—I liked not a part of her news. It seems plain from what she says that the Spanishers discovered Darien before the Scots, and I fear there will be trouble anon."

But Vance leaned over and patted his arm, saying cheerfully:

"Ease your heart, sir, ease your heart. If the Spanishers prove troublesome, the English Navy will be sent thither in the settlers' defence. We have the word of King William for that."

Five

(i)

MARALYN'S departure had thrown poor Nick Hammond into a mood of dull despair in which he remained sunk for many months. He was in his early twenties now, and a journeyman, but his mind had not kept pace with his growing body, nor had he learnt any self-control. He was extraordinarily indiscreet in his political talk, and it was a marvel to Michael that he had not got himself hanged before this, but probably Nick and his Jacobite club were too unimportant to excite the hostility of the Government. Yet, for all his recklessness and indiscretion, the young man was without question loyal to his ideals, both to his cause and to his lost Maralyn; and his burning sincerity, pitiful enough in the boy, was almost tragic in the man.

In the spring of 1699 Nick suddenly disappeared. When his absence was discovered by his master, Vance was at first angry and then anxious. Despite all Nick's failings, the brewer retained a fatherly affection for him, and still continued to regard him as the poor parish lad, dependent upon his master for everything.

"Pray God the youth has not miscarried," said Vance, as he lingered to discuss the matter with Michael in the counting-house. "They say the press-gang is hugely busy again because we are like to have another war with France over this vexed question of the Spanish Succession, and Nick is a likely stalwart lad and a great frequenter of ale-houses. If he returns not by tomorrow I shall be minded to put up an advice for him in Paul's."

Nick was absent three days, and on the fourth morning he reappeared in the brewhouse with a sheepish expression, bleary eyes, and a dirty napkin swathed around his head. He confessed frankly that he had been upon what he described as an "extra-ordinary guzzle" in a good tippling society at the Peg and Wassail ale-house somewhere in the neighbourhood of Moor Fields, and that he and his companions had come into collision with the watch. A constable of the watch and his henchmen had arrested several of the company on the charge of disturbing the peace, and had immured them in the Poultry Compter, but Nick had managed to escape after getting himself a broken head, and had lain hidden for three days in case a search was being made for him. He did not give the reason for this "extraordinary guzzle", though he had neither the means nor the temperament for such debauchery, but Michael made a shrewd guess that the young man had revolted from his own lowness of spirits and had decided to drown his sorrows for once. Mr Vance greeted his re-claimed journeyman with a mixture of relief and reproach, and taking him into the yard walked up and down with him for half an hour, lecturing him in a fatherly manner upon the perils of low company, in conclusion bidding him remember the dictum of the Water Poet that "Ale neither hurts nor kills any but those who abuse it immeasurably and beyond bearing".

It was typical of Mr Vance that, partly to keep Nick from the low company of which he had warned him, and partly to atone for any harshness which might have crept into the lecture, he should follow it up by an invitation to supper. Nick accepted gratefully, and when the hour came sat down at the hospitable board with Mr Vance and Michael, Mrs Vance supping above-stairs as was usual nowadays. Michael, observing the journey-man, decided that his debauch had done him good; he seemed more alive than he had done for a long while, and not so deter-mined to wallow in romantic gloom. From Nick, Michael trans-ferred his observation to Nan Huggins. He had noted how, during the past three days, her ordinary demeanour had suffered a change; usually she was as cat-like in her behaviour as in her facial appearance, lazy, aloof, and faintly contemptuous of the world at large. But directly Nick's disappearance had become known she had grown fidgety, forgetful of her duties, restless and disturbed. Michael had caught her on one occasion with her ear to the keyhole when he had been discussing Nick's absence with his master in the counting-house. And now that Nick had returned she seemed fairly to purr with pleasure, yet with a certain ferocity, as though her delight had more of the wild-cat than of the domesticated tabby about it. The presence of her master made her hold her tongue tonight, but she made up for this enforced silence by her assiduous attention to Nick's requirements, ready with the tankard before he had drained his can, springing forward to pick up his napkin when he dropped it, and lingering to look back at him with plain lust in her eyes as she retired into the kitchen to fetch another dish. Nick appeared to noticed nothing of all this and paid no sort of attention to the girl; only once Michael observed him jerk his head rather sharply when Nan brought her face unnecessarily close to his in serving him with food.

As the cloth was being cleared, and Mr Vance was in the act of lifting the hinged seat of his chair to reach for his pipe and tobacco-box in the recess beneath, there was a noise abovestairs as of someone falling. Conversation died instantly and all four of them remained arrested in their various attitudes; then, as a whimpering cry broke out, Vance slammed shut the upraised seat, and his ruddy face pale, cried out: "My wife! God save us, she has suffered some fit! "—and rushed from the room. They heard his feet spurning the stairs, then the opening and shutting of a door and his voice raised in anxious enquiry.

The two men stood looking after him for a moment; then Nick went towards the tankard of ale which was being kept warm on top of one of the fire-dogs, and made to lift it; Nan was before him, and as she filled his can she contrived to bring her body very close to his with a certain ugly suggestiveness. He took so sudden a step backwards that the ale was spilled upon the floor; then, turning abruptly, he murmured to Michael some conventional anxiety about Mrs Vance. Before Michael could answer, Nan, still standing by the fire, gave vent to a short, derisive sort of laugh.

Nick banged his ale-can down upon the table, flung round upon her, and slapped her face so hard that she staggered backwards. There was an instant of complete silence. Then:

"Maybe that will make you laugh t'other side of your face,

you spiteful bitch!" snarled Nick, extraordinary venom vibrating in his voice.

"Why, you swaggering clown!" whimpered Nan, nursing her reddened cheek, tears of pain and humiliation in her eyes, "how dare you lay your hand upon an unprotected girl?"

Michael who had been shocked for the moment by sheer surprise, stepped between them. His experience told him that the balm which the "extraordinary guzzle" had laid upon Nick's over-wrought nerves was deceptive, and that he was in fact in that state when a man is capable of making an ugly scene out of nothing.

"Come, Nick," he said quietly, putting a hand on the journeyman's arm, "let's keep the peace, for there is one abovestairs who is sick."

But Nick jerked his hand from his arm and continued to glower at the girl, his eyes red with a senseless rage.

"You're nothing but a shameless punk," he raged, thrusting his face towards Nan. "I'm sick of your pawings and your lewd looks and your whispered invitations; why don't you go upon the streets and have done, for I tell you I have no market for your goods and never shall have." He fished in his pocket, brought forth a couple of coins, and flung them violently at her. "There's twopence, you whore; 'tis sufficient to bribe your way into the Hole at the Poultry Compter, and doubtless you will get it back with interest in a bout with the knucks in quod."

Her lips drew back over her teeth, and she fairly spat at him:

"It ill becomes you to name the Poultry Compter, Nick Hammond, for I could send you there in the twinkling of an eye if I chose, and not for tippling at an unlawful hour, neither; ay, I could send you to the Whitt, if I chose, and the Three-Legged Mare, if it comes to that. I know where you spend your evenings, talking treason with the Lads of the Lion——"

"Now am I minded to lay more than a hand upon your cheek, you filthy drab," yelled Nick, beside himself with rage. "I am minded to put my two hands round your false neck and to squeeze the life out of it—so!"

As he made to suit the action to the words, Michael sprang at him and tried to drag him off.

"Agad, Nick, what a-devil are you doing? Take a hold on yourself, man, or you will do that which you will repent."

Nick wrestled to free himself but paid no other attention to him, as he continued to rage at the girl:

"That's the tune of it , is it? You'd turn informer, would you? Because I won't pander to your lust, you'd play the female Judas. Now marry hang me, I'll have your blood, you lousy stinking jilt. Let me alone, Master Pennington, let me alone, I say! 'Twere a charity to all mankind to stamp upon this louse that she may bite no more. Stand off, sir, stand off, d'ye hear? Else will I pink you first and strangle her afterwards."

Wrestling with the frantic man, Michael cried at him:

"Nick, Nick, you are clean mad. I implore you, I command you, recollect yourself and where you are. This is your master's house, man, and this your master's serving-maid. Nick, listen to me. 'Ounds, I'll make you listen. You did not come with the rest of us to bid farewell to Miss Maralyn, but she, ere she went away, commended your welfare to me, and asked me to befriend you for her sake. It is for her sake that I implore you to make an end of this unseemly brawl."

During the last few sentences Nick had gone limp in the restraining hands, and now, keeping his face turned away, he muttered hoarsely:

"Did she in truth say that? Did she remember me ere she left?"

"Her last words ere she left were of you, Nick, I swear it," answered Michael gently. "And you must not make her grieve to hear how you have thought to abuse her father's hospitality."

Nan broke the pause which followed, broke it with a repetition of her ugly, provocative laugh. Instantly Nick's hands reached out again in longing for her throat, but she, her former terror giving way to frustrated malice, leaned back against the chimney-breast and chastised the absent Maralyn with all the filth and venom her tongue could command. Michael, now sickened as well as seriously alarmed, cried at her:

"Get out of here, Nan, get into the kitchen, or by God I'll lay a hand on you myself!" Then, forcing himself into a sort of calmness, he added more soberly: "Nan, and you too, Nick, for the love of heaven remember there is a sick woman above-stairs."

But Nan, her lust for Nick turned to thwarted hate, her mean soul fain to vomit a long-repressed spite, laughed again, and changed her loud vituperation to a sly sneering:

"Oh, sick is she, my poor, poor mistress? Alack, the time of life is upon her, or she grieves for her absent daughter, or she has the falling sickness, or the plague, or the dropsy, or the ague. Call it one or t'other, my masters, it goes by many names, but where I come from we speak plain and we call it gin-fever. Ay, gin-fever," she snarled into the sudden silence, "Madam Geneva's very own disease. Poor mistress! She cannot sleep, and then she lights upon that which will make her sleep, and she says it is mint sweetmeats and her husband believes her because the odour of mint is on her breath and because, forsooth, he cannot suspect his genteel spouse of condescending to so mobbish a habit as lapping up of gin. The woundy fool! She finds much benefit from taking the air, says she to her sweet daughter, and charming Maralyn, good, innocent Maralyn, begs her to go a-marketing every morning that she may take this wondrous London air which has worked the miracle aided by magic sweetmeats. Oh, that was rare! But then sweet Maralyn must be gone overseas, and there comes one in her place who is not so easily bubbled, and by and by poor Mistress Vance discovers that she cannot rise of a morning to go to the diddle-shop for her dram, that indeed she cannot rise at all until she has had her dose of Geneva, and so the poor drudge Nan must be let into the secret, and Nan is a good girl, an excellent little wench because she never lets fall a word of all this to the stupid clown of an ale-brewer, to the doting husband, the—the——"

So the words died on her lips, for at last she saw him standing there, the stupid clown of an ale-brewer, the doting husband; and so dreadful was the pain upon his face that even she was silenced.

(ii)

"Nan," said Michael at last, forcing himself to speak steadily, "get you to the kitchen and stay there."

"Nan," said Vance, in a voice which from its very dullness compelled attention and obedience, "stay you where you are."

So they stood, the four of them, Vance still by the door, holding it partly open, Michael still mechanically grasping Nick who had gone limp in his grip, Nan facing them all, her lips drawn back over pointed teeth, her slant eyes narrowed, very feline indeed in her defiance. It was Vance who broke the silence.

"You have been carrying spirits to your mistress, say you, wench?"

She wriggled her shoulders. He was not at all formidable, and yet there was something about him at that moment which frightened her more than the frantic Nick had done a while ago when he had sprung at her throat.

"Yes, I have. She asked for them, demanded them. My duty is to obey my mistress." (She put every ounce of sneering spite into those words.)

"How long has this been going on?"

"For as long as I have been in your service, master. And before. Oh, make no mistake of that! If you think that I——"

"She—drinks—spirits," muttered Vance in a queer, unnatural voice, speaking half to himself and half questioning Nan.

"Drinks 'em?" cried Nan, recovering her insolence. "She's pickled in 'em."

Michael's breath, hissing with pain, merely emphasised the silence.

Again it was Vance who spoke. He turned to Nick Hammond, looking not at but through him, and with a piteous blind man's gesture groping for his hand.

"Nick, lad, I must bid you good night. I ask your pardon for so unmannerly a dismissal, but my wife—is—is not well, and I am not good company. I regret—I say I regret we cannot have our songs and ale, but—we'll make up for it another time, another time. Good night again, lad; I will see you in the morning in the brewhouse."

Nick gaped at him and would have spoken, but Michael hustled him out, pushed him along the passage and out of the house with scant ceremony, shut and bolted the outer door after him, and returned. A tableau greeted him, Vance still standing flaccid in the middle of the room, Nan still facing him from before the hearth, half house cat ingratiating, half tigress defying, her carefully dressed hair falling back from its twin peaks like a cat's ears flattened.

Michael came up to Vance and took his arm.

"Turn her out, sir," he said curtly. "She has deserved no less."

The brewer started, stared at him, and passed a vague hand over his mouth.

"No, no," he murmured, as though waking from a dream, "she is bound to me and I am responsible for her welfare."

"She has behaved herself so, sir, that she merits no care from you."

"No, no," said Vance again, with a dreadful kind of patience. "She is a poor girl earning her bread in my service and has a right to my protection. Moreover, she has but obeyed her mistress's orders . . ." His voice broke and died. Then, rallying himself, he said heavily to Nan: "Get you to the kitchen, my wench, wash the dishes and then go to your bed." He came stumbling forward and sank down into his enclosed arm-chair, groping for it as for some familiar comfort, his hands caressing the arms which were shiny from long service.

Nan, without a word, perhaps humbled, perhaps merely sly, took the cloth, went into the kitchen, and shut the door. Then there was silence, a daunting kind of silence, unbroken by the loud clatter of dishes, punctuated only by the faithful clock. Michael came and sat down at the table near his employer, aimlessly stroking the worn oak of the board. At last Vance fixed his glance upon him, and asked sharply:

"Is it true?"

"It is true, sir," answered Michael tonelessly; and then he shut his eyes because he could not bear to look upon that defenceless face and the soul which saw the last slender hope vanish. Michael continued after a moment, still stroking the table and following the action of his fingers with his eyes: "I could go upon my knees to ask your pardon, because I have not spoken of this to you before. I have guessed it for a long while now, and often have resolved to make you cognisant of my suspicion, but I could not, because I lacked the courage, or the brutality, call it which you will."

"Yes, yes, I understand, indeed I do," murmured the brewer, with a limp gesture. (You could see his slow mind revolving and revolving, like the works of a broken clock from which the face is removed.) "Wert ever a kind young gentleman. I understand; think no more of it." He rose abruptly, walked with an uncertain step to the fire, stooped and threw on a log, straightened up again, and stood there with his back to the room, his shoulders drooping. "Is there aught that——?" he jerked out, leaving the sentence unfinished.

Michael clenched his hands and answered steadily:

"No, sir, there is nothing, nothing we can do. I was a coward to keep the truth from you at first; I should be a craven indeed to buoy you up with false hopes now."

As though he had not heard, the other stammered:

"A g-good physician . . . or c-country air perhaps. . . . You are a c-countryman yourself, sir. Maybe that p-pure air of which you have so often s-spoken——?"

That stammer unmanned Michael more than all the rest, for it brought back one of the worst memories of his life, of how King James had stammered in his speech when they told him that Churchill, his best friend, had betrayed him. But, forcing himself to a semblance of control, Michael rapped out almost harshly:

"I tell you there is nothing, sir; it has gone too far. Deny her spirits now and she will turn frantic. To be kind you must be cruel. Administer the poison for which she craves until—until she has no longer any need for it. It is the only way."

There was a very long pause, during which Michael tried in vain to shut his ears to the strange muffled sounds that came from the figure at the fireplace. Then at last a noisy nose-blowing

164

told him that the sturdy mechanism of a simple mind had survived the blow and was limping on again.

"The King should be told of this, sir, indeed he should be. I mean of the plague it is becoming. You warned me of it long since but I would not listen; I said it was only a vice of the mob. I was a blind fool, but I could not believe that decent folk would stoop to such wicked folly. Yet so it is. I hear the same story everywhere; near every tradesman sells the stuff and, what is worse, encourages his customers to drink it upon score, so that they partake of it very freely, and then, at the week's end, not being able to discharge their shot, are forced to carry their goods to the pawnbroker. They tell me there are gin-booths set up even in the Poultry Compter, that the very prisoners may make their ill condition worse by sharing in the common vice."

He came slowly back to his chair, shaking his puzzled old head in a doleful manner. Lowering himself gruntingly into his seat he continued:

"There is an acquaintance of mine, a cooper, a very honest man with an excellent business, but last week he did a flit to the moon, as the saying runs, leaving nought but debts behind him and his wife and children on the parish. They say 'twas gin which ruined him and I can believe it now. And then there was the tenement on Cornhill burnt and wholly destroyed by fire because some client of—of Madam Geneva (I speak the abominable cant of the vice, you understand me?) took a candle to bed with him. They tell me there are gin-shops in the City whereon they dare to set a notice boldly displayed for all to see: 'Drunk for a penny. Dead drunk for twopence. Clean straw for nothing.' His Majesty should be made cognisant, Mr Pennington, or half the City will be ruined. Already mine own trade is fallen off apace because men are forsaking honest malt liquor for these hellish spirits. I must speak of it on Monday at Brewers' Hall. A petition perhaps. I am well acquaint with two or three of the Worshipful Wardens of our Company, and will venture to bring the matter to their notice."

"I am well assured that Mr Bunch would second you in this, sir."

"Bunch!" snapped the brewer, with something of his old spirit.

"A man who poisons his customers' bellies with beer would care not a fart to see 'em burnt up with gin." Then he continued in his former agitated tone: "They tell me mothers give it to their children, ay, and that pregnant women poison the fruit of their womb with it ere the babe comes forth; ay, and it is a fact that crimes of violence are increased of late, rape and murder and the like, and I will stake my life on it that gin is the cause, for it inflames the brain and makes men mad. I would not have believed——"

He broke off, and Michael, not looking at him, heard him nibble at his nails.

"I would Maralyn were home," went on the patient, bewildered voice. "She would know what to do. She always knew what to do, that wench. I scoffed at her old wives' remedies many a time, God forgive me, and at her meddling with pure barley-oil by an infusion of herbs and berries, but I will confess she has cured many ills by such concoctions, and though maybe it is scarce fitting that a tender wench should learn of so—so sad an affliction which has befallen her own—her own mother, yet there is a spirit in the girl which makes one confide in her and rest confident she will contrive some way out."

Again a long silence. Michael had nothing to say. He was drained of strength, sapped with sheer helpless pity, and he could find no comfort to offer. After a while he roused himself to suggest that Mr Vance should go to bed and take some rest.

"No, sir, no," said the brewer, smiling. He sighed sharply, and then, with an apologetic air, smiled wanly again. "But go you to your couch, and God be with you. I—I have somewhat I must do." He glanced at Michael with a kind of embarrassment. "Mr Pennington, I was never—ahem! —one to take much comfort from religion. I do confess it frankly. I go to the Sacraments once a year because it is the law of the land, and I carry my household to church every Sunday because I take it to be a healthful thing that every human creature should get down upon his knees one day in the week, it being a posture which—ahem! —puts us in mind of what we are and a sovereign remedy 'gainst pride. But for the rest, I strive to do my duty and love my neighbour and deal honest with all men, and I trust—ahem!

—God Almighty will accept such service from a laborious man and bring me to salvation. Yet there are times, sir, when religion is the only thing left us, and then we must try to pray."

He wandered over to his shelf of books and searched among them for a volume which ordinarily was taken down but once a week. When he had found the big prayer-book, and was coming back with it to the table, Michael met him with outstretched hand.

"I will bid you good night, sir. There is nought I can say but only this: my prayers and good wishes are yours entirely, and my services, such as they are, are ever at your command."

Vance took the other's hand and held it as though he did not know what to do with it. His lips mumbled soundlessly, and his poor eyes blinked as though from a blow.

"Thank 'ee, thank 'ee," he murmured. "Art a good friend to me, lad." He groped for his chair and sat down, laying the prayer-book upon the board in a gingerly manner as though it were fragile. "Ay, His Majesty should be told of the evil," he went on. "He is a good man, say what you will. My lords and gentlemen of the City of Westminster care little for the grievances of mechanics and shopkeepers, but His Majesty has care for all his subjects. I know what you would say: that he brought gin over with him. But that was rare stuff, sir, out of reach of the poor. He would be shocked if he knew that half the City were ruining themselves and their families with these crude spirits sold cheaply by the compound distillers. I would His Majesty were a trifle more easy to come at; they tell me 'tis a huge matter to get a private petition to his notice. And then doubtless this impending war troubles and preoccupies him; ay, that would be it. Ah well, we must do what we can for ourselves, Master Pennington, until such time as His Majesty has leisure to listen to our grievances."

And with an air of resolution Mr Vance opened the prayer-book, determined, it seemed, to seek the assistance of the King of Heaven while the King of England was occupied in martial matters.

(iii)

When Michael came downstairs next morning, a little earlier than usual for he had not been able to sleep, he saw no signs of breakfast, and venturing into the kitchen found it sordid with unwashed dishes and occupied only by an indignant Tiger yowling to be let out. It was plain that Nan had run away. Beset by the helpless feeling of the male in a domestic crisis, he wandered about, peeping into cupboards and fingering pots and pans; at last, turning his attention to the fire, which in the kitchen was never let out, he raked among the ashes till he found a small glow, and set to work vigorously with the bellows. Having succeeded in this occupation, he rose from his knees, dusty but triumphant, snatched up the great kettle, and filling it with water from a jug he found, placed it on the hook above the flames. He had just accomplished this when his master appeared in the doorway and blinked at him in great perplexity. Michael briefly explained the situation.

"The silly jilt," was all the brewer said. "How will she find honest work without a character?"

"She has broke the terms of her indentures, sir," observed Michael curtly, "by running away. She should be pursued and brought before a magistrate that she may learn her lesson."

"Nay, let her go, let her go," said Vance, drifting into the kitchen and staring dully upon the uncomforting disorder there. "She is a silly wench and will punish herself; God forbid I should add to her chastisement. Bread now, where is the bread? Bless me, that is a strange thing, that I know not where the bread is kept in mine own house. What are you doing with that kettle, sir?" he demanded, suddenly sharp.

"I really don't quite know, sir," said Michael diffidently. "I thought a kettle was commonly put on at this hour. Perhaps some tea——"

Vance fairly glared at him.

"Tea, sir? In my house? Tea, sir, for breakfast? And what is wrong with ale, pray?"

The necessity to deliver this rebuke seemed to stimulate the

168

brewer, and by the time the 'prentices came yawning in he was able to make a jest of the situation, and girding himself with a dirty safeguard which Nan had left behind her, set an example by washing the dishes. And not even when it was discovered that Nan had not left her situation empty-handed, but had snatched up such petty valuables as she could come at before she made her flight, would Vance take steps to seek her out and haul her before a magistrate, merely repeating that she was a poor silly wench who knew no better. Michael was surprised by this attitude at first, for Vance, with all his kindness, had a strong sense of justice and prized honesty as the chief among the virtues; but when his master steadily refused to engage another servant, Michael began to understand.

"We do very well, sir," asserted Vance, when they discussed the subject. "Our wants are simple and our hands are willing. As for food, sir, while we have ale we shall not lack for sustenance."

Michael drew his own conclusions from this strange attitude. On the one hand the brewer shrank from exposing his wife's vice to a stranger, and the state of his business made him feel that he could ill afford to feed another mouth.

The months that followed were gloomy and difficult in the extreme. The blow Vance had suffered on that dreadful night seemed to have inflicted on him a queer, hazy state of mind which threatened to become permanent. Constantly he would forget that there was no one to cook the meals and would come trotting in to dinner, rubbing his hands in anticipation of a good hot meal. Then, seeing the empty board, he would blink and mutter; then become shamefaced and apologetic, and thrusting money into the hands of one of the 'prentices would bid the lad run to the nearest cook-shop. Sometimes he would trot into the house in the middle of the morning and bawl for Maralyn to fetch him something he required; then, half recollecting himself and grinning sheepishly, he would murmur: "'Uds, I grow foolish. The wench is overseas. But methought there was a serving-maid, a slant-eyed jilt named—named—bless me, I shall forget mine own name next. Pooh, it doth not signify a fart, sir, not a fart," he would mutter, and go trotting back to the brewhouse, puzzling his simple head over a situation he could never seem to get straight in his mind.

But he never once called for his wife on these occasions, nor did he ever mention her in conversation. His slow brain had seized upon the fact of his wife's condition, and held on to it like a bulldog, to the exclusion of all else. He waited upon the invalid assiduously, allowing no one near her save himself, guarding her most jealously. Only he permitted Michael, by silent consent, to fetch her the fatal dram which she must have, in larger and larger quantities, day after day. With the patient resignation of his kind he had accepted the fact that the poison must be administered. There had been one or two dreadful scenes at first, when Vance had tried to make a stand, had endeavoured to argue with the patient, to cajole her, even to bully her. Then she would fly into something ominously like madness, would fling herself about the room, smash the furniture, tear her hair and curse him, until at last he would come scuttling out of her chamber, his neckcloth awry, his face ashen, his eyes huge with bewildered agony, and snatch from Michael the dram which at the same time killed and soothed. Mrs Vance never left her room now, and no one save her husband knew how she progressed. But Michael guessed something of it, heard at night her bouts of drunken laughter or tipsy raving, and saw the shadow deepen day by day over the face of her husband. His imagination supplied the details, and, raging helplessly, he cursed the Government which not only permitted this fatal vice, but even fostered it; cursed also the dangerous patience of "laborious men".

The most piteous aspect of the situation was Vance's insistence on keeping up a pretence that his wife was suffering from some ordinary ailment. The neighbours gossiped openly of her vice, the 'prentices sneered and giggled; still Vance shut his ears and clung to that love of respectability which was the hall-mark of his kind. To the neighbours' hints and significant enquiries he would answer stolidly: "Mrs Vance is not so well today because of this humid weather. She was ever affected by such conditions, being of a most delicate constitution and subject to a glandular disturbance of the heart." (Heaven knew where he had picked up this expression, which meant nothing to him nor to anybody else.) "Yet she presents her service to you, neighbour, and speaks of you ever in a most kind way. I would I could invite you to visit her, but the physician told me some while since that she must not exert herself in the least nor suffer any excitement." And so on. Meantime, Vance tended the poor creature with clumsy tenderness, washed her, made her bed, swept out her room at dead of night, and disappeared from the brewhouse every morning half an hour before the usual time to lock himself in the kitchen. There he wrestled with the invalid's meal, which often as not would come down untasted, and once Michael caught a glimpse of him through the window he had forgotten to shade, standing in the midst of chaos, girded with one of Maralyn's old safeguards, his face streaming with sweat, and his eyes regarding, with hurt bewilderment, the charred remains of some joint he had been endeavouring to roast upon the spit.

So the shadow deepened over that once cheerful house, as the dust gathered on the furniture in ever-thickening layers. There was no savoury smell of cooking now, no pleasant clatter of pots and pans; the spits lay in their rack above the chimney-shelf, collecting cobwebs, and the great pot which had cooked so many rich stews hung empty on its iron crane; the brass and the pewter, Maralyn's pride and joy, were slowly tarnishing; the once well-scrubbed table was disfigured by stains and grease; mice made an evil odour and stole the food from under the very nose of a Tiger who seemed to have lost heart with his master; the rushes on the floor, unchanged, stank and rotted; and the linen, ill washed by some creature in a garret, grew grey and torn.

Vance appeared to notice nothing of this general decay, and the 'prentices made the lack of a hot dinner the excuse for dining at a tavern. As for Michael, though he noticed it and grieved over it, he felt himself defeated by the situation. He did what he could, rose early in the morning to rouse up the kitchen fire with the bellows, sometimes clumsily wielded a besom, and even attempted, now and then, to try his hand at cooking; but he knew all the while that the situation was beyond him, and concentrated his energies in an attempt to cheer his afflicted master.

He needed some cheering himself, for, apart from the domestic situation, he had several causes for anxiety at present. First there were the rumours circling round Darien. Mr Vance still trotted down to the letter-office every day, but only once was his patience rewarded. In this second letter, which was very much shorter than the first, Maralyn informed him that the settlers had landed and had taken up their abode in wooden huts, that the rainy season was upon them and kept them much confined, that certain necessities were lacking and that the *Dolphin*, one of their sloops, had been dispatched to seek these in the Barbados, which, being an English colony, would certainly supply them. Their efforts to find either gold or silver were still fruitless, but digging continued and hopes remained high. She ended rather abruptly, but with her usual careful formality. She was, and ever would be, their loving dutiful daughter, Maralyn Moray. And that was all.

But so far as Michael was concerned it was not all. In the taverns and the coffee-houses he heard rumours, ugly and persistent rumours which could not lightly be dismissed, and certainly could not be discussed with Vance, who appeared oblivious of them. Something had gone wrong with the Darien venture; someone, either maliciously or with criminal ignorance, had given false information in the first place. There was no gold and there was no silver; the climate was anything but paradisal; and the natives were hand-in-glove with the Spanishers. More ominous still, the Governor of Jamaica had received positive orders from King William that he must not supply the Darien settlers, and had issued a proclamation to his own colonists accordingly, "as they will answer the contempt of His Majesty's command to the contrary at the utmost peril of their lives." Later came the story that the *Dolphin* had struck a rock and had been forced to run in to Carthagena for repairs, and that the Spanish Governor there had seized the ship and put the crew in irons. This bunch of rumours, taken together, made anxious food for thought. William had encouraged the Darien venture; he had given his consent to an Act of Parliament promising the colonists protection and aid; but he had done this at a time when the whole of Scotland was seething with indignation over the

Glencoe massacre and was demanding the punishment of certain officers in William's service, whom William refused to give up to justice. And behind William, who had no love for Scotland, stood his masters, the English landed interest, seeking always a monopoly in everything, including overseas trade. So the lengthening shadow spread itself over that tiny colony who lay in a "crabb'd hold" upon a strip of swamp which they had named, defiantly, New Caledonia, a pitiful handful of pioneers ringed round by hostile Spaniards and treacherous natives, confidently making an appeal for help to English colonists forbidden to succour them.

And secondly there was Moll.

Moll was changing, slowly but surely, and it was not a pleasant change. Sunday by Sunday she came to the Crown, but she seldom wanted to go abroad nowadays and see the sights; she pleaded fatigue as an excuse for her desire to sit quietly in the tavern. If this had been all, Michael would have thought little of it; she was no longer young, and it was true that those of her trade aged early. But it was not all. She, always so open and so frank, had become oddly secretive; she, so completely unpossessive, had grown curious about his affairs, continually plying him with questions as to where he had been, whom he had met, what he had been doing. And when he answered her as best he could, she would sneer:

"Quite sure 'twas not the brewer's wench you met, eh? Fie, have you made no assignation with the pretty Maralyn after all these years?"

He could not understand such jealousy; it was so utterly unlike the Moll he knew, and it was so deep-rooted that she would not even accept his word that Maralyn was overseas. She seemed to harbour a mysterious suspicion that he had invented the whole story of Maralyn's departure for the Americas. So fantastic a suspicion bewildered him; and he was equally bewildered by the curious change in her likes and dislikes, and by the sudden storms of ill-temper which would fall from the clear sky of her equanimity.

For instance, there was the Easter Monday on which Moll insisted on visiting Hockley-in-the-Hole, the new establishment in

Clerkenwell which had just ousted from favour the old arena at the Bankside. The famous giant, Miller, was to meet another gladiator in a "trial of skill", and Moll adored such contests. For some weeks past she had been her old self, and as she and Michael sat in the "pleasant cool gallery for gentlemen" that day she was all smiles and wit, while the crowd gloated over the blood from the spectacular flesh wounds of the combatants. At the conclusion of the contest she excused herself, and was absent so long that Michael went in search of her. Finding her at length in a drinking-booth (he noticed that she swallowed down whatever she was drinking as soon as he appeared), he suggested that they should leave, as a bull-baiting was the next item and neither of them cared for this brutal sport. But, to his astonishment, she insisted on staying, and when he began to argue flared up at him, and accused him of being womanish and puritanical.

Much against his will, he followed her back to the gallery in time to hear the proclamation of: "A brindled dog from Spitalfields Market to fight against a fallow-coloured bitch from Whitechapel; to fight ten let-goes apiece at the famous Newington bull for half a guinea each, the dog or bitch which goes farthest in, or fairest, wins the money." The bull was fastened in the arena by a chain of fifteen feet in length, and had a huge rosette stuck between its eyes with pitch. A pair of oxen's horns were fastened on to its own, but they were provided with a sheath to minimise the risk of goring. The dog and bitch, each attended by its owner, were held in front of the chained animal until the signal was given to release them. Like most contests of the kind, this was not a baiting to the death, and it was obvious that the bull was an experienced animal and knew his business. He took things very coolly at first, kept his feet close together to avoid an attack from underneath, and presented a horn at the advancing enemy. Both his antagonists were high-bred bulldogs; they remained silent in attack, crouched low on the ground, and then rushed for the throat, their masters encouraging them all the while with the cry of "Go again! "

But presently the bull succeeded in getting the bitch in the hollow between his horns; her master rushed to break her coming fall by offering his back but, with a roar of triumph, the bull

174

tossed her plumb into the lap of Moll as she sat in the gallery. The experienced and courageous bitch was not at all discouraged, but immediately bounded over the tiers of seats and rushed back to the fray; the dog by this time had got his eye-teeth in the famous grip of his breed in the bull's neck, and men were rushing to force open his jaws with staves.

But Michael did not see this conclusion to the fight, for all his attention was taken up with Moll. She had turned white as death when the bitch had landed in her lap, but immediately afterwards had started up, and with colour flooding her face, had begun to scream out curses at the bitch's owner, working herself into a veritable frenzy, and anon including in her vituperation the crowd, the bull-ward, the owner of the establishment, and the world in general. Now a Hockley crowd was not the kind to take such abuse with meekness; it gave her back as good as it got, and soon began to show signs of not confining its fury to its tongue. A free fight threatened, and Michael, alarmed and disgusted, endeavoured to drag Moll from the scene before the advent of the constables. She came; but immediately they were outside she rounded on him, accused him of forcing her to witness a spectacle she loathed, dragged up all his past misdemeanours, real and imaginary, told him she never wanted to see him again as long as she lived, and lastly, spitting in his face, flounced off and left him.

Had this been but an isolated incident, Michael would have explained it away by the shock Moll had received when the bitch had landed in her lap. But it was not an isolated incident. Again and again he found Moll acting clean out of character; she was perversely determined to view sights which she had always loathed and despised; she would be all smiles one moment and a raging tornado of fury the next; she would twist his most innocent remark into an insult; she would take offence at nothing; and she took pleasure in indulging in the most unwitty obscenity when in his company.

Michael was revolted, bewildered, and most desperately sorry for her. After one of her rages, she would weary him with gushing promises of repentance, and he knew that the old Moll, the real Moll, was there beneath all this horrid change, fighting

175

some battle which was hidden from him. After months of it, he forced himself to face the idea that Moll was becoming a gin-addict. He knew something of the vice by now, but it was hard to believe that Moll had succumbed to it. For Moll was a crafts-man in her way; she took her trade seriously and had never allowed herself any diversion or pleasure that would interfere with business. Besides, she was never one to conceal her own weaknesses, yet, when he taxed her with spirit-drinking, she vehemently denied it, and he never smelled it on her breath. The truth of it was that he did not guess the cunning and the self-shame with which a secret gin-addict could hide her vice. And neither did he realise how necessary he himself had become to Moll as she grew older, how her feeling for him had not only intensified but had changed, that the warm affection had become a hot hunger, the healthy friendship altered to a greedy posses-siveness.

So the year progressed and died, and with it died the seven-teenth century.

Overseas, in exile, King James awaited his release from a long life of sorrows, while his son, that delicate, spirited, black-eyed boy of twelve, attended High Mass at Notre-Dame and was accorded by the Archbishop of Paris the same honours as the King of France himself. In England, William sat uneasily on his stolen throne, "driven mad", he said, by a Parliament who inso-lently upbraided him for his recent absence in Holland, an absence which had not the former excuse of a campaign. At St James's Palace the Princess Anne mourned the death of the ten-year-old Duke of Gloucester, her heir, while the Whigs were busy pushing through an Act of Settlement which should give the throne upon her death to a race of German princelings, and the Tories, emboldened by the eminent accession of her who was their patroness, talked loudly of impeaching the great Whig potentates. The Jacobites celebrated the Prince of Wales' birth-day with defiant jubilation, certain vessels in the Thames even venturing to fire salutes, the Oak Club gave itself a lavish dinner and applauded an excellent new loyal song, and the mob amused itself by raiding a Whig mug-club and burning in effigy William's new male favourite, Arnold von Keppell. Scotland was uneasily preoccupied by the Darien venture, trying to disregard disquieting rumours and to take comfort from the confident attitude of the Council of that Company in Edinburgh, who were busy drawing up rules for the government of the colony, declaring proudly but with a certain ambiguity, that "The commands of Holy Scripture are to have the full force and effect of laws within this settlement".

Meantime, gallants began to stiffen their full coat-skirts with whalebone, to affect leopard-skin muffs, to wear stays beneath their waistcoats to ensure the even fit so essential to a man of fashion, and, lounging in the bow-window of the modish White's, to debate with all due gravity whether the new fashion of hair-powder had come to stay; the City merchants paraded in their several walks on 'Change and eyed askance the increasing throng of Jewish stock-jobbers; the City Companies began to throw open their hallowed membership to whomsoever would buy a place; the City craftsmen wrestled with the intricacies of new taxes and duties; the lottery-offices did a brisk trade; the Bank of England, firmly established, waxed fat and flourishing as a tenant of Grocers' Hall; the National Debt rose higher and higher, and so also did the Mortality Bills, as Madam Geneva extended her dominion over London, driving poor Sir John Barleycorn further and further from his ancient stronghold.

And Nathaniel Vance, his trade falling off apace, his wife's malady growing steadily worse, his daughter overseas and his son estranged from him by money, still brewed his ale with the same care and craftsmanship, looked confidently for the abolishment of the new taxation when peace was secure, believed in the promises of politicians, took it for granted that England was still ruled by a king whose prime business it was to administer the ancient laws and secure his subjects from tyranny, debated petitions against gin with his Brethren at Brewers' Hall, and sought relaxation in a quarrel with John Bunch over the respective merits of ale and beer.

PART THREE

One

(i)

ON a certain Sunday, early in the new year of seventeen hundred, Michael came home earlier than usual from the Crown. Moll had been very fidgety and restless all day, and presently had told him that she had an evening engagement; Michael had never questioned her about her movements, and on this occasion she did not enlighten him as to the nature of the engagement, only he sensed that she half dreaded it, half yearned for it. For weeks past she had been her old self except that now and then her cheerfulness had seemed a trifle forced and she had lost much of that vitality which had been her most striking characteristic. As he walked eastwards this evening a suspicion crossed his mind that her appointment tonight was with Madam Geneva.

He stopped in his walk and stood hesitant, his mind a turmoil of doubt and anxiety. Ought he to return and try to follow her, to seek her out and endeavour to dissuade her from the orgy she contemplated? It would be, he knew, of very little use, for he was aware by now of the dreadful hold gin had over its victims, but Moll was his dear friend and he could not let her destroy herself without an attempt to save her. On the other hand, their friendship was based on non-interference with each other's private affairs, and although she had violated this condition lately, that was no excuse for his acting in the same manner; nor had he the right to interfere for he had nothing to offer her in exchange for her present condition. The nature of his work prevented him from accepting any other responsibility, condemned him to the loneliness of the unattached. And, from a more practical point of view, he realised that it was exceedingly unlikely that he would be able to find her tonight, however diligently he sought her; if in truth she was a gin-addict, she had taken enormous pains to pursue her vice in the strictest secrecy.

He walked on again through the ill-lit streets, which somehow seemed to have changed in character during the last ten years. The smell of gin was everywhere, overwhelming the ordinary odours, the shops had a secretive air as though the goods in their bow-windows were but a blind. Respectable citizens slunk furtively, with backward glances, down the steps of areas, and the usual swarm of beggars was increased by ragged, white-faced children, many of them pigeon-chested, humpbacked, or with shins rounded in front like a scimitar, who pestered the passer-by for a coin. They were the children of Madam Geneva, neglected by mothers who spent their time at the gin-shop, by fathers who pawned their tools and household goods for spirits, children driven on to the streets as soon as they could walk, to pilfer or to beg their bread.

The dwelling-house of Mr Vance had a lanthorn swinging above its door, a lanthorn often unlit during the last two years. But it was lit this evening, and this was the first thing Michael noticed as he came into Bird-in-Hand Court. That light seemed to raise his fallen spirits most strangely; it was like a beacon on the shore to the lost mariner. It shamed him, too, for his depression and discouragement, so that he squared his shoulders and walked briskly across the court. He paused a moment before the door and smiled up at the lanthorn, swinging gently in the night wind; and as he so stood he heard an odd sound from somewhere within the house. It was not, he was sure, the too-familiar whine of the gin-sodden Mrs Vance, and yet it resembled it in its helplessness and imperious demand. A cat, he thought, or maybe only some house-sign creaking; he shivered involuntarily, and shook himself a little, and lifted the wooden latch.

It was dark in the entry, but when he opened the door of the living-room he was dazzled and blinded by the candlelight which filled the room with a soft radiance. He blinked to clear his vision, and so saw, flitting busily about the room, a female figure. Then he blinked again more violently, because he thought his eyes must be playing him some trick. The figure had its back

179

to him; over its black gown was tied a snowy safeguard; and all its movements were tantalisingly familiar, swift yet unhurried, deft and unself-conscious.

Then the figure turned, and he cried out something, he knew not what; for it was Maralyn Moray.

(ii)

She dropped him a little curtsy as she came to the table with a dish, and said, quite easy and natural, "Good evening, Mr Pennington." So dumbfounded was he by her sudden appearance that he could not return her greeting, but merely stood there, gaping at her.

"You are in good time for supper," she said, still moving composedly about her tasks, "and must join us; I will set another cover."

At last, rousing himself from his bewilderment, he murmured a conventional greeting, and then, his eyes straying to the table, noticed there for the first time the figure of her father. Vance sat in his own arm-chair, leaning heavily against the tall wooden back, his arms hanging over the sides, his face pale, his eyes vacant. He took no sort of notice of Michael, but went on staring into space.

Michael, feeling suddenly limp himself, came and sat down at the board, watching Maralyn as she bustled in and out of the kitchen fetching the supper, with Tiger stalking on stiff legs behind her, purring like a kettle. Already, or so it seemed to Michael, the forlorn house was revivifying like a flower to the sun; there was an unfamiliar smell of cooking, the fire burned brightly, the hearth was swept, the top layer of dust had been removed from the furniture, and the foul rushes had been hastily gathered up from the floor. The meal which Maralyn set upon the table was a simple one, cabbage soup, brawn with mustard, and bread of it, but it was cooked to perfection and laid out with care. Maralyn grimaced a little as she set out the greasy, ill-washed knives and spoons, but catching Michael's eye she smiled instantly, and murmured: "We shall soon have these cleanly again." Yet despite her composure he had sensed already a subtle change in her, though he could not decide upon its nature; only he noted that she seemed to smile with her mouth rather than with her eyes as of old, and that she did not hum to herself as she used to do.

The girl was about to take her seat at the table, when from upstairs there came again that strange little mewling cry which had puzzled Michael before he had entered the house. Instantly, and without a word, Maralyn hastened from the room; her feet padded softly on the stair; there was the opening and shutting of a door and presently the two men heard again that old familiar singing break the horrid silence of the house. But now it seemed to Michael as though she sang consciously and with a purpose, and not any longer spontaneously and to herself.

Vance and his clerk sat at the table for a while without speaking, each intensely occupied with his own thoughts. Then Vance shifted in his chair, passed his hand across his face several times, glanced at Michael without seeing him, and muttered:

"It must be done. Ay, it must be done. For all our sakes she must be got into some—some hospital."

"Of whom do you speak, sir?" asked Michael, bewildered anew.

The brewer glanced at him again, and started, as though becoming aware for the first time that he was not alone. Then he said abruptly:

"Of my wife, Mr Pennington." He leaned forward, joining his hands together on the board, and began to twist his fingers together in an agony of agitation very pitiful to watch. "It would not be fitting, sir, to keep her here now. There is an infant, d'ye see? A babe but a few weeks old, Maralyn's son. The child is weakly, and it would not be fitting. . . . The physician told me plainly a while since that Mrs Vance should be removed to—to some hospital, you understand me? But I could not do it. Yet now it must be done. But not—not Bedlam! " he cried, almost shrieking the name; and then he dropped his head upon his hands and remained as still as a stone.

Michael gripped his own hands tightly together to steady himself. His head was buzzing, and it was difficult to concentrate on this old trouble so soon after the shock of Maralyn's sudden reappearance.

"Mr Vance," said he at length, "you have honoured me in times past with your confidence, and this encourages me to ask you to be plain with me now. Is Mrs Vance's condition, then, so—so melancholy?"

The head was raised, and two haunted eyes stared into his.

"She raves, sir. There are times when I am hard put to it to prevent her laying violent hands upon herself. I dare no longer give her a knife to cut her meat. . . . The poison itself hath lost its power to soothe her, but with fiery malice inflames when it doth not render insensible. A week since, a physician came a-prying while I was abroad, carried hither by some meddling neighbour, and when I returned he told me plainly that she was —she was mad, and must be put away." His voice broke, and dreadful involuntary spasms twitched his throat. "But not Bedlam, sir, not Bedlam, for Jesu's sake," cried the poor man, as though pleading with a judge. "I went thither once when I was 'prenticed to my father, and being cruel in the way of young men, I deemed it sport to bait poor frantic folk chained and fettered in filthy straw like condemned men in Newgate Hold. No, no, not Bedlam, for the love of Christ, not that." He was shaking all over, his lips so violently a-tremble that they could scarce articulate his words.

Michael reached out a hand and gripped his arm.

"Not that, sir, indeed. There is no need for such a desperate course. If Mrs Vance must leave your care, why, then we will find some private lodging for her in the country with a kind nurse. Why, sir," he continued, saying whatever came into his mind in order to give the brewer time to recover some composure, "you must needs bear with me when I cry up the blessings of the country, for you must recollect that I am country-bred and sucked in with my milk a firm belief in the benefits of pure, wholesome air and quietness. If you will permit me, I will make some enquiries; the most of my father's tenants were beggared by the enclosures made by their new lord, yet I despair not of finding out some honest family, attached to my house in the days of our prosperity, who would count it an honour to receive your wife into their household and tend her as carefully as her goodness deserves and her melancholy condition requires."

Vance's tortured eyes searched his face during this discourse, and now the poor mouth opened to reply, but speech would not come for some moments. In a manner ludicrous if not so tragic, the lips opened and shut, and opened and shut again, like a fish's; but no sound issued. Then at length a hoarse voice murmured:

". . . Infinitely obliged to you, sir, for your courtesy and interest, but you must understand, I could not afford . . . my business . . . exceeding fallen off of late . . . such grievous and increasing taxation, and then this beastly habit of drinking spirits. . . ." The broken words trailed away into silence, and Michael found nothing to say. Then suddenly Vance drew his shoulders back, clasped his hands afresh upon the table, and staring straight before him said, curtly and with a complete change of manner:

"It grieves me to have to inform you, Mr Pennington, that I must dispense with your services at the end of the quarter."

"I—I am sorry, sir," stammered Michael, taken aback by this sudden and harsh dismissal, "that I have offended you, or no longer give you satisfaction. My private activities, perhaps——" Then he stopped abruptly, for he had encountered the other's glance, and understood. "Mr Vance, may I appeal to you on mine own behalf? I have nowhere to go if you turn me out. I have ventured to look upon this as my home during the years I have had the honour to serve you. All my humble affairs would fall in ruins if I must seek other employment. 'Tis true I am very little use to you, not being bred as a clerk, but if you will please to allow me to seek to repay in some small measure your past kindness by serving you in future without payment, I would be eternally in your debt. I am not young any longer, and you must understand——"

But then the words choked in his throat, the silly, stilted words he had snatched at as an armour for them both. Vance stared at him, and again came that comic, tragic, silent opening and shutting of the mouth. Then, with a prodigious effort, the older man regained his self-control.

"I thank you, sir," said he simply, "and am infinitely obliged for your offer. I will—ahem!—I will think on't, and let you know." Then the thought seemed to strike him that perhaps he had sounded ungracious. So he reached over his square, work-worn hand, and patted Michael's shoulder. "My dear lad, I really am sensible of your worth and kindness and will strive to be worthy of your good opinion. . . . Excuse me, sir, excuse me," he added hastily, "I think I hear my wife call. We will speak further of these matters. Pray excuse me now; I must go see what my wife lacks."

Michael rose with him, went to the door and opened it for him. Vance, with an immense, unconscious dignity, made him a little salutation in passing. For a while after the brewer's footsteps had died away up the stairs Michael stood looking after him. Then he returned to his chair, flung his arms across the table, and buried his head between them.

(iii)

A voice said quietly: "Your meat is grown cold, sir; I will heat it for you."

He jerked his head and saw her standing there, waiting to take up his plate. Her self-control, combined with that odd, indefinable change he had sensed in her, flicked him like a whip, and, ashamed of himself, he drew his sleeve hastily across his eyes, rose, and bowed to her.

"I thank you, mistress, but I—I am not hungry. If there is aught I can do to serve you——" He broke off awkwardly and made a vague motion to collect the dishes.

"Your pardon, Mr Pennington, but you must eat and so must I, and since we may not have the pleasure of my father's company this evening, if you please we will sup together." She took the dish from him with a little gesture of apology and went into the kitchen. When she returned ten minutes later, Michael had got a firm hold on his emotion, and stood waiting to bow her into her chair. She arranged the food with all her old carefulness, dropped him a small curtsy, and sat down, motioning him to do likewise. Then, having served him and herself, she took up her knife and spoon, and began steadily to eat.

Playing with his own food, unable to swallow a mouthful, he wondered at her, eyeing her in surreptitious glances. She wore the rather absurd loose white dog-collar such as had been fashionable for widows forty years before; her hair was covered by the conventional crape head-dress, tied beneath her chin, and black ribbon bows made her black gown yet more sombre. He noticed that the gown was darned and patched in several places, and dimly remembering to have seen it before, guessed that it was an old one newly dyed. Her face was tanned and the skin slightly coarsened; it was thinner, much thinner than when last he had seen her, but this ageing effect was counterbalanced by the complete absence of lines. The really noticeable physical change in her was in her eyes; the perpetual smile in them was gone completely, and now and then he glimpsed behind their mildness a kind of haunted look.

She said suddenly, not looking up from her plate: "Alec is dead."

His knife clattered to the floor; he had indeed guessed, but he had been unprepared for the bald, calm statement.

"He was slain by the Spanishers," she continued, steadily eating. "They crucified him. They made me a witness. That was in June last."

"The—the Spanishers," he stammered, scarce knowing what he said.

"They sent an expedition against us and there was a skirmish. They took some prisoners and Alec was of the number. I went to their camp to see if I could do aught for him. They were about to slay him, and they constrained me to see the execution. But they did not molest me, and anon they sent me back, telling me I must be sure to describe to the settlers what I had witnessed and that Alec's fate would be the fate of all our people unless we went away from Darien. You see, the Spanishers regarded it as their own territory, and indeed it is true that they discovered it many years before we went there, and likewise they knew that the English colonists in the Barbados and other places were forbidden by the English Government to give us countenance."

"But William swore to protect you."

"So it is said," said Maralyn tonelessly. "However that may be, he sent not one soldier, not one ship, refused to answer our appeals for help, and forbade, as I have said, the English colonists to render us assistance or to give us hospitality. You are not eating, Mr Pennington; is your meat not to your liking?"

She lifted her head and looked him full in the eyes. And then he knew what he ought to have guessed from the beginning, that the food was as tasteless to her as it was to him, that nine women out of ten would have refused to make a pretence of eating, and that the effort she was making to be sane and normal was the most gallant thing he had ever witnessed. He took up his knife again, murmured something, and doggedly began to eat.

"You must pardon me, Mr Pennington," the quiet voice continued determinedly, "if I spoil your supper by discoursing of unpleasant matters, but you see, I feel as though I had suffered some nightmare, and that I must speak of it to someone or——"

"Nightmares should be described and shared," said Michael, catching up the pause and trying desperately to imitate her careful matter-of-factness. "Then we see them in their due proportion and after a space they lose something of their horror."

"I thank you. You see, it was very—difficult. Apart altogether from the Spanishers, I mean. You see, we had been misinformed on many matters. The climate proved very unhealthful; when the rainy season came the land was little better than a swamp, and there was much fever. And then there was the jungle; it grew as fast as we could clear it, and with the half of our company sick it encroached upon us in a very fearsome manner. And the natives, though not unfriendly, were in fear of the Spanishers and dared not aid us. And there came no reinforcements or provisions from home; and our Council grew hugely quarrelsome after a time, and so distrustful of each other that they appointed a new president every week. It was mighty difficult," she repeated, doggedly warding off the silence which threatened to fall if she finished speaking, and despairing, perhaps, of ever going on again. "And then there was the sad business of the *Dolphin* sloop."

"I heard rumours of that affair," said Michael, steadily putting food into his mouth.

"You see, the Spanishers at Carthagena seized the vessel and flung the crew into jail. Our Council remonstrated, and sent a copy of the Act of Parliament whereby King William had countenanced the venture and given it his protection. But the Governor of Carthagena tore it up, and called us rogues and pirates, and sent his prisoners to Seville, where they lie to this day, and they say will be executed for piracy. Then we had tidings, brought us by a Frenchman, that the Spanishers were gathering a huge force to attack us, both by land and by sea, so soon as the rains were over, and such of us as remained got off in two ships; for we could not have withstood them, weak as we were in arms, and sick besides, and despairing of help from any man. The vessels were separated by a fearful storm, and one of them, I believe, drifted to Sandy Hook; but the one in which I lay, after a most hazardous voyage, reached Scotland safely three weeks since."

"Three weeks? Then you——"

"You see, I was not very well. You see, my son had been born on the voyage. I lay a while at Leith till I could get me some strength, and then I made the journey into England."

"You came by coach, mistress?"

"Oh no. You see, I had no money. No, sometimes I walked, and sometimes charitable wagoners let me ride in their carts. I managed rarely, and here I am."

"Yes," he said, staring at her, "you managed rarely. You always have. You always will."

She threw him a puzzled glance, and went on hurriedly:

"You see, there was the child to care for; I could not leave him to perish. There was a woman on the ship, a midwife; she told me I would die when my child was born. You see, I was not very well, and the voyage was passing troublesome. There were three hundred souls aboard and the vessel was not a great one. And food was short, and water likewise. But I could not die and leave the child to perish, and by the mercy of God we came safe to Scotland." She stopped dead on the word. When she continued, there was for the first time a hint of emotion in her voice. "Scotland is ruined, Mr Pennington. She ventured her all in the Darien venture, near every man in the kingdom investing his savings. And now the great enterprise has failed, and I know not what will become of Scotland. Mr Pennington, it is a dreadful thing to say, but I can find it in my heart to be glad that Alec died when he did, for he did not see the last hope vanish, he did not know that we must give up, nor that where the brave New St Andrews was to be built, there would be anon but jungle, inhabited only by the sloth and the baboon. He could not have borne that, and would have run mad with sorrow and with anger, for he believed so fervently not only in the success of the enterprise but that King William would keep faith with us."

"And you, mistress?" said Michael earnestly. "Are you not angry at that broken faith?"

The mild, bewildered eyes looked into his for a moment, and then dropped.

"Oh no," she said, "no, I am not angry. You see, I do not understand these great matters. Since I landed in Scotland, I have heard men talk, Englishmen I mean, upon my journey south. And it seems that King William's failure to keep his word had somewhat to do with trade. It would be bad, they say, for England's trade, to have succoured us. I cannot comprehend what they mean. You see, trade means to me—well, brewing good ale and selling it honestly, and so with all other crafts. But I suppose 'tis not so simple as that. But I am sorry. Scotland has never been anything to me, though I married a man of that nation, but I know what would be my state of heart if I saw England ruined and her people beggared."

"William broke his sworn word," said Michael harshly. "You cannot get away from that."

She drew herself up a little, and answered severely:

"You must not say such things, sir; it is not fitting. I am sure that there is good and sufficient reason for this seeming breach of faith. King William is our Sovereign Lord, of Scotland as of England, and is pledged to protect all his subjects impartially. He is no tyrant, like the late King James. He is the Protestant hero, and came hither to rescue us from arbitrary power."

188

She waited for him to speak, but he only sighed and smiled and shook his head. How powerful was continual propaganda! How ineradicable this reverence for the Sovereign. An excellent thing indeed, such reverence, but only while there was a Sovereign. How long would it be, he wondered, before the Vances and the Maralyns of England woke up to discover that behind the purple and the ermine there was only a dummy, dancing to the strings pulled by a wealthy faction. After a pause, she pushed her plate aside, and went to close the shutters at the window, but with her hand upon them she hesitated, and stood looking out into the London night.

"London," she said softly, speaking her thoughts aloud, "how I have yearned for it, the smell and sight and sound of it, these weary months and years. Darien was beautiful with its burning skies and rich vegetation and the gorgeous birds and the rest. But all the while I was homesick for London, for fog and rain and muck, for the rumble of the hackneys and the trotting of the chairmen's feet, for begrimed brick and the creak of the signboards, for the sober sparrows, and for the odour of the new ale." She broke off, half turned to him, and a blush crept up her cheek. "Lord, how I run on! I will mull some ale for you, sir, because the night is cold, and then I must go see if my son lacks for aught. You see, he has been but weakly, and he needs my constant care."

"So do we all."

"I—I know not what you mean by that, Mr Pennington."

"The human race needs you, Maralyn, your ready service, your courage, and your ability to contrive a way out when there are others to care for. I knew my faith in you was not misplaced; I knew it when I bade farewell to you in the inn-yard. You and your like will save this poor world yet."

She stared at him, and there was a kind of outrage in her eyes. He had transgressed her narrow code; all her instincts revolted against such talk. He realised this, and continued briskly:

"Your father needs you sorely, Mistress Maralyn. Your mother——" But the practical beginning petered out, and for the life of him he could not go on.

"My mother is very sick," said Maralyn evenly. "I know."

"You know? But how much do you know, I wonder?"

"I have seen her, Mr Pennington." She came back from the window and went to tend the fire. Her tone was steady but somewhat abrupt. "I know the nature of her malady and the pass to which it has brought her. But I have thought already what we must do, though I will not speak of it tonight. Yet will I speak of it to you anon, Mr Pennington," she added, "for I tell you frankly, I intend to make so bold as to seek your aid."

"I am honoured, mistress, and pledge my word to serve you as I may."

"I thank you, sir, you are mighty kind. And now I recollect I have not thanked you for all your service to my father while I was overseas. I know he has come to depend upon you in many things outside your duties as his clerk, and though he is not given to say much, believe me, he is grateful."

He said heavily (conscious all of a sudden of a profound fatigue):

"It has been a privilege to serve him, mistress. Never had any man a better master." He folded his napkin with slack fingers, and added: "I must bid you goodnight now, for I have work to do." Then he recollected that this was Sunday and that Maralyn was ignorant of his private activities. So he murmured lamely: "I must be up betimes tomorrow."

But he need not have worried, for her simple mind had seized upon a single word and its familiar associations.

"Work," she said, turning from the fire and smiling on him, "that is indeed a blessing, sir, and one we prize too lightly. What would we do if we had not to rise early in the morning and go a-marketing or add up figures in a ledger or wield the mash-stick? And poverty, too, that can be a most rare blessing. While we must pinch and scrape, and make tomorrow's dinner out of this day's leavings, and turn an old gown and patch a coat, there is no time to—to think of other things. Were I a great lady now, with nought to do but make my toilette and read reports of the Paris modes and walk in the Park and yawn away the hours till it was time to go to the play, what would I do, having so sorrowful a heart in my bosom? For you see," she said, as though telling him this for the first time, "Alec is dead." She

190

stopped and looked steadily at him, as if she were challenging both him and herself to lose control. "I should wake the night long and refuse my meat and be no manner of use to anyone, whereas now I must eat and sleep that I may work. You stare at me. Do I speak foolishly?"

"No, indeed, you speak most wisely. And yet, I know not. Because we are men and women, we have other duties besides manual work. We have minds, Mistress Maralyn, and we must use them, and there are other matters we must think upon besides baking a pie and entering figures in a ledger, ay, and even brewing of good ale."

He was smiling at her as he added those last words, but she did not return his smile. That new haunted look had crept into her eyes again, and she said, breathlessly and with a strange urgency:

"No, no, it is not good to think upon these other matters. It is —it is dangerous to think that way."

He said no more, but bade her goodnight; but as he climbed the stair he found himself wondering whether those words of hers had any hidden significance, and whether it was only of Alec that she dared not allow herself to think.

Two

(i)

THE terrible experiences which had befallen Maralyn during the Darien expedition seemed to have changed her curiously little. She took up her old life at her father's house as though she had never left it; she even sang again about her work, though Michael suspected that there was a lack of spontaneity about that singing. She worked continually, yet had time and to spare for the little graces, for playing on the clavicytherium to her father in the evening, taking her baby for an airing, stopping to greet a neighbour, tending the flower-pots on the ledges. The sordid existence which her family had endured during her absence smoothed itself out into the old harmonious routine, the tarnished pewter shone again, the linen was fair and white and neatly patched, dust and cobwebs disappeared, and gravy dripped with a comforting odour into the shallow pans beneath the spit. She spoke freely of Darien when questioned, but always of superficial matters, describing the look of the country and the habits of the natives; but she never spoke of Alec, nor of the way in which King William had behaved to the colonists.

Not many days after her return she came into the counting-house one morning, shut the door carefully behind her, bobbed a small curtsy, and sat down upon the chair which Michael hastened to place for her. She seemed rather tense and nervous, and her hands kept pleating up her safeguard while she talked.

"I have taken the freedom of intruding on you, Mr Pennington, because it is necessary I have private speech with you, and this being a Monday, my father is gone to Brewers' Hall and will not be home till noon. What I would say concerns my mother.

I had hoped that maybe I could ease her condition, since I have some little skill in nursing and in the preparation of physics, but now I know 'twas a vain hope, and that no physic in the world has power to heal her. Moreover, my father is wearing himself out with his constant attendance upon her, and is so set upon concealing her condition from the world that he will scarce let me have access to her. I honour him for his delicacy and tenderness, but the time is past, sir, for keeping up such a show."

"I understand you, mistress," murmured Michael, leaning against his stool and fraying out a quill. "Therefore, some hospital, perhaps——"

"As you say, sir," she broke in hurriedly, "but you know there is but one such which would take her, and that is—that is not to be thought of." She paused, and licked her lips once or twice. "My father has said to me that he would agree to your suggestion of carrying her into the country if we could find some honest family to take her in and care for her, but you see, we cannot contrive this without money, for there must needs be someone constantly with her, since the fever is grown so fierce and malignant that God knoweth what she might do to herself if not restrained. I must tell you, Mr Pennington," she added quickly, as he was about to speak, "that it never was our custom to accept charity from any man, be he never so friendly and willing, for we are resolved to earn what we require, and if we cannot earn, why then we do without."

He had nothing to say to this; he had been about to suggest that it was possible he could find one of his former tenants who would undertake the care of Mrs Vance without payment for the sake of an old master, but Michael had learnt something of City pride by this time, and he knew it would be useless to argue the point with this citizen's daughter.

"I need not tell you, sir," continued Maralyn, "that my father's trade is greatly fallen off, for you have charge of his books and know full well the sad state of his affairs at this time. And I see not any hope of improvement, for the malt and the ale taxes are rising apace, and then they say we are to go to war with France again, and likewise this wicked rage for gin has made men forsake malt liquor. You must not think that such things daunt us; trade rises and falls, and sometimes times are good and sometimes they are bad, and when they are bad we learn to live more modestly and to work harder and to wait with patience for better days. But however hard we work, and however modestly we live, I fear me we should never contrive the moneys necessary for lodging my mother in the country and paying for the attention she requires. All this being so, I am resolved to seek aid from my brother."

"From Nat!"

"Why yes, Mr Pennington, from Nat. He is my brother. Moreover he has no family, and I know he has a great business. He was boasting of it when he came to visit me on my return. And since we needs must seek for aid, it is fitting we apply ourselves to him; he knows not the real desperateness of his mother's condition, but when he does know I am very sure that he will freely succour her in all that she requires, and indeed it is his plain duty so to do, for he is my parents' only son."

She had spoken the last few sentences with a hint of defiance, but now she seemed to grow nervous again, and pleated her apron harder than ever.

"Mr Pennington, I am about to ask of you a huge favour."

"Mistress, you may command me to the limit of my power."

"I thank you, I thank you," she said hurriedly, and looking suddenly very like her father. "It is this: that you will go to Lombard Street and apply yourself to my brother on my behalf."

Michael stared at her, somewhat taken aback. She continued quickly:

"I ask what I should not, maybe, but you must understand that I am mighty ignorant of business matters, and therefore I should be but a poor advocate in my mother's cause, for you see, Nat is a hard man to deal with, I know he is, though maybe 'tis not proper I should speak so of mine own brother. Besides, it is scarce fitting that I, a female, should approach him in his office, and having but little acquaintance with his wife I am reluctant to call upon him at his house. Nat and Susan have not been very—very friendly to us all these years, maybe because my father has never concealed his disapproval of this new banking which Nat has espoused, and I cannot bring myself to intrude upon them without invitation, especially on such a matter. But you, sir, being a gentleman, and well acquaint with business, and having likewise a most excellent address (if I may say so), are most fit to—oh, Mr Pennington," she burst out, her eyes filling suddenly with tears, "I know I should not ask it, indeed I do, but I am desperate, and that is sober truth."

The naked appeal, so uncharacteristic of her, rent his heart. He came quickly to her and seizing her hands fondled them almost fiercely within his own.

"Mistress Maralyn, I will go and with pleasure, and am proud that you have honoured me with your confidence." Then he saw that her eyes, dry again, were regarding him with a faint rebuke. He dropped her hands, and said, with a change of tone: "But I cannot promise that I shall meet with success upon this errand. Your brother is indeed a hard man, and if I mistake not, his wife is even harder."

"I do not ask you to approach Susan, Mr Pennington," said Maralyn stiffly. "I ask you to apply yourself to my brother in his office. And it is my mother's son, and not some Jew, with whom you are to deal. I say again, Nat is big with affairs and doth not come to visit us except at Christmas and such like, and I am sure he has no notion of my mother's desperate state. Give me leave to suggest that you make your call upon him when the brewhouse closes, when you will find him at his desk, for I know that he doth not put up his shutters till eight of the clock."

He bowed to her without speaking.

"One thing more, sir," said Maralyn, preparing to depart. "I beg of you to say nothing of this matter to my father. He is mighty proud, you see, and exceeding tortured in his mind at present because of my mother and because he cannot succour her as she requires. When you have applied yourself to Nat and gained his aid, then will I make all plain to my father. And sure he cannot refuse the help, freely offered, of his own son."

Michael had his doubts about the help being freely offered, but he kept such doubts to himself, and promised to do his best. That very evening, as soon as the brewhouse closed, he set off eastwards along Cheapside. The weather was cold and dull, with a dry, teasing wind which made a sordid scurry of the refuse from the fruit and vegetable stalls as he came into the Poultry. He was just crossing Stocks Market, very preoccupied with his thoughts, when a familiar voice said at his elbow:

"So the quill-driver has given himself an evening off. Fie, fie!"

He turned sharply, and there was Moll. In that moment of seeing her so unexpectedly he realised how long and sad a road they two had travelled since the days when such an encounter would have filled him with excitement and with pleasure, for the first emotion of which he was conscious this evening was anxiety as to her mood. Then he noticed that she was wearing a green bird's-eye hood, and the sight of that took his mind back to that day, so long ago, the most bitter day of his life, when he had drifted aimlessly down the Strand after losing his master and renouncing his mistress, and had become aware of Moll, wearing just such a colourful and becoming hood, tripping along beside him, full of nonsense and vitality and comradeship. He stopped dead as the memory hit him, and smiled with an old gratitude.

"Damme," said Moll, leaning against one of the foot-posts and quizzically regarding him, "but the sun is pleased to come through the cloud after all. God save you, sir, when first I spied you, you walked as if you had as aching a heart as a broken merchant coming near the Compter."

"Moll," said Michael, "you are very well met, though hang me if I know what you are doing in these parts."

Her eyelids flickered a little, and she began to fidget with a ribbon on her cloak, not looking at him as she replied playfully:

"Give me leave to inform you, Master Pennington, that the City, jealous though she is of her privileges, yet deigns to permit a poor 'foreigner' to walk and talk within her sacred liberties. And there are times of late when I swear I tire of the town gallants, and then it pleases me to intrude upon this hallowed ground and snatch a City beau from under the very skirts of a City punk, who is as angry to see me as a milkmaid when you cry 'Wo-ball!' "

He said nothing, only stared at her, feeling warmth flood his heart. Here indeed was the old Moll, his dear friend, his perky London sparrow, pranked out in borrowed plumage and delighting to steal by her wits the provender of greater birds.

"And having thus laid bare my errand," continued Moll, taking his arm and walking along beside him with her familiar lilting step, "do you be as plain with me, pray, and tell me the nature of the mission which tears you from your quill-pushing, and whether it permits a poor honest town punk to give you her company upon the road thither?"

So they walked on together, arm-in-arm, Moll chattering of this and that with all her old vitality, until they came to Lombard Street.

"'Adsheart, how quiet it is here," exclaimed Moll, gazing about her. "I thought it would be all a-hum like the rest of the City. What cit puts up his shutters before eight or nine of the clock? Maybe the poor bankers have no custom."

"It is far otherwise, I do assure you," said Michael. "They are vastly busy there behind those shutters, counting their gold ere they lock it away in fettered trunks, writing little figures in a ledger whereby they make one man rich and another poor by the stroke of a quill, filling in bank-notes whereon they promise to pay that which has no existence save on paper, cogitating upon what terms they will make this merchant a loan whereby he may pay his Customs duties, and planning how they will speculate with this other merchant's gold to their own advancement without making him one penny the richer."

Moll guffawed.

"Now, marry come up, how sweet a life is this they live in Lombard Street!" cried she. "I vow 'tis the simplest way of growing rich that ever I heard. Sit on your arse and pass a miracle; that's rare. Damme, they're out to rival the Almighty."

He answered nothing but walked on, scanning the tall brick houses which rose up on either hand, houses unpretentious, discreet and drably rich, protected from the street by facades of wrought iron, entered by doors solid and handsome, the windows blinded by shutters, no signboards cheerfully creaking, no 'prentices calling "Buy! Buy! Buy!", no goods displayed for sale, a hidden community, a secret citadel, its unseen tentacles reaching out further and further over London, over England, over the lives of men.

He said goodbye to Moll at Nat's house, which stood eastwards of 'Change Alley. She winked at him and put up her face-guard as she tripped away. He watched her as she went, as confident here as in her native territory, a jaunty highwaywoman out for prey. Then, summoning his resolution, he lifted the heavy knocker and applied it to the door. The dull thunder reverberated down the street, affronting the wealthy silence.

(ii)

He had to wait some while before the door was opened by a young man in decent black, who looked him up and down, noted his shabbiness, and snapped at him:

"Well, sir?"

"I desire to see Mr Nathaniel Vance."

"My master is engaged. What is your business with him?"

"My business," said Michael, keeping his temper with some difficulty, "is of a private and personal nature. You will be good enough to inform Mr Vance that Mr Pennington brings him a message from his family."

The clerk peered at him round the half-closed door.

"Well, sir, I do not know. . . . My master is not accustomed to seeing persons without an appointment. However, pray wait, and I will deliver your message."

With that he closed the door firmly, and Michael heard him slip the bolt home before his footsteps retreated down the passage. Michael, half amused, half irritated, wondered whether the fellow suspected him of unlawful designs upon the house. The clerk returned after a while and grudgingly informed him that Mr Vance would receive him. The visitor was admitted, the handsome door carefully rebolted after him, and he was marshalled rather than ushered down a gloomy passage into a sort of ante-room, where he was left to himself. It was a room entirely impersonal; it had a table and some stiff chairs, and that was all. The window, which looked out upon an area, was heavily barred, and the brisk-voiced striking-clock was firmly nailed to a bracket. There was another door, communicating with some inner room, and he guessed that this would be Nat's private office; he heard the low hum of conversation proceeding from thence, and presently could make out Nat's voice and another which seemed vaguely familiar. After a while, this second voice was raised in emphasis, and Michael recognised it as that of Frank Maynard, Nat's old friend and unsuccessful rival in love.

"'Ounds, man," cried that voice, genial even while it contained some irritation, "this is the most damnable folly that ever I saw. I tell you, 'tis the richest and safest venture of the age. All the world knows by this time that the National Debt is not as other debts, that it is in very truth permanent and will remain so. I told you how 'twould be, seven years ago, but you would not believe me. Once admit the lengthy indebtedness of the State to private moneylenders, and there can be no return to the old methods. 'Sbud, doth it mean nought to you that this Debt, which began to the tune of one million pounds, is risen, but seven years later, to thirty millions? D'you recollect telling me that the original million could be repaid within a twelvemonth? Well, it was not so repaid, and shall I tell you why?"

Nat's voice replied, but so quietly that Michael could not catch the words. The other's answer, fairly shouted, echoed it however:

"Because of the prolonged war, forsooth! I tell you, this Debt would have grown to be accepted as permanent, war or no war. The Government has discovered that 'tis possible to effect a mortgage upon the whole of the population of the realm, and henceforth their first thought, whenever they need extraordinary moneys (and that is always nowadays), will be to enlarge the Debt. And if you speak of war, Nat, are we not to have another? These Partition Treaties signify nothing; the whole of Spain is against partitioning the realm, and when their King Charles dies (which must be soon, for his sickness is mortal) he will leave Spain, both the Old and the New, to Philip of Anjou, Louis's grandson. And will our William stomach that? Ever since the late peace he has been straining like a greyhound in the leash to be at Louis's throat again, and here is a rare excuse. And if you demand of me how I come to be so knowledgeable, why, I will answer you fair and square: it is because the Government must needs be plain with me regarding its policies since it desires some more of my money. Ay, it is cap-in-hand again, my gossip, and tells me that if I oblige it I may have what interest I choose to name and a knighthood thrown in for good measure. And I say frankly I have deserved such an honour; have I not served my country in her hour of need?"

Michael caught Nat's reply to this speech, not because it was spoken loudly, but because of the biting quality of the tone:

"For my part, I desire no knighthoods and never have. I prosper, and I earn my prosperity by honest business."

"There speaks your father's son! There speaks the outmoded sit-on-his-arse mechanic! But let me require you to answer this, mine honest, hard-working cit: where would you be now if you had not first plunged and ventured your all in the Million Lottery? Journeyman to a goldsmith or skimming your father's ale. There's no wealth to be gained in this brave new age save by speculation and adventuring; moreover, that man is a fool who will work for gold when he can have it by sitting in his elbow-chair and receiving it from a grateful Government."

There was the harsh scrape of chair-legs and an angry murmur from Nat, but immediately Frank's voice came again, this time propitiating:

"How now, Nat, wilt take offence so easily! 'Uds, man, you must not take me ill. If I upbraid you, 'tis because I love you and long to see you prosper."

"And Susan prosper, eh?"

"And Susan prosper, certainly." A hearty laugh. "By heaven, Nat, will you be for ever raking up that old business? Think you I am so beastly a creature that I would harbour a grudge all these years, or so much a dog-in-the-manger that I would not desire my lost mistress's prosperity because she was wed to another? Nay, not a word further, but good night. Come dine with me next Tuesday and we will speak of these matters again if it please you, and if it please you not, at least you shall admire my fine new chariot and go with me to see this droll of

Mr Congreve's called *The Way of the World*; they say 'tis vastly amusing. And by and by, when I am made a knight, I will carry you both to Kensington and show you His Dutch Majesty, and amuse you by a sight of his new male favourite, the prettiest thing out of a petticoat that ever you saw; and I will present you to our masters and his, the great lords; our masters, Nat, who are so deep in my debt that they positively fawn upon me, as the rich City merchants fawn on you because you have the power of the purse."

Again that hearty laugh, and then a murmur of farewells, an opening door, retreating footsteps, then one pair of feet returning briskly. In a moment or two the door of the inner sanctum opened, and the figure of Nat appeared on the threshold. Michael rose and bowed.

"I can give you no more than half an hour," said the banker, in the tone he might use to a lackey. "I am very much engaged with business at this time."

Michael bowed again without speaking and walked past him into the office. Nat, following him, shut the door, and motioning his visitor to a chair, himself sat down before a large writing-table whereon were neat piles of papers, goose-quills, some deed-boxes and a couple of ledgers, and, incongruously, a pair of laced and scented gloves.

"Now, sir," said Nat curtly, "be good enough to state your business."

As Michael talked, describing the sad condition of Mrs Vance and the falling off of her husband's trade, he was observing the banker closely. He had not seen Nat for some while, and never in his own domain. The first thing which struck Michael was how rapidly and prematurely Nat had aged. He was still in his twenties, but so set was his mouth, so sallow and lined his face, and so dull his eyes that he looked forty at least. He wore a dark sober suit of good broadcloth, and his neckerchief was twisted carelessly round his throat in the fashion called a Stein-kirk from the battle of that name in '92. It seemed that in office hours he affected the peruke, a dark one with bunches of curls on the forehead, but he had confined the long curls at the nape of his neck in a black silk bag, as did sportsmen and travellers.

The wig accentuated his look of maturity. But apart from this physical appearance, he seemed really to have aged unnaturally; the frank insolence of his boyhood had hardened into an air of permanent contempt, and there was an air about him which made Michael guess that he was a stranger to joy or contentment. His whole personality seemed to be overlaid with that curious dry inhuman mask which sits upon all men who deal exclusively with figures in a ledger.

When Michael ceased speaking, Nat said with undisguised impatience:

"So far, you have told me nothing that I did not know before."

"You were aware of your mother's melancholy state?"

"Mr Pennington, I am not a fool. I saw my mother when I visited my sister a fortnight since on her return from overseas. It needed but a glance to assure me that my mother was raving mad."

"Give me leave to say, sir, that it seems mighty strange to me that you have not acted on your knowledge."

"I am not a magician, sir, to cure my mother's malady by the wave of a magic wand."

"No, sir, you are a topping banker, and what your mother requires is not magic but money."

"I really must beg you, sir," said Nat thinly, "to be a little more explicit, even at the risk of your deeming me stupid. If my father wishes a loan from me, he should come to me himself, and then I will please to see what I can do for him. I never was one to mix sentiment with business, sir; if I desired a barrel of ale, I should go to my father and pay the just price for it, and if he desires a loan from me he ought to come to me and pay the just rate for it."

"Master Nathaniel," said Michael, restraining a burning desire to hit Nat as hard as possible upon the chin, "I do not think you can have understood what I have told you concerning my master's business. He is not in a position to buy succour for his wife, else would he have done so. Yet succour she must have, and therefore, since his pride will not permit him to ask charity from any man, his daughter, your sister, appeals to you through me, on your mother's behalf."

"I think I begin to understand you," said Nat, his expression hidden by the deep shadow cast by his forehead curls. "My mother must be got into Bedlam, but this is passing troublesome at present for the asylum is over-full, they tell me, by reason of the influx of persons whom gin hath turned frantic. Well, sir, I have some influence with the Common Council of the City, and will do what I can to procure her admission."

"You do not begin to understand me, sir," said Michael, tugging at the rein of his self-control. "It is the desire of your father that your mother be placed under the care of some honest family in the country, and therefore am I come from your sister to desire you to provide the necessary expense. I trust I have made myself plain."

"I can see," said Nat, ignoring the sarcasm, "not the slightest reason for such expense. The realm has provided a house of refuge for those in my mother's melancholy condition, and what the realm offers, its subjects should accept of."

"Am I to understand, sir, that you would be content to see your mother placed in Bedlam?"

"Mr Pennington, you must know that my family is sprung from honest trading stock; I mention this because I have heard that you were born of a different sort of people, and therefore have other notions in your head. We are used to earn our bread or to go upon the parish; you inherit your upkeep, and if your income fails you seek charity from kinsfolk or marry an heiress. It is possible that you have spoken to my sister of some of these foreign notions, for I hear you are very familiar with her, and she, being a female, and impressionable, may have imbibed ideas improper in one of her station. I think——"

"Permit me first to tell you what *I* think," interrupted Michael, dangerously sweet. "I think you are a louse, Master Nathaniel Vance. You may not agree; why, then, Moor Fields are conveniently near; would you care to step thence with me and settle the matter man to man?"

Nat continued to stare at him from under the shadow of his foretop.

"A duel, eh? Bless me, Mr Pennington, we shall never make a cit of you. Your town gallants use the Moor Fields for what they call their affairs of honour; we citizens are too busy with our trade to indulge in such foolish recreation."

"Then it seems we may insult one another with impunity. Very well. I will name you further a beastly hypocrite, and to back up my insult I will make so bold as to enquire of you whether, were your wife to turn frantic, you would be content to see her immured in Bedlam?"

"I should not be content. The case is entirely different. (You will observe, sir, that I ignore your insult, which I consider beneath my notice.) If my wife suffered such a misfortune, I would have the means to put her away privily. It would seem that my father has not the means. Therefore must he accept of the public charity."

"You are of the opinion that you owe your parents nothing?"

"Financially, nothing at all. I set myself up and, having established myself, I have maintained my wife and myself by hard toil and careful business."

"So likewise has your father."

"With this difference: my father has failed. He has failed because he will not move with the times; he keeps up this silly feud with the beer-brewers, he insists upon the virtue of quality over quantity, he scorns to adulterate his ale though it is come to be the accepted practice of his craft, he refuses to sell to those tavern-keepers who lace their ale with gin to their customers' demand. If a merchant refuses to give the people what is to their taste he must needs expect ruin."

"The people, sir, sometimes ask for poison, as at present."

"That is their affair. A man must pay for sticking to outmoded principles and mixing sentiment with business, Mr Pennington, and the price is high. My father is paying that price, and pray God it will teach him a necessary lesson. But you cannot expect me to pay his debts for him."

"Meantime your mother must be chained in filth at Bedlam, to be baited by 'prentices and misused by keepers?"

"You are of a romantic disposition, sir. My mother is mad, and mad folk are unaware of filth or baiting."

"Your father is not mad and neither is your sister. They are very capable of feeling, and they are in dire distress."

"I am willing to commiserate with them and to give them the comfort of my presence by calling upon them, though I must add that they appear to have survived these many years without that comfort, and that my father at least has never concealed from me that the business I have chosen is hateful to him and never could secure his approval. But my father, it seems, retains his proper pride and makes no appeal to my charity; it is my sister who, having married a penniless 'prentice and being left destitute with an infant on her hands returns to live upon her father, now makes appeal to me through her—her proxy, shall we say? And now, sir, if you have nothing more of consequence to say to me, I will wish you a good evening."

He rose; but as Michael resolved to cast his rage from him, and make one last appeal to the man's better feelings, there was a step in the passage, the door flew open, and Frank Maynard stood upon the threshold.

"I left my gloves," he began; then, seeing Michael, bowed, and said: "Your pardon, Nat; I knew not that you were engaged. Why bless me, sir, I know your face; I'll swear we've met before."

"My name is Pennington, sir," said Michael. "I had the honour of making your acquaintance many years ago at the Exchange tavern."

"'Sheart, I do recall the occasion," exclaimed Frank in his hearty way. "You preached us a sermon on the evils of the lottery."

"Mr Pennington is a sweet pretty preacher," sneered Nat, "and lavish with his sermons upon every occasion. He has just concluded one to me."

"Why then that's two you've had tonight, Nat," cried his friend, laughing. "'Sblood, but you're a hardened sinner to convert. I was at him for an hour or more ere you came, Mr Pennington, crying up the excellence of investing in the Debt."

"Yes, I heard you, sir," said Michael quietly. "You spoke mighty loud and I was in the ante-chamber."

"Why that's brave. Then you will not refuse to back me up. Now, Nat, do you look to yourself; here are two preachers and but one congregation, and what chance has one against two?

Come now, Mr Pennington," added Maynard, seating himself and beginning to jingle the coins in his pockets, "do you take the field first, for I have had my say."

Michael looked from one to the other; and in him there crept a mounting tide of fury, so overwhelming that it swept aside discretion.

"You desire a sermon on the National Debt, sir," he cried. "Why then, by God, you shall have it! "

(iii)

He stood there facing them, and began to pour at them the spate of words that went racing through his brain.

"The Revolution Government, like all usurping governments, has needed friends to retain itself in power. The best friend to any usurper is a successful foreign war, which pleases the people and reflects glory on the victors, but foreign wars, especially if they be prolonged, cost money, more money than can be raised by a set of great lords, be they never so wealthy. The Revolution Government has given abundant proof of this its need, and has taxed, both directly and indirectly, has laid duties upon everything conceivable, and has encouraged its subjects to gamble away their savings by giving them public lotteries. But still the amount raised falls short of the expenditure, and so they have recourse to a loan, which becomes a multiplicity of loans, and the lenders are the really moneyed men, the bankers and the rich City merchants and the Jews and the foreign financiers. Now these moneyed men, these obscure and useful men, cannot be other than greatly concerned with the Government and all its policies; if you lend a man money you have him in your mind. And if you lend a man sufficient money you have him in your power, and he knows it; he takes care to make you the civility of his hat whenever he meets you, he is at pains not to offend you, he learns to respect your wishes and to pay attention to your demands, be they never so intolerable. This Government of ours, which is founded, not upon law, not upon Divine authority, not even upon the will of the people, this Government,

I say, itself a wealthy faction, is gotten into the debt of private moneylenders; and one day it may find itself so deep in their debt that it has become as much a puppet as once it made the king."

Maynard, who had listened with every appearance of enjoyment, clapped his hands as Michael paused for breath, and would have spoken, but the other swept on:

"Already money, in reality nought but a convenient token, has gotten unto itself a sinister new value, a new grip upon the mind of the nation. The lotteries serve as an example of what I mean, the itch for unearned wealth which is infecting all conditions of men. The introduction of Dutch methods of finance, as exemplified by the banks, has quickened the pace of this infection; a poor 'prentice can become rich overnight by winning a benefit in a lottery, and by entering figures in a ledger the banks can create money which has no reality in gold. Nor is there any longer the check of the Sovereign upon the ambitions of the wealthy, since the Sovereign himself is become the puppet of the wealthy. There is nought a man may achieve nowadays without money; you cannot wear a crown nor wage a foreign war nor expand your trade nor become a knight nor give decent sanctuary to the unfortunate. The rule of money is a hidden rule, and does not have to face the broad daylight of publicity, as does the rule of a king or of nobles. It will sacrifice for its own dark ends not individuals only but nations; it will provoke wars, if wars can gain it a harvest of investments; it will destroy a whole people if it can squeeze a profit from the instruments of destruction. Money has no masters, no friends, no ties, no traditions, no country, no morals. There is no appeal to it, because it is inhuman; it has no bowels to be moved, no heart to be touched. It has no nationality, and yet is greedy to control all nations; it would make all men slaves, binding them with golden fetters. Money is necessary to an unlawful and therefore an insecure Government, and he who can supply that money is necessary to it likewise. Take your thought one step further, and you will perceive that one day such a man will become that Government."

"Bravo! " cried Frank, springing from his chair and seizing Michael's hand. "I never heard such eloquence. Mr Pennington, you should have been a politician, or at least have entered the Church. Your talents are wasted as a clerk, sir; damme they are! I'll grant that what you say is a trifle too open to be blazed abroad, but it is true, sir, every word of it almost, and since, sir, you know me to be one of those same moneylenders of whom you spoke, you will not be surprised to find me hugely happy to know that I and my like may look in time to be the rulers of this nation. How now, Nat, you sit there mum; what say you to this excellent sermon?"

"I say it is a somewhat dangerous sermon," said Nat, keeping his eyes on Michael. "For by his own admission, Mr Pennington is disaffected towards the Government."

"Might I suggest then," snapped Michael, "that you lay an information against me, sir? 'Twould not be so rich an investment as the National Debt, but at least it would be money for nothing."

Then, before either of them could speak, he walked out of the room and left the house.

(iv)

He had retraced his steps down Lombard Street and had come as far as the entrance to Stocks Market before he became aware that he did not walk alone. He turned irritably, and beheld a green bird's-eye hood bobbing along through the dusk. A hand was thrust through his arm, and Moll's voice said to him:

"I perceive by your look that the mysterious errand which brought you hither has gone all awry and that you are in a rare depression, so it is left to me as usual to put a little heart into you. The evening is young, my friend, and we will shake the dust of the City from our feet and go upon our old territory, where we shall find some sport, I promise you."

Michael answered nothing, scarcely hearing her. The rage which had possessed him in Nat's office had been driven out by an image which made him faint with pity: Maralyn expectantly awaiting his return, her eager questions, her confident trust in her brother's sense of duty, her bewilderment and despair which must follow his tale of failure. Receiving no reply, Moll ran gaily on, describing her encounter with some of the City prostitutes and the wordy battle which had ensued when they discovered her intention of poaching upon their preserves, a battle from which, it seemed, she had emerged a complete victor.

" 'Damme,' said I 'think you to compete with me, my jilts, that have had courtiers and great lords for my gamesters? I learnt my trade in a more genteel school,' quoth I, 'than in this nest of mechanics wherein prigs and 'prentices are your flash bowmen and the highest bidder for your favours is but some fat merchant who lives in terror of his wife's tongue if he be but one hour late for dinner. I angled for salmon, mine honest whores,' said I, 'while you exclaimed with delight if you landed a minnow. Have a care how you provoke me,' said I, 'or I will bilk you of every gallant between Aldgate and Temple Bar. Ay, let me alone a while, and I'll be as well known hereabouts as Amen to the clerk.' And then they taunted me, and, said they: 'Maybe you had the King himself for suitor?' Whereat I answered 'em: 'You are clean outmoded, friends, and sound as stale as last year's news-sheets. *Imprimus* (which means firstly, for I perceive you lack education), the King is a Sodomite and beds with none but he-whores. And *secundus,* when one of our trade would fly after the highest game nowadays, she sets her cap at the great lords in the Ministry, for 'tis they who are now the masters of the realm.' (This much of your lectures I remembered, d'ye see?) 'And among these new masters of ours,' said I, 'there is scarce one that hath not solicited my favours; I swear I have but to crook my little finger, and they all come a-running.' And then, to back up my boast, I told 'em some stories of the Court, common stuff in truth, and such as can be learned in any town tavern where the gossips gather, but a rare novelty to them, poor souls, and they lapped it up as a housewife the cozening of a tallyman. 'Od rot you, Michael, you're not listening."

He neither heard nor spoke, but walked on, staring straight before him, his hands twisting together behind his back. Moll, half exasperated, half frightened by his manner, began to cajole him, begging him to call a hackney and drive to the Crown for a bowl of punch, but still he paid no attention. Then, suddenly, as they came into the Poultry, he stopped dead in his tracks, and muttered:

"I must tell her, yet I cannot tell her. She will be waiting. How am I to make her understand, she so simple and so good, the heartlessness of money?"

A brittle voice said at his elbow:

"She? So you had an assignation after all. So I was right."

" 'I am desperate,' she said to me," continued Michael, not hearing the interruption. "There were tears standing in her eyes. I have never seen them there before. She has endured so much and has been so steadfast. How am I to deal this further blow to one already so severely afflicted, so trusting, and so patient? I cannot do it; and yet I must."

There was complete silence for a moment. Then:

"The brewer's chit," snarled Moll, her voice shaking with fury. "I might have known it. 'I am bound for Lombard Street,' says you, 'on some private business of my master's.' And I near believed you, the damnable fool that I was, you had me fairly bubbled. You had not the face to tell me it was business of your mistress's, you stinking coward! "

And with that, planting herself in the path in front of him, she struck him in the face.

He staggered back from the force of the unexpected blow, and stared at her in a dazed kind of fashion. They had been crossing Compter Alley when Moll had made her assault on him; it was a long passage that led up to the Poultry Compter, with the Red Cock, an eating-house, on one corner and the Rose tavern on the other; both these houses had a lanthorn over their doors, so that he could see her face quite clearly. So evilly transformed was that face by a rage he could in no way comprehend that he could scarce repress a shudder. As one awaking from a dream, he blinked at her, smiled vaguely, and putting up a hand rubbed his stinging cheek.

"Why, Moll," said he, with a rueful laugh, "what crime have I committed to earn so sharp a chastisement?"

"I have borne with you," said Moll in a low trembling voice, and continuing to confront him in a menacing manner, "long and patiently. I have endeavoured to respect your silly prejudice against strong waters, even when I craved for a dram till I was like to run mad if I could not have it; I have laboured to entertain you even while you refused me the courtesy of so much as pretending you gave me your attention; I have endured your sermons, listened to your pesty dull lectures on matters which interest me not a fart, and have held my tongue when you have cried up brewers' jilts and fine ladies to my face. I forgave you even when you told me plainly you were ashamed of me and offered me money to be rid of me. I have journeyed about the town with you and gaped at curiosities like a country yokel when I might have been resting in my bed. But now I will endure no more. I have done, I tell you. Miss Modesty can have you and welcome, and I'll warrant you'll find her a kind companion to one who loves kissing in a corner." And with that Moll burst into a storm of tears.

Bewildered, embarrassed, horribly helpless, even more horribly nauseated, Michael put his arm around her and drew her into the shadows of the alley. He said hesitantly, choosing his words:

"Sweetheart, for all these failings and misdeeds you have catalogued, I can but ask your pardon and swear that they have been the outcome only of my trust in your friendship. With a friend, Moll, a man is apt to be tactless because so sure of understanding. As for this evening, I did not lie to you when I said I was bound for Lombard Street on private business of my master's, though maybe I should have added that such business was entrusted to me by my master's daughter."

"Ay," sneered Moll, wriggling away from him, "maybe you should have added that, since your head is stuffed so full of her that you rave about her even in my presence."

"Moll," he said, giving her a little shake, "what means this jealousy? Can you not believe me when I tell you that my master's daughter is nought to me but a young woman I admire for her goodness and courage? She is scarce even a friend, for she knows nought of me save that I am her father's clerk."

"I cannot but recall," said Moll harshly, "that you are singularly capable of making a fool of yourself over young women with whom you are not intimate, though you long to be, and who may be denied you because of your political opinions or some silly code of honour. Must I remind you of the Lady Eve?"

"If I made a fool of myself over Eve," said Michael steadily, "you bore with me then and put me eternally in your debt by your friendship and understanding."

"Did I so? Well, let me tell you I am not minded to do you the like service in connection with this City jilt, the brewer's wench."

"I need not such service in connection with Mistress Maralyn, for I am not in the least in love with her nor she with me. But I stand in need of your friendship, Moll, now and always."

"So much in need of it, forsooth, that you talk to yourself in my company and pay me not the least attention when I speak to you."

"I can only crave your pardon. The truth of it is, I am fearful for my country and sorrowful for my master's family. You have encountered me at an ill hour, Moll, tonight, but forgive me, dear, and do not cast me off."

She stared at him a while in silence through the darkness. Then she said sulkily:

"You have a cursed knack of making me seem in the wrong whenever we fall out. But harkee now, I'll strike a bargain with you. If you will go with me to the Crown for a whet, and afterwards to my lodging, I will forget what has passed this evening and things shall be between us as they were before."

"I am sorry, Moll, but I cannot go with you this evening. The errand which took me to Lombard Street is not yet completed, for I must return to her who sent me and make known to her that I have failed."

"In plain language, you prefer her company to mine."

"I do no such thing. By heaven, Moll, you twist my words like a hanging judge. I tell you this poor girl is in sore distress which anon I must make more grievous with my news. Do you think it likely that if I followed my inclinations I would prefer a most difficult interview with her to a merry evening in your company? You and I have, please God, a-many evenings in which to be merry; do you grudge a suffering woman one evening in which the most that I can offer her is my sympathy?"

"So it is sympathy, is it? Lord, under what cant names doth it parade here in the City! "

"You are determined on sticking to an evil suspicion," said Michael, his voice hardening. "But at least you might allow the poor girl her fair name, howsoever you are resolved to sully mine."

"You will not go with me?"

"It is not, I will not. 'Tis, I cannot, Moll."

"You may juggle with words as you please, Michael. I will stay plain, and say to you that if you do not, then you had best look to yourself."

"Is that a threat?"

"You have got my meaning exact, Michael Montague. You do ill to thwart me, and so you had best take care."

"Moll," he said, cold and quiet, "threats ill become a friend, so ill indeed that I can scarce believe 'tis my friend who utters them. I will wish you good evening, for it grows late and my errand will not keep."

But as he made to go she grasped his arm, and with a swift change of mood began to plead with him, exerting all her charm, beseeching him to let her have her way this once, whispering broken words of love, imploring his forgiveness, vowing she never could betray him, nestling her head against his shoulder. He gently disengaged himself, and said wearily:

"Moll, it is of no manner of use, I do assure you. I cannot go with you tonight. I will call a hackney for you, since you are weary and it is a long step to your lodging."

She stood back from him, and her look was ugly.

"You may spare yourself the pains," she snapped. "Go tumble the brewer's wench but mind this: I'll have my revenge on you for this night's work, God rot me if I don't."

He said nothing; nor could she see his expression for the darkness. He lifted his hat to her and, walking briskly along the Poultry, was soon lost in the London night.

(v)

She stood where she was for a while, staring after him, scarce able to believe that she had failed with him, that he had left her, torn by conflicting emotions, rage, self-pity, wounded vanity, and a kind of shame. She had come into the City this evening on purpose to spy on him; unable to eradicate the unreasonable jealousy which had tormented her ever since that day she had seen Maralyn at the Tower, and which had grown steadily ever since, she had resolved either to confirm her suspicions or allay them. In her heart of hearts she knew that they were unfounded; what she did not know was that her own character had become warped since that evening at St Bartholomew's Fair when she had made the acquaintance of Madam Geneva for the first time, and that her senseless jealousy of Maralyn was conceived and nourished by gin. It was gin that had made her spy on Michael, even while her better self despised such spying and confidently expected a negative result. But his mysterious errand to Lambard Street, his obvious distress and preoccupation, his talking to himself in so obsessed a manner concerning Maralyn and, above all, his obstinate refusal to give Moll his company for the remainder of the evening, all seemed to confirm her worst suspicions and to justify a jealousy which she had deemed baseless.

Bitter triumph and outraged pride made havoc of her shallow mind and lonely heart. He had forsaken her, not for his work, but for another woman. Of late she had come to resent his absorption in his political activities, but her acceptance of that absorption was of very long standing, dating, indeed, from her first acquaintance with him, and if he had told her tonight that he could not go with her because he had his writing to attend to, she would have stormed, she would have argued and protested, but she would not have experienced the keen hatred and thirst for revenge which now racked her. He had rejected her, openly, brazenly, in favour of the brewer's chit; he had insulted her who had given up so much for him (she really believed this as she stood here raging, intoxicated not now by gin but by pique, self-pity, wounded vanity), and she would have her just revenge.

She began to walk towards Cheapside, jostled by the crowds. The shutters were up and the City was turning to its brief hours of pleasure; craftsmen and their wives walked arm-in-arm towards the cockpit or the bear-garden, crop-headed 'prentices elbowed their way into the ale-houses, and the merchants' sons, apeing the town beaux with their curled wigs and long walking-staffs, ambled elegantly in the direction of Kiftell's coffee-house. Moll glared at them all as though she hated them, and scanned the houses beside her for something she required. Presently she stopped before an area, and peering down spied a blue light set above a door; a familiar odour assailed her nostrils, and a crooked notice-board announced briefly "Gin Royal". She jerked up her head in a kind of pitiful defiance, and groped her way down the steps into the gin-cellar.

It was a filthy place, unlighted save by a lump of tallow stuck in a basin; the wretched flame cast shadows round the cellar, half concealing, half revealing the human forms which occupied it. There was no cheerful talk and singing here, no mellow laughter or good-fellowship or comfortable hum of gossip; gin was not as ale and wine, convivial; gin begot secrecy and shame and moroseness; gin inflamed and bred hate or despair. Those evil emotions seemed to permeate the atmosphere; a woman was cursing aimlessly in a long stream of profanity; a man growled at his neighbour like a vicious dog. There was foul straw upon the floor, the straw provided free for the clients of Madam Geneva when she had overthrown them; from the forms already prone upon that straw there came strange animal noises, grunts and groans and primeval squeals. When you came in here, you must either get as quickly as possible into the same state as the rest of the dreadful company, or you must flee the place in terror and disgust. Moll bought a double dram for twopence, and swallowed the crude spirit in great gulps, gasping with the fire of it; so she passed swiftly from stage to stage of the mental and physical process familiar to the gin-addict.

Shame went first. It went at the same moment as there came a weakness of her limbs which made her sit down quickly on a stool against the mildewed wall. Next there disappeared the consciousness of her surroundings, of the filth, the stink, the proximity of the most degraded of humanity, the sliminess of the wall against which she leaned. Then, from the fumes of the raw spirit there arose thoughts like demons, twisted and evil, mean, crawling thoughts foreign to her nature but more powerful than her flaccid will. Self-respect had withdrawn, and reason, and fundamental decency and justice, but although they had withdrawn they had not altogether vanished, for these things were strong in Moll. So, through the miasma of foul thought which seemed to come from somewhere outside of her, there loomed the pitiful remnant of her better self; and it seemed to her that these two forces wrestled with one another, locked in mortal combat, to which she was a mere spectator, and that the combat took on the form of a wordy battle raging in her mind. . . .

"I have done with him and he deserves it. He has slighted me and all that's left to me is vengeance."

"You will never have done with him because you love him, and he deserves nothing but well of you."

"There was his precious pure Eve, and now the brewer's jilt."

"Eve was lost to him long ago, and the brewer's jilt is nought to him but a friend."

"So he says."

"And if he lies? What claim have you upon him? What claim has he ever made on you? You have insisted ever that you and he were free."

"I grow old and lose my looks. It is mean and cruel to desert me now."

"It is you who would desert him, and out of childish spite."

"I'll not take second place to City wenches. He should be taught a lesson."

"Take care what you say."

"Revenge is sweet, and it lies ready to my hand."

"Take care, take care what you say."

"I know that which would make him Ketch's client tomorrow."

"For your own sake, if not for his, take care."

"I have but to seek out Tom Fields, his old acquaintance, and lay an information, and Master Michael Montague, the Jack pamphleteer, would lie in Newgate tomorrow."

But then, like a cloud of outraged phantoms, her better self rose up upon her, overwhelming her with shame, with fear of herself, with panic. She found herself upon her feet, panting and gasping and clutching at the wall. But through the clamour which filled her aching head the voice of Madam Geneva whispered:

"You have but to stumble out of the cellar and hail a hackney and bid the driver carry you to Kensington. The drive will refresh you, and when you are come to Tom Fields you will be able to lay your information plainly and make him understand that all he has to do is to go to Michael's garret next Sunday while you entertain the victim at the Crown; a search of his papers will reveal——"

"No! No!" she shrieked aloud, and staggered towards the counter, and thrust out her measure and tipped the fresh dram down her throat all in a moment. Then, feeling the last stage of gin intoxication come upon her, she sank down with powerless limbs upon the verminous straw of the cellar and burrowed into it, her body seeking its refuge as her mind sought the safety of insensibility.

Three

(i)

MICHAEL laid down his quill, leaned back in his chair, and stretched his cramped fingers. It was April 23rd, 1702, the day of Queen Anne's Coronation, a public holiday which he had occupied as usual with his writing. All day long the squeaking of his quill had been accompanied by the thunder of the London bells and the roar of the crowds in Cheapside; now, as the evening drew in, the crude glare of a hundred bonfires flickered redly through the window on to his littered table.

King William's death, so long expected, was sudden when it came. On the twentieth of February, in this new year of 1702, his favourite horse Sorrel stumbled over a molehill in the park at Hampton Court and threw him, breaking his collar-bone. Official bulletins assured the nation that there was no cause for alarm, but gossip leaked out that those piercing cold eyes of his had grown strangely vacant, and that the thin bloodless lips could scarce articulate the vindictive order for a Bill of Attainder against the son of the man William had so greatly wronged. By this Bill, young James could be put to death without trial if ever he fell into the hands of his enemies. William signed it on March 7th, and next day, to the indignation of his physicians who had just issued a bulletin announcing that His Majesty was suffering "but a short fit of the ague", he died. The Privy Council, already entirely preoccupied with scrambling for places under the new Sovereign, hurriedly passed a vote to bury him "decently and privately"; and that was the end of William of Orange, the Protestant hero, the Liberator who had come to rescue England from Popery and Arbitrary Power.

And here sat Michael Montague, alias Pennington, a man approaching middle age, clerk to a decaying brewer, employing the Coronation holiday in writing tracts in which he told the people of England, not the things they wanted to know, the titbits of gossip, the inside scandal of the Court and the Ministry, not even about the chances of young James, but about the increase of the National Debt, the spread of gin-drinking and its consequences, the menace of the banks, the evils of the Party System, the reason behind this Government drive for Union with Scotland, the sinister power of the landed interest— dull, practical matters set down in plain language, matters unromantic, but concerned with the life and liberty of the average man and woman.

He was tired, tired to death; he was filled with that mortal fatigue which overtakes at times the champion of a lost cause. For twelve years now he had been striving to make the common people aware of their danger, and for all the effect which he could see he might just as well have held his tongue. The menace was there before their eyes; landlord after landlord was driving the smallholder from the ancient common lands and making him a wage-earner; because of the huge taxes, hundreds of small shopkeepers were being forced to put up their shutters and work for a master instead of for themselves. Land and money and all the power that went with them were becoming more and more concentrated into the hands of a few. Yet the citizens of London went about their business, grumbling a little but always hoping for better times, shutting their eyes to unpleasant facts, each man busy with his own petty affairs, determined, each and every one, "not to meddle in politics" and to "leave great matters to great folk".

With an exclamation of impatience, Michael rose, pushed aside his papers and straightened his tired shoulders. The roar of a London enjoying a fine free show seemed to mock him, and despite his weariness he knew he could not sleep. He put on his plain wig, rearranged his neckcloth, and went downstairs for a chat with Mr Vance.

The brewer was sitting in his enclosed arm-chair, his short legs stuck out before him, his Sunday coat and vest unbuttoned, and a pot of strong-ale clasped upon his stomach. He had pitched his wig into a corner, where it lay looking like a floor-mop, and he was smiling all over his red face with repletion and content.

"Aha, come in, come in with you," cried Vance heartily. "Maralyn, wench, another pot of ale. Bless my heart, Mr Pennington, you look as fatigued as I feel, but not so cheerful. I shall not be cheerful in the morning, I promise you that." He slapped his plump belly with a grimace. "I did eat freely of goose-standard at Brewers' Hall and I shall pay my reckoning for it, as I always do for such gluttony. But it was worth a bellyache, troth it was. Maralyn, sweetheart, remind me to take a purge ere I retire."

It was the first time for six months that Michael had seen his employer either so gaily dressed or so cheerful. Mrs Vance had died in the previous autumn, and the widower had arrayed himself in conventional black, even to the soles of his shoes. His grief had been pitiful to see, even though he knew it to be a most providential and merciful solution to a desperate prob-lem; the poor gin-fiend had been on the point of being carried off to Bedlam when death had signed her release. Vance, so desperately determined to conceal the true nature of her malady, had been open and candid in his grief; he had wept even before his 'prentices, and had gone about with the heart-rending bewildered look of a lost child. But lately he had recovered a little, his trot had regained something of its former briskness, and he had begun to smile again. He possessed that rare and genuine humility which values the smallest blessing; and the fallen state of his business served to help him put aside his private grief, for he was constrained to work even harder than of old. Moreover, he had a daughter devoted to him, courageous, tender and efficient, and as compensation for his disappointing son he now had a little grandson who one day, he was sure, would prove a good brewer in the old style, inherit the business, and carry on the tradition of a race of craftsmen. So he bustled to and fro again among his mash-tuns and fermenting-vats, his little legs moving briskly around his odorous domain, his com-fortable paunch making a small mountain beneath his leathern apron, his experienced nose and eyes and fingers testing the gravity of his beloved ale. And often after supper, encouraged by Michael and Maralyn, he would forget the lack of that family circle who had shared with him so many a convivial evening, and would fetch the Water Poet or Chaucer or Herrick from their shelf and recite aloud the virtues of English ale; or, sitting in his enclosed armchair, his shaven head a-shine, his coat removed for comfort's sake, would beat time with his ale-can to the old ballads he loved.

"It would seem you have hugely enjoyed this day's ceremony, sir," said Michael, sitting down on the brewer's right hand and bowing to Maralyn who came in from the kitchen with a fresh tankard of ale, "from which I would suppose that you are glad the Princess Anne hath gotten her the crown."

"Why, I am heartily glad of it, sir, and so is all London."

"I know it, Mr Vance, and am in labour to learn the reason for this general rejoicing."

"Tut, lad," said the brewer reproachfully, "that should be mighty plain. For first this princess, now our gracious Queen, is of the legitimate Royal House, born here in London and, though she be wed to a foreigner, has lived in England all her life; she declared publicly this day that she knew her heart to be entirely English, a declaration foolishly resented by the admirers of the late King. Next I believe her to be of a most excellent heart, altogether a more worthy person than her late sister, King William's wife, and firmly attached to the Church of England. I know that she betrayed her royal father, but I am sure she sincerely repented of it afterwards, and that she was led away upon that occasion by evil men. I do confidently expect that with her accession the Dutch invasion of our trade will cease, that there will be no more inconvenience to the realm by the Sovereign's repeated absence from it, and that many abuses brought over from Holland with the late King will altogether vanish." He took a deep draught of ale.

"But tell me, sir," pursued Michael, "what of the Succession? Queen Anne is no longer young and 'tis improbable that she will bear a living child. When she dies, what then?"

"Now marry come up!" cried the brewer. "You would coffin the poor lady on the very day she gets the crown."

"But is it in truth the will of the people of this realm," persisted Michael, "that when she dies the ancient crown shall devolve upon yet another foreigner, upon a race of petty German princelings who cannot speak the English tongue and who admit freely that they have no interest whatsoever in England or her welfare?"

"It is not the will of the people, sir," cried Vance emphatically, "and God forbid such a calamity ever befall us. As for the Act of Settlement, that was William's doing, and Queen Anne, who pretends no love for her German kinsfolk, will see that it is repealed."

"But if it is repealed (which I think most unlikely), and you will not have the Hanover princes, who will you have to reign over you?"

"Bless me, you hang as firm as a leech!" Mr Vance then glanced nervously over his shoulder, and continued in a undertone: "Why, sir, there is ahem!—a certain Young Gentleman overseas can claim by hereditary right, and who cannot be obnoxious to the nation as was his misguided father. But mark this, Mr Pennington," added the brewer, wagging an emphatic forefinger and looking very severe, "the next King will not be a Papist. No, saving your presence, sir, England will never again stomach a Popish monarch."

"Not a German nor a Papist," sighed Michael humorously; "neither George nor James. Faith, Mr. Vance, you will be hard put to it to find a successor. Maybe the Shah of Persia would suit you? He has as much right to the throne as George, and is not a Papist like James."

Mr Vance regarded him reproachfully; he considered the jest to be in bad taste.

"We do not despair, sir," said he loftily, "of hearing that the—ahem!—Young Gentleman before mentioned has consented to throw off his Papist superstitions and has embraced the religion of his martyred grandsire. Come now, I will be plain with you. That lad is dear to me and to all honest Englishmen, and to Queen Anne, his half-sister, likewise. We cits pay little heed to

222

Jacobite gossip, but it is plain to us from the reports of impartial observers overseas that the lad is a brave, good, gallant lad, sweet-tempered, tolerant and just, and I'll warrant that if he but consents to repudiate the religion in which he has been bred, a religion for ever hateful to his English subjects, there's scarce a man within this realm but will welcome him over when Her Majesty ends the reign she is now beginning, always provided that he comes not over with a French army at his heels."

Michael looked attentively upon his employer for some moments without speaking; then he rose and began to pace the room. His thin face was flushed and when he spoke there was restrained feeling in his voice.

"As for the French army, that will never come over if the Young Gentleman has his way. I had the honour to serve his father and never met a man more violently English. If the son inherits the father's desire, he will be content to wait for the invitation, freely given, of his own subjects. But, Mr Vance," continued Michael, pausing by the brewer and speaking with great emphasis, "if his subjects combine such invitation with the intolerable condition that their native-born prince betray his conscience and renounce, for the sake of a throne which is his by right and law, his own integrity, they may wait till Doomsday and he will not come. If he did accept the throne on such a condition, then I tell you plainly that I for one never would accept him."

"You're an obstinate Papist, sir," cried Vance indignantly, "and that's the truth of it."

"So little am I an obstinate Papist that I swear to you I care not if King James be Catholic or Church of England or Dissenter so he be sincere in his beliefs and sticks by 'em. You will not have your King dictate to you in matters of religion, and you are right; how, then, do you justify yourselves in dictating to your King in these selfsame matters? Tell me plain, what faith would you place in a prince who came over on the condition you have mentioned? Would you not say, ay and with reason, that such a prince desired only the power and the glory, who grasped at the kingdoms of this world at the expense of his place in the next? A man's method of worshipping his Maker

223

must be decided by no master save his own conscience. It has been the Stuarts' habit to insist that no man's conscience, neither their own nor their subjects', should be forced. The late King James asserted that dictum in almost those precise words. But if you, and the people of England, will not extend the like tolerance to your lawful ruler, you will find yourselves with a German hireling on your throne and a self-interested faction a-ruling you, and may say farewell to your liberties, one by one. And God damme, sir, you will have merited your slavedom!" He stood breathing quickly, his face pale, his eyes blazing. Then he forced a smile, made a swift bow, and with a low, "I beg your pardon, sir, and will wish you a good night," turned and left the room.

Vance sat a long while after the other's footsteps had died away up the stair, staring into his emtpy ale-can, while the bonfires of Queen Anne's Coronation sent shafts of savage light through the shutters and the drunken crowds surged and huzzaed in Chepe. Maralyn came in from the kitchen presently and began to set the room in order for the night, carefully smothering the fire with ashes, and depositing in its straw-lined box a tabby kitten, Tiger's successor. At last Vance sighed heavily, and muttered:

"Jesu, but 'tis a troublesome world to understand. All a laborious man demands is to be governed justly; his concern is with his mistery and he has not the understanding nor the leisure to attend to weighty affairs of State. And why should he so? There is one who should be as wholly taken up with government as he with his craft. But now it seems there is not one any longer, but—how ran the word?—a faction. I do not understand what he meant by that word. Pooh, pooh, he's a malcontent and always has been, yet a good lad at bottom, ay, a good honest lad. Pray God Her Majesty will take off these horrid taxes and put down this vile gin. I would she were a man; the times are passing troublesome and a strong male ruler would have been a blessing. But God's will be done."

"You are weary, sir, and should be gone to bed," said Maralyn, bringing him his candle.

He threw her a glance of mingled affection and irritation.

224

"Ay, ay," said he, heaving his fat person out of the chair and taking the candle from her, "it has been a busy day and a glorious one. But not a good trading day, my wench, as it should have been. Why, I mind me how, at King James his Coronation, we laboured at the mash-tub day and night for a week beforehand to supply our customers with the ale in which to drink his health. But now half of 'em have deserted us for the distillers and t'other half for the beer-brewers; shame on this City which would toast its new Sovereign in such rot-gut. Ay well:

" 'Thus men consume their credit and their wealths,
    And swallow sicknesses in drinking healths,
    Until the fury of the spiteful grape
    Mounts to the brain, and makes a man an ape.'

"Thus did John Taylor censure wine; but now it would seem that even the grape is superseded and men choose to drink their hell beforehand in consuming liquid fire."

He shook his cropped head dolefully, yawned, and trundled off to bed.

(ii)

Ever since Maralyn's return from Darien, Michael had observed her with some curiosity.

In all the time that had elapsed since then, he had never once seen her give way to grief. If she had shed tears at her mother's death she had shed them in private; she had been the prop and stay of her father in his bereavement, had managed all the funeral arrangements, and had made harmonious the difficult family gathering afterwards. She had, indeed, betrayed some agitation on the occasion when she had appealed to Michael to seek help for her mother from Nat, but it had been only for a moment, and immediately he had responded with warm sympathy she had withdrawn into her shell again. Her self-control was doubtless very admirable, but Michael could not help being faintly repulsed by such stoicism, and there were times when he suspected that the astonishing stolidity which had manifested itself in her ability to eat and drink on the night of her return, and to discuss with calmness her husband's tragic death, was not only apparent but real.

For her courage, her efficiency, her continual, unstinted giving of herself in service to all, Michael admired her to the full; only he wished sometimes that she was a little more human, that everything about her was not quite so perfectly ordered and composed. He was not in the least in love with this girl, but he intensely desired to establish his faith in her as a type. He had known, in a moment of illumination when he had bidden her farewell in the yard of the Saracen's Head, that such faith was justified; but the moment had passed and now he could not be sure that it had not been the product of mere emotionalism. The Maralyn who had returned from Darien with her life in pieces round her, and who so patiently and without complaint had stuck them together again, was doubless a young woman of heroic virtues, but in his more cynical moments he was convinced that she was likewise something of a prig. Her soul, he thought, was like her body, neat, trim, clean, and permanently childish. The bitterness of life, its temptations, its weaknesses, its passions, to these she was a stranger. He had known from the beginning that she was slow-thinking; now he had come to believe that she was incapable of using her mind at all except about the simple tasks that lay to her hand.

Having formed this opinion of Maralyn, Michael was very much astonished when one morning, as he slipped into the house to fetch a clean handkerchief (for he was suffering from a cold in the head), he heard from the kitchen the sound of abandoned weeping. He stood stock-still in the passage; at first he thought it must be a neighbour who had come to Maralyn for comfort in some domestic crisis, but the longer he listened the more was he convinced that the noisy sobs came from Maralyn herself. He hesitated, reluctant to intrude himself upon her privacy, yet curious to learn the cause of her grief and anxious to comfort her if he could. It must be, he reflected, some very great matter which had broken down that formidable composure and had burst the bonds of a self-control he had deemed unbreakable. His curiosity and his concern for her presently overcame his diffidence, and quietly crossing the living-room he pushed open the kitchen door, which had stood ajar, and remained upon the threshold, staring.

Maralyn sat at the well-scrubbed table, her arms flung across it, her head buried between them, her shoulders heaving with her sobs. Her mob had slipped back from her curly hair, which was tumbled about her head in most unusual disorder. On the table there was evidence that she had been pastry-making; a rolling-pin was flung down in a heap of flour, and near it stood a jug of water, a bag of salt, and some lard. The kitten had leaped upon the table and was licking the lard unrebuked. In the centre of the board lay some pieces of broken china, neatly piled together.

He stood there for several moments before she became aware of his presence. Then her head jerked up and he saw her tear-blotched face and woefully swollen eyes. She passed her arm swiftly over those eyes, attempted a smile, put a hand to her dishevelled hair, and murmured:

"Oh, Mr Pennington, I—I pray you excuse me. I did not know that anyone was here."

"You are in sore trouble, Mistress Maralyn," he said very gently.

Her lips trembled violently again as she stammered:

"Y-yes. You see, I have b-broken my m-mixing-bowl."

He stared at her, amusement, relief, incredulity, and something very like exasperation struggling for the mastery of his mind. She continued to make foolish, ineffectual little efforts to order her appearance, and said, pointing to the heap of broken china and then letting her gesture stray vaguely round the room:

"You see, it meant all—all this to me. It was more than a—a mixing-bowl; it was in a manner of speaking a friend. It belonged to my mother before me, and ever since I first learnt to bake I have used it. I know I must sound mighty silly, Mr Pennington, but somehow I think that when you care for things like that, and treasure them and work with them for many years, they come to have a kind of life, a share in your own life maybe. I cannot make this plain to you, because you are a gentleman and vastly clever and understand books and writing of accounts. I am sure you never felt that way about your ledgers. But for me, when things like that perish, I cannot but recall the hands which used to employ them and the happy times when they were whole, when my mother was alive and—and Alec. Alec used to steep his hands in that bowl when he had the chilblains. I am a foolish girl, I know, but it seems to me that there is a kind of benediction in these things, and that when they go there is a kind of death. You'll laugh at me, but sometimes I—I talk to the things I work with, to the fire when I light it and to my pewter when I polish it, and—and there is a sort of comfort there."

He asked, not knowing he was going to ask it:

"I wonder are you lonely? Is it possible you can be lonely?"

Misinterpreting the tone of the question, she hung her head, and murmured:

"Yes, I am lonely, and I know it is wicked and ridiculous that I should feel so when I have my father and my son and so many kind friends."

"We are all lonely," he said, "because we are human creatures. But I did not think that you——" He broke off, and then added apologetically: "I had no sort of right to ask you that prying question."

She did not contradict him. She stood up and smoothed her crumpled safeguard, then went round the table to pick up the kitten and set it on the floor with a little smack. Then she began to knead her dough on the board, but he noticed that her fingers were unsteady and that her eyes kept straying towards the piteous heap of broken china which had been a friend. She said with an effort, not looking at him:

"You have a mighty troublesome cold, Mr Pennington. I will make some hum anon and you must drink it hot ere you go to bed." Then she glanced at him, swift and shy. "Pray now, forget you saw me weep; it was vastly foolish, but the—the truth of it is I do not sleep very well o' nights, and that disorders me."

"You do not sleep?" echoed Michael, astonished anew by the idea of the composed and tranquil Maralyn tossing restless in her bed.

"No. You see, I am fain to think when I should be sleeping."

She answered his unspoken question by adding quickly: "No, not about Alec. Alec is happy; I am sure of that. I know that he is with God in Heaven, for he was a very good man. But I am not at all clever, you see, and I cannot understand certain matters which—which yet I cannot get out of my mind. I mean —about Darien."

He was silent, suddenly and intensely interested.

"You see," she continued, doggedly mixing her dough, "I cannot choose but think about Darien because I was there and I saw it all, the hardship and the heroism, the hopeless fight against odds. And then I visit my mother-in-law and she speaks of nothing else. She is herself an Englishwoman, but her husband was a Scot and she spent her married life in that nation, and she has many friends of her husband's nationality and she tells me what they are saying, and I cannot choose but think about it," said poor Maralyn of the limited vocabulary. "You see, Mr Pennington, it is sober truth that King William promised by what they call Letters Patent under the Great Seal to protect the Company of Scotland Trading Overseas, and yet he not only refused to send us aid but instructed the English colonists to refuse us help in our dire necessities, and he would not so much as receive my Lord Basil Hamilton whom the Company sent to London to lay the case before His Majesty. And all their later petitions and addresses were in vain, it seems, and Scotland declares roundly that King William broke the word he had never intended to keep." She glanced at him again, and now there was something resembling horror in her eyes. "That is a most dreadful accusation to be made 'gainst any man, much more 'gainst our Sovereign, and maybe the Scots make it but out of their bitterness, for they are ruined as a nation. And I know what King William's admirers say: That he promised protection without knowing what he promised. It may be so; I cannot tell. I hope it is so. But yet I cannot choose but think that King William should have known what he did or that at least, when the settlers were in such sore distress, he should have succoured them."

"You forget that he promoted a scheme of Union," said Michael dryly.

"Oh yes, indeed," said Maralyn, not recognising the sarcasm, "and I do trust and pray that such a scheme will comfort and revive that poor ruined nation. But then, you see, there was Glencoe."

"Yes," prompted Michael, watching her closely, "there was, as you say, Glencoe."

"Alec used to talk about Glencoe, although as a Whig he hated the Highlands and deemed their people but barbarians. Yet for all that he was a Scot, and a human being likewise, and as such he abominated broken faith and bloody massacre. King William signed the order for that frightful deed; that is common knowledge. Again I know what is said by his partisans: that he did not read the order. Well, I am but an ignorant woman, yet is it passing strange to me that the King, our ruler, the maker and executor of our laws, the protector of our lives and fortunes, should sign his name at the head and at the foot of a State document and neglect to read what was written in between, that he should twice affix his signature to an order for massacre and walk away not knowing what he had signed. And then he did know in the end, you see; when the whole dismal story became public, I mean. And yet even then he would not punish the murderers nor would he succour the survivors. Sometimes when I think on these things it comes into my mind that he had no care for his kingdom of Scotland. But then I begin to think further, and there is a most horrid notion comes into my head: maybe he had no care for his kingdom of England either." She looked at him with wide eyes and laid a hand over her mouth. "I think I must be a very wicked woman to have such thoughts come to visit me and certainly it is wicked to speak them aloud, but indeed I have never done so till this moment."

"Except maybe to your pewter when you polish it," said Michael softly. "Pray pretend I am a piece of pewter, Mistress Maralyn; I promise you I am as incapable of betraying your confidence."

She did not seem to hear him. She went on rapidly, swept as it were upon a tide of dammed-up speech:

"I know the people of Glencoe were robbers and heathen savages. Everyone knows that. But there were women and children and old men and sick folk who were murdered with the fighting men of the tribe. That likewise is known. And I cannot choose but think sometimes: suppose it had been me and little Alec and my father? If we had been bred up in such a wilderness we should have known no better than to thieve and defy the law and cling to Popish superstitions, but that would not have justified any man in murdering us in cold blood by treachery, sending soldiers amongst us who ate our cakes and drank our ale and lay under our roof until the hour when they rose up to butcher us. I lie and sweat in my bed sometimes to think of that horrid, that dreadful brutal deed." Tears ran down her cheeks again, and she trust her knuckles hard against her mouth as though to keep back the sobs which rent her. "There is one frightful tale I have heard them tell at my mother-in-law's about a child's hand lying lonely in the snow. They never found the child; it was just a little hand lopped off, a hand which maybe had been playing with some toy or scratching in the mud to make a pie when one of those vile murderers dismembered it. Don't the great lords in Government ever think upon those things, I wonder? They too have sons and daughters. And the King? He had no children, so maybe it did not mean so much to him if he heard such stories, but as for me, I cannot choose but think upon it, for it might have been my little Alec's hand, my little Alec's hand!" Her shoulders shook and the frustrated sobs racked her poor tight chest beneath the snowy safeguard.

"They were King William's own subjects," she said after a while, swallowing her tears and speaking with a kind of desperate resolution as though she must say all that she had to say now or never speak again. "Yet it is true that they were rebellious and hot for Popish James. Very well then. But when King William permitted the tragedy of Darien, and refused to succour the Scots in the hour of their need, he meted out the vengeance of Glencoe upon subjects obedient to his rule. And they hated him, the Scots. And you cannot blame them. I cannot. I know that. And yet he was our King and the Protestant hero, and came hither to deliver us from Popery and slavery, Scotland as well as England. I know not what he did for us except tax us and take away our trade to give it to his Dutchmen and bring in gin. I cannot choose but think upon gin because it killed mine own mother and has near ruined my father's trade. But I know what he did to the Scots and I cannot forget it. I wish I could. I wish to God I could, then maybe I should sleep o'nights."

Her fingers were kneading and kneading the dough again, and her downcast swollen eyes stared into it. He said nothing but waited for her to continue, waited in an anguish of hope and fear. Her simple mind was bewildered, her inbred faith in politicians shaken, and because of her experiences and her honesty she was being forced to think. Was not this what he had laboured for, to make the common people think for themselves, to question, to investigate the truth of propaganda? Once let them perceive that the Glorious Revolution had borne evil fruit, and they would be half-way towards demanding The King Again. But Maralyn's next words disillusioned him.

"Well, King William is dead," she said more calmly, "and now we have an English-born Queen to reign over us. I doubt not Queen Anne will succour poor ruined Scotland and foster the trade of England and make illegal this distilling of gin, then all will be fair and joyful again." And then she grimaced a little because she had noticed that the dough she was kneading was stained in places a dirty pink.

"I think you cut your finger when you broke that bowl," said Michael.

She lifted her hands, scanned them hurriedly, clasped them together, and turned towards the pitcher which earlier she had filled at the Conduit.

"It is nothing," she said almost curtly. "Just a little scratch. I' faith, Master Pennington, 'tis nearly noon. You must excuse me or there will be no dinner today."

He took the hint and left her. But as he went back to the counting-house his mind answered her in a desperate appeal. A little scratch, only a little scratch. Nowadays life is full of little scratches for little people. But sometimes an accumulation of little scratches on mind and body will make even little people begin to think, as they have made you think, whether you will or no, my dear. Only you will not pursue your thoughts to their conclusion; you are ashamed of them; when they reach a certain point you grow frightened and take refuge in a vague hope that all is for the best and that great men in Government must know what they are about and have your welfare at heart. Will the day ever come when you will not only think but understand, and understanding, demand, repent, revolt? Will the little people of this poor realm endure the little scratches until the whole body is disfigured, for ever refuse to face facts or to meddle in great matters? Will they go on telling their troubles only to mixing-bowls and pewter candlesticks, forget their grievances in a can of ale, rally their sense of humour, snatch at every excuse for optimism, turn their backs upon first principles, and insult their intelligence by accepting a lie as truth because it is printed in a newspaper or mouthed at them by a politician?

He sat upon his stool completely idle until the bell rang for dinner, fraying out his quill, and resisting with all his will a temptation to despair.

(iii)

Mr Vance returned from Brewers' Hall one Monday in a very thoughtful mood. It was not, however, until after supper, when Maralyn was washing the dishes, that he mentioned to Michael the matter which had made him so pensive.

"Pray a moment, Mr Pennington," said he, as Michael was about to say good night. "I am exceeding troubled in my mind and would take it friendly of you if you would discourse with me upon a certain matter."

Michael bowed without speaking and returned to his chair. Mr Vance sat silent for several minutes, staring hard at the table; then he crashed his first upon it and cried out:

" 'Tis this hellish spirit-guzzling again. It grows worse and worse and the Bills of Mortality tell a dreadful tale, the excess of burials over baptisms mounting higher every year. I cannot now recall the precise figures disclosed to us this morning, but I know they shocked me as they did all the Brethren. There can be no explanation other than the spread of this abominable vice, for London is growing, the price of foodstuffs is low, and the Plague is altogether disappeared (please God). Yet the weekly bills tell us that the death-rate increases, and they say that scarce one child in ten survives beyond the age of five years."

He paused, fished out his handkerchief, and blew his nose loudly.

"The Brethren," he continued earnestly, "have made investigation into the matter. Reports from the hospitals show that increasing numbers of sick folk are admitted suffering from dropsical and consumptive diseases which arise, say they, from the imbibing of this demon gin. Likewise have there been vast numbers of fires in various parts of the City, caused by the many stills set up in crowded places, and by the mischievous carelessness of these compound distillers who are always fuddled with their own poison. Deeds of violence of all kinds increase, and so likewise does poverty, because the workman sells his tools and the housewife her pots and pans that they may purchase that which will certainly destroy them. It is a madness, I tell you, a veritable madness, and if it be not checked our rich England will find herself as poor as Scotland and as depopulated as the kingdom of the Turks, which opium has rendered barren."

Michael was about to speak, but the other went on in a low, hurried voice:

"I heard a dreadful story this morning, Mr Pennington, but one among many, 'tis true, yet somehow it hath stuck in my mind more than the rest. There was a woman went to fetch her infant from the workhouse that she might carry it for an airing. It was newly clothed by the parish. She—she strangled it, Mr Pennington, and laid it in a ditch; then she sold the clothes to a pawnbroker for one-and-sixpence and spent the money in a ginshop. In her inflamed intoxication she confessed the deed to her fellow-wretches in the cellar where she passed the night and one among them informed upon her. They say she gloried in her crime and boasted of her cunning." Tears stood in the old man's eyes. " 'Ounds, sir, what strange creatures are men that they hunger and thirst after that which will inevitably destroy them, drive them to such unnatural deeds, ruin their families,

234

and undo in a night the trade they have laboured to build up through many years of toil."

"Yet can you altogether blame them?" asked Michael. "Gin is so cheap, so warming, brings such forgetfulness of misery and hardship ere it inflames and maddens. There is every temptation given to the poor of London to buy this poison, and the poor are easily tempted. Yet I do recall that you said to me, when we discussed this evil upon a former occasion, that Queen Anne would certainly abolish it."

"So I did, sir, so I did," said the brewer, in a slightly offended tone, "and so she will when she is made cognisant of the scourge. And she is to be made cognisant, sir, without delay. Our Company is resolved to petition Her Majesty; a document is already drawn up, of the which I did make a careful copy this morning, and will even read it to you now, if you will have patience."

He drew a sheet of paper from his pocket, smoothed it out upon the board, affixed his iron-rimmed spectacles to his nose, and solemnly began:

" 'The humble Petition of the Worshipful and Ancient Company of the Brewers of the City of London, etc. etc.' (I will not plague you with the preliminaries, sir—ahem!) '. . . That the prohibition of gin would be greatly advantageous to the Kingdom, and would prevent the destruction of Your Majesty's subjects, many of whom have been slain by the drinking thereof, it not agreeing with their constitutions. Before gin (which is now become common and is sold not only in the spirit-shops but by men of all crafts and misteries) came over, in England we drank strong good ale and—ahem!—beer; and all laborious people (which are far the greatest part of the Kingdom), their bodies requiring, after hard labour, some strong drink to refresh them, did therefore every morning and evening use to drink a pot of ale or a flagon of strong beer, which greatly promoted the consumption of our grain and did them no great prejudice; it hindered not their work, neither did it take away their senses, nor cost them much money. We therefore humbly petition, etc., etc.' This document, sir, is entitled: 'The Grand Concern of England explained in Several Proposals to the Consideration of

Her Gracious Majesty,' and is to be presented at the Guildhall by our four Wardens for the approval of the Lord Mayor. It is hoped that other Companies will be persuaded to draw up the like petitions, that every craft in the City may unite in putting down this abominable vice."

"Every craft, sir? What of the distillers?"

"The Distillers' Company, Mr Pennington, should be the most forward and zealous, for they have suffered keenest by having their charter overridden, their right of search taken away, and their trade thrown absolutely open. Why, these new buccaneer distillers are even freed from the statutory obligation of serving a seven years' 'prenticeship."

"Therefore is the Distillers' Company rendered powerless and is become, I undersand, much decayed. Meantime, the distilling trade continues to receive ever fresh favours from the Government, and this trade, sir, spreads itself among all sorts of men. The malt distillers, they who produce the raw spirit, are few in number, 'tis true, but the compound distillers abound, and retail the crudely adulterated spirit they concoct; likewise any man is free to distill on giving notice to the Commissioners of Excise and by paying the Excise Duty, which is made negligible."

"It is against such rascal distillers, sir, that we are especially petitioning," said Vance loftily.

"But that is by no means the end of it," continued Michael. "By an Act of William, any man is free to retail spirits without the justices' licence required from ale-house keepers. In practice this means that every other shop sells the poison, and from what I hear it has come to be their most profitable commodity. Therefore, you will have against your petition not only the landed interest, which makes a huge profit out of its surplus grain by selling to the distillers, but likewise every petty shopkeeper, not to speak of their customers. You will have in arms against you the very turnkeys in the prisons, the vendors of various commodities in the streets, the constables of the watch, the parish nurses, the keepers of workhouses, all of whom find their toil made lighter and their pockets enriched by selling gin. And

236

lastly, and most formidable, you will have against you the Government itself."

"Stuff and nonsense, sir!" exclaimed Vance angrily. "The abominable Acts of which you speak were made by King William, and I say that good Queen Anne will repeal them."

"They were made by the masters of King William, the landed interests, and the masters of Queen Anne, the selfsame landed interests, will see to it that they are not repealed. Nay, sir, do not mistake me. I wish your petition every success and am entirely with you in your resolution to adopt such a course as you have described, only I would have you aware of the strength of the enemy you are determined to fight, and I doubt the power of the City Companies against a taste which is become so dangerously universal and which has been so blatantly encouraged by the Government."

"Nay," said Vance, smiling upon him, "I'll not have our petition put out of countenance by one who himself is resolved to fight this evil, though in a less lawful fashion, if I may take the freedom to say so. For I must tell you that one of our Brethren did show me a most excellent tract this morning which concerned this very business of spirit-drinking. He told me his wife had been handed it in mistake for a play-bill, and when I read it I was sure I recognised your hand. It was most admirably writ, sir, most excellent." He bowed to Michael, who smilingly returned the salutation. "I gave it to my friend, John Bunch, and said I, we should circulate such a rare tract among the Brethren, but he would have none of it. 'Tis plainly the work of a Jack, said he, and the Jacks are ever forward in seizing upon any excuse for stirring up mischief and promoting disunity."

"Alas, the Jacks can do no right," said Michael dryly.

"Well, sir, you must confess that they have proved themselves noisy and troublesome with their raiding of the Whig mug-clubs and their breaking of windows, and their nasty intrigue and plotting."

"There are times when to be noisy and troublesome is the only way to remove an evil."

Mr Vance regarded him in disapproval.

"It is the way of the mob, sir, a lawless, vulgar way. The method of respectable, laborious men is, and has ever been, a petition to the Sovereign or to Paliament, such petitions being acceptable to law and custom."

"And if they fail?"

"This one will not fail, sir," said the brewer complacently. "You will find that Queen Anne has care for her subjects and that, so soon as she is made cognisant of so damnable an evil, she will destroy this demon gin."

Four

(i)

MARALYN walked quickly down the Strand one January afternoon in the year 1707. It was a raw day, patched with fog, and a cold wind from the river blew up the streets on the south side. Maralyn was well huddled into her hooded cloak, partly to keep warm, partly to efface herself as much as possible. A true daughter of the City, she both feared and distrusted this London which lay outside the City liberties. She ventured hither only when, as now, she visited her mother-in-law, whose green-cellar was in Bedfordbury, a district of small and narrow streets lying between St. Martin's Lane on the west and Bedford Street on the east. Ordinarily she went through Drury Lane to reach it, but on coming into that thoroughfare this afternoon she had seen a great press of footmen around the door of the playhouse, going in to hold the seats for their masters and to display their fine livery, and so had turned back timidly.

Despite her dislike of this London, she regarded with naïve wonderment the famous street down which she was walking. It was vastly busy with coaches, chairs, and these new chariots, very rich in carving and gay with coloured harness, affected by the gentry. Maralyn caught a glimpse or two of fashionable occupants, of ladies who had just discarded the *commode* and looked curiously short without that tall head-dress, of gentlemen wearing their hats in the new Ramillies cock (named after Marlborough's great victory of the previous year), and sometimes of children dressed like their elders, very gallant and pretty in a curled wig or a set of pinners edged with colberteen.

Here, as in the City, the 'prentices stood at their masters' doors, but their incessant chant of "Buy! Buy! Buy!" seemed to her oddly obsequious. The old palaces of the nobility awed her with their vastness, though many of them had been partially demolished to make room for the streets which had been built after the Restoration, and at least one was divided into shops. The side streets were quiet now, for it was the hour when ladies rested before dressing for the evening's frolic, and when gentlemen were gaming or gossiping at these clubs which had sprung into being of late. Yet the Strand itself was always busy; merchants stepped briskly into the chocolate-houses to keep a business appointment, a party up from the country pressed eagerly towards the menagerie at Exeter 'Change, the office-keepers of the theatres hurried round the houses of their wealthy patrons to inform them what pieces would be played that night, clerks ran out at the cry of "Fine writing-ink!" from the man who carried a little barrel on his head and a funnel and measure at his side, fashionable tradesmen's wives sallied forth for an afternoon's shopping at the New Exchange with one of their husband's 'prentices in attendance, and porters, resting their loads on the board set for the purpose on the tavern walls, crowded the benches beneath. In the narrow entrance to Salisbury Street, which led down to the river and was known as the Whores' Nest, finely dressed prostitutes ogled the passers-by through their face-guards, and a crowd gaped at some horse-breakers who were leading their nervous charges in the direction of Lincoln's Inn Fields. It was all very gay and colourful and marvellous, but to the City-bred Maralyn it was also vaguely wicked, a street of luxury rather than of honest trade, full of dull, over-large houses and suggestive of idleness and of wealth misspent.

She breathed a sigh of relief when at last she turned down one of the narrow alleys on the northern side, crossed Chandos Street, and came into Bedfordbury. It had been built in the year 1635, and, like most such districts, had once enjoyed a fashionable era. But now the tall, narrow houses were let off into tenements, with mean shops and eating-houses and poor little taverns on their lower floors. There was always a stench of decaying vegetation here, for the stall-keepers in Covent Garden market had a habit of pitching their refuse over the wall of the church-yard of the fashionable St. Paul's, which stood upon the other side of Bedford Street, despite the angry remonstrances of successive churchwardens.

Maralyn's mother-in-law had her green-cellar in an alley called Slug Lane. The odour of rotten vegetables warred here with a stink of fish, for a fishmonger, trading under the favourite sign of The Dolphin, had his shop on the ground floor. A flight of uneven stone steps led down to the cellar, with a broken hand-rail beside it, and from the open doorway in the area there issued the flickering glow of a rushlight, and a woman's voice mildly scolding.

Maralyn's relations with her mother-in-law were somewhat difficult. Mr Vance, good man though he was, had all the snobbishness of the City craftsman, and knew and rigidly observed the status given to each trade by immemorial tradition. Trades ranged from the "genteel" at the top, through the "dirty genteel", the "genteelish", the "ordinary", the "mean", to the "mean, nasty and stinking" at the bottom; moreover, there were different grades within the same trade, depending on the reputation for craftsmanship enjoyed by the master and the size of the apprenticeship fee he was thereby entitled to demand. Brewing came into the "ordinary" class, but the excellent reputation of Mr Vance put him in a high grade within the trade itself. A green-cellar, on the other hand, especially a green-cellar run by one woman and an apprentice, came very far down in the scale on both counts, and while Mr Vance received his sister-in-law very graciously on the rare occasions when she came to visit him, he never dreamed of calling upon her in her own domain, particularly as that domain lay outside the City liberties and hence, in his opinion, gave to its owner no kind of status at all. He made no protest against the dutiful visits of Maralyn beyond impressing upon his daughter that such visits must be undertaken purely from motives of charity, and must take place only on Sunday afternoons. Maralyn had experienced some difficulty, therefore, in persuading him to allow her to comply with a very urgent summons from Mrs Moray senior, begging her daughter-in-law to call upon her on this afternoon in mid-week.

Maralyn had inherited her father's snobbishness, but this was not the only reason that made her visits to her mother-in-law a duty rather than a pleasure. Alec had always been a hero in his mother's eyes, but since his tragic death he had become something more like a god, and she expected her daughter-in-law to join in her morbid worship. The one room behind the shop, which served the poor widow for sleeping-chamber, living-room and kitchen, was crammed as full with relics of Alec as the apartment of some devotee with those of a patron saint. His picture, crudely executed by some strolling painter at a fair, formed the centre-piece of the collection, and reigned upon the chimney-shelf with a jug of wilting greenery on either side of it. Upon the wall was nailed the battledore with which he had played as a boy, and as witnesses to the various stages of his education there were ranged upon a shelf a small array of books, from a battered horn-book to an edition of Dryden's translation of Ovid's *Epistles*. His very quills, long dry, stood in a jar, and in a press, as Maralyn very well knew, lay folded a suit he had outgrown, a patched bedgown, and the City flat-cap he had discarded the day before he left London for Leith, when his mother had presented him with a cheap imitation beaver as a parting gift. Mrs Moray was desperately poor and some of these piteous relics might have brought her in a few shillings had she sold them, but such a sale would have been sacrilege in her eyes, and, moreover, their company brought her the only kind of pleasure she had left, a melancholy, gloating obsession with the dead.

The widow herself was one of those vague women who live always in a muddle and are incapable of order, either mental or material; yet like many such women she got things done in the end, and could be extraordinarily obstinate and self-willed. If you gave her advice, she listened to it in a quiet and apparently receptive manner, smiling all the while and murmuring at intervals "Yes, yes, you are perfectly right," and straightway acted in a manner exactly contrary to the advice given, in a futile, seemingly hopeless manner, yet managed to achieve the desired end. Her business never prospered, but on the other hand it never failed; she had her regular customers, who came to her more because they seemed to be hynotised by her incessant stream of talk than for the excellence of her goods; her cellar was always in a state of chaos, yet she always in the end found what she wanted; she had the most complete disregard for time and would loiter vaguely round her "relics" when she ought to have been serving customers or going to market, but on the other hand she kept open to extraordinary hours in the evening, and was quite ready to serve some housewife, harassed by unexpected company, with potatoes or cabbages at ten o'clock at night. She had that habit of the very poor, maddening in the extreme to those in different circumstances, of never throwing anything away, because "it might serve for something some time". And, sure enough, "it" generally did so serve, turning up in the most apt manner on the most unlikely occasions, and appearing in the most unexpected of new guises.

Maralyn, although she never carried her efficient housewifery to the lengths when it becomes a vice, yet had inherited her mother's love of order and punctuality, and therefore found Mrs Moray's chaotic establishment both irritating and depressing. But she was very sorry for the little woman, admired her courage in keeping up without complaint a lone battle for existence, and being possessed of a strong sense of duty, never failed to visit the green-cellar on a Sunday afternoon. This was the first time she had been summoned hither, and her apprehension regarding the reason for such a summons, combined with a sense of guilt for having deserted her own household on a weekday, made her return Mrs Moray's greeting with a nervousness she could not quite disguise.

"I received your message, Mother, and hastened to comply with it. I do trust there is nothing gone amiss?"

"Amiss? Oh, nothing, nothing in the world," replied Mrs Moray, smiling vaguely upon her. "Dot," she added, turning to the hunchbacked 'prentice who was her only assistant, "do you mind the shop as I told you, and be sure to put aside those sprouts for Mrs Turner. And the onions, Dot, no more than a pound to each customer, mind; they are short this year because of the blight and really it is wonderful that we have any to sell. And if any enquire for pickled cowcumbers, Dot, I think there are some in the box wherein I kept the sparrowgrass last summer; if they are not there they are sure to be somewhere else and you will find them if you search diligently. Bid them broil the potatoes, Dot, and then they will not turn black; say the crops have never recovered from the great storm of—I cannot quite recall what year it was but I think we shall never see a fair potato crop again, and I do thank God my Alec never lived to see such times, for he was exceeding fond of a white and mealy potato. Mara, my love, come you into the back room and I will make some tea."

It was Mrs Moray's habit either to abbreviate the names of her acquaintances or else to invent a pet name for them. No one knew why the poor hunchback should be addressed as Dot, and Maralyn's father would have been horrified to have heard her called "Mara", which sounded, indeed, like an illiterate pronunciation of a certain useful vegetable. Mrs Moray who in person was small and wispy and dressed in vague clothes, and whose complexion was colourless from living in a cellar, led the way into the back room and set about the infusion of tea, a weed Maralyn had been taught to look upon with even worse disfavour than the wicked hop, but which was Mrs Moray's one vice and luxury. Tea was still enormously expensive, even the inferior varieties, but somehow the widow always managed to have some in her caddy, even as she always managed somehow to pay her way.

"It will soon be time for the snowdrops," said she, hovering in front of Alec's picture and rearranging the carrot-tops which drooped in the two jugs, "and that will be a glad time for you and me. It is horrid to give him nought but greenery, but he will be so happy to know we are to attend the meeting this evening; that will be even better than snowdrops for our darling. Mr Walker is to speak, you know, and he is a vastly knowledgeable man, I am sure, and will tell us all about this nasty business. The English are set on having it entire, and that is a beastly thing for those whose forebears resisted so bravely the Romans and the Danes and the—Turks, I think it was, and other would-be conquerors whose names escape me for the moment."

"Mother," cried the bewildered Maralyn, slipping desperately into the pause, "I swear I do not understand a word you say. What is this nasty business of which you speak?"

"Why the Union, Mara, the Union, my love," replied her mother-in-law reproachfully, as she wetted the tea. "You know all about that, I'll warrant you do, knowing how our dear Alec would have interested himself in such an affair. He would have opposed it with great firmness, Mara, as I know very well, being his mother and well acquainted with his mind, and you and I must do the best we can in such an affair now that the Lord has been pleased to take him. We will drink a cup or two of this excellent tea, and then we will hasten to the Presbyterian church against Leicester Fields where the meeting is to be held, and dear Alec will go with us in spirit, and Mr Whitehead, the minister, who is an Englishman, and a most worthy person, will make plain to us what is to be done."

Maralyn regarded her in speechless horror. A vision of her father floated up in her mind, her father who detested Dissenters only a little less than he hated Papists. The word meeting, too, made her think of crowds and raids by constables, of disreputable Jacobites and other malcontents; and she could not help revolting, though she succeeded in hiding such a feeling, against Mrs Moray's assumption of knowing everything about Alec, alive or dead. But beneath these more superficial objections to the programme mapped out by her mother-in-law lay a deeper, more indefinite kind of fear. She did not understand this fear and shrank from investigating it, only she knew it dated from that day when she had broken her mixing-bowl, and had given way to grief, and had spoken aloud to Mr Pennington certain shameful secret thoughts. Since that day she had never been quite sure of herself and had played a kind of hide-and-seek with her own mind. She had tried with all her might to put public affairs out of her thoughts and to concentrate upon the duties of that state of life to which it had pleased God to call her. And she had succeeded tolerably well, though it had been a strain, how great a strain she did not know as yet. And now here was her mother-in-law insisting upon making her learn all about this Union; Maralyn knew absolutely nothing about the Union except that it appeared, from the general talk, that Scotland did not want it. And she desired to know nothing; she wanted above all things to shut her ears to public affairs. Particularly was she anxious to shut them against the affairs of Scotland, for were not those old indecent, almost treasonable thoughts of hers the outcome of Glencoe and Darien? She could not, of course, say anything of all this to Mrs Moray; she merely murmured that she must return to the brewhouse very shortly to put her father's supper on the fire.

But like all vague, obstinate women Mrs Moray was terribly hard to deny. She took it for granted that Maralyn was as anxious to attend the meeting as she was herself, and she refused to accept any hint to the contrary. As for Maralyn's practical objections, she swept them aside with a brief, smiling, and pious: "My love, Alec's wishes are more to us than a supper," and, gently removing the younger woman's cup, bustled about in a futile way to find her own cloak and hood. Before she could collect her scattered wits, the hapless Maralyn found herself being piloted gently but firmly down the street, while the brook-like voice at her side babbled on ceaselessly and vaguely about the Union, its injustice, and the merits and demerits of the public men connected with the scheme, the whole subject being, it seemed, at the same time cloudy in Mrs Moray's mind and very vital to her heart.

(ii)

Mrs Moray shepherded her reluctant charge across St Martin's Lane and down Bear Street into Leicester Fields; the latter were still so termed, though they had been for many years turned into a square surrounded by great houses, and were still used by the town gallants as a duelling-ground. Leicester House, the home of the Sidneys, formed the boundary on the northern side, and running along the side of this, on the north-east corner of the square, was Cranbourn Alley, or, as it was known locally, Dirty

Lane. Down this passage, famous for its vendors of bawdy ballads, went Mrs Moray and her companion, and presently came to a modest brick building tucked away among shops and taverns. This, it seemed, was the Presbyterian church. Mrs Moray was late as usual, and the bare, ugly interior of the church was already packed as she marshalled Maralyn through the entrance, yet she managed in her seemingly futile way to find seats for herself and her daughter-in-law near the front.

Cold with nervousness and a strange apprehension, Maralyn stole timid glances round her. The church was dominated by a vast pulpit which had a kind of lower deck for the clerk. In a row beneath this pulpit sat half a dozen men, facing the congregation, and among these she recognised Mr Walker the hose-factor, Alec's old acquaintance. These men had notes in their hands and were busy studying them. The pulpit itself, with its sounding-board and hour-glass and large Bible laid out on a dusty velvet cushion, was empty at the moment, both in its upper and lower storeys. Despite herself, Maralyn began to feel some interest as she studied the congregation. It seemed a very representative gathering of the trading class, yet she was astonished to observe that there was no order of precedence. In St Pancras' church, the master craftsmen and their families occupied the front pews, the journeymen sat immediately behind, and behind them again sat the apprentices, while at the very back, under the galleries, were accommodated the charity children and the bedesmen and women, and ranged in a row with their backs to the communion table the watermen had their traditional place. But here, master craftsmen and journeymen and 'prentices were mingled together and seemed to find nothing strange about it. She noted, too, that there was a curiously tense air about the whole congregation; the men seemed to have forgotten their business and the women their housewifery in an affair of more importance; the 'prentices refrained from giggling and whispering, and the very children behaved with an unnatural sobriety, staring with wide innocent eyes upon the vast pulpit and speaking to their parents in a sedate whisper. This solemnity and attentiveness of a gathering so representative of Scotland's trading class, this forsaking of their trade by laborious men upon a weekday, impressed themselves upon Maralyn, the widow of a Scot and the daughter of a tradesman, and, rather conscience-stricken, she set herself to remember all that she had heard during the last few years concerning the proposed Union.

It was but odds and ends of gossip and did not make much sense to her. There had been talk of a Union, she recalled, soon after the failure of the Darien venture; she remembered hearing the ale-conner say to her father that "Scotland is to be starved into a union with us, and that is the truth of it". The phrase had stuck in her mind because of its ugliness, but because of her determination not to think upon public affairs she had refused to investigate the meaning of it. Somewhere about the year 1704 she had heard stories of riots in the North; the Scots were hungry and desperate and had demanded unrestricted trade with England as compensation for the loss of Darien. And then, last year, Maralyn had been told that thirty-one Scottish Commissioners had arrived in London to debate with those of England an "entire" Union. Immediately, fresh tales of riot and insurrection had come filtering down from the North, frightening tales of wild Highlandmen swarming into Edinburgh to league with the Lowland malcontents against what they regarded as the threat to Scottish independence, of stones thrown at the windows of those lords known to be in favour of the measure, and of the rioters being pelted with white roses as they stood in the pillory. Some said that the Horse Guards had been brought into the city to overawe the populace, a measure never adopted in Edinburgh before.

So much Maralyn remembered, a hazy impression as of an anthill disturbed by some incomprehensible uneasiness. And she had no wish to comprehend it; she sensed that there was danger in such comprehension, though she could not tell why. She did not understand the Scots, though she had married one, but having shared the Darien tragedy with them she had come to admire them and to lose that inbred prejudice against them which was rife among the City trading class. It was not, therefore, that she had no interest in their welfare as a nation. It was rather that a dim fear haunted her lest an understanding of the Union business might continue the work which Glencoe and Darien had inaugurated in her mind. Fresh from the horrors of the broken faith which had wrecked Darien, she had cried at Michael Pennington: "It is not good to think upon these matters. It is dangerous to think that way." If there was moral cowardice in that cry, there was also a genuine humility. She was a working woman, the daughter of a small tradesman, and as such she was not fitted to judge public men and their actions. To refrain was, indeed, to shut one's eyes to many things, to the strange refusal of the Government to abolish the gin scandal, to Her Majesty's ignoring of a certain petition presented by the Brewers' Company against spirits, to the heavy burden of taxation which rose higher every year. But there were times when to shut one's eyes was the only thing to do if one would live peaceable and continue to be a good subject and to remember who one was. Were she better educated, and a man, she would understand the reason behind these grievances; but since she was a very ignorant woman, she had best ignore public affairs and occupy herself with the matters she understood.

Yet now it seemed that, whether she would or no, one public affair was to be forced upon the attention of Maralyn Moray; for here came the minister, Mr Whitehead, to make all plain.

(iii)

As soon as she saw him there in the pulpit, she knew that here was an impressive personality. His outward appearance was extraordinary enough, for in that clean-shaven age he wore a black beard which climbed up his cheeks to meet his low-growing hair, and in place of the surplice to which she was accustomed in men of his calling in church, he was garbed in a black gown with two little bib-like bands at his throat. But she soon forgot these details in her intense interest in the man himself. Never had she seen such large, steady eyes or a face that had so much rugged power in it. He spoke deliberately and naturally as though in conversation with friends, yet the simple words and manner filled her with a feeling of awe, as though he had been some biblical prophet.

"My brethren, we are met together here this day, not as men of one communion in matters of religion, nor yet as men of one nation, but as the children of that God Who is the foundation of justice and the source of liberty. We believe that the matter now being debated yonder at Whitehall concerns not the quarrel betwixt two parties or two nations, but trespasses upon the sacred rights and privileges of human creatures. It has been asked of Scotland that she sell her birthright for a mess of pottage and, unlike Esau, she has refused. Therefore is she to have her birthright wrested from her, and this is an offence to God as well as man. I tell you this, being myself an Englishman; yet, please God, I am a Christian first. As for you, the principal among you being of Scotland, you must be doubly concerned with so intolerable an act, and I am sure that the destiny of your own nation, the ancient independence and the national liberties for which your fathers so often ventured their lives, will persuade you to put by all differences of creed and party and opposing views in lesser matters, that you may unite in the fight for liberty and fundamental justice which has called you to this church today. You are to hear the voices of several speakers, each representing some opposing sect, religious or political; but I believe, nay I know, that you will find that all, from whatever viewpoint, arrive at the selfsame conclusion: That a nation is not to be bought and sold, that Almighty God Who gave to men the aweful gift of free-will gave it to nations likewise, and that if it can be done by lawful means, this proposed Union is to be prevented, being altogether abhorrent, not only to all true sons of Scotland, but to all righteous men."

He ceased, yet remained standing where he was, making a small gesture with his hand towards the row of men seated facing the congregation; and immediately one of them sprang up, came briskly round the base of the pulpit, and entered the lower tier.

This first speaker was in striking contrast in his manner to the minister. He began by flinging wide his arms and in a voice of doom exhorting his audience to "Remember Flodden!" Then came a dramatic pause; and then, in a spate of fiery eloquence, he rehearsed the wrongs which Scotland had suffered from her stronger neighbour throughout the centuries, the repeated ravaging of her southern counties, the burnings of Edinburgh itself, the bribery, the treachery, the cynical bad faith which, he asserted, had been the hall-mark of the "auld enemy" throughout countless ages. He did not disclose to which party, if any, he belonged; his was the simple and effective eloquence of the patriot. He possessed a keen love and exact knowledge of old glories; he described old sorrows as though he had himself experienced them; he became Scotland, high and low, rich and poor, Presbyterian and Episcopalian, Highland and Lowland; and in an admirable flight of fancy he depicted Caledonia, venerable with age and honour, striving to shelter beneath a tattered plaid her children threatened by the ruthless Saxon and spurning the defiled riches offered by alien hands.

"It wad be lang," he concluded, "before sic trash makes up for Flodden."

His audience received his rhetoric in a silence more eloquent than tears.

He was followed by a most precise and dry little man who consulted notes and gave his hearers careful statistics. He spoke with the charming accent of Aberdeen, and stated proudly that he was indeed the son of a woollen merchant of that town. He had studied the whole matter from the point of view of the trading classes, and stated his conclusions somewhat in this manner: the English wished to exploit the Scots and force them to share in the recent taxes with which the southern kingdom was being burdened by the war against France. But Scotland had no quarrel with France. She would be made to share, moreover, in this sinister National Debt, which was growing year by year and which certainly was no affair of hers. The English land-tax would be put upon her likewise, which would be an intolerable burden and injustice since her immemorial habit was to pay such dues in kind. The trade with France, an hereditary trade, would be debarred, and as a very questionable substitute she would be given trade with England, the terms of that trade being dictated by English merchants. "The poor will cry in vain for ale and bread", was the gloomy prophecy with which this speaker ended his discourse.

Next came a rabid Presbyterian, a spiritual descendant of John Knox. Employing all the old tricks of thumping the pulpit cushion, beating his breast, weeping, and leaning so far over the ledge that it seemed he must land at any moment in the laps of those who sat in the front pews, he denounced the Union as a truckling with a prelatic nation and a Cause of Wrath. Maralyn found him very difficult to follow, for he referred to the sponsors of the Union under biblical names and intermixed quotations from the Old Testament so freely with his own denunciations that she grew more and more confused. Those among the audience who were of his persuasion punctuated his discourse with fierce ejaculations and savage encouragements. In an effective but obscure alliteration, the speaker affirmed that if they permitted the Union they would find themselves "blastit wi' Bishops and Belials", and in a last wild flight of denunciation he consigned to perdition Popery, Prelacy, the Pretender, England and the Union, everything, in fact, except the "true Kirk of Christ's Evangel". There was an exhausted kind of pause when he sat down.

Several other speakers followed, and lastly there arose Mr Walker the hose-factor, the friend of Alec in his apprenticeship days. He was a little sandy man, a man you knew instinctively carried a foul pipe somewhere about his person and who would draw on it and puff and speak and then draw and puff again, who liked his dram and could carry it, who knew his way about, was perfectly at home in all sorts of company, and could be depended upon to find a way out of all sorts of dilemmas and to suck the cream off all sorts of gossip. Canny: that was the word which came into your mind when you met Mr Walker the hose-factor.

He stood in the lower deck of that vast pulpit with as much ease as if he had been standing at his own house door. He made a mechanical gesture to reach for his pipe, recollected himself, grinned, and clasped his hands behind his back. He looked upon the audience in silence for a while, upon men and women, already swayed and emotionalised by so many speakers. He regarded them with a serious face and an incipient twinkle, and then he began to talk in a confidential fashion and with an indefinable accent which yet was as the very breath of the North.

"Harkee, friends, I'm a plain man, a kind o' travelling man, who meets all but to say fareweel, and has no bit ground in a' Scotland or England he can ca' his ain. There are many like me, and 'tis for them I speak. Whiles we sit, when the day's wark is over, and we think. Ken ye of what we think, neighbours? Why, maybe 'tis o' the Honours of Scotland lying snug in Edinburgh Castle, or o' the Estates debating the affairs o' Scotland in the Tolbooth, or maybe 'tis of a burn wherein we paidled when we were bairns, a bit croft and kail-yard, or a half-forgotten sang. For wheresoever we roam these things abide, and the knowledge that they so abide is our comfort and our peace at last. I ken not why this should be so, but I ken it is."

He paused a while and his glance roamed over his audience in a gently ruminative manner, while he rocked backwards and forwards on his feet.

"Now, if ye are wishful to hae the facts concerning this Union, neighbours, I can gie you them; guid grief, I came hither wi' them at my fingers 'ends. I ken what Queensberry is promised out o' it, and Stair, and Marchmont and Mar and the rest. I could gie you it exact, pounds, shillings and pence, though it wad burn my tongue as it wad offend your ears to hear the sorry tale o' it. For make no mistake about it, neighbours; Scotland is being sold by Scots lairds to English nobles for money down. But I'll not descend to it. Instead, I'll tell ye this. If yon swankies have their way and this Union is made law, a plain man like me willna dare to think, when day is done, upon the Honours of Scotland; they'll be lying snug in the Tower yonder, to be stared at for a curiosity by those Saxons who have tired of their ain rarities. The Estates will sit no langer at the Tolbooth; the affairs of Scotland will be debated at Westminster, if there is time to spare for sic clish-ma-claver after those of England have been thrashit out by my Lords and Gentlemen. As for the sangs we learnt when we were bairns, I dinna think we'll want to mind them, for an auld sang will be ended and there'll be no heart in us for national airs. And for our burns and our crofts and our kail-yards, they will have gae'd the way o' our laws, and Scotland hersel' will have become a kind of raree-show, a place whereto men travel for to glow'r at the ancient manners of a dying race, and exclaim, putting up their quizzing-glasses: 'Och, what a humorous wee country is here! Damme I'll buy me a demesne here for a mere sang, and come hither to refresh me with game and venison and mountain air when I have made my fortune on 'Change.' And thus will they benefit Scotland, neighbours; they will turn out the crofters and build muckle palaces for themselves, and preserve our natural food by making it sacred to their ain love of sport, and they will gar our people become their hired men, the ha' folk o' rich lairds, even as they have made the peasantry of England. And in return for giving them our freedom, we are to hae the leavings of their trade when they hae finished wi' it. Och weel, maybe I'm a wee bit daft, but I'd no feel very easy with siller in my pocket got by selling my native earth, and the price of my liberty is so high that there is not gold enough even in rich England to purchase it."

He had spoken entirely without emotion, and now, with a little nod to the congregation, strolled back to his seat. The minister came forward again to the edge of the upper deck of the pulpit, and made known to his hearers that there was a petition got up to be presented to the English Parliament, that it bore near upon one thousand signatures, that if there were some here present who had not yet signed they were invited to do so now, and that then it would be carried, that very evening, to the door of the House of Commons.

"When there was debate at Westminster concerning the demonstrations in Scotland against the Union," he continued quietly, "a certain English Minister was pleased to declare that it was but 'the whine of the rascal multitude'. We intend to give him the lie in this teeth, brethren, by means of this petition, signed by all sorts and conditions of Scotsmen, good subjects of our Gracious Queen, living here in London. Now, by the Common Law of England, the subject has a right to petition Parliament, so such petition be humble and decent and presented in a peaceable manner. I, being an English subject, claim my Common Law right to present such a petition, and I invite ye all to follow me to Westminster to be a witness to this mine act."

(iv)

At some later period of time, Maralyn found herself walking down St Martin's Lane in the direction of Charing Cross, hemmed in by men and women who marched in orderly procession, some of them carrying torches (for the early dusk was falling), all of them silent and purposeful, while a little distance ahead, all alone, like some strange general walked the black-bearded, black-gowned figure of the minister.

It was all too fantastic to be true. It was absurd to imagine that she, Maralyn Moray, the daughter of a City brewer, a quiet, self-effacing working-woman who had made so firm a resolve to ignore public affairs, was really and truly walking in a procession down the London streets amid a crowd of people strange to her and hostile to her race, with the intention of supporting a Presbyterian minister who was determined to present a petition against a piece of national policy. Either she really was in a dream and the meeting, the speeches, and the petition were all part of it, or else she was mad. And something whispered in her mind that it was a dangerous sort of madness.

And yet, though apprehension and even thrills of a wild terror made her mouth dry and her heart race, there was a kind of unfamiliar enthusiasm which sustained her and drove her forward. The whole fantastic episode of that afternoon had carried her away as never in her life had she been carried away before, and she was goaded forward as, like little tongues of flames, disconnected sentences leapt up to light a kind of conflagration in her simple mind. "It is the end of an auld sang"; "I ken what Queensberry is promised out o' it"; "Remember Flodden"; "The subject has a right to petition Parliament"; "I, being an English subject, claim my Common Law right"; "The price of my liberty . . . the price of my liberty." It was Alec's voice that spoke those burning words; they had crucified Alec; King William had crucified Alec; King William had crucified Scotland, but good Queen Anne would take her down from the cross. But it was not only Alec's voice; it was her father's also. Her father had petitioned Queen Anne against this demon gin; maybe he and his Company had no right in Common Law to do that, but they could claim custom for it, and yet Queen Anne had not listened. But Parliament would have to listen; it would be compelled to listen to an English subject petitioning it, because that was his right by Common Law. She understood this and held on to it as though it were a rock in a stormy sea.

The procession had halted and she had halted with it. She was in the rear ranks and she could not see what was happening there in front. A voice was speaking in her ear, Mrs Moray's voice, but she did not recognise it; she was deaf to everything but her own tumultuous thoughts. The dusk was falling rapidly, but she could make out the outline of a gate-house against the sky; scraps of conversation from those around her drifted into her ears and out again: "King Street Gate; they say it narrowly escaped the fire of '96"; "He would not have us to go with him to the door of the House but to stay here lest they complained of so great a concourse"; "The Commissioners are sitting yonder at the Cockpit"; "Pray God the petition is in time; they say that Stair and Mar are hot to bring all to an end and claim their reward." Dusk turned to dark as she stood there, forgetting where she was or who she was, light-headed from hunger and fatigue and emotion; the torches spilled great pools of ruddy light like blood upon the ground and figures swayed and fidgeted in the glare. There was talking now, but she could not distinguish any words; she saw a man's face turned over his shoulder, the mouth gabbling rapidly to someone behind. Then many faces were turned and a strange mutter, like distant thunder, surged through the crowd, and instantly her old instinctive fear and hatred of the mob and of the dark leapt up in her and she shrank into herself, cold with apprehension. Someone was jostling his way in her direction from the front ranks, speaking to those around him as he passed; whatever he said seemed to stir the crowd into an even fiercer animation, for they began to gesticulate and to surge backwards and forwards, and a woman's voice cried shrilly "Shame! Shame!"

Then in fainting terror she felt her arm grasped by a firm hand, and a voice she knew said sharply:

"Harkee, mistress. You're Alec's wife, and for auld acquaint-

ance' sake I have sought you out to bid you run hame while
there is time. I'll take care of the auld lady yonder, but do you
gang back to your father's house and make haste about it."

"What is it? What is it?" she whispered, staring fearfully
upon him.

"They have arrested the minister," said Mr Walker the hose-
factor tersely, "and they hae sent for the Foot Guards to disperse our folk."

"No," she said, with a hand to her mouth. "No, it is not
true."

"They called in Mr Whitehead and he owned the petition at
the bar," continued Walker rapidly and inexorably, "then, he
withdrawing, the petition was read. The House was pleased to
resolve that 'The said Petition is scandalous, insolent and seditious, tending to subvert the established government of these
realms', and it was ordered that Mr Whitehead be taken into
custody as guilty of promoting the petition."

She stared at him, her face bloodless, her mind whirling, a
deathly coldness occupying her body. Then with a cry she
turned and began to push and thrust her way through the multitude, one thought possessing her to the exclusion of all else:
to get back to the City, to the brewhouse, to her kitchen, to her
housewifery, to the dear safe stable things to which she belonged.

(v)

She ran without pausing until she came to St Clement Dane's.
There, leaning against the railing which enclosed the graveyard,
she stopped to get her breath; it was quiet here, for most folk
were in the taverns; some link-boys trotted by, going to seek
custom outside the Duke's Theatre in Portugal Row, and a few
furtive figures slunk along the side-walk, but that was all. She
was come out of ear-shot of Charing Cross where, she reflected
with a shudder, the Foot Guards would be busy dispersing a
crowd of bewildered, indignant men and women who had gone
thither so confidently and so peaceably to present a petition to
Parliament; but the mere thought of those men and women made

her begin to hurry eastwards again, and she was sobbing as she went and muttering to herself, striving with all her will to push from her, not the memory of the menace she left behind, but something yet more frightening, something she carried with her in her heart. It is no concern of mine. I have my father to consider, and my son. And I have a supper to put on the fire. I was mad to go to that church. Those people seemed peaceable, but my Lords and Gentlemen at Westminster do not arrest men without just cause. The Edinburgh mob burned the articles of Union, they say, and pelted the chair of Mr Daniel Defoe who was sent thither to persuade them to accept the measure. That was rebellion. Parliament fears that there will be the like revolt here unless it acts with firmness. I did not read the petition; doubtless it was—what was it?—scandalous, insolent, and seditious, as they said, or they never would have arrested the minister. Anyway it is no concern of mine. I did not set my hand to the petition, thanks be to God, so they cannot harm my father. I am a law-abiding housewife of London City. I have nothing to do with great matters and petitions and the Union. It is no concern of mine. I have my father to consider, and my son. And I have a supper to put on the fire. . . .

Thus she muttered to herself, over and over again, repeating these sensible, sane phrases in order to crush down the bewilderment, the clamorous questions, the sneaking self-shame which possessed her inmost heart. But the something within her would not be easily crushed. It was a seed sown there long ago by the story of Glencoe, watered by the experience of Darien, nourished by the spectacle of her own mother dying mad from gin, a seed of doubt and of deep questioning of all she had been taught to believe infallible. It had grown without her knowing it, and even now, though it was a hardy plant, she did not recognise it for what it was. It had grown every time she had talked in her loneliness and deep uneasiness to the new-lit fire and to her pewter when she polished it. Glencoe and Darien and gin had made her think, really think, for the first time in her life, and although she had known from the first and by instinct that such thought was not only improper but dangerous, destroying peace of mind, she had never been able completely to recapture her old absolute faith in all she had been taught to believe without question. And now today such thought had driven her to a stupid, a dangerous, a fantastic action, to going to a dissenters' meeting-house and listening to, even being fired by, seditious speeches cunningly wrapped up in patriotism, to marching in a public procession and risking arrest. . . . Thinking with a shudder of the Maralyn who could do these things, of the Maralyn she had fostered so unconsciously for all these years, experiencing for the first time fully the pounce of her secret mind, she felt as one who, going to open a familiar cupboard, sees a lion spring out.

Cheapside at last, dear, orderly, sober Cheapside. But perhaps because it was so orderly and sober she looked upon it with a sense of shame. Her father would be waiting for her, reproachful, anxious, supperless. She could not face her father; not just yet, not until she had regained some self-control, some common sense, not until she was sure she would not shout aloud to him the fragmentary doubts which racked her and tossed her poor simple bewildered mind to and fro like a toy boat on the ocean. She was cold and dishevelled and deadly tired; she realised suddenly that she was walking the streets of London at night; for the first time in her life, unescorted, she was doing that which no respectable woman or prudent man ever did do, she was braving the City streets after dark. When she thought that, she began to run again; to her mental anguish were added the physical terrors of footpads, of drunken bullies, of kidnappers, of pimps in search of prey, of the dreaded Mohocks; she was wholly possessed by fear, in body and in soul, as she came at last, panting and exhausted, into Bird-in-Hand Court and to her father's door.

So utterly beside herself was poor Maralyn that she ended that day with an action more uncharacteristic, more crazy even, than her marching in procession to petition Parliament. She raced up the stairs, burst open a door, and stood breathless, filled with a slowly mounting tide of horror at herself, in the garret of Michael Pennington.

(vi)

It was empty.

In the first engulfing of relief she leaned weakly back against the door, thankful only to find herself alone and safe within doors. Then, after a while, her glance began to stray around the room. She had never been up here since Mr Pennington had come to live in the house; it was his room, his domain; sometimes she had been half minded to offer to clean it for him, but had never made that offer because she was shy of him, not only because he was of a different class from herself but because she sensed, without ever articulating the thought, that he was a man with a secret. She did not know the nature of that secret, but she was vaguely afraid of it, and of him. Yet he was always kind and considerate; he worked hard and had stuck faithfully to her father in good times and in bad. Little Alec adored him, and her father trusted him, and the rabble of apprentices, though they gaped at him and gossiped freely about him (she had heard them), gave him a grudging sort of respect. And although he had a disconcerting habit of disregarding the conventions in which she had been reared, as when sometimes he used her christian name or spoke in a manner rather too free, she was perfectly aware that as a woman she had nothing to fear from him, and that in heart and action he would never give her anything but a respectful friendship.

Something akin to awe fell on her as she stared around the miserable garret in which his private life was lived. Her father had told her that he was an author, that he was engaged upon some learned treatise; she had accepted the story readily enough, though sometimes she wondered a little because he never appeared in print so far as she knew, and it must be, she thought, some very monumental work that was not yet completed after all these years. But she did not understand such things and, at least in the past, her habit was to dismiss from her mind matters which she could not comprehend. A little excitement stirred in her now, seeing his inferior quills, shortened to a few inches from constant sharpening, lying in a brass standish, his books standing in a neat pile upon the floor, and a little trunk in one corner, a genteel sort of trunk which obviously had seen better days, which might have contained at one time or another fine clothes or important documents, which might even have accompanied a gentleman upon the Grand Tour. Scarce knowing what she did, she moved a little nearer to the table; it was sad to see so pretty a standish tarnishing for want of a good clean. She bent down to rub it with a corner of her cloak, and now she thought she could make out a crest and motto on it. Then, at a slight sound from behind her, she whipped round with a startled cry; and there was Michael Pennington standing in the doorway.

"I am exceeding honoured by this visit, Mistress Maralyn," said he, uncovering and bowing to her, with only a very faint hint of surprise in his smile. "You desired to see me? Will you not sit down and give me your commands?"

She sank into the chair he placed for her, staring at him; then, before she knew what she was about, her pent-up emotion found relief in a burst of rapid speech.

"I was carried by my mother-in-law to a meeting of protest against the Union at a—a church. They seemed a decent sort of people. I did not want to go, but Mrs Moray insisted. There was much talk. I did not understand it all, but it seemed to me that all were against the Union though of different opinions in other matters. There was a petition got up to present to Parliament, and the minister carried it thither after the meeting, he being an Englishman and claiming his right by Common Law so to do. We all went with him to witness his act. But they arrested him, and said the petition was—was seditious and mischievous, and more besides which I cannot remember, and they sent the Foot Guards to disperse us, and then I, being very fearful, ran home. I had no supper prepared and my father would be anxious and it was no affair of mine. I ought not to have gone. I know not why I let myself be persuaded. But Mrs Moray——" She broke off, then added in a low voice as though compelled to it: "Mr Pennington, is it indeed true that according to the Common Law the subject has a right to petition Parliament?"

"It is true, mistress."

"Then why did they arrest Mr Whitehead? He went thither

peaceably, and he was a good man, though maybe mistaken in his views. I did not read the petition, and perhaps it was seditious, but I am sure he did not intend it so, for from his speech and look I am sure that he was a worthy, honest man and no malcontent. And from all that I have heard it is plain the greater part of the Scottish nation is against this Union, and it is not right, it cannot be right, that so weighty a matter should be decided without the protests of the people being heard. Maybe they know not what is good for them, and that, like children, they desire that which will certainly harm them. Yes, that would be it, I suppose, and I am sure our Government must know best about such affairs. Yet I cannot understand why they should arrest Mr Whitehead, an Englishman and a good subject, when he acted peaceably and according to law."

He said nothing for a moment, but came and sat down on the table, folding his arms and staring at the floor. Then he raised his eyes and met hers and held them, and said:

"When King Charles the First stood in that same House of Commons at his illegal trial he said: 'I am not suffered to speak. Expect what justice other men will have.' I think he was a true prophet, Mistress Maralyn. Today you have seen the Common Law overriden; what more is wanting to convince you?"

"To—to convince me?"

"Of the peril in which you stand."

"I know not what you mean."

"Let me remind you of somewhat else which was said by King Charles on the occasion I have mentioned. 'If power without law may make law, may alter the fundamental law of the kingdom, I know not what man there is in England can be sure of his life or anything that he may call his own.' Of what can you be sure, after today?"

"I am but an ignorant woman and know nought of these great matters. But I had hoped that you—oh, I know not what I hoped."

"Perhaps that I would explain away the tyrannical act you have witnessed, that I would give you comfort and assurance that all was well. But all is not well, and I do not think comfort is what you need, for it suggests forgetfulness, a closing of the eyes, and that is dangerous. I would rather prick you into activity, you and your like, rouse you out of sleep, open your eyes to the stark peril which confronts you. For you are in peril, Maralyn, in deadly, urgent peril, you and all of us. Unless we face that peril, and take steps to escape it, it may be in a little while too late, and we will find ourselves enslaved."

"It would not be permitted——"

"By whom? By the Sovereign? It is not so very long ago that you were made aware how little power remains with the Sovereign, when your father's Company petitioned against the scandal of gin and the petition was ignored, not, you may be sure, because Queen Anne is in favour of ruining her subjects, but because the great ones in the realm find themselves enriched by gin. Who then will not permit the enslavement of the people? Parliament? Today you have seen a cynical overriding by Parliament of the ancient and most sacred Common Law because a brave man dared to voice the protest of a whole nation."

She sprang up and cried at him:

"We shall not permit it, we, all decent laborious people."

At that he too leapt up, and she was astonished by the fire in his eyes and voice:

"Ah, if I could but believe it! You could stop the rot, you and yours; but will you? Are you even convinced that it is there? Of all classes and degrees of men the most difficult to arouse and unite are the decent trading people of England. You are immersed in your craft and in the problems of your daily life; you are content to leave affairs of State to your rulers, and you were right when your ruler was a lawful ruler, the ancient guardian and protector of your lives and liberties. But you are wrong, and dangerously wrong, when you are content to leave them in the hands of a greedy, self-seeking faction, which itself is getting more and more into the power of mere wealth. Yet you could save yourselves if you would but act now.'"

"I don't understand. I don't understand. What is it you would have us do?"

"Get back the King."

"You mean——" She did not finish the sentence but stared at him, horror slowly filling her eyes. Then she took a step backward from him, and whispered, with mingled revulsion and incredulity: "You're a Jack! Yes, that is your secret, Master Pennington; you're a Jack."

He smiled at her.

"Yes, Mistress Maralyn, I am a Jack. What then?"

"What then? Why that is—is treasonable, rebellious, wicked. It means the Pretender and assassination plots and vulgar rioting and a fetching over of the Pope and the French army."

"You have learned your lesson very well, my dear," he said bitterly. "You learned it with the criss-cross row in your horn-book at your mother's knee, and it has stuck. They are clever, those who crammed your generation with such stuff; God damn their rotten hearts. Yet is there one item, Maralyn, which you forgot in that list of evils which the name Jacobite calls up in your mind. Arbitrary power; you forgot that, you know." He paused and smiled one-sidedly. "Or is it possible that you have had your stomachful of arbitrary power this day?"

She said nothing; she was leaning weakly against the chair-back, and so pitiful was the look of bewilderment upon her face that he made an involuntary movement to take her in his arms like a hurt child. But she drew back instantly, and straightened up, and walked quickly past him to the door without a word.

"Are you going to denounce me, mistress?" he asked gently. "Sure it is your duty if you deem me dangerous and a rebel."

She glanced back at him from the door, and there was a kind of dignity in her look.

"I am going to put my father's supper on the fire, sir. That is my duty, and that, at least, I understand."

PART FOUR

One

(i)

T H E Act of Union received the Royal Assent upon the 6th of
March, 1707, and the City taverns and coffee-houses began to
forget Scotland in more exciting matters. A new light was appearing at Court, and its name was Abigail Masham; she was a mere
bed-chamber woman, but it was whispered that she had two
hours' private talk with Her Majesty every day, and was beginning slowly but surely to oust the all-powerful Duchess of
Marlborough from the royal favour. The Whig lampoonists began
straightway to choose Masham's large red nose for their favourite
theme, and the Duchess tried some of her famous rages in an
effort to bring Anne to heel. For Masham was the friend, some
said the mistress, of Robert Harley, and Harley was the accepted
leader of the Tories. By 1711 the Duchess had been officially
dismissed, Harley was Chancellor of the Exchequer, Anne,
surrounded by Tories, was speaking of herself as being freed
from a long captivity, and Marlborough, returning from his
last campaign, found his dismissal from all employments already
decided upon.

Thus ran the great world; but in the little world of the Cock-
on-the-Hoop brewhouse those years were less exciting. Mr
Vance still zealously pursued his "mistery", relaxed among his
authors, and dined and quarrelled with John Bunch; he was bewildered and cast down by the Queen's ignoring of his Company's petition against gin, increasingly worried over the falling
off of his trade, and maliciously gratified over the new tax imposed on hops. Maralyn worked harder than ever in the brewhouse, cared for her growing boy, and resolutely sang about her

work; but she seemed sometimes preoccupied as though she had thoughts which troubled her, and it might have been re- marked by an acute observer that she took pains to avoid being alone with Mr Pennington, and that her manner to him had be- come rather constrained. Michael himself still totted up accounts in his ledgers, retired to his garret in the evenings, and disappeared every Sunday on his personal affairs. But he frowned a good deal as he pored over his ledgers, often sallied forth to collect outstanding debts and returned empty-handed and de- pressed, looked very grey and drawn sometimes in the morn- ing, as though he had stayed too long at his writing overnight, and had a dogged air about him as of a man refusing with all his will to admit defeat.

These years then, whatever they signified in the larger world, brought to the tiny world of a City brewhouse only a kind of melancholy attrition, a slow fatigue and decay. Vance and Mara- lyn and Michael were all growing older, which was in the nature of things; but it seemed that they were all growing older in spirit, and that was not. Mr Vance's father had died at the age of eighty-four with a can of strong-ale in his hand, sitting in the enclosed arm-chair now sacred to his son, roaring out the air of *The Leathern Bottle,* his heart permanently young and carefree and only his digestion fatally impaired by a long series of ban- quets at Brewers' Hall. His son was but sixty, as hale a man as his sire, as excellent a craftsman, as confirmed an optimist. Mara- lyn's face and figure had retained to a remarkable degree a look of youth. Michael had the healthy constitution of the country- man, a constitution which will defy all kinds of hardship and privation. Yet there was in all three of them this slow attrition of spirit, this sad, scarcely perceptible wearing out of the heart by ceaseless, petty friction from outside circumstances, as a stone will become hollowed through the years by the constant drip of water.

Of all that household, only poor Nick Hammond seemed the same.

They did not see much of Nick nowadays, for long ago he had gone to lodge in some mean room in a tenement off Cheapside, and his evenings were spent with his poor little Jacobite club. He

266

worked hard in the brewhouse and never gave his master cause for complaint, though Mr Vance suspected with indignation and amazement that Nick's mind was not entirely occupied with the mistery of brewing ale. Nick was still the fanatic, still the hothead who must always endanger his cause, his comrades and himself by unbridled zeal. Often such men die young or turn cynic. Nick had done neither. The light burned strong behind those over-large eyes of his, his heart retained its simplicity, and his mind did not develop; in his late thirties he was as burningly sincere and as incapable of concealing his feelings as in his teens. The new set of 'prentices sneered and giggled at him as spitefully as the old had done when he himself had been of their number; he still flushed up crimson when Maralyn addressed him, still devoured her with his eyes, still adored her with the fierce, innocent, and almost sublime worship of the boy. He had loved her and lost her and had learnt since that she never could be his, that she was faithful to the memory of the dead Alec; but none of that made the slightest difference to his piteous devotion.

It was the same with his Jacobitism. His wretched little club had never achieved anything except a successful raid on some Whig club of the same type, and the failure of the attempt of 1708 seemed to have sealed the fate of his cause; but Nick never despaired of a successful revolution in which he himself should take a leading part. What would happen after that revolution was accomplished he did not trouble to enquire. He would have given his life to bring back King James; exactly what King James would do when restored, or in what way his restoration would benefit England, was not Nick's business. He did not argue thus with himself; he simply never gave it a thought. The vice of the masochist was mingled with the virtue of the martyr in his nature, and his secret pastime consisted in seeing himself in all sorts of unpleasant situations, facing perils and doing daring deeds for the sake of his ideal. He played perpetually the game which is proper only to children, the dangerous and fascinating game of confounding enemies and pleasing idols by an imaginary, horrible, but always dignified sacrifice of life or limb. He composed dying speeches which brought exquisite tears to his eyes over the mash-tub, and when he walked down Cheapside to his miserable lodging of an evening, in fancy he was walking to the scaffold between the ranks of an admiring multitude.

He was a child also in his love of secret societies, cant names, passwords and fantastic plots. He would go without his supper any day for the pleasure of rapping in a certain secret manner on the door of the cellar wherein met his club. The small-beer in which he drank the health of "The little gentleman in black velvet" (the mole which inadvertently had caused the death of Dutch William) tasted like nectar because of his enthusiasm for the toast; and the wild plot and counterplot, the ceaseless, futile intrigue which went on underground among those of his party, made the most dreary day and the most humdrum task exciting and delightful.

Yet all the while, unknown to himself or anyone else, there lay somewhere deep down in poor Nick Hammond a potential nobility which one day might appear to startle himself and his friends.

(ii)

In the late autumn of 1711 Maralyn fell seriously ill.

The apothecary, the poor man's doctor, whom Mr Vance hastily consulted, diagnosed a quantan ague and bade the brewer send for a barber-surgeon. That worthy arrived with his lancet and basin, threw a handkerchief over the patient's face that she might not see the blood, and bade her squeeze the ball of worsted he placed in her hand in order to make the veins swell. Then, bidding the anxious father hold the basin at the correct distance, he touched a blue vein with his lancet and a jet of blood leapt forth, part of it spurting into the basin and part over the surgeon's clean apron, to that gentleman's extreme annoyance. Having decided that the case required bleeding *ad defectionem*, as it was called, he took eight ounces of blood from the patient, two and a half for health and five and a half for the ague. He was much put out to find that Maralyn had not fainted as was customary, crossly ordered her a dose of taraxacum mixed with Rhenish wine, pocketed his fee, and withdrew. Maralyn, very white but smiling, soothed her anxious father, asked him to infuse some betony, rosemary and wormwood in clear ale, and to take away the basin of blood lest it frighten her son. Then, having attended to these practical matters, she quietly swooned away.

It was not a quantan ague from which she suffered; it was a complete breakdown of mind and body. She was no longer young, and behind her lay years of physical overwork and mental strain. With her old dogged courage she set herself to the task of recovery, refusing to see the apothecary or the barber-surgeon again, dosing herself with the home-made remedies with which her store cupboard was always stocked, and resigning herself to a short rest in bed. She was not so successful in her task as usual, for it was many months before she could leave her room.

To Mr Vance's anxiety for his daughter's welfare was added the worry resulting from the lack of her services in the brewhouse. For many years now, Maralyn had been her father's right hand in his craft, and now that she was laid by he was left with only Nick Hammond and a handful of apprentices. For a while he set himself to make the best of the situation by working harder than ever himself, but he was in late middle-age and the herculean task of doing his own share and Maralyn's as well was plainly beyond him. After a month or so of this hopeless struggle, during which his health began to suffer, he went out early one morning dressed in his Sabbath attire and with his wig upon his head. On his return he came trotting into the counting-house, sat down promptly and thankfully upon the chair Michael hastened to place for him, paused for a moment or two to get his breath, cleared his throat, and addressed his clerk in a solemn but somewhat nervous manner.

"It cannot have escaped your notice, Master Pennington, since you have charge of my books, that my trade is sadly fallen off of late years. Ahem! Yet, though I can ill afford his wages, it is become necessary that I engage another journeyman. My daughter, even when she is recovered (which pray God will be soon), must not be permitted to exert herself at the brewing as she has done in times past, and I shall be hard put to it to feed my household unless I have more skilled labour. I need more 'prentices likewise, as I very well know, though 'tis a great matter to support them during the long term of their indentures. And I will not follow, sir," cried Vance, with a look in his eyes as though he argued angrily, not with Michael, but with someone whom he had seen lately and who had insulted him, "I say I will not follow, sir, the abominable custom lately resorted to by certain masters I could name, I mean that of taking a 'prentice for the sake of his fee and afterwards being rid of him, either by ill-treatment so that he runs away or by tempting him to some species of misconduct which will justify the cancellation of his indentures without an order from a magistrate for the return of any part of the apprenticeship fee. 'Uds, sir, when I think upon such rogues as these, who consider not either the justice of God nor the sacrifice made by the lad's parents to ensure his maintenance and instruction in some honest trade, nor yet the responsibility they accept towards the lad himself, I am sure there is no punishment contained in the statute-book severe enough to be meted out to them."

Mr Vance, glaring more fiercely than ever upon the innocent Michael, paused to trumpet upon his nose.

"Now, sir," he resumed more calmly. "I have considered well and carefully mine own position, and I am convinced I must engage a journeyman and likewise one more 'prentice; that is the least I can make do with if my business is not altogether to fail. Now a good journeyman, a topping workman (and I will have no other), cannot be got for less than fifteen shillings a week, and Bunch tells me he pays twenty-five. As for the 'prentice, it has never been my custom to accept the children of the labouring poor, whose offspring are often sickly and ignorant, especially since this gin mania is come upon the City, but strong, well-grown lads whose fathers are used to bind their boys to the better sort of trades and to masters of good repute. But beggars, sir—ahem!—cannot be choosers, and I am willing at this time to take a lad for a mighty low fee, so he be industrious and willing, even though he be the son of a labourer. I will ask no more than five pounds with him," concluded Mr Vance modestly, "and I may tell you that I have a boy in mind I think will answer my purpose."

He then drew from his pocket a paper, which Michael could see was covered with writing and figures, many of them erased.

"Be good enough, Mr Pennington," said Vance, handing him this document, "to cast your eye over these estimates and give me your opinion upon 'em. And be sure, sir, to let me know if, in your view, I have anywhere erred."

Michael studied the paper carefully. He guessed that it was the result of much laborious meditation and of many hours of wrestling with figures; Mr Vance's skill with the mash-stick was unquestionable, but he would have been the first to admit that to him the pen was a clumsy instrument and that his knowledge of arithmetic was sadly lacking. But he was essentially a thorough and conscientious man, and having faced the fact of his new poverty, and resolved upon a remedy, he had not shrunk from desk-work. The result now lay in Michael's hand. Upon this paper Vance had worked out, first the total sum of paying a journeyman fifteen shillings a week for a year; from this he had subtracted what he thought would be added to his own business by the journeyman's labour. Then there followed the more teasing matter of the 'prentice; Mr Vance had considered it necessary to work out roughly the cost of feeding and otherwise providing for the lad, and he had done it somewhat in this manner:

"Breakfast: Bread and cheese, twopence. Dinner: Chuck beef or scrag of mutton or sheeps' trotters, cabbage or potatoes or turnips, bread, fivepence. Supper: Bread and cheese with radishes or onions, twopence and a halfpenny. A good dinner on Sundays, sixpence. For making two blue frocks of good strong dowlas, three shillings. For a best suit for Sundays, of serge, with a pair of stout shoes with iron buckles, fifteen shillings. Money for the pocket, per week fourpence. For a prayer-book and Bible, three shillings. A thrum-cap, sixpence." And so on.

"You will observe, sir," said Mr Vance, waving his hand towards the paper, "that I have not itemed ale. No workman of mine shall ever want for free ale while he is in my employ. As for the rest, I have reckoned by the prices of this current year, which, as you know, is a year of dearth and therefore prices are high. It is as well to be on the safe side, for one never knows what God is minded to send us. Well, sir," added the brewer, very brisk and business-like, "do you approve my reckoning?"

"I think it most neat and excellent, sir. But I must take the freedom to point out to you that you have not deducted from the grand total of expenses the apprenticeship fee which you will receive."

"Now, by St George!" cried Vance, slapping his thigh, "nor have I. 'Sheart, what an old fool am I! Five pounds, sir, five pounds is the tune of it. Pray now, Mr Pennington, make the sum for me, like the good lad you are. It makes a difference, sir," said the brewer, rubbing his hands in delight, "it makes a vast difference, I promise you."

"Nor have you reckoned in," continued Michael, making the simple correction, "the earnings of the 'prentice, which will be yours entirely."

But Mr Vance waved this aside.

"Nay, sir, nay, I have not bestirred me to do this. They earn but little, these lads, for several years, for all their time is taken up with learning their new craft, and we must not hustle them. You must not expect to find old heads on young shoulders," added Vance, glancing out of the window into the yard, where the sturdy little figure of his grandson, eleven years old now, could be seen, busily shovelling used grains into a countryman's cart. Then he crossed his short legs and, turning on Michael a very solemn face, resumed:

"Now, sir, this reckoning hath given me a notion of the round sum I shall require to justify me in engaging a topping workman and another 'prentice, and it is one hundred pounds. With that sum safely locked away in the strong-room of Mr Green, the goldsmith, I may feel confident in taking on such new responsibilities. But I had it not, nor nothing like it; and so I was constrained, sir, to borrow it."

Michael jerked up his head and looked at his employer with a certain anxiety.

"From Mr Bunch, sir? I do trust it was from some such friend."

"Bunch!" snapped his master, mightily affronted. "Certainly not, sir, certainly not. I—ahem!—I will own, sir," he continued, growing rather red, "that the pesty wine with which Bunch regaled me when I dined with him last week so far o'erthrew me that I blabbed to him of my necessity, and I will confess further, sir, that he straightway offered me the whole sum, ay, and vowed he would not take a penny interest on't. But I refused it, sir, I refused it; you must not deem me ungrateful, but I have my pride, and I will not, sir, I say I will not condescend to put myself under obligation to a concocter of that whip-belly vengeance called beer."

He paused, but Michael made no comment. Mr Vance uncrossed his legs, fidgeted with a button on his coat, cleared his throat, and at last blurted out in a tone of defiance:

"I borrowed the hundred pounds from Nat."

"From Nat? By way of business?"

"Of course, sir, of course. Mr Pennington, I have never borrowed before from any man, d'ye see, and I could not go to the Jews, and I would not go cap-in-hand to any of my neighbours, nor to Mr Green, who is a friend of mine, an old friend, and I—ahem!—I would not have such cronies know that—ahem!—that the Cock-on-the-Hoop was in desperate straits for money. But Nat is a banker, and so is accustomed to such—such deals; I went to him, you understand, purely in the way of business, and he has obliged me with a loan."

"May I ask upon what terms?"

"Why, naturally, sir, he demanded some—ahem!—security. He assured me 'twas the accepted custom of his craft. I could not at first bethink me what security I had to give, but he was pleased to point out to me that I had—ahem!—my brewhouse and my dwelling-house likewise."

"He took—your brewhouse and your dwelling-house—as security—for the loan of—one hundred pounds?"

"He assured me 'twas the custom, and I——"

"And interest likewise, I presume?"

"Naturally, sir, naturally. He was careful to point out to me, sir, that though the rate was somewhat high, such interest could not be termed usury. It seems that—ahem!—usury is—now what was it he said? Let me see; ay, I have it: usury is interest upon an unproductive loan. But this loan, being productive——"

"You have a copy of the deed of mortgage, Mr Vance? May I see it?"

Vance fished in his pocket and drew out a document. His hand shook a little as he handed it to Michael. The latter scanned it for some while in silence, then he lifted a flushed face and said thinly:

"Mr Vance, do you understand what is writ here? This loan is to be repaid within two years; if it is not so repaid, or if at any time the interest falls into arrears, your son is at liberty to seize upon your brewhouse and your dwelling-house, with all the goods which they contain. I really think you would have done better to have gone to the Jews."

"Pish, sir," cried Vance irritably, "you speak as though my son were some monster. He explained to me that such a bond is the accepted custom of the bankers, and told me himself that he knew my proper pride would forbid me to have a loan upon any other terms. Naturally he would not stick by the terms if I did suffer the misfortune of becoming so altogether destitute as not to be able to repay. You have but little faith in my skill as a craftsman if you deem me unable to make that loan productive, and you have but a poor opinion of my son if you deem him so unnatural as to be willing to see his own father put upon the parish for the sake of one hundred pounds."

"My opinion of your son, sir, is based upon mine own experience of him. I have not forgot how he refused to aid——" But then Michael stopped abruptly and caught his lip in his teeth, for he had remembered just in time that Nat's refusal to aid his demented mother was a secret between himself and Maralyn.

"Well, sir?" snapped Vance, very red and wrathful. "Whom did my son refuse to aid, eh? Tell me that, this instant, sir, for I will have it."

Michael feigned sulkiness.

"He refused to aid a friend of mine who was in sore distress."

"My son is a business man, sir, and lends not but upon proper security and just interest. It is the—ahem!—the very foundation of good banking, sir," continued the poor man, obviously racking his brains to recall snatches of a lecture lately made to him and which had been at the same time incomprehensible and impressive, "that money should be lent only upon proper security. A banker, sir, trades with—ahem!—money, as I trade with ale, and expects as I do reasonable return for his labour. But I see what 'tis," he added severely, "you are set against this banking system because it came over from Holland with King William, and therefore you will have no good in it."

"I have always understood, sir," said Michael wearily, "that you likewise could see no good in it. I do recall some words of yours which——"

"We must move with the times, sir, we must move with the times," interrupted the other hastily. "It is the considered opinion of the City that banks are come to stay, and that——"

"Mr Vance," broke in Michael, leaning forward and speaking with the utmost earnestness, "I do implore you, take back that hundred-pound bill to your son, receive in return your deed of mortgage, tear it up, and then go you to Mr Bunch and say you have bethought you, and that you would be mighty obliged to him if he will lend you the sum required. Bunch is a good man and your friend; borrow from such an one if you must, but for God's sake do not put yourself into the hands of a banker."

" 'Ounds! " cried Vance, jumping up from his chair, "how dare you tell me what I must do, sir! I'll thank you to mind your own business, sir. I came not hither today to consult you on this matter; I came to have the skilled advice of my clerk as to certain accounts and estimates I had drawn up. When I desire you to meddle in my affairs I will say so, Mr Pennington, and until then I would be obliged if you would keep your place."

Michael looked at him for a moment in silence. Then he rose and made a formal bow.

"Then I can only crave your pardon, sir," said he stiffly, "for anything wherein I have presumed."

Vance sniffed, blew his nose, and turned abruptly towards the door, which Michael hastened to set open for him. But as he was about to walk into the yard the brewer paused, turned back, and spoke over his shoulder to Michael. His voice sounded oddly muffled, and his shoulders drooped:

"He's mine own son, d'ye see, and if we begin to distrust the fruit of our loins the world becomes a sorry place. But harkee, Master Pennington, not a word of this to Maralyn. Wenches are strange cattle, and—and understand not business."

Then, without waiting for an answer, he trotted off to his mash-tun.

(iii)

Time, the inexorable, moved on.

Seventeen-thirteen brought the war to an end with the Peace of Utrecht, and England had leisure to concentrate upon the pressing question of the Succession. For Anne was failing fast. She took to her bed; then rallied sufficiently to be able to review her household troops. She began to talk weakly, and to lean more and more upon her favourite, Masham. It cannot be long now, said the politicians, and the place-hunters and the Whigs and the Tories and the Jacobites; it cannot be long now. On Christmas Eve, Mr Vance came in late for supper, having stepped out to the Dagger for a whet; he seemed very agitated, and burst out without preliminaries:

"They say Her Majesty is attacked by a virulent fever and lies at death's door. God help her, and this poor realm."

Then he set himself to entertain his household in the festive manner required by the season, and it was not until the gathering had broken up, and he and Michael were alone, that he touched again upon public matters.

"The Queen may die at any moment, Mr Pennington; such is the opinion everywhere. There is a general feeling of uneasiness throughout the City; stocks are falling upon 'Change and trade is dull, for men will not buy and sell till they see what may befall us. I called upon my son today, to wish him and his wife a happy Christmas (and I must tell you in passing, sir, that he hath shown himself most kind regarding my mortgage and says it may run on, seeing that I have paid the interest regularly—ahem!), and he tells me there is rumour of French troops assembling on the coasts of France, and that the Pretender is holding himself in readiness for a call to bring him over. God help us all, for these are troublous times."

"I see not how they can mend until this nation makes up its mind whether it will have James or George."

Vance moved restlessly in his chair.

"I know what you would be at. You would persuade me that we cannot be easy again without we fetch over the Pretender. Well, I know not. When William died I did accept Queen Anne with contentment and thanksgiving, not only because she was an Englishwoman and of the ancient line, but because methought she would abolish many evils. But now I cannot say with honesty that my hopes in this respect have been realised. Poor soul, I am sure that she has done her best, yet her reign hath brought us little except war abroad and dissension at home; moreover, taxes are mounting yearly and this beastly spirit-drinking grows apace." He paused, then sank his voice to a confidential undertone. "They tell me hopes run high among those of your way of thinking, Mr Pennington, for the Queen gave a negative answer to two separate addresses from the Lords requesting her to demand the removal of her half-brother from Lorraine, and likewise is it known that when she closed the session of Parliament in July she omitted the now customary assurance of her determination to support the Hanoverian Succession. They say she detests her German kinsfolk, and that she has altogether refused to invite the Electoral Prince hither upon a visit, though pressed to it mighty hard by the Whigs."

"He will come upon something longer than a visit soon," said Michael.

"Why how now? Do you discount the possibility of a Stuart restoration?"

"I see but one chance of a permanent restoration, Mr Vance, now or at any time: The demand of the people of England for the King's return."

"The demand quotha? What, sir, would you have us act

like the vulgar mob and endeavour to force the Government's hand by violence?"

"There would be no need for violence if you but spoke with a united voice, Mr Vance. The voice of a whole people is more feared by a government than is armed revolt."

Mr Vance passed this over, and resumed:

"Nay, now I think the Pretender has an excellent chance, sir, for the Whigs are clean out of favour with the Queen, and Oxford and Bolingbroke rule all between 'em. They say that Bolingbroke is in open correspondence with a Certain Gentleman."

"I put no faith in any member of that class, let him call himself Whig or Tory, who drove out the late King James in order to seize upon the supreme power of government. Nay, I would sooner have a thoroughgoing Whig than these whiffling fellows, for with a Whig I know where I stand; so determined is that party to retain the power it stole, that it will foist upon England a German barbarian, and it says so openly. The German barbarian will be mighty useful to our masters, sir, since he speaks not a word of English, has not the shadow of a claim to the throne, and boasts that he understands nothing of English affairs. As for Oxford and Bolingbroke, the first knows not what he wants from hour to hour, and the second favours James because the coming of George would destroy him."

"Pish, lad," said Vance gently, "you grow disheartened."

"No, sir, but I grow older, and the longer I live the more am I convinced that nothing good can be got by the game called party politics. It is a game in which truth and honour are thrown overboard, wherein avarice is made to seem a virtue, and wherein he who can mostly neatly betray a colleague to his own advantage gets the prize. Yearly are we presented with the beastly spectacle of Ministers of the Crown convicted of having taken a bribe or indulging in peculation, a crime punished only because some rival of the Minister convicted hopes to climb into his place. Likewise do we see men put into the greatest offices, wherein they must decide questions which affect the welfare of the whole realm, having as their sole qualification for such office the fact that they are the sons or the nephews of some ambitious politician who desires their support to foster his own greatness; we see the awful responsibility of government passing into the hands of those untrained and unfit for it, untutored in the duties of such lofty stations, and set therein only because they are members of the party in power, or because their wealth has given them a stranglehold upon that party."

"Nay, Mr Pennington, nay, I cannot believe that things are so ill as you would have me think."

"I know you cannot believe. You refused to believe that your liberties were in danger even when one of the first acts of William on his coming over was to suspend the Habeas Corpus; even when, in 1707, a subject who used his Common Law right to petition Parliament was arrested for that act. Yet you accept without question the word of the politicians when they tell you that William came over to safeguard your liberties, and that King James would lead you to the feet of the Pope and make you slaves. You will wake up one day, Mr Vance, and see things as they are. Pray God that awakening will come ere it is too late. For there may come a day when the tyranny of wealth and self-interest has gained so great a stranglehold upon you that you are powerless to burst your bonds asunder; ay, and there may even come a day when you will demand The King Again and fail to find him."

Vance said nothing, but stared into his ale-can. In the silence the bells of the City chimed the hour of midnight, the melodious bells of St Mary-le-Bow answering the deep chimes of the Jesus Bells of Paul's School, the peevish tones of St Pancras interrupting the pretty harmony of St Mildred-in-the-Poultry. Those bells announced that it was the anniversary of that day so long ago when a King had come to His people who would have none of Him.

Two

(i)

A N N E died upon the 1st of August, 1714.

She left behind her an unsigned will believed to have been made in favour of her exiled half-brother, a nation dazed by the twists and turns of recent politics, a James the Third sitting penniless in Lorraine awaiting a call from England, and a George sitting comfortably in Hanover, declaring that while he had no wish to exchange his German beer for English ale, or his fat German mistresses for the insipid ladies of England, he had heard that the English Government was minded to give him a good fat salary if he would accept the throne, and would allow him a yearly visit to his dear Hanover.

He landed in England on 18th September, followed by his son, whom he heartily loathed, and by his mistresses, who somehow or other had contrived to elude their creditors. His wife, whom he had incarcerated in the Castle of Ahlden twenty years previously, after the murder of her lover, Königsmark, he left behind in her prison. He had not deemed it necessary to learn even a few words of English, but he had been very well instructed in more important matters by the Earl of Dorset, who was sent to bring him over, so he conscientiously cut all the Tories who flocked to fawn upon him, and showed an admirable consciousness of his position by his affability to the Whigs. He was much gratified to learn that Parliament had voted him a Civil List (a polite new term for salary) of seven hundred thousand pounds.

The day of his landing was disturbed by riots in certain English cities, Oxford so far forgetting herself as to burn him in effigy to the cry of "No George!", but London merely stared at him in stupefied amazement, not quite able to believe her eyes, and indeed in all her long history there had never been so curious a spectacle. George, who in appearance was rather like a pug-dog, quarrelled openly and noisily with his son in the state coach; he had his Calvinist chaplain with him, though he was not the type to make difficulties over the religious question and had published his intention of conforming to the Church of England. Behind him came his German secretaries and German chamberlains and fat German ladies, all of them chattering in their own tongue; and there was a bodyguard of negroes, the captives of George's wars.

In the days that followed, poor Nick Hammond lost what little self-control he had ever possessed. He made no pretence of working, would start up suddenly from the dinner-table, shout out an oath, and rush from the room, and so beside himself was he that he would blurt out his hopes and his fears to his master, making a habit of coming in nightly after supper so to do. Mr Vance had always retained a special kindness for this lad whom he had taken from the parish, and was very patient with him now, though obviously alarmed lest Nick's openly expressed opinions endanger not only the journeyman himself but his master's household.

"The honest party," Nick would rage, "did nothing when Anne died, nothing in the world. They sat on their arses and let George come over without one blow for it. And this after all their fine promises. The great ones have trimmed; look at Wyndham, he was the right hand of Bolingbroke and hot for James, but now speaks in favour of paying the Hanover troops out of the English Treasury. And the King himself, what did he do? Sat tight at Bar and trusted in Heaven and French promises. Why did he not land and take his chance?"

"Possibly," said Michael, "because he has a sense of his responsibilities and will not plunge this kingdom into civil war without a likelihood of success."

"I believe he might have succeeded," mused Vance, before Nick could retort, "if he had but cast off his Papistry. They say the Papists themselves have entreated him to abjure or at least to dissemble his religion."

"And do you know his answer?" asked Michael. " 'How could ever my subjects depend upon me, or be happy under me, if I should make use of such a notorious hypocrisy to get myself among them? I know their generous character could not but detest the crime itself and him that should be guilty of it.' "

"Bah! " cried Nick, and relapsed into sulky mutterings.

But during the winter and summer that followed a change came over the journeyman. His eye lost nothing of its fevered brightness and his mind was obviously as far from his work as ever, but now his ravings were all on a new note, a note of hope, of excitement, of frenzied expectation. The name of Mar was constantly upon his lips, also those of Bolingbroke, Wyndham, and Ormonde once more; he thrust under Vance's nose a crude picture of Ormonde he had bought in the streets, and in a thrilling whisper commented: "Ormonde's impeachment for High Treason reached Richmond only to find my lord flown, and you and I, master, know whither he has flown." He was full of such mysterious hints, picked up at his club or in some tavern. "There's a ship lying at the mouth of the Spey unloading arms night after night. Pretty soon there will be another with a yet more precious cargo." His toasts multiplied with bewildering rapidity; to the English names were added Scottish ones, Glengarry, the Bishop of Edinburgh, Drummond, Gordon. Presently he bought a cheap pistol and would sit polishing it every night at Mr Vance's table, to the brewer's extreme apprehension and dismay. "I will be needing this anon, master," exulted poor Nick. "Ay, I'll be using it soon in a gallant company."

But Michael was too preoccupied just now to pay much attention to the journeyman, for he knew now beyond all doubting that something great was in the wind. London herself seemed to have turned Jacobite overnight. Jack ballads were sold openly in the streets and were bought as fast as they could be printed; Baker, the publisher at the sign of the Black Boy in Paternoster Row, boldly displayed in his window the popular edition of Lockhart's *Memoirs Concerning the Affairs of Scotland;* Marlborough was hissed as he attended George to a service at St

Paul's; a slightly intoxicated gentleman walked into the colour-yard at St James's Palace, drew his sword upon the flag, abused the Hanoverian, and gave a cheer for his lawful Sovereign; and when the Whigs brought in a bill for offering one hundred thousand pounds reward for the capture of James, if he should land, Wyndham denounced the outlay and was cheered by the Tories.

But Michael knew his London by this time and he valued but little such fickle enthusiasm; it was Scotland that claimed his interest. The murmur of discontent which had succeeded the silence of despair in the North was rising to a shout, a shout which might be followed soon by the clash of arms and the screech of war-pipes. While the English Jacobites insisted upon the bringing over of foreign troops before they would rise, the Scots were sending urgent messages to James, imploring him to give the signal to rise even though the French would do nothing. They lacked only, they said, a commander of experience; it was a lack that was to ruin them and their King.

That the spirit of revolt in Scotland was formidable was proved by the attitude of the Government. It began to call up its reserves, formed a camp in Hyde Park, sent thither a strong train of artillery from the Tower, and made a clean sweep in the Horse Guards of those officers and men reported as being wavering in their loyalty. Marlborough was sent to review the troops and made them a long, almost deferential speech beginning "Gentlemen". Suspected Jacobites in the Commons found their names struck out; a proclamation ordered all Papists and Non-jurors to forfeit their arms and to keep within five miles of their residences; the Oath of Allegiance was to be administered to every person supposed to be "disaffected". The measures of the Government grew more severe with its growing alarm; for merely turning his back upon two Whigs who were belauding George, a butcher was whipped at the cart's tail from Stocks Market to Aldgate, and died of it, and for wearing mourning on the anniversary of King Charles's martyrdom, a tanner's 'prentice was sent to Newgate for a year. Jacobite ballads were called in and burnt by the common hangman, and a reward was offered for the discovery of the author of the tracts written by Michael, and another for his printer, Richard Derrick.

The confident expectation of a northern rising induced the timid Tories to show their colours, for they found themselves permanently out of favour with George. They were rather obscure colours, it is true, and it was the dead Anne's portrait, rather than that of the living James, which could be discerned upon them. The Tories had discovered that Anne had been a veritable paragon; in an address of congratulation to George they concentrated entirely upon their grief for the death of Anne; they celebrated the anniversary of her coronation by hoisting her portrait over the Conduit in Cheapside, burned a picture of George on the same spot, smashed those windows not illuminated in the dead lady's honour, and were somewhat unreasonably disappointed when this show failed to arouse the enthusiasm of the City. The City indeed, while heartily disliking George, was chiefly alarmed for its trade in the event of a rising, and the thoughts of the average citizen were entirely preoccupied with fear for his person and his goods if those barbarians the Scots should make a descent upon London.

The London mob did not share either the timidity of the craftsmen or the ambiguity of the Tories. It gave itself a grand time raiding Whig clubs and taverns, and its vengeance was so swift and terrible upon informers that those persons suspected of being so, posted up bills in the City affirming their innocence. Printers and authors, protected by the mob, poured out broadsheets and ballads harder than ever; all day the book-women were busy thrusting their wares into hands eagerly outstretched to receive them, shoving them under doors, and crying such dangerous literature boldly in the streets. And throughout all this season of alarms and excursions and arrests, Michael Pennington's quill squeaked into the small hours of the morning, begging the people of England to demand The King Again.

It was only his reason that impelled him to reiterate that old message now; his inclination was far otherwise. The remnants of his youth rose up to tease him, to bid him seize the obvious chance, to foster with his pen this imminent rising in arms. So tortured was he in his mind that night after night he paced the room when he should have been sleeping, and at least one member of his master's household noticed that his nails were bitten to the quick. He had resigned himself long ago to the belief that he himself would never live to see the King come back; he had convinced himself that a restoration brought about by a section of the people, and by the employment of armed force, could never be permanent; but now, for the first time since 1688, there was excuse enough for the hope of an immediate and successful counter-revolution, and because he was both human and humble he caught the new enthusiasm, and was racked by doubt. Was it not presumptuous to set up his conviction against that of his King, who, it seemed, was ready to lead a rising in arms?

He became scrupulous and searched his conscience. Was he perhaps a physical coward? Was he perhaps afraid of Tyburn? It will end in the halter; so he had told himself many times since first he had joined the ranks of those who fought for a defeated cause; such work as his could have no other end. Perhaps advancing years had made him over-cautious, pusillanimous? Maybe he really had lost hope. Why otherwise did he refrain from joining in, nay, overtopping, the shrieking chorus which urged to revolt? Why did he hesitate to write his life away in one wild, glad, soul-satisfying broadside which might well turn the scale in favour of all he held most dear? Why, otherwise, in the name of God, did he still continue to grind out the old dull stuff which had proved futile after twenty years of toil?— the unanswered appeal to the common people, the drab, sober, uninspiring appeal to tradesmen and housewives, who cared for nothing in the world but to pursue their blameless lives in peace and quietness, who were incapable of thinking of anything except buying and selling and baking and marketing, who saw the Common Law abrogated under their noses and ignored it, who found themselves burdened with ever greater taxes and grumbled a little and forgot their troubles in a can of ale, and who obstinately continued to believe, despite the evidence of their experience, that the Revolution of 1688 had rescued them from slavery.

But he could not do violence to his reason, and he knew, in

the deep heart's core of him, that his inability was not caused by cowardice or by middle age. In youth he had narrowed his life to a single purpose; he had so narrowed it of his own free choice, deliberately. In his middle forties he was as incapable of deserting that purpose as he was physically incapable of walking ten miles without fatigue. What he had set himself to be, that he was; the lessons he had learned by painful experience he could not unlearn, the values he had set up he could not pull down. He knew, if he knew anything at all, that the restoration of the ancient form of government was supremely necessary to England; and he knew in like manner that such a restoration could not be lasting if won by conquest, if brought about by a faction or by weapons similar to those which had in the first instance defeated it.

And lastly he knew that, in this year of 1714, it was not the voice of a united people that was upraised to call the King home. He could distinguish in the clamorous tumult of the day the shrill cry of the fanatic, the fickle enthusiasm of the mob, the deceitful undertone of the trimmer, the raucous shout of the eternally disaffected, the burning conviction of the zealot; but he could not hear the solid, dull, sober demand of the ordinary man and woman. The King could not be secure without the people, and the people could not be free without the King; they were mysteriously one, and to separate them was to separate the head from the body. But the people did not yet realise their need of the King. It was his, Michael's, business to convince them of that need; and he would go on trying to do it, he had to go on trying to do it, until either he was successful or his enemies put an end to his work by sending him to Tyburn tree.

(ii)

The year seventeen-fifteen came upon a London apprehensive to the point of panic, and in tavern and coffee-house nothing was talked of but the national situation.

There were disturbing rumours of a growing discontent in the Army, because the men were given rotten clothes and then punished for having holes in them, and on George's birthday the Foot Guards paraded the streets with rags stuck up on their bayonets, yelling "Look at our Hanover shirts! " Others stripped off their coats and flung them over the wall of St James's. Feeling grew tenser every day. An eclipse of the sun in April made all men fear some impending calamity. In vain the astronomers, Dr Halley and Mr Whiston, told the town there was nothing but what was natural in it. "That is all very well," retorted superstitious London, "but there has been no such eclipse in England since the days of Stephen the Usurper." Recruiting for James was carried on almost openly in the coffee-houses and at street corners, and officers with his commission in their pockets were arrested in the Horse Guards. On May 8th, several persons in disguise proclaimed King James at Manchester, and on the 29th, the anniversary of the Restoration, the rejoicings were more public and more general than at any time since 1688.

At the beginning of July a proclamation was posted in London declaring an invasion to be imminent and ordering all Papists to withdraw at least ten miles from the City on pain of death. The Lord Mayor and Common Council of the City forbade the holding of St Bartholomew's Fair because it was considered dangerous to have a crowd of people assembled in one place. The party news-sheets kept London's nerves on edge, one side assuring its readers that all idea of an invasion was ridiculous, the other discovering treason everywhere, the *Flying Post* going so far as to assure its startled subscribers that the Pretender's picture was being passed from hand to hand among the Tories in the King's very drawing-room, and that one of them had been seen to kiss it.

On July 24th, the Earl of Mar, nicknamed Bobbing John and notorious for his trimming even in that age of trimmers, was dismissed from his employments under George, straightway went in disguise to Scotland, and issued invitations to every Jacobite in the North to meet him at Braemar with all their followers. In vain did James send an urgent message that preparations for a rising were not complete, and that hasty action would ruin all. Upon the 6th of September, Mar set up the Stuart standard at Braemar, proclaimed King James the Third, and began his march south.

When the news reached London, bringing panic in its train, Nick Hammond burst in upon his master, who was sitting with Michael after supper, and announced his immediate intention of going North to join the rising. Mr Vance gaped at him, then leaped from his chair, rushed to the door of the kitchen, in which Maralyn was busy washing the dishes, shut and bolted it, and leaning against it enquired with wrath whether Nick had taken leave of his senses.

"No, master," snapped Nick, "I have come to them. Men are needed up yonder, and I must go."

"I took you from the parish," raged the trembling brewer; "I fed and clothed and instructed you, and have behaved towards you for twenty years as though I were your father, and this is the way you reward me, to leave my employment when most I need your services and without even due notice given."

"There is a greater service which now I must enter," said Nick solemnly, "and a greater master whose call I must obey. I ask your pardon, sir, with all my heart, but I am resolved, and nought you can say will shake me."

"You would turn rebel," stormed Vance, indignation and a genuine fear for the lad's safety wrestling for the mastery of his mind, "and let me tell you what will be the end of you. You will swing on Tyburn tree when you might be working at an honest trade."

Vance continued for some while to argue with his journeyman, but it was plainly useless. Nick, who was dressed for travelling and carried his belongings in a little bundle under his arm, was about to withdraw, when he hesitated, looked at his master and away again, and at last blurted out:

"May I take my leave of—of Mistress Maralyn, master?"

"'Ounds, you may not, you rogue. Get you out of my sight; and if you return from this mad and wicked venture with a whole skin you may seek employment where you will, but you will not find it in my brewhouse."

Nick bit his lip, turned very red, and sent one glance of indescribable homage in the direction of the kitchen. Then he made the others an awkward bow and left the room. Michael followed him to the outer door and laid a hand on his shoulder.

"I would not take it too hard, Nick," said he. "Our master is put out by your deserting him, but he has an affection for you and always will have. I will carry your message of farewell to Mistress Maralyn. Good luck, lad," and he held out his hand.

Nick took the hand slowly, staring at him through the dimness. Then he turned without a word, and walking resolutely across Bird-in-Hand Court was soon swallowed up in the bustle of Cheapside.

In the following months, his outraged master forgot all about him. King George prorogued Parliament, suspended Habeas Corpus, and was described in the news-sheets as being "pleased to take notice of the horrid rebellion in Scotland"; Bolingbroke was attainted and fled to France; Thomas Forster, lately a member of the Lower House, gathered considerable forces in the north of England and captured Preston for King James. From Oxford came the news that a recruiting party had had their big drum cut to pieces and their persons maltreated by a vast multitude who shouted out "King James is the true King! No usurpers!" Night after night there were brawls in the London streets, and sober merchants trembled behind their shutters as they heard the raging of the mob outside. Stocks and shares rose and fell like meteors, trade was nearly at a standstill, London was placed under martial law and the horse-militia of the City paraded daily in the Moor Fields; trimmers nearly lost their reason by their effort to be polite both to George and James, and every night witnessed a raid upon some club, cook-shop or ale-house where the Stuart supporters gathered. The cries of the street-vendors were altogether drowned in the thunder of party slogans: "An Ormonde! High Church and Ormonde!" "No Hanoverians!" "Down with the Pretender, the Pope and the French!" "Huzza for King George and the Protestant religion!" "Huzza for King James and liberty!"

Maralyn listened and observed as she washed the dishes and the clothes, and baked and went a-marketing and worked at the mash-tun. She had recovered from her illness long ago, but she had never quite regained her former tranquillity. When an honest and simple woman once begins to ponder upon deep matters she finds it difficult to shake off the habit. Hard as she tried, Maralyn Moray had never been able to rid her mind of certain uncomfortable impressions made upon it by Glencoe, by Darien, by the gin scandal, by the arrest of a peaceable subject in the teeth of the Common Law. Every now and then, despite herself, she opened that familiar cupboard inside her mind and the lion leaped out, the lion of her secret thoughts; and worst of all she knew that in herself she possessed the capacity for revolt, that when she had marched in that procession to Westminster she had been fired with some measure of the enthusiasm which had burned so strongly in the breasts of her companions. This knowledge terrified her, for to what might it not lead? She could never be sure of herself again, even as she could never be sure of the faith of public men. Nor could she ease herself by confiding her troubles to another. Her father would be shocked, and as for Mr Pennington, she knew him now for a Jack, who would seek to seduce her soul with wily arguments, with Jesuitical craftiness.

But with the advent of this rebellion she began to feel better. For here, she told herself, were the consequences set out before her eyes of that spirit of revolt of which she herself had not been entirely guiltless. It was wicked and mad to wish to bring in the Popish Pretender; it was mobbish to brawl in the streets and break windows and upset peaceable citizens; it was altogether beastly to disorganise trade and ruin the nation by civil war. As for James himself, she knew nothing of him save what she had been taught; she never could think of him without his inevitable companions in a Fifth of November procession, the Pope and the Devil; his very name suggested warming-pans and whispering Jesuits and Irish troops a-murdering. Let this then be a lesson to her, this horrid rebellion; let it fix in her mind, once and for all, the consequences of doubting the wisdom of the established Government. Not, of course, that she had ever hankered after the Pretender, but the habit she had contracted of secretly criticising the Government and its policies might ultimately lead to that. She did not understand high matters, and she had no business to try to understand high matters; her housewifery, and the care of her father and her son, should occupy both mind and body to the exclusion of all else. It had been so once; it must be so again. The effort she must use to make it so was her punishment for her secret presumption.

But although she had no sympathy whatever with the rebellion, she could not help grieving and worrying over a certain rebel. Nick had disappeared to join the Pretender's forces; so much her father had told her, briefly and curtly, and had bade her never mention his name again. But, while she obeyed her father's command, she could not compel her thoughts to shun the forbidden subject. She had known Nick Hammond from childhood; they were nearly of an age. His gauche adoration of herself, so unconcealed, was irritating and improper, but it was pitiful, and even a little flattering, and it had endured without the slightest encouragement on her part; she had even, though she did not know it, come to count upon it.

So when she heard that Nick had gone to join this horrid rebellion she was properly grieved and shocked, but she was also fearful for the safety of this misguided weakling. She was irritated too, because she could not for the life of her conceive what had made him do it. He was earning a decent wage as a journeyman at an honourable craft; he had the best master in the world, as he himself had often acknowledged; what could have possessed him to throw all this away, not to speak of inconveniencing his master, by running off to join a pack of malcontents who were pledged to bring in Popery and the French and arbitrary power, and whose end must be the gallows or the Plantations? So he lay in her thoughts, willy-nilly, a child who had never quite grown up, a naughty, wilful child for whom she felt a mysterious responsibility.

She was awakened in the pitch-darkness of a night early in November by the sound of galloping hooves; they seemed to drum incessant and imperative in her ears as she tried to sleep again. Then a door opened noisily somewhere, and there were voices; then a shout and the sound of windows being thrown open, and the swell of voices thickened. She felt her heart begin to race with an odd, sickening apprehension; it is the Papists, she thought, out to fire the City; or it is the Irish come to cut our throats; or it is the Pretender and the Scots and the French. The streets will run with blood, they will take away our trade and make slaves of us; they will bring in the tortures of the Inquisition. . . . Then, gathering her courage, she got out of bed, found her hooded cloak and a pair of shoes, ran down the stairs, unbolted the outer door and slipped out into the court. A full moon was drifting in and out of clouds and by its light she saw a little knot of people gathered on the corner by Le Bere Tombeth; they were talking and gesticulating as though in a frenzy of excitement, and she saw the figures of men and women run past in Cheapside itself. She drew nearer to the group, keeping in the shadows so as not to be seen in her undress, and presently, through a medley of voices all speaking at the same time, she was able to pick up stray sentences, enough to tell her all she needed to know:

"Utterly defeated . . . fled to Perth . . . Argyll is certain of forcing him out of it . . . terms refused at Preston . . . Sheriffmuir finished Mar . . . rebellion over . . . huzza for King George and my Lord Argyll! . . . a rare sight at Tyburn anon . . . five hundred prisoners . . . a public holiday . . . utterly defeated . . . utterly defeated . . ."

But she could not feel at this moment the joy and relief which should have overwhelmed her at the realisation that the rebellion had failed. For with the eyes of her mind she saw the shadowy forms of five hundred men limping down to London, driven like bullocks to the shambles, defeat behind them, death or the Plantations before them, and among them, perhaps, Nick Hammond. . . .

(iii)

As soon as it was clear beyond the shadow of a doubt that this most ill-managed and most futile rising was really defeated, all the Tories began to speak contemptuously of the "rebels", all the trimmers vowed most feverishly that they were and ever had been staunch supporters of King George, and all the gentlemen who had ventured to express in public a preference for James retired unostentatiously to their country seats. The Government meantime, conscious that it had experienced a very narrow escape, combined tactfulness with a firm hand; it kept several companies of horse and foot in and around London, ordered the Riot Act to be read again, and announced that the entry of the Jacobite prisoners into London would be made the occasion of a public holiday. In other words, if the mob would behave itself, it should be given ample compensation for the loss of Bart's Fair.

It was a cold grey day, with patches of snow lying untidily upon the roofs, when Maralyn hurried in a furtive manner from her father's house with a basket upon her arm, and joined the stream of people who were trudging westwards, *en route* for Highgate Hill.

The crowds surged about her, laughing and chattering in high good spirits, dragging children with them, carrying food and drink; even the mob which had so lustily disturbed the peace in favour of the rising now went merrily to witness the dereliction of its heroes. London's appetite for this spectacle had just been whetted by the hanging of four Jacobite captains who had tried to secure Oxford for King James, but even Tyburn could not offer a greater treat than this, when five hundred to a thousand prisoners were to be herded into London after a long and weary march from the North. And besides the chief spectacle, there were to be raree-shows and tumblers, booths selling gingerbread and saloop, and of course gin, and the latest fashions to admire and the quality to gape at, and even, some said, a sight of several of His Majesty's Ministers who had promised to grace the scene with their presence. Yes, there was to be all the fun they had missed at St Bart's this year, and later they would be able to go down to the waterside and see the fettered wretches being herded aboard ship as slaves for the Plantations, and then there would be Tyburn again, and not just everyday hangings either, but the rare and entrancing spectacle of the quartering-block, the disembowelling-hook, and the smoking cauldron.

But Maralyn had never cared for the brutal sights in which her age delighted, and each step of the way to Highgate was for her a painful effort. She was driven thither by sheer pity; Nick might be among those wretched prisoners, a Nick defeated, desperate, friendless, without hope, disillusioned once and for all. The punishment he must now endure cancelled out his crime, she thought. For a mad ideal he had forfeited the things which she and her kind, and his kind too, prized so highly: respectability, personal liberty, his craftsmanship, his niche in society, his reputation as a decent honest citizen. It was right and just that he should pay this price for his folly and his wickedness, but she could not find it in her heart to deprive him of the only things left him: her pity and her friendship. He would need a friend upon the last stage of that dolorous journey; he would need too the things which only she could give him, the material things which can always comfort such childlike creatures as he. And so she had packed into her basket a cake she had baked, a bottle of her father's strong-ale, a wash-ball, and a shirt which she had made herself on purpose for him. When they came from the wars, the things men needed were food and drink and cleanliness and a friendly face; she had all these to give him and, whatever his fault, she had it not in her heart to withhold them. So strong was her pity for him that she was prepared to hand them to him in public, to him, a declared and convicted rebel; and one side of her, the not so pleasant side, was fully aware of the obligation under which she would put him by this unselfish act.

As she trudged along, shoved and jostled on all sides by the multitude who hemmed her in, she wished that she had told her father of her intention of going to Highgate. She had not done so because she was vaguely ashamed of her errand; she had risen very early that morning and put the dinner in the iron pot over a slow fire and had told her father that she had some business which would take her abroad for the morning. That was true, and he had accepted her statement without question, for he trusted her implicitly; only because she knew that he had imagined, and that she had let him imagine, that the business she had mentioned was innocent and everyday, her conscience pricked her when she thought of him. Moreover, he might have offered to accompany her if she had told him the whole truth; he was the kindest of men and he had a real affection for poor

Nick. And his sturdy presence would have comforted her in this horrid crowd, which was composed so largely of the lower sort of people, the mob. Maralyn had an inbred contempt for the mob, but she was not only contemptuous; she was afraid. She knew the mob and its ways. There was no controlling it when once it had decided on a particular sport, and it was no respecter of persons.

It was noon when at last she reached Highgate. The crowd was already so great upon the hill that she could get no further than the point where the lane ran off over the Heath to the village of Hampstead. There was a little tavern just here, with a small green before it on which stood a cluster of old elm-trees; she got her back against one of these trees, and so remained, weary, depressed, and very nervous, wedged into the restless multitude.

It was strange to see a London mob heaving and surging in this peaceful little place. Between the heads of the people in front of her she could see a clear space kept in the centre of the road; a company of Foot Guards, in easy scarlet coats and black gaiters, with their hair arranged in the Ramillies-tie and with their firelocks in their hands, pressed back the crowd on either side, and down the clear space there passed the chariots and coaches of the quality, and innumerable Whig processions. There was a cart in which sat effigies of Ormonde and Mar, the first with an emblematic padlock on his sword, the second with a paper pinned to his staff: "I have sworn sixteen times to the Protestant religion, and I ne'er deceived you but once." After them came the Pope and James the Third, riding backwards like traitors, with Bolingbroke in dutiful attendance and in an absurd Court dress, with the motto round his hat: "Perjury is no crime." Beside the carts bearing these dummies walked men dressed to represent the Pretender's nurses, beating upon warming-pans, while others flourished banners on which were painted satirical pictures: here a very fat Truth stood with her foot upon a snake and opened the door of a cupboard to disclose the Pretender as a child, with a Monstrance in his hand, his body being pushed up through the roof by Father Petre; there Queen Mary of Modena, his mother, sat by his cradle while her Jesuit confessor familiarly caressed her.

It was a great day for the Whigs, and they were taking full advantage of it. The Williamite Club marched proudly by, all bedecked with orange favours and roaring out *Lillibulero*. The Calf's Head Club had gone one better with an excellent pageant of a bear dressed up as a Highlandman, with a Pope and a Pretender holding each a chain attached to its paws, while a very realistic Devil goaded it from behind with a pitchfork. The cries of rival parties which had so deafened the town during the last few months had given place to a triumphant chorus composed solely of Whig slogans; and prominent among the names roared out with such enthusiasm was that of Robert Walpole, not so long ago committed to the Tower on charges of notorious corruption, but now newly made Chancellor of the Exchequer and First Lord of the Treasury. His brother-in-law, Lord Townshend (vulgarly known as Turnip Townshend), was the nominal head of the Government, but Walpole was the darling of the Whigs, who looked upon him as the coming man. Had he not pushed through the impeachment of Bolingbroke and had he not declared that a ferocious punishment must be meted out to the Jacobite lords concerned in this hellish rebellion? The estates of those lords would be declared forfeit anon, and that would mean pickings for Walpole's admirers. The Kit Kat Club proudly displayed the hero's likeness painted on canvas and strung between two pikes: a fat and jolly face with thick dark brows, a face which looked as though its owner cared for nothing in the world except good food and choice wines.

When the Whig processions grew a trifle monotonous, there were always the fashions to admire. In front of the handsome coaches of the gentry there trotted the running-footmen with their long staffs and comical petticoat-breeches, and through the glasses of those vehicles glimpses could be caught of gentlemen whose waistcoats had lately shrunk sufficiently to show some inches of black velvet breeches, whose cocked hats were delicately furred along the edges, whose manicured hands fingered in turn the jewelled snuff-box, the quizzing-glass, and the wide black ribbon, called a solitaire, which was attached to the bag of the powdered wig; glimpses too of ladies whose faces had broken out into a perfect rash of patches, whose waists were so pinched it was a marvel they could breathe, and whose limbs were incommoded by this recent revival of the verdingale, now called a hoop. These ladies peeped out of the windows of their conveyances, holding dainty masks before their faces or sniffing at silver pomanders, and exclaiming "La!" in wonder and contempt as they looked at the vulgar multitude.

The hours went by, but the crowd was patient. Family parties sat down upon the ground and picnicked off the food they had brought with them; some built a fire to keep themselves from perishing in the icy wind, and sat around it telling stories and singing ballads. And then there were the side-shows, this new Punch and Judy, tumblers with their coloured hoops, conjurers thrusting bodkins through their legs and blowing fire out of their mouths, mountebanks promising a cure for every ailment. The laughter, the singing, the brawls, the invitations from rival showmen, the restless surge of feet, the rumble of wheels, the rattle of swords and occasional trumpet-note, all these combined into a cacophony to dizzy the mind and confuse the senses; the warring stinks of sweat and ordure and gin and food and cheap perfume drugged the brain and sickened the stomach. But Maralyn stood sturdily against her tree; her nose and ears were accustomed to such ill-treatment, for she was London-bred, her body was used to great fatigue, and her mind was as the minds of all women of her type: it was capable of extraordinary tenacity in adhering to a certain fixed resolve. She would have stood here, if need had been, until the Day of Doom, sustained by the knowledge that she had carefully arranged beforehand for the needs of her household. When at last her duty here was done, she would go home and tell her father the truth, tell him where she had gone and why; and then, having eased her conscience in this particular, she would forget poor Nick, and take up her normal life again with the comforting assurance that this dreadful rebellion was defeated and that London's liberties had been preserved.

She did not know what hour it was (for she had lost all count of time), when at last the rumour ran like wildfire through the crowd that the prisoners were coming. Instantly, necks were craned and heads turned in one direction, the showmen's booths were deserted, children were snatched up and lifted shoulder-high that they might get a view of the sport, and the surge of the crowd was so great that the soldiers hastily screwed their bayonets into the muzzles of their firelocks and formed a hedge of steel to keep the road clear. Beneath one of Maralyn's elmtrees stood a bench, and this being now vacated by a couple of boys, who ran off to try and push their way into the forefront of the crowd, Maralyn picked up her skirts and stepped on to it, supporting herself with one arm against the tree-trunk. Standing thus, she had a good view of the road and would be able to scan the faces of the prisoners in her search for Nick; how she would reach him when, or if, she saw him, she did not know; hers was the type of mind which can think of only one thing at a time.

Suddenly and strangely the savage roar of the crowd seemed to lessen, and now there could be heard the slow thudding of horses' hooves and the squelch of feet through the slush. Soldiers, horse and foot, came marching down the road, and between them, hemmed in by them on either side, came all that remained of Mar's and Forster's armies. A whispering broke out around her: the prisoners were to be divided presently into four bodies, one for the Fleet, the second for Newgate, the third for the Marshalsea, the fourth, the great ones, for the Tower. That was my Lord Widdrington with his two brothers, and there were the Earls of Carnwath, Nithsdale, and Winton; they rode without bridles and with emblematic halters round their necks. Here came my Lord Derwentwater, so young and handsome, the idol of the North; and there, fettered together, came Thomas Forster and his chaplain, Mr Patten. Behind these came the gentlemen volunteers on foot, fettered or free according to the caprice of their guards. Last of all in the long procession came the rank and file, many of them Highlanders; the crowd craned and exclaimed to see these strange half-naked men, with their hairy faces and ragged tartan, their bare knees and blue bonnets. The guards goaded them with hand and voice, the enthusiastic Whigs beat warming-pans under their noses and roared *Lillibulero* in their ears. A company of Argyll's triumphant horse carried in their midst Mar's captured standard, the standard set up so short a while ago upon Braemar. It was carried reversed by its enemies, who threatened it with their bayonets, spat upon it, and sometimes scooped up a handful of dirty snow to fling at it, but in the soiled and tattered blue and gold of it there still showed plainly the strangely desperate motto: "For our Lives and Liberties."

Squelch, squelch, went the weary feet through the slush. On some of those begrimed faces there was despair, on others bewilderment, utter weariness on all; but on the one for which Maralyn had looked, and which now she found, there was something else, something as simple and unmistakable as it was shocking and incongruous: it was peace. Her satisfaction at seeing him was straightway swallowed up in numb bewilderment; even from where she stood she knew instantly that here was a Nick she had never seen before. There was an ugly scar on his face and he limped; his clothes hung in tatters and his flesh was grey with dirt, yet he walked with head up, not in defiance but with a kind of quiet pride. His hands were fettered in front of him, but he had given his arm to a poor old man, his fellow-prisoner, who hung on to him, half collapsed from fatigue and terror; she saw how the ancient kept looking up into his supporter's face, as a child looks up for comfort to its mother. But Nick looked neither to right nor left, and so great was the change in him that she shuddered as though she looked upon a ghost. He, so undignified, seemed now the very embodiment of dignity; gone was the posing, gone too the unnatural fire in his eyes. There was no trace of the old theatrical Nick in the man who walked wearily but contentedly as if to his home after long travel. His glance was preoccupied, as though he saw, not the hostile multitude nor the ranks of his comrades in distress nor the triumphant soldiery nor the desolate winter's scene, but some bright vision which his eyes had captured after long pursuit, and held, and would hold, to the end.

Then she shook herself free from this ridiculous fancy, reminded herself of the duty which had brought her here, and putting aside her timidity, even her modesty, jumped down from her perch and began to jostle her way through the crowd, disregarding hostile faces and obstructive elbows and lewd remarks and curious stares, until, by sheer force of a single-minded resolution, she found herself abreast of Nick, separated from him only by a moving hedge of scarlet uniforms and fixed bayonets. Then she trotted along to keep pace with him, and shouted at him, flourishing her basket:

"Nick! Nick Hammond! It is I, Maralyn. Harkee, Nick, I am come to greet you and to bring you some comforts. You will be the better for them. Oh, pray, sir," she implored a soldier who turned to stare at her, "permit me to speak with him, to give him my basket; you may look for yourself, there is nought in it but a clean shift and a cake and some ale."

"His sweetheart, eh?"

"No, no, a friend. But he was my father's journeyman, and a good lad until seduced by those Jacobites. Pray now, for pity's sake, let me come at him."

"You may not come at him," said the soldier, regarding her with a rough pity, "but I will give him your basket. Hallo, you there! " he called to Nick. "Here is a friend of yours. Call out a word of greeting, man, for you will not see her again. He'll be speedily under hatches in the Fleet, mistress, ere he sails for Hanging Island, for he's a notorious rebel who distinguished himself at Preston and will certainly swing."

Squelch, squelch, went the feet; and the dishonoured banner flapped in the icy wind above the doomed heads, proclaiming its piteous motto: "For our Lives and Liberties." He was looking at her now, but it was not Nick who looked at her; she did not know him, she who had known him for so many years. She had come to pity, but he did not need her pity, this stranger who inhabited Nick's body. He did not even need her carefully prepared comforts; he took them and passed them on to the old man at his side. And then, most intolerable of all, he pitied her.

"Have no fear," he said, "for this is not the end. The King will come back, let them do what they will to prevent him."

"How dare you! " she gasped. "How dare you suggest that I have share in your treason! "

But he only smiled patiently upon her; and then his glance

300

strayed upwards, and following that glance she saw, as the flag streamed in the breeze, the mottoes on the once-white pendants: "No Union" and "Remember Darien".

And then fear seized her by the throat. The lion had sprung out of the cupboard again and had taken her unawares. She knew in that moment that there were things, mysterious, dreadful, awesome things, which were so powerful that they could change a piteous poseur, an irresponsible fanatic, into a martyr; a familiar, slightly contemptible dependant into a being strong, unfamiliar, who had found his manhood in adhering to a cause defeated. She knew that there were things, whether good or ill she could not tell in this crazy moment, which were so important that they could make a man despise food and drink and a clean shift and popularity and respectability and personal liberty and friends and common comfort, that were so powerful, so insidious, so peremptory, that they could make a man sacrifice for them all that the world holds dear, and give him contentment in facing for them ignominy and death; and she knew also in that moment, but only for a moment, that liberty and honour and justice are so precious that nothing in the world is worth while when they are absent....

He was gone, gone from her for ever; and in a hideous topsy-turvy it was she who needed him. It was she who was lost and despairing and lonely, she, the charitable, law-abiding, sensible Maralyn, who had steeled herself to come hither and do what she could for a declared and defeated rebel. It was monstrous, it was ridiculous, it was shattering; but it was none the less fact. Later she would comfort herself by the conventional explanation: he is hardened by his experience as a soldier, he has been seduced by Jesuitical pleading, he was always easily led; his dignity at the last was a pose like all the rest, or perhaps he was buoyed up by a childish satisfaction in being a martyr for his ideals. But this comfort was far away; now, in this horrid moment, she saw things quite otherwise, for the cupboard door was still open and the lion held her by the throat. Its claws scratched words upon her mind in letters of blood: For our Lives and Liberties. Remember Darien. I am not suffered to speak; expect what justice other men will have. Is it possible you have had your stomachful of arbitrary power this day? Our Company presented a petition to the Queen but she ignored it, humble though it was. You are in peril, Maralyn, in deadly, urgent peril. Unless you face that peril, and take steps to escape it, in a little while it may be too late, and you will find yourselves enslaved. For our Lives and Liberties. . . .

And then, mercifully, she became aware that she was about to faint; mercifully, because that was the kind of contingency with which she could grapple. It was human, ordinary, and familiar; it drove the lion back into his cupboard, and for a while she could forget that he was lying in wait for her there. She must force her way out of the crowd and go home. She had done what she had come to do; she had fulfilled her duty. At least she had seen Nick, or rather she had seen someone who had Nick's features and body, and she had done her best to comfort him. It was not her fault that he did not need her comfort and was ungrateful and a hardened rebel. Neither was it her fault that, as she feebly pushed her way out of the mob, the last thing she heard was the squelching of weary feet and the last thing she saw was a tattered banner with a desperate motto:

"For our Lives and Liberties".

Three

(i)

YOUNG Alec, Maralyn's boy, was growing up. He was almost exactly as old as the century, its senior only by a few months. The terrible circumstances surrounding his birth had not, it seemed, affected him either in mind or body; he was spare and wiry like his father, and possessed the high cheek-bones and sandy hair of his father's race. Indeed there seemed to be very little of his mother in him, except that he had inherited her strong constitution and efficiency; in manner he was extremely reserved, was not much given to laughter, and had a fondness for his own company and for book-learning.

Mr Vance had taken it for granted that his grandson would choose to become a brewer, and the old man had every intention of apprenticing the lad to himself at the usual age. But at the time of Maralyn's illness, when her son was eleven, Alec had evinced so strong a desire to work, and Mr Vance was so short-handed, that the brewer had decided to apprentice him then and there. It had been an enormous satisfaction to old Vance to find his little grandson so keen; he was too simple to realise that young Alec's keenness was for work in the abstract and that he did the tasks which lay to hand for lack of others. It came, therefore, as a very great and bitter shock to Mr Vance when, in 1718, young Alec, newly out of his indentures, announced his intention of engaging himself to his Uncle Nat. Mr Vance pleaded, protested, expostulated, all in vain; young Alec's mind was made up and his plans complete. Uncle Nat had promised him a position in his bank and was ready to receive him. Alec possessed that curious, stone-like quality which is one of the less pleasant of Scottish characteristics; he listened patiently and respectfully to his grandfather's remonstrances and arguments, but he would not allow himself to be diverted from his purpose by them, and he would never allow sentiment to interfere with business.

His mother, no less than his grandfather, was hurt and bewildered by the lad's decision, for she was as unshrewd as her father and as conservative. The thing which wounded her most deeply was the suddenness with which Alec had announced his decision; why, she asked him again and again, had he said nothing of his intention all these years? He replied simply and frankly that Uncle Nat had advised this silence; it was kinder, Uncle Nat had maintained, not to worry his grandfather before it was necessary. Uncle Nat did not desire him as a 'prentice; bankers, it appeared, did not take 'prentices. They required young men of sound education and a talent for figures. Uncle Nat was pleased to say that he, Alec, possessed such a talent, and would do very well in his office. But, cried the distressed Maralyn, did he owe no debt to his grandfather for caring for him and instructing him all these years? He was aware of none that he had not repaid, he answered; he had worked hard in the brewhouse, had entered it at a very early age in order to oblige his grandfather, and now felt free to pursue the life he had chosen and in which he knew he could succeed. (He was most horribly reasonable.) He would continue to live at home, if it pleased his mother, and would pay her a weekly sum out of his wages for his keep. That would be, he asserted calmly, an additional repayment to his grandfather, if she felt that he was still in the brewer's debt, and would assist the latter in the fallen state of his finances.

"But," wailed Maralyn, "how is it you have come to discuss all this business with your uncle whom you see so seldom?"

"We have discussed it upon several occasions," replied Alec gravely, "when my uncle has been pleased to invite me to his house of an evening. I did not mention such invitations to you, because I was aware that your relations with him were not of the most cordial. I did not consider, however, that such family feuds concerned me. My uncle is a clever man and has made a fine business for himself; he says I can do the same if I apply myself to my work. He says I have an eye for money—why, Mother, what ails you that you look at me like that?"

She could not answer him, but turned away that he might not see her tears.

(ii)

When Alec had been working for his uncle for some eighteen months, a gentleman called at the bank after it was closed for the day. It happened that Alec was working late; he did this more from inclination than from necessity, for he had that curious type of mind which finds its real and only romance in figures, ledgers, and mental sporting with money. When the heavy knocker sounded he looked up from his desk with a frown; not only did he dislike interruptions when he was thus engaged, but he knew that a summons at such an hour usually announced a broken merchant soliciting a loan. With his lips still moving to the tune of his sums, he got off his stool, groped his way to the outer door, and opened it a few inches, a curt refusal of admission on his lips. But fortunately he did not articulate the words, for he perceived, just in time, first that a very handsome coach was drawn up before the door, secondly that a powdered footman in a splendid livery stood deferentially holding a link, and lastly that there waited upon the doorstep a fat, round-shouldered gentleman quite obviously wealthy. Immediately the gentleman spoke Alec recognised his voice; it was that of Sir Frank Maynard, his master's old friend and reputed the richest bachelor in London.

"Good evening, good evening," cried Sir Frank, with his usual heartiness. "You work late, I perceive, like your good master. 'Sheart, what a world is this when a topping banker of Lombard Street must burn the midnight oil to keep himself from the parish!" He gaffawed at his own jest. "But keep up a good heart, young sir, for I am come to inform your master of a way in which he need not open another ledger and yet become as rich as the Bank of England. May I enter?"

Alec admitted him, coldly polite. He did not like Sir Frank Maynard, but he was very curious about him. He wanted to know just how Sir Frank had made his money. Alec was interested in money in the abstract, just as he was devoted to work in the abstract, and he had the same curiosity about this financial phenomenon as a devotee of racing might have about a horse which had won some famous race without the necessary qualifications. It might be, of course, a mere accident; it was certainly not an accident he would wish to see repeated. He had enough of the Vance in him to make him convinced that honest craftsmanship alone merited reward. But he likewise had enough of the financier in him to make him desirous of investigating all such accidents as a guide for the future.

Apart from his wealth, Sir Frank was not, in Alec's eyes, a desirable friend for his master. The young man was shrewd, and on the occasions when he had met Sir Frank socially at his uncle's house he had observed a certain by-play which went on between Maynard and Nat's wife. It was nothing very much, an exchange of glances, a particular tone of voice, an undercurrent of vague intrigue; but he had rightly interpreted this by-play. And Alec, though he did not concern himself with other people's morals, had a great admiration and even an affection for his uncle and was loyal to Nat's interests. He was convinced that Maynard was but biding his time to do Nat some injury, and although he was sure that Nat was Maynard's equal in business acumen, he guessed that his uncle was capable of being persuaded against his better judgment by his masterful wife. His infatuation for Susan was still his one weakness; to please her he was ready to do much; to hold her, Alec suspected that he was ready to do anything.

His distrust of Maynard, his curiosity concerning his wealth, and his loyalty to his master, must be the excuses for what Alec did on this particular evening. For when he had ushered Sir Frank into the banker's presence, the young clerk came quietly into the unlighted ante-room to his master's office (that ante-room where Michael Pennington had waited so long ago) and, not to put too fine a point upon it, prepared to eavesdrop. Perhaps this was not the first occasion; at any rate he seemed perfectly satisfied that he could hear what passed, remaining himself undetected.

It appeared that Maynard was treating his old friend to a very serious lecture. His hearty tones came plain through the intervening door, but subdued to a note of great gravity.

"Now hearken unto me, Nat. I care not how much you know already; I am resolved to state my case, and to state it I must rehearse the history of the whole affair, that it never may be said hereafter that I did not make you acquainted with all the facts necessary to convince you."

Here a slight pause ensued. Then the visitor continued briskly:

"Now with the wars of the last reign, the National Debt rose to the tune of fifty millions. Included in this was a floating debt of ten millions, and I need not tell you, my friend, that such a debt can be demanded for immediate repayment at any time by its creditors. Oxford, at that time still Sir Robert Harley, was uneasy concerning this floating debt, and formed a scheme whereby he could fund it. His proposal was to call together the creditors of the ten millions, to give them certain advantages by incorporating them into a company of merchants, and to offer them the monopoly of the trade secured to England by the Treaty of Utrecht. He promised further to foster their interests, especially any ventures of theirs in the South Seas, and if they would consent to forgo their right to immediate repayment upon claim, he would set aside the Customs as a guarantee to pay them the interest upon the sum owed. In this way he would make his floating debt irredeemable and feel secure against any sudden claim for it. Well, Nat, as you know, the thing was done, and the company so privileged, formed of the old creditors of the ten millions (of whom I was one), became the South Sea Company."

Again a pause, but still Nat said nothing. Sir Frank cleared his throat and continued:

"By the beginning of the year 1715 Sir Robert Walpole had become the rising man. It was no surprise to those who knew him when he was made Chancellor of the Exchequer. He has a head for finance, as he showed most clearly when he was Treasurer of the Navy in 1710, and I tell you the man is set for a long reign as First Minister. He is most excellent in business;

307

he appeals to the vulgar because he is outwardly genial, coarse, and speaks like a country farmer. He is an artful rather than an eloquent speaker, but artfulness pleases the mob while eloquence goes clean over its silly head. He is strong for the Hanoverian Succession, which commends him to such as I, because the Hanoverian Succession secures the National Debt and all that appertains to it. He has an eye firmly fixed upon the main chance all the time; and that is the kind of man we need today and tomorrow. Had he been born fifty years earlier we might have seen his head fall on Tower Hill; and that, my friend, would have been a huge misfortune for all men of business like you and me."

Sir Frank laughed gruffly, blew his nose, and went on:

"From 1715 until 1717 Walpole was working on a new scheme in regard to the Debt, or rather he was elaborating and adding to Harley's old one. The Debt was costing the Government anything from seven to nine per cent. The Government, of course, got this interest from the pockets of its subjects, but the thing was becoming troublesome and there was discontent in many quarters. During these years the Pretender's attempt to return was quashed and the House of Hanover firmly established. This settled security at home enabled Walpole to borrow at a lower percentage, and with the money to pay off such annuitants of the National Debt as would consent to receive hard cash. To find this money at a lower percentage he turned to the South Sea Company and succeeded in raising near upon five million pounds. Thus the case stood until last month. But now, Nat, now it stands in a vastly more tempting guise."

There was a small sound like a sigh, and Nat's voice said wearily:

"I know what you are about to say. I know all about this scheme for reducing, I might almost say for paying off, the National Debt. The South Sea Company is to take over the Debt as it stands, something over fifty-one millions. The two groups of annuitants, redeemable and irredeemable, are to be approached, and the suggestion made to them of an exchange for their claim against the Government for South Sea stock; the Company has consented to receive from the Government five per cent only for seven years, and after that four per cent, and further, to allow this debt to be redeemable at the pleasure of the Government. I say I know it all, Frank, and I know likewise that I care not a rush for it." A pause. "What are you trying to do, Frank? Sell me South Sea stock? If so, you are come upon a fool's errand."

There was the harsh sound of chair-legs being dragged into a new position. Then Sir Frank's voice again, this time with the indulgent, deliberately patient tone of a mother towards a foolish child.

"Harkee, Nat, let us tabulate the advantages, first to the Government, then to the annuitants, and then to the South Sea Company, for it is plain to me that you cannot have considered well upon the business. The Government will exchange the burden of finding eight per cent to pay for a debt largely irredeemable, for the far lighter task of finding, first five, and later only four, per cent, for a redeemable debt, and will, moreover, have but one creditor instead of many. The advantage to the annuitants is not so plain. As matters stand, the Government is pledged to pay them eight per cent; why, then, should they exchange their claim on it for stock in a company which will pay them but five or even four? Yet cast your mind upon the expansion of overseas trade, Nat; you know as well as I that the potential wealth there, especially in the region of the South Seas, is unlimited, and that a company with a Government guarantee of monopoly there will be able to increase its dividends indefinitely. The man who sacrifices his eight per cent for five does in reality cast aside that eight for ten, for twelve, for twenty, for fifty, in the future. Stay! Let me finish. What is the advantage of this scheme to the South Sea Company? It will receive a regular income from the Government securing its permanent prosperity, and meanwhile will become the one great financial agent in the realm blessed with unlimited opportunity for enrichment. Let me repeat, friend: it has secured to itself the greatest monopoly in history, and behind it stands the Government, its debtor, identifying one interest with t'other. Can the Bank of England itself feel more secure?"

"I will answer that question with another," Nat's voice said dryly. "Precisely what is it you require of me?"

"Nat!" The name was spoken in accents of deep reproach. "Nat, what have I ever required of you but that you shall advantage yourself by hearkening unto me when I show you how you may do it? It is as your friend that I am come to you now, as so many times before. If I say to you (as indeed I do say): Put every penny you possess into South Sea stock, what can it advantage me? I have so much gold already that I vow it embarrasses me. Nat, my dear old gossip, be advised. This financial deal will receive the Royal Assent in the new year; so much is certain. Thank God we can be certain of these things beforehand nowadays, for we have to do with a group of business men and not with a despot. King George will do as his Ministers advise; nay, let us have the thing plain and honest and say, he will do as he is told. And to speak more plainly still, Nat, the Ministers will compel His Majesty to give his assent because their interests are involved. For I need not tell you, friend, that such a scheme as this could not be carried through without certain—er—gifts to the leading men in Government. It was the same with the Union; in all such schemes money is the best persuasive. To buy support for the South Sea scheme it was necessary to promise ten thousand pounds' worth of stock to Charles Stanhope, fifty thousand to Sunderland, thirty thousand apiece to the two Craggs, the one Postmaster-General, the other a Secretary of State; and Aislabie, as Chancellor, naturally looks to have the greatest prize of all."

"And Walpole?" Nat's voice asked sharply.

A low laugh answered him.

"Ah, Walpole! Think you so excellent a man of business would refuse to share in so rich a harvest? Walpole is bought, never fear; but that is a thing we do not talk about, Nat, if we are wise, even within these walls. Now see what you have here. You have a company whose affairs are normally prosperous, now guaranteed by Government, soon to be secured by the Royal Assent to its monopoly, protected further by the self-interest of all the leading Ministers; is it hard to guess what will befall? If you buy stock at one hundred pounds a share today, those shares will be worth two hundred tomorrow; in six months' time I'll wager they'll be worth a thousand, and be hard to come by even at that price. For not only will the annuitants be persuaded to give up their claim upon the Government in exchange for such obvious advantages, but the whole nation will run mad upon the thing. Nothing else will be sold on 'Change but South Sea stock, and 'Change Alley will be as crowded with folk rushing to invest as Smithfield of beasts upon a market-day."

"It may be so. I care not a rush one way or t'other. Certain I am I do not intend investing one penny-piece in South Sea stock."

There was the sound of a fist being crashed upon a chair-arm.

" 'Ounds, I but waste my time! 'Twas the same with the Debt. Why a-devil did you not stay at your father's mash-tub if you are so nice, so shy, so set against bettering yourself?"

"I have bettered myself and shall continue so to do without resorting to the stock-jobbers. I do very well, I thank you, by pursuing my chosen trade, and have all the money I require."

"Nay, Nat, that's plain selfish. Come now, would not Susan like fine to be riding in her own coach and play the great lady? Would it not please her to——"

Again the harsh scrape of chair-legs, and Nat's voice was for the first time upraised.

"Susan does very well likewise, and I will thank you to leave Susan to me. Agad, do you think me such a fool that I see not what game you would be at? So blind that I have not suspected all these years your intention of making me a cuckold? I tell you——"

"Nat! For God's sake forbear saying that which you would afterwards repent. Tush, man, let's forget the South Sea Company; nay, to the devil with the South Sea Company, say I, if it would cause you and me to fall out. Alack, that my oldest and most valued friend should have been harbouring against me all these years, so groundless a suspicion."

There was a murmur from Nat which the unseen listener could not distinguish; then the hearty voice boomed out again:

"Say no more, gossip, say no more. We are both grown heated, and since the cause of our difference is this South Sea Company it never shall be mentioned again betwixt us. As for the other matter, why, I am persuaded you spoke hastily, and I for my part have already forgot it. Our friendship is too healthy a ground ever to bring forth that ugly weed suspicion. Come now, Nat, will you not offer me a whet? I came hither to make you rich; it seems you will not be made rich, but at least you will permit me to drink your health."

For the last time there came the sound of chairs being moved, and then footsteps and the clink of glasses. Alec slipped quietly from his concealment and returned to his stool in the outer office. But he made only a pretence of working for the remainder of that evening; his mind, shrewd but slow-moving, was churning over and over the late conversation, a conversation which troubled him oddly.

(iii)

It was to Alec's credit that he went to his master next day and told him frankly that he had overheard the talk between Nat and Sir Frank the previous evening. Nat stared at him a moment in surprise; then he said dryly:

"It would interest me, Nephew, to learn how you came to overhear that conversation."

"I stood in the ante-room and listened, sir," replied Alec, with commendable frankness.

Nat bit his lip for a second; then burst into a laugh.

" 'Sbud, but you're plain, whatever else you are."

"I have your interests at heart, sir, and I would not see you bilked."

"You think Sir Frank came hither to bilk me?" asked his master, his brows together, his eyes half searching and half angry.

"I think Sir Frank is, maybe without desiring to be so, the enemy of honest banking," replied his clerk, not answering the question directly. "And if I may take the freedom to say it, master, I like not this South Sea scheme. Money should talk soft; when it shouts it is like to be dangerous."

"Now marry come up!" cried his master, leaning back in his

chair and staring at the grave-faced youth, "you have a head upon your shoulders for one so young. Tell me more, Nephew, pray tell me more of your notions."

"I think, sir," continued Alec, quite composed but speaking slowly in time with his slow mind, "I think it is never safe to bribe men in the Government."

"You are right there, lad, agad you are. A Government is apt to change."

"More than that, sir, a Government such as we have now will have no mercy upon its own members if they are convicted of corruption. It cannot afford to have mercy, for its own life is at stake. And if the Ministry were to be convicted, the Company itself would fall."

Nat stared at him for a long time in silence. Then, with a curt gesture of dismissal, he turned back to his desk and took up his quill.

During the next few months young Alec followed with close attention the fortunes of the South Sea Company. Nor was he alone in this preoccupation, for at least one of Sir Frank's prophecies was quickly fulfilled: the investing public plunged and South Sea stock rose and rose. Even before it became known that the Royal Assent would be given to the deal between the Government and the Company, the shares had stood at twenty-five per cent premium. George gave his assent on April 7th, 1720, and within a week a hundred-pound share was greedily bought at three hundred; within two months the Company had persuaded two-thirds of the annuitants to give up their claim upon the Government, and had stepped into their shoes.

But there now occurred something which Sir Frank had not prophesied, yet which he and his friends ought to have foreseen. The rage for speculation, once started, could not remain content with the South Sea; companies of every kind were floated, springing up like mushrooms overnight, and so great was the mania, so credulous the public, that no man stopped to ask himself if a project were practical before he invested in it. There were companies for "assurance of seamen's wages", for "breeding and providing for bastard children", for "planting of mulberry-trees and raising of silkworms", for "importing jack-asses from Spain", for "curing the gout", for "insuring marriages against divorce"; one company went so far as to announce itself as "an undertaking which in due time shall be revealed", and its shares were greedily bought. At the root of all this madness lay the astonishing rise in South Sea stock; the ignorant masses saw in the importation of Spanish donkeys as good an invest-ment as trading in the almost mythical South Seas. By July, one hundred and four such companies were advertising themselves in the news-sheets, and London had completely lost her senses. In the coffee-houses and the taverns, in the street and in the workshop, nothing was talked of but the day's doings upon 'Change; the mania was greater even than that which had followed the institution of the State Lotteries; great men hazarded their estates, little men their savings; national and international affairs were alike forgotten; stock-jobbing became the principal and indeed almost the only trade; and Anglican and Dissenter, Whig and Tory, forgot their old quarrels in a mutual infatuation.

The South Sea Company, seriously alarmed, brought pressure to bear upon the Government to act against its rivals. Upon August 11th a Royal Proclamation was issued, to take effect within ten days, laying very heavy penalties upon any promoter who should issue for public subscription shares in any company not duly chartered. No less than eighty-six of the new "bubble companies" collapsed overnight, and many more tottered. The immediate effect was to raise the value of South Sea stock yet higher; there came a moment towards the end of August when it reached one thousand pounds a share, or ten times par; and it was in the midst of this dizzy moment that Nat sent for young Alec to come to his private sanctum and announced to him that he had decided to invest everything he had in South Sea stock.

"You say everything, sir?" enquired Alec quietly, after a pause.

"Everything," snapped Nat. "Every penny which lies in my bank. Mine own private fortune was not sufficient, for I must tell you, what doubtless you know already, that South Sea stock is exceeding difficult to obtain at present, and it was only through the courtesy of Sir Frank Maynard that I was able to come at a block of shares. A friend of his has recently died and the widow, being timorous, desired to sell out her late husband's South Sea stock, to sell it entire and at once; I had not wherewith to buy so great a block of shares without assisting myself by the moneys in my strong-room. Sithee, Alec, this is a private talk; it must go no further." He spoke in a strange, biting tone, and he did not look at his nephew but down at the quill he was fraying.

"It would seem that your mind is changed upon this business," remarked Alec, in his slow, stolid way. "You now believe it to be all that its promoters claim for it, all that Sir Frank described?"

"I know not what I believe," cried Nat irritably. "There are times when I deem it the greatest cheat ever foisted on a nation. But my wife——" He broke off and bit his lip. "You have my leave to go, Alec; but be sure and keep close what I have said."

It was the dinner-hour, but Alec did not go to dinner. He put on his flat-cap and walked up Lombard Street towards 'Change Alley. He desired to ponder and to observe; and he was of the opinion that in the circumstances he could best do these things in the very centre of this raging pestilence of speculation. The heat was stifling, and he took off his cap and fanned himself with it. This whole summer had proved unhealthy; the weather had continued humid, without breezes, strangely oppressive. He remembered to have heard men say that they feared a return of the old Plague which had not been seen for thirty years and more. But when he came to 'Change Alley he forgot about the weather; used as he was by this time to a City gone mad, he yet could scarcely credit the sight which met him here.

'Change Alley was one solid wedge of people, all moving in the direction of Cornhill. It was the representative nature of this concourse that most astonished young Alec. Ladies of fashion jostled citizens' wives, the decorous damsel the woman of easy virtue; the three-tailed periwig and gold-topped cane of the modish physician were wedged in beside the blue petticoat and canvas jacket of the sailor; the single spur of the postilion jagged the decent black gown of the dissenting minister; the hanging-sleeves and green brief-bag of the lawyer were set beside the blue frock and cropped head of the apprentice; the white frock of the baker made conspicuous the scarlet coat and black gaiters of his neighbour of the Foot Guards; the scarred face of the gladiator pressed close to the prim countenance of the waiting-woman; two great figures of the literary world, Mr Pope and Mr Gay, pushed their way along, one on either side of a verminous beggar; and most astonishing of all, a bishop in his lawn sleeves was elbowed by a Billingsgate fish-vendor.

Alec joined the stream and was carried with it on to Cornhill. Here the crush was even greater, for besides the crowds of pedestrians there was every kind of vehicle. The ancient coaches of the country squires were rammed against the new chariots of the London beaux; small farmers had come up a-horseback and travelling tinkers sat astride their donkeys; up and down Cornhill, as far as the eye could see, were lines of sedan-chairs, forsaken by their bearers, who were scrambling to invest their shillings with their betters. Meantime the ballad-mongers, most persistent and most adaptable of all the London street-hawkers, cried their wares to the topical tune: *"Merry Remarks upon 'Change Alley: to a new Air called The Grand Elixir; The Philosophers' Stone at Last Discovered; The Stock-Jobber turned Gentleman.* Buy my new ballads! Buy!"

As Alec tried to squeeze his way towards the Royal Exchange, he caught snatches of the talk which hummed around him: "They say the Company's ships are returning from the South Seas laden with ingots of gold as huge as footballs." "The Treaty of Utrecht gave them a share in the slave traffic." "It will be the richest company the world has ever seen." "Silver will be as plentiful as iron." "Free trade is promised with all the Spanish colonies." "Last week Mr Smith was ripe for the Compter, but today you may see him riding in his coach." "A month since, Miss Robinson was earning her living at twopence a bout, but now has bought a decayed earl for husband and is a countess." "It is sober truth that Master Brown was considering a flit to the moon to save himself from the bums, and now he is a knight and has the entrée to the King's drawing-room." "It is guaranteed by the Government; it cannot fail." "My daughter is to be married shortly and I have ventured her dowry in it." "I said to him that he must wait a little for his money since I needed it to make my fortune." "I helped myself from master's strong-box, d'ye see?—but 'tis not robbery. I'll repay it next week, when I'll buy myself out of my indentures at the same time."

It was like being in a madhouse; it was a nightmare; and yet it was real, it was here before his eyes, all the world buying South Sea stock, the sober City of London caring for nothing, thinking of nothing, doing nothing but buying South Sea stock. And his master, that careful banker, that honest craftsman, that respected uncle, that shrewd financier, he likewise had caught the frenzy and had pledged everything he had, and everything he held in trust for his customers, in order to buy South Sea stock at the word of his wife.

It was hot, dreadfully, ominously hot. Women and even men were fainting with it; the burnished sky pressed down upon that crazy multitude like the hand of hell. Alec ought not to have forced his way into the Exchange; he had no business there, and he had seen enough while he was wrestling his way along 'Change Alley and across Cornhill. It was foolish and unnecessary to squeeze his way into that seething pandemonium, and all he achieved by his wilfulness was to cannon into a gentleman and topple him over like a ninepin. The gentleman's name (though Alec did not learn it then or ever) was Mr Henry Fordham; the gentleman really had a very good reason for being here today (though this also was never disclosed to Alec). Poor Mr Fordham had invested during April in the Welsh Copper Company; it ought to have prospered because it was quite genuine and Mr Fordham knew that the Prince of Wales had given it his patronage and had cleared something in the nature of forty thousand pounds. But unfortunately for Mr Fordham it was among the companies abolished through the jealousy of the South Sea promoters; Mr Fordham had lost heavily, and although he was a very rich man indeed he did not like losing, heavily or otherwise, in any venture; it was an insult to his shrewdness and it weighed upon him. He had come here today,

317

therefore, to make up that loss by investing in South Sea stock.

None of this was known to young Alec Moray and, indeed, none of it concerned him. What he likewise did not know, but which was to concern him very nearly, was that Mr Henry Fordham was not feeling at all well; that he had come upon 'Change today against the advice of his physicians; that he felt even hotter than the atmosphere warranted; and that he had that morning vomited, in the strict privacy enjoyed by the rich, it is true, but still had vomited in the same way as common men vomit when they are suffering from some infectious fever.

Alec, with all his faults, possessed the instinctive courtesy of his father's race. He hastened to assist Mr Fordham to his feet; he offered sincere apology for his clumsiness; he dusted Mr Fordham down with the latter's handkerchief, and then, perceiving that the article had become much soiled in the process, produced a clean one of his own. The encounter terminated with mutual expressions of goodwill; it ended also with Mr Fordham pursuing his goal in possession of Alec's clean handkerchief and Alec leaving 'Change with Mr Fordham's soiled one held in his hand. He did not know, poor Alec, what to do with an obviously rich merchant's soiled handkerchief; he did not like to throw it away for he had a great reverence for money and all its contacts. When he walked wearily into his grandfather's house that evening, he still had not discovered the proper way of disposing of such an article, but was unconsciously mopping his hot face with it.

But Maralyn, his mother, knew very vividly what to do with Alec. She took one look at him and then hustled him off to bed; then she ran as fast as she could to the nearest apothecary, knocked him up, and demanded some saffron, some red nettles, and an ounce of hedge-rife, praying with all her anxious soul the while that these herbs, when mixed with honey and ale, would prove as sovereign a remedy as Culpeper's *Herbal* declared them as a cure for the rare and the dreaded black jaundice.

(iv)

The God to Whom she prayed vouchsafed her an answer; Alec survived.

But it was a fight, and the toughest one of this poor woman's life. It was not merely the black jaundice that she fought; it was also some strange and frightening dementia in the patient. In his fever he raved, dreadfully and continuously: Uncle Nat and the South Sea Company, these were the two names which he repeated over and over again. In his delirium he seemed to wrestle with some frightful problem which centred round Uncle Nat and the South Sea Company, and although she did not understand what it was that troubled him she was vaguely alarmed, and would not let the neighbours sit with him lest, like Lady Macbeth, he said what he should not. She and her father and Michael Pennington took turns at watching by his bed; and one day, when his watch was ended and he was relieved by Maralyn, Michael came out of the sickroom looking very preoccupied and went across to the brewhouse to find his master.

The steam from the open copper in which the liquor was heated made the place dim, but he could distinguish the stout little person of the brewer by the mash-tun. Vance was instructing one of his 'prentices in the art of mashing.

"Now sithee, Tom, there is one golden rule to guide you: when you are able to see your face in the mash, then is it at the proper temperature. And then the mash-stick, Tom—nay, now, that is the fork, which is not employed till later—you must hold it so, and not so—— Well, Mr Pennington, what is it, what is it? I am much engaged."

"Your pardon, sir, but I would have private speech with you."

The brewer frowned.

"Pish, this is not at all a convenient hour. Howsoever, if the matter is pressing—Dick," cried he to his journeyman, "come hither if you please and instruct Tom in the use of the mash-stick till I return."

He trotted out into the yard and across to the counting-house, followed by Michael. When the door was shut, the latter began quickly:

"Mr Vance, I have been sitting by your grandson and in his fevered talk he said that which you should know without delay. It seems that his uncle has ventured all he has in this South Sea Company."

Vance stared at him.

"Pooh, the poor lad raves."

"I know it, sir, but I think there may be truth in his ravings. He gave a mighty circumstantial account of his uncle's action."

"Well, well, it may be so. Nat was mad in love with the lottery when he was a lad, and maybe the same mania hath bitten him now, for I count this speculation but another lottery. Yet I see not how this concerns me, sir, nor why you deemed it so important that you must needs carry me from my mash-tun in the middle of the morning."

"Mr Vance," said Michael slowly, "the loan made you by your son has never been repaid, and——"

"I know it, sir, I know it," snapped Vance, interrupting him in a testy manner. "Yet have I kept up the interest and Nat has never plagued me for the capital sum. I would have repaid it had the state of my trade allowed it; you should know that; but in evil times like these, when spirit-drinking grows apace, it is a great matter to maintain my family and pay my journeyman and——"

"Mr Vance, if your son chanced to lose the sum he has invested in the South Sea Company (and from what I have learned from Alec's ravings it is composed of his customers' money besides his own), he would be ruined, and the first thing he would do would be to call in every debt to save himself from dishonour and his wife from the parish. I tell you this that you may be forewarned. He would most certainly foreclose upon your mortgage if——"

He broke off, for there was the sound of running feet in the yard. Then the door of the counting-house burst open and Maralyn stood there, her face flushed, her mob awry, her eyes shining like stars.

"He is better!" she cried in a shaking voice. "He knew me! He spoke my name and asked for a draught of milk. He will live, Father; Alec will live!"

Then she threw herself into her father's arms and great tearing sobs began to rend her. The old man, with tears running down his own cheeks, looked over her shoulder at Michael and, awed as a child by some undreamed-of happiness, murmured brokenly:

"God is merciful to those who trust Him, Master Pennington. He has spared my grandson and will provide for me. Ease your mind, sir, ease your mind, for the Lord has care of laborious men."

Four

(i)

ON a Sunday early in the September of that same year Michael set out as usual towards the Crown in Russell Street to spend the day with Moll. A long while ago now, Moll had set herself up as the mistress of a brothel on the Bankside, her clientele being chiefly sailors; but she still came regularly every Sunday to meet her old friend at the Crown, unless she was what she vaguely described as indisposed, which meant that she was recovering from a bout of Madam Geneva.

Michael had come to dread the Sunday meetings; the sight of this withered old woman, the grey complexion of the gin victim plastered over with paint, the sunken eyes unnaturally bright, the lovely figure grown angular with age, filled him with a mixture of disgust and fierce pity; nor could he disguise from himself any longer the fact that, with passion so long dead between them, they had nothing in common wherewith to maintain their friendship. And Moll was utterly changed in temperament; it was not now as it had been when first she had succumbed to the prevailing vice and her fits of temper and jealousy were but occasional disturbances of their comradeship. Nowadays it was rare to find her equable, and there were times when she would fall into so sudden and noisy and unreasonable a rage that she seemed on the brink of madness. But his loyalty would not let him forsake her, and so Sunday after Sunday he went to meet her at their old haunt.

As he walked westwards from the City today he felt a curious uneasiness grow in his heart. He tried to tell himself that the unhealthy weather was to blame; he observed how the old habit, lapsed since his youth, of carrying a packet of cloves in the hand, had returned, for all men continued to fear another outbreak of the vanished Plague. Indeed, fevers of all kinds had been rampant in London this summer, most of them the result of the excessive gin-drinking, for the crude spirit undermined the health, lowered the resistance, and ruined the constitution of the strongest. The unhealthy weather, too, had bred pestilence. A thunderstorm was needed, he thought, and glancing up at the sky he noted that indeed there was that hard, copper-bright tint in the blue of it which often presages thunder, and that the clouds, piled in the west, were tinged with saffron. The air was stifling, without a breath of wind.

But the prosaic explanation of the weather for his uneasiness of heart did not satisfy him. It seemed to him that London looked restless instead of busy, overstrained, on edge, awaiting some catastrophe which could not be long delayed. Men whispered sibilantly together, oblivious of their surroundings; groups stood arguing fiercely; brawls broke out with alarming suddenness; people wandered aimlessly up and down with pre-occupied glance. It was this mania of speculation, he supposed, that had set London's nerves a-jangle; he had heard the most fantastic tales of late, of a society turned topsy-turvy, of beggars become wealthy overnight, of great fortunes lost in a few hours, of two hundred new coaches appearing on the streets, of three thousand new gold watches sold by the goldsmiths, of innumerable embroidered coats finding their way on to backs which previously had been content with sober broadcloth. He had heard, too, of the hundreds of families reduced to sudden penury, of the innumerable tradesmen ruined, by the abolition of so many of these "bubble companies", and of how Bedlam was become packed to suffocation by a multitude of folk whose nervous systems could not endure the strain of not knowing whether they would be penniless or fabulously rich upon the morrow. It must end soon, he reflected, this lunacy of stock-jobbing, this nightmare of credulity and avarice, but he did not see how it could end save in some great tragedy.

As he came into Fleet Street, and pushed his way through the streams of people going to morning service at St Bride's, his heaviness grew upon him. He was here among the scenes of his youth, scenes for ever infested with old memories of that first era when he had drawn a spiritual sword never afterwards to be sheathed, memories of plot and counter-plot, of youthful enthusiasm and vigour, of first love, of heartbreak, of piteous, white-hot hope. He had known this street when it had seethed with rumours dangerous enough to upset a dynasty, when the fathers of this crowd who now believed so sincerely the lies of stock-jobbers had swallowed with the like credulity the tale of a supposititious prince foisted on the nation by means of a warming-pan, of mythical hordes of Irish coming over to cut Protestant throats.

He came through Butchers' Row and turned right into Drury Lane, and his heaviness deepened with every step he took. The tall old houses he had known in his youth greeted him with a changed and melancholy aspect, and presently he could see, over the roof-tops which cut hard lines in the burnished sky, the statues which adorned the roof of Chesgrove House. A sword of pain stabbed at his heart. Chesgrove House, a hive of crawling humanity now, a nest of poor tenements, but once the grand new garish London seat of Lord Chesgrove, the father of Eve Barrowes, once a shrine which had housed a goddess, the incongruous, unworthy shrine of a female paragon, named, perhaps appropriately, Eve. In a sudden spasm of self-fury he dug his nails into the palms of his hands and told himself that it was silly, it was altogether inexcusable that, in late middle age, he should sentimentalise like a boy over the thought of an Eve who, even in his far-away youth, had proved no goddess but a very human woman who had made the sensible choice between love and respectability. But as he turned into Russell Street, and saw ahead of him that familiar sign of the Crown, and heard the comic creak of the board as it swung in a hot little wind which seemed to have sprung up from nowhere, a queer feeling fell upon him, a premonition not to be denied, that his past was about to overtake him, that some seed sown in youth was ready and ripe for the harvest.

He did not enter the tavern by the front door; he went round the side by the skittle-alley and came into a narrow strip of garden, protected by a high mellow wall. He knew the Crown, every inch of it, and he knew the habits of the friend who was as familiar with it as he was himself. And there she sat already, in the shade of a gnarled old walnut. She held her face-guard before her to protect her painted complexion from the sun, and she was dressed in green, the colour which suited her best and in which he always saw her in his mind's eye. The old heady scent called Eau d'Auge, to which she had remained faithful, greeted him like a challenge from the softer scents of flowers and sun-baked earth. There was a little table set before her, and on it stood a bowl of the Crown punch, ice-cold, with slices of lemon floating on its rich brown surface. Moll thrust out a friendly hand to him, and chuckled, and said:

"You are late, or I am early. It signifies not which. Only it is well that you are come, else would you have been constrained to call for another bowl of punch, for I must tell you I have such a thirst upon me that I shall drink this day as though I had twelve pound of sponge in my maw. Come, sit down, and dispense this nectar, and let us comfort one another."

"Are you in need of comfort, Moll?" he asked, sitting down beside her on the round seat and taking up the punch ladle. (It was poignant in his present mood to find here the old Moll, the genial friend, the merry companion, the easy, stimulating comrade of those days which suddenly had seemed to come so near to him that the thing called time became a mystery.)

"Marry am I. This cursed heat is bad for trade; when a man is so hot he can scarce think upon a bed without loathing, his thoughts will be far removed from coupling. All things droop in the heat, my friend, and I will tell you this: if there is no marrying or giving in marriage in heaven, most certainly there is no whoring in hell."

"I think there will be thunder anon," remarked Michael, looking up into the sky which now was drawing a dun-coloured curtain over its burning face.

"Thunder will do well enough," said Moll, spitting out a lemon pip. "Anything spectacular is good for my trade. Many a man has lost his fortune and found his manhood at the self-same moment. And a good, rousing storm, if it does not bring a man to his knees brings him into a posture a deal more pleasant for him and more profitable for a poor bawd."

She rattled on in this strain for some while, completely her old self, and presently he began to talk to her of his political hopes and fears, and of the heaviness which had weighed on him as he had walked from the City. She listened patiently, now and again throwing in some shrewd remark; it was marvellous to have her thus, and to confide in her as he had used to do.

" 'Tis like being with a father-confessor, Moll," he murmured, idly playing with a twig of the walnut near his cheek, "to sit here and talk with you."

Moll, mock-indignant, made the obvious answer.

When the smell of dinner penetrated to their sanctuary Moll suggested that they should dine in private ("because I am all out of humour with hell, of which the kitchen will be today a kind of ante-chamber"), and then each of them delighted the other by murmuring spontaneously, "The old Tapestry." For this was one of the private rooms of the Crown, a room they had hired sometimes when Michael was in funds or when the charm of their own company had made them long to avoid the crowded kitchen. All taverns possessed such rooms for the convenience of business men who wished to discuss some deal in private, or of attorneys who had a case to thrash out with their clients. But to Michael and Moll the Tapestry Room of the Crown in Russell Street was their own sacred domain, full of their memories, and of nothing but their memories. For youth has a trick of annexing such places, a trick which age itself, with all its disillusionment, cannot quite forget.

They dined well in their sanctum, on viands whose exact nature Michael instantly forgot, if, indeed, he ever knew it, for he was lifted from the depths of his heaviness on to the heights of a strange exaltation. They sat in the bow-window and ate and drank, and exchanged foolish merry badinage with the old familiar serving-man, and in intervals looked down into the street, their own particular street, to which she had introduced him when his youth lay in pieces round him and his heart was broken. He felt blessedly aloof from the restless, jostling crowds who, upon his way hither, had made him feel so exasperated and so pitiful. The wine of an old comradeship, recaptured so unexpectedly, had as it were intoxicated him, so that he felt like flinging an orange rind on to the roof of a passing coach and chuckling at his prank like some urchin. He murmured presently, out of this gay, irresponsible exuberance:

"It is a mad world, sweetheart. Like to an ant-hill disturbed."

"It will be madder on the morrow."

"Now what do you mean by that?" he asked carelessly, still gazing idly through the window.

"I mean that your ant-hill will be shaken by an earthquake tomorrow. For rather is it a world of bubbles, friend Michael, and the giant bubble, the South Sea Company, is ripe for bursting."

Her words went down and down into the depths of his mind and at last touched bottom with a kind of soft bump. He turned a bewildered face to her; and then, all of a sudden, the words she had spoken became alive, and his own private world, of memories and of a new lazy contentment, collapsed like a card-house. In a sickening somersault he became what indeed he was, a middle-aged man, deeply and permanently disturbed in the fibres of his being for the welfare of the world which was his chief concern, the world of England, of London, of laborious people, of little men and women, the world which now restlessly, aimlessly, surged by beneath his window, dreaming of unearned gold.

"The South Sea Company, the giant bubble, is ripe for bursting."

(ii)

He managed to say presently, deliberately keeping his glance withdrawn:

"You are pleased to jest."

"Am I so? It will prove but a sorry sort of jest, my friend, for all the fools who have plunged."

"But you must be mistaken, Moll. The Directors have just promised a dividend of fifty per cent."

She laughed.

"As a last hope of bolstering up a company which is tottering on the brink of ruin. La, Michael, it is passing strange that I, a poor bawd, should be more knowledgeable about this business than my little City clerk."

"Don't mock me, Moll, for God's sake. If you have private information let me share it. If you withhold it, it may mean the total ruin of an honest man."

She wriggled her shoulders irritably.

"I have given you what private information I have. You cannot expect me to recall the pesty details, for the jargon of the City is plain gibberish to me."

He took her hands and, steeling himself to patience, began to drag the details from her, translating her rambling fragments of talk into the language of finance, until at last he had gathered a coherent story. It seemed that Moll had an old client who had blabbed to her what she called "the whole business" the previous night. This man was one of the few of the old annuitants of the National Debt who had refused to receive South Sea stock in exchange for his claim upon the Government, but, a week or so since, he had decided to come in with the rest and had deposited his securities with the Company. He was told, however, that he must receive his stock written at the price of eight hundred, so that for his twenty-thousand-pound claim upon the Government he must be content with but three thousand of the Company's stock, though other men with the same claim were receiving six thousand as late as July. Furious, he demanded the voiding of his contract, but was met with the terms of the purchase he had signed, whereby nominees of the Company were given power to fix the price. It was his opinion that the Company was in a very bad way, else why should it treat late-comers like himself with less generosity than it had extended to the other annuitants? Also, he said, the Jews were beginning to avoid South Sea stock, a sure sign that the ship was sinking.

"And moreover," concluded Moll, "I will tell you this from mine own observation. In my trade I meet all sorts and conditions of men, and from the general talk of late I have gathered that the investing public, seeing so many companies put down, has begun to ask itself, overlate, what security there is in any such undertaking, ay, even in the dazzling South Sea itself. And when such fools begin to ask themselves that, my friend, the end is in sight. From lapping up the lies of every stock-jobber, they'll become such doubting Thomases that they'll disbelieve the Giants of St Dunstan's when they strike the hours."

"Yet the Company cannot fail," he muttered. "The Government stands behind it, and if need be will force the Bank of England to come to its aid."

"You think that, eh?" She smiled cryptically upon him. "Michael, my love, I think you must have caught this speculation madness and will not confess to it, else what means that white face, those trembling hands? Well, if you have, you had best sell out while there is time, and to cozen you into it I will tell you a secret; but mind, it must go no further, for it is the kind of secret which, if let out, will get one snabbled in the twinkling of an eye." She leaned towards him and whispered: "Sir Robert Walpole, who, as you doubtless know, has made a handsome pile out of the South Sea venture, has just sold out his shares at the top price of a thousand. There, sir! That is what made my client so sure that this giant bubble will go the way of the small ones."

Michael had been pale before; now he was ashen. Sweat stood out upon his forehead, and his lips trembled so violently that for a while he could not speak. Then, staring at Moll but not seeing her, he muttered:

"Walpole has sold out, eh? Walpole has a huge ambition and is well versed in the art of financial corruption. He showed that when he was Treasurer of the Navy. He has made his pile and can afford to let the South Sea down into the pit. He is capable of riding the storm which will follow better than any man in Government; he will sacrifice, wholesale, friends and foes alike, in order to appease the national fury; the whole structure of the Ministry will be shattered, and that will suit his game, for from the wreck will emerge one man (himself), the man who played for moderation, who worked to expose corruption in high places, who threw overboard the Jonahs, and who retained his nerve when the nation had lost theirs. Walpole, half aristocrat, half plutocrat, the very man, the very type, to bridge the gulf between aristocracy and plutocracy, the incarnation of the Revolution."

"A sweet pretty speech," said Moll dryly. "And now dismount, I pray, from your spavined hobby-horse, and let us have some more of this excellent Canary."

He paid no attention but continued:

"And yet it cannot happen so sudden and so sharp. If the Company must fall there will be a space before the final crash; the thing will slide downhill slowly——"

"I never knew you so timorous in facing facts," snapped Moll. "Be ruled by me, my friend, and sell out. My client swears that the hundred-pound share bought yesterday for a thousand will have dropped by tomorrow to five hundred, or even less. Did you ever see the excellent droll they played one year at Southwark Fair? A man climbed a rope hanging from the church spire, hand over hand, until he was so high he looked like a louse on a beau's foretop, and then—presto! —he was back upon the ground."

He said nothing, but stared down upon the hot and busy street. At first he did not see the street; he saw the garden in which they two had sat so happily and lazily before dinner. He saw the brown grass and the baked earth, and in the earth a crack. The fierce sun of greed had dried up the world of London, and it too was cracking before his inner eyes. Soon the crack would widen, the earth would gape, the decent houses and the sober streets would totter, and men and women—little, ordinary, too-credulous men and women—would awake to find themselves falling in a falling world, would see all their bright dreams disappear in an earthquake of wholesale ruin.

And then his gaze steadied, and he saw the street again, with its shuttered shops and its strolling 'prentices in Sunday attire and its hackneys a-clatter and its tradesmen and their wives out for an airing. Then the scene telescoped itself into one figure, and he stared upon that figure as though he saw a ghost, and cried out something he knew not what; for the figure which walked so briskly in the direction of Covent Garden, with a basket upon its arm and a kerchief tied neatly under its chin, was that of Maralyn Moray.

(iii)

For a moment he stared; then a kind of frenzy fell upon him, so that he sprang up and cried:

"I must go, Moll; I must go now, at once."

"Whither must you go? Pox on't, what ails you now? You are like a Jack-in-the-box and turn me dizzy. What a-devil makes you rave like a Bedlamite?"

"It is the South Sea Bubble," he stammered, scarce knowing what he said. "Ay, a bubble like all the rest. I tell you I must be gone."

But Moll also had looked down into the street and had seen the figure of the brewer's wench.

"So it is the South Sea Bubble which makes you so hot to leave me," she snarled softly. "Now, as I hope to be saved, the South Sea Bubble takes on a most unexpected guise today."

He did not hear her. His mind was tossed upon rough waves of thought; he could not steady it yet from the double shock of seeing in imagination a cracking world and in reality the figure of Maralyn walking so unconsciously through it. He had forgotten Walpole now, had forgotten abstractions and politics and theories; he saw the practical and immediate crisis staring at him, the little private crisis of the Vances; he saw a problem to be solved at once, but could not find solution. Only he knew that some instant action was imperative, and that the first thing he must do was to reach Maralyn and warn her of the peril which threatened herself, her father, and her son.

"I tell you I must go," he raged. "I cannot stay for explanations now. It is ruin and destruction for those I serve if I do not act immediately."

She sat staring up at him with a dangerous calm, and said distinctly:

"You will not leave me now. If you do, Michael Montague,

331

you will never see me again, nay, nor the brewer's chit neither, for I will put you in that place wherefrom you shall not stir till you step into Jack Ketch's cart. I threatened you once in the same fashion, but 'twas an idle threat. I promise you 'twill not be idle this time."

Her eyes held his, but he saw, not her snarling face, but a strange phantasmagorical vision of all his roots and his work and his past and his present being disintegrated, of his public and private worlds whirling in a sickening nightmare of chimneys tumbling and a sharp scent reeking and a green hood like a cave and a multitude of workworn hands toiling at a million tasks and money falling like golden rain and a man sitting astride a nation, riding it hideously, a man with a fat and jolly face and the vision of his own interest fixed in front of him like a distorted grail. Then he shook his head and blinked, turned clumsily, knocking over a stool, hammered down the stairs, jostled his way through the crowded entrance of the tavern and debouched upon the street; and at last came out of semi-delirium to see a pair of mild brown eyes gazing up at him with an expression of mingled astonishment and reproach. He recovered sufficiently to take off his hat and bow to her. Then he seized her arm and gabbled:

"Maralyn, I must have speech with you. It is a matter of life or death."

"Why, Mr Pennington, I—I cannot stay now. I am promised to call upon my mother-in-law and I am late already. I visit her every Sunday," added Maralyn irrelevantly; and she tried to disengage her arm. Her eyes added plainly: "I think you must be drunk."

"You cannot visit her today," snapped Michael, retaining his grip. "You must return with me to the City. Upon the way thither I will tell you what I have discovered, and we will strive to think what we must do."

"Nay, Mr Pennington, you really must permit me to hasten to Bedfordbury and inform Mrs Moray that I cannot be with her until later. 'Tis the least I can do. She will be expecting me, and 'twould be mighty discourteous and unkind to——"

"I tell you that unless we act immediately you and your father will be ruined."

Without giving her time to expostulate further he began to drag her in the direction of Drury Lane, but as he went he felt his glance impelled upwards, and there he saw, standing at the window of the Tapestry Room, the figure of Moll. His glance met hers, and in her eyes he saw his doom, he saw a friend turned implacable enemy, and he knew that the presentiment he had experienced upon his way hither had not been an idle fancy, and that here among the scenes of his youth his fate had been sealed.

He got a hackney in Drury Lane and directed the man to carry them to Cheapside. During the drive he must decide what he must do, but the first thing was to make Maralyn understand the peril.

"Listen, mistress. I am about to betray your father's confidence, but it cannot be avoided and you would learn the truth shortly in any case; 'tis kinder to let you hear it from me, and besides I need your help. In 1711, when you were very sick, your father, being pressed for money, borrowed the sum of one hundred pounds from your brother. As security for this loan, Nat demanded your father's brewhouse and his dwelling-house, with all which they contain. Your father, though he has kept up the interest, has not found himself able to repay the principal, and Nat has let the debt run on, being free to foreclose at any time should he demand the principal and your father fail to find it. Do you understand what I say?"

She stared at him, and even in the dimness of the hackney he saw her face whiten as he looked at it. There was bewilderment and horror in her eyes, but she managed to murmur faintly:

"Yes, yes, I understand."

"Now, I have just learnt that the South Sea Company, in which your brother has invested all he has, stands upon the brink of ruin. When it crashes, or rather when your brother learns that it is tottering, he will seek to lay his hands on every penny owed him, he will foreclose on every mortgage, call in every loan. We must face facts, Maralyn; Nat has never shown himself merciful in the past, and it is impossible he will do so in such a crisis of his fortunes."

"I cannot believe——"

"You must believe," he interrupted harshly. "Nat will foreclose unless he is prevented. How to prevent him is the problem on which we must bend all our thoughts."

She said nothing, only stared at him. He could not bear that helpless, bewildered gaze, and he turned his head away in order to escape it. But now he could see through the window of the coach the crowds in Fleet Street, and instantly there returned the evil vision of a falling world, of ants running aimlessly hither and thither before being swallowed up in wholesale destruction. He jerked his head, clasped his hands tightly together, and forced himself to concentrate upon the practical problem which confronted him.

"I suppose that the first thing to do is to consult with your father. Maybe he could borrow the sum from his goldsmith."

"My father is dining at Brewers' Hall. It is the Charter Feast, you see. Besides I am sure——"

"Then must we act without him. Harkee, Maralyn, it is unlikely that your brother will have got warning of the state of the South Sea Company, for the affair is secret at present. Therefore must we lay our hands upon the hundred pounds today and obtain from him your father's deed of mortgage. But it must be done this very day. Tomorrow will be too late, for there will be whispers of the coming crash on 'Change and Nat will not fail to hear them. Yet how to get the money? Maralyn, within the next twelve hours we must have one hundred pounds. We must beg it, borrow it, steal it if need be, but have it we must and will."

"It is a very huge sum," murmured Maralyn, who obviously had not understood half of what her companion had gabbled at her so fiercely.

"A huge sum! Pish, 'tis a trifle." He laughed suddenly and

334

shortly in a kind of snort. "A man in this town had a twenty-thousand-pound claim upon the Government—a man, say I? A score of men. And Walpole, what is the tune of the sum he has made out of the shares he has just sold to a duped public? And what is the sum-total of all the bribes to Ministers which made the hoax possible? One hundred pounds! Why, a man pays that for a gold watch; there have been three thousand gold watches sold to the new wealthy men of the South Sea Bubble during these last few months. And yet in all this great town of new wealthy men there is not an hundred pounds to spare for the saving of one honest craftsman from ruin. But by God I will get it, if I have to turn tobyman and hold up a coach on Hampstead Heath."

"Oh, pray, Mr Pennington, do not jest about such things. And pray do not speak so loud. The coachman might chance to hear you, and a jest of that nature is sufficient to bring a man to—to Tyburn."

Then he turned and smiled at her and said gently:

"I am meet for Tyburn, Maralyn, and have been these many years. But you cannot hold up coaches in daylight, and you must have a horse and a face-guard and reasonable youth." They jolted on for some way in silence. Then, suddenly, he slapped his hand upon his knee and cried: " 'Sblood, what a fool am I! Why, there is Jack Bunch. I mind me how your father told me he had blabbed of his trouble to Bunch and how that good friend had offered straightway to lend him what he required, but he would not have it so. I'll go to Bunch; I'll state the case to him and throw myself upon his mercy. If I come not forth from his house with one hundred pounds in my purse you may call me a Dutchman."

"Mr Pennington," said Maralyn, in a low and trembling voice, "you really must listen to me. You must not borrow from Mr Bunch on my father's account; my father would die of mortification."

"He will die of a broken heart if I do not borrow."

"You do not understand what I would be at," pursued Maralyn obstinately. "My father has never sought for charity and never will. He has his proper pride——"

"And pride has its proper place," snapped Michael, "a place at present usurped by stark necessity." Then again he turned to her with gentleness, took her fidgeting hands and held them strongly. "My dear, you must strive to understand the desperate case we are in. If your brother forecloses on that mortgage, Maralyn, as assuredly he will do unless we are able to forestall him, your father's brewhouse and his dwelling-house will pass from his possession for ever; and, more than that, the very meaning of his life will pass likewise. He is old, and yet I know he could face poverty with a stout heart and with the courage of his sturdy race and character. But the passing of everything he has ever loved and striven after, the destruction overnight of that piece of solid craftsmanship which is his inheritance and which he regards as a sacred trust, the wresting from him of his mash-tub and his vats and his copper and his books—his books, Maralyn, Chaucer and Herrick and the Water Poet—and last, but by no means least, the loss of his independence and his ability to maintain his family, those I think he could not face, be his courage never so high, his heart never so dauntless. You spoke a while ago of proper pride, and here indeed it has its proper place, in the hearthstone of home, in the tools of a trade, in the independence of a skilled craftsman of London City."

She stared at him, and her eyes filled with sudden tears. He pressed her hands and said softly:

"Maralyn, I crave your answer. Will you go with me and plead your father's cause with Mr Bunch? Will you share with me that humiliation, that you may share with me later the triumph, when we lay before your father that deed of mortgage and watch him tear it up?"

She could not speak, but she nodded vigorously. Then she snatched her workworn hands from his grasp and buried her poor face in them.

(v)

The next hour or so was very sober and prosaic. They alighted at the sign of the Old Swan in Bucklersbury and bade the hackney wait for them. They plied the knocker of Mr Bunch's dwelling-house, disturbing the Sabbath calm. They learnt from Mr Bunch's sister, who opened to them, that, by the greatest good fortune, the master of the house had not gone to Brewers' Hall, because he was suffering from an attack of the gout. They were ushered into the presence of Mr Bunch, who was sitting with his bad leg propped upon a cushion, and prevailed upon him to give them a private interview. Then, baldly and briefly, Michael stated the case and solicited the brewer's help.

Michael had retained an uneasy doubt as to Bunch's reaction to this request, but he discovered now that he had underrated the beer-brewer. That good man did not understand all that was told him about the South Sea and its imminent crash, for he distrusted the stock-jobbers as heartily as did Vance himself, and it was his pride to boast that he "knew nought of such iniquities". But he did understand that Nathaniel Vance, his old crony, was in the most desperate straits for the lack of one hundred pounds; he understood likewise that Nathaniel Vance junior, whom he had always detested as a saucy young jackanapes, could be cheated out of his pound of flesh if he, Jack Bunch, produced the hundred pounds there and then. Having got these concrete facts firmly wedged in his mind, he heaved himself out of his chair with many grunts and groans, shouted to his sister to bring him his cap and a stout canvas bag, and announced his intention, first of going to the goldsmith who had charge of his moneys, and then of accompanying Michael and Maralyn to Lombard Street.

" 'Twill do me more good than a flagon of my best beer to see yonder Jew-hearted usurer bilked," said he heartily.

So they went out to the waiting hackney and drove to Goldsmiths' Row; here Mr Bunch knocked up his friend Mr Green and demanded a few minutes' talk with him. He returned to the hackney with a beaming smile and a canvas bag which bulged and jingled. He seemed to have forgotten his gout and was in the best possible humour, enjoying in anticipation the besting of Nat and the forthcoming ruin of all those fools who had invested in the bubbles. The latter spectacle would, he asserted, teach the City a timely lesson, and when the madness was past the citizens would return to sober craftsmanship again and would forget their troubles in his beer.

"But harkee, Mr Pennington," said Bunch, the words jolted out of him as the coach bumped up and down over the cobbles, "not a word to Vance about my lending of this money. I know him and his woundy pride; he'd never forgive me for settling his debt with money earned by that poor weed the hop."

"But how am I to explain the obtaining of the money?" asked Michael, in some dismay.

"Say you found it, sir," replied the brewer vaguely. "Ay, say you picked it up. Stay!" he added, slapping Michael on the shoulder. "Say you plunged in the bubbles and sold out your shares in time."

Bunch's appreciation of his own jest occupied him during the remainder of the drive, but Michael had to make an effort to join in the good man's mirth. There was a sickening doubt in his mind as to whether Nat could be persuaded to yield up the deed of mortgage without Mr Vance's signature to a receipt. In any case the interview must be handled with the utmost delicacy, and Michael therefore set himself to persuade the militant and jubilant Bunch to leave the matter in his hands and to remain in the hackney while Nat was being interviewed. Bunch proved difficult to persuade, and might indeed have refused outright (so strong was his shameless anticipation of seeing Nat put down), had not Maralyn proved an unexpected ally.

"I cannot help but feel that Mr Pennington is right in this matter, sir," she said timidly. "My brother might take it into his head to resent your presence, and then all would be ruined."

Bunch, who had a great admiration for his old friend's daughter, grudgingly gave in, and handed the canvas bag into Michael's custody, only begging them to remember that if they needed an ally, or if there was a rascally head to be broken or a

Jewish arse to be chastised, he, Jack Bunch, would be waiting outside the house and would have much pleasure in executing these punishments on their behalf.

A servant admitted Michael and Maralyn and bade them wait in the hall. The fellow's manner had less of insolence in it than of preoccupation; he gave the impression of being devoured with that half-guilty curiosity and enjoyment which some "scene" in the master's household never fails to arouse in his kind. Michael himself was convinced, as he stood in the sober hallway, that somewhere in the house a domestic crisis was in progress. He heard voices talking incessantly, not raised, but one against the other in sustained bitterness; and when at last Nat came out to them Michael noted the man's agitation, though it was admirably concealed behind a mask of cold formality. In that moment he was sorry for Nat, not knowing why; perhaps it was because he felt that Nat too was but an ant, absorbed in his own futile activities and unaware that the whole ant-hill was soon to disintegrate.

Upon the way hither Michael had endeavoured to rehearse the manner in which he would make known the nature of his errand to the banker. But he had not been able to concentrate, and now he found himself saying the first thing that came into his head:

"I am come, Master Nathaniel, from your father, who lies very sick of the gout." (He heard Maralyn gasp at this unexpected and to her quite incomprehensible lie, and went on quickly, raising his voice a little.) "I beg your pardon for that I have intruded upon you on a Sunday, but my master's mind would not be set at rest until I had despatched for him a trifle of business which is troublesome to him. It seems that he owes you the sum of one hundred pounds, and I am come to repay it."

There was a profound silence, in which a roll of thunder grumbled over the roof-tops like ominous drums. Then Nat jerked his head towards his sanctum, turned on his heel, and led the way. When they were all seated he said stiffly:

"I really am at a loss to understand why my father should be in such haste. I do not transact business on a Sunday, as he very well knows. But since he seems so concerned to have this debt repaid, and is stricken with the gout, I will send a clerk tomorrow to his brewhouse and the necessary formalities can be despatched."

Michael licked his lips. He had no knowledge of the laws which govern mortgages, and he did not know how far he could press Nat to take the money now. To persuade him to do this was of the first importance, for it was unlikely that tomorrow he would escape hearing rumours of the coming crash and then it was possible that by some trickery he might seize on the brewhouse, which would be more valuable to him than a paltry hundred pounds. Michael felt pretty certain that the banker had heard no such rumours so far; his manner was, indeed, preoccupied, but not to the degree it must have been had he learnt the fatal news.

"Why, sir," said Michael, sinking his voice to a confidential undertone, "since you are my master's son I will tell you privily that Mr Vance's trade is sadly fallen off of late and that he has been much concerned to know what he can do to restore it."

"Such concern is somewhat over-late," sneered Nat.

"It may be so. But I must tell you that my master has a business deal impending which he hopes will prove a remedy, but which cannot be carried through unless his brewhouse is free from mortgage."

"Indeed?" said Nat indifferently.

"Ay, sir, that is the way of it," gabbled Michael, fearful all the time that the truth-loving Maralyn would make some interjection which might ruin all. "You are acquainted with your father's old friend and rival, Mr Bunch, the beer-brewer? Well, it seems that Mr Bunch is minded to buy a share in Mr Vance's business, upon what terms I need not discuss. But I must tell you that Mr Bunch is engaged to call upon your father this very evening to debate upon the matter, and therefore is my master in labour to have this debt cleared off without delay."

It sounded horribly unconvincing to poor Michael, and he sweated as he awaited Nat's comments.

"My father," remarked Nat, not troubling to disguise his contempt, "was always nice upon such trifling points of honour,

340

but it would interest me mightily to know where he has obtained the money to pay off this debt."

A curt demand that he should mind his own business sprang to Michael's lips, but he dared not offend the banker at this ticklish moment.

"Why, sir," said he with a show of reluctance, "I myself was so fortunate as to win a trifle upon 'Change, and have put it at your father's disposal."

"So?" Nat's lips curled and his eyebrows went up. "You surprise me, Mr Pennington. I mind me how set you were against the public lotteries years ago. 'It demeans the kingdom and excites to cupidity,' said you. Well, for my part I can see but little difference between the lottery and stock-jobbing, but doubtless you have satisfied your tender conscience on the point." He paused, but Michael said nothing. "Well," added the banker, "I will oblige my father in this matter if I can."

He rose and left the room, returning presently with a ledger and some papers. Sitting down at his desk he opened the ledger, turned the pages, and ran his finger down some columns. Michael, sick with relief, filled with a desire to get out of this house and have the business done with, sat silent, and Maralyn, who had not spoken a word, fiddled nervously with the handle of her basket.

"H'm," said Nat presently, "I find here that the interest is paid up to date, and indeed it is my custom to have it paid quarterly in advance." And then, drawing a legal-looking document from the pile of papers, he went on: "Here is the deed of mortgage. You will be good enough, sister, to receive it on my father's behalf. I must add that I am breaking the habit of a lifetime in thus transacting business on a Sunday, but as my father is about to do the only sensible thing I have ever known him to do as a tradesman, I am willing to waive such irregularity. He is about to act upon the principle that the combining of a multitude of small firms to form a few great ones best benefits the nation."

Before Michael could stop himself he had asked:

"You would apply that maxim to all trades, sir, including the bankers?"

"Certainly," replied Nat calmly. "Indeed I may tell you that I have it in my mind to buy up several bankers anon. Such merging is a sign of the times and the keynote of progress."

"I remember that the landlords applied something of that principle when they enclosed the common lands," said Michael in a head-voice, "with the result that England has no longer a free peasantry."

"She has in its place," retorted Nat, "a large body of labourers who have no longer to fear how they may support themselves and their families, since they have become wage-earners and are secured from want by the prosperity of their lords. If my father had put by his foolish pride, and had been content to work for some great brewer instead of for himself, he would not have found himself in the straits he is in now."

Michael's fingers itched, but he managed to restrain himself, and, without a word, took up the canvas bag and counted out the gold upon the table. Nat re-counted it with expert fingers, scooped it into a drawer, which he then carefully locked with a key he took from a string around his neck, and rose.

"You will present my service to my father," he said to Maralyn, "and convey to him my heartfelt approval of the step he is taking."

Before Maralyn could answer, Michael hastily expressed his gratitude to the banker for his kindness and hurried her out of the room. As they neared the outer door, another opened behind them and someone called Nat's name. Michael observed how the banker started and turned pale; looking over his shoulder, he saw the figure of Susan Vance silhouetted in a doorway. She stood with her hands upon her hips and her head a little tilted to one side; she said nothing, but stood there waiting for her husband to obey her call. Michael, overwhelmed by a sudden pity for this strange man who combined in his character so much hardness and so much weakness, was about to ask Nat to give him a few minutes' private talk that he might warn him of the forthcoming crash on 'Change, but Nat, with a stiff bow to his sister and a curt nod to Michael, turned hastily and hurried to his wife like an obedient dog.

342

(vi)

But the moment the outer door had closed behind Maralyn and Michael, the latter forgot all about Nat, his domestic crisis and coming tragedy, for relief flooded him with so overwhelming a wave that he felt faint. The thing was done, Vance's ruin was averted; in a mad and toppling world at least one decent craftsman would retain his independence, his sanity, and his self-respect, at least one ant would survive the disintegration of the ant-hill.

The roll of thunder had grown to a series of ear-splitting cracks as once more they drove through the streets of London on the last journey of that eventful day. Huge drops, single now, but soon to merge into one solid sheet of rain, fell noisily upon the coach-roof, and they saw through the "glasses" how men looked anxiously up at the leaden sky and began to quicken their pace to escape the deluge. They were blissfully ignorant as yet, these anxious citizens, that a greater deluge was about to overtake them, a cataract of ruin which would sweep them away. But the pity in Michael's heart was dulled to an ache, for he was drained of emotion; mentally and physically he was exhausted, and feeling was numb. It was as much as he could do to answer Bunch's eager questioning regarding the late interview, and to join in the latter's uproarious laughter at the tale.

"'Uds, sir," cried Bunch, "you have mistaken your trade. With such a talent for cozening you should have been a tally-man."

"Or a politician," murmured Michael with dull bitterness.

They set down Mr Bunch at his own door, and pleaded fatigue as an excuse for refusing his pressing invitation to come and celebrate their victory in his best beer. So at last they splashed up to the entrance of Bird-in-Hand Court, and saw and heard familiar things, the well-known tumble of roofs, the harsh creak of the well-chain, the red lattices of Le Bere Tombeth and the Lion, the closed gates of the brewhouse yard,

the golden cock upon his hoop, the flowerpots on the window-
ledges, the arms of the Brewers' Company proudly carved in
plaster, all drenched and sodden in the rain. At the rattle of
their hackney the door of Mr Vance's dwelling-house burst
open, and there was the brewer himself, in his Sunday clothes
and old-fashioned monstrosity of a wig. He came running out
to them, and cried anxiously:

"Bless me, bless me, what's this? I did not look to see you
home so soon, Mr Pennington, and with my daughter. Maralyn,
my love, is all well with you? I feared for you in this storm,
I vow I did."

"All is well, Father," said Maralyn, "all is very well." And
then, to his surprise and embarrassment, she put her arms
around him and hugged him tightly, kissing him again and
again upon the cheek. His old face, creased with lines of laughter round the eyes and with just a few wrinkles of care around
the mouth, stared at Michael over her shoulder in comical
bewilderment.

"There, wench, there; here's a great to-do in the public eye.
Come in with you now unless you would have us drowned. And
you likewise, Master Pennington. We'll take a pot of mulled
ale together, lest you have gotten you a chill in this pesty
storm."

But when they were come into the house Michael said to him:

"Mistress Maralyn has much to tell you, sir, and I will not
intrude. Likewise I think I should return whence I came, for
I left a friend most unmannerly and would make my apologies
if I can."

"But your friend is here, sir," said Vance, smiling at him.

Michael stared at him; and something cold closed on his
heart.

"Ay, sir," continued the brewer, bustling into the living-room,
"he is yonder abovestairs, and so has saved you a journey. A
gentleman arrived just after I returned from Brewers' Hall, and
asked if you were in. When I told him no, he said that you were
expecting him, that he knew you very well, and that, if I pleased,
he would wait in your room for your return. I supposed that
you had given him an appointment to wait upon you here, and

therefore did I show him to your chamber. I do hope, Mr Pennington, that I have not done amiss," he added, for it seemed to him that the other was looking at him with rather an odd expression.

But Michael smiled at him, and answered:

"No, sir, no indeed. I will go up immediately and see my— friend. For it is true I have been expecting him." And then he added, as if to himself: "I have been expecting him for many years."

He bowed to the father and daughter, and began to climb the stairs. He heard from the living-room Vance's cheerful voice, and smelt the good odour of mulled ale. He was conscious of no emotion save a great weariness of mind and body; the bombardment of heaven's artillery, which crashed and cracked over London, seemed to beat down thought. Before his tired eyes little vignettes kept passing: Bunch's parlour, swathed and shrouded in his sister's "knotting", the silhouette of Susan with her hands upon her hips, Vance's monstrous foretop nodding as he trotted out to meet them, the cracked earth of a garden, a figure in green at a window, a row of decayed statues on a roof, Maralyn's smiling eyes, the crowds in Cheapside hurrying home to escape the storm. These things were passing from him, were already of the past; he was done with them and they with him, for this was the end of an era, the era of Michael Pennington, the brewer's clerk. For Michael Montague, Jacobite pamphleteer, there remained the last short stage of a long journey, at the end of which he would climb another stair, a narrower stair, a stair from which there would be no descending.

So at last he came to the door of the poor little garret which had been his home for so long; he opened it quietly, closed it behind him, and leaned back against it. A figure straightened up from bending over a trunk, a figure once very familiar to him in the long past. The trunk was open and piles of papers from it lay upon the table, spilling over on to the floor. But Michael did not look at these things, these precious things, for they too were of the past; he looked at Tom Fields, once his fellow-Pensioner at the Court of King James the Second, now some official at the Court of King George the First. Tom Fields turned and looked at him, and for a while they stood thus without speaking, noting the change which thirty years had wrought in each of them.

"Why, how do, Tom?" said Michael at last, smiling. "You have tracked me down, it seems."

The other cleared his throat.

"I have tracked you down, as you say, Michael," he said curtly; but it was the kind of curtness a man employs in order to cover some emotion. "I am come here to arrest you; you know that?"

"I scarce thought you were come to shake me by the hand," said Michael dryly.

"As a man who values friendship, I am sorry," pursued Tom Fields, still curt and short. "As a good subject of King George, I am glad. You have done a great deal of mischief during the past thirty years, my friend."

"You flatter me. Well, it would seem that you have helped yourself to my secrets," he added, indicating the scattered papers and the open trunk.

"It was my duty."

"I know it, Tom. I hope you'll get the reward; there was a price put on my head during the Fifteen rising and I suppose it is still there." He came and leant against the table. "Pray tell me, Tom, just out of curiosity, what kind of a post have you under the Hanoverian?"

"I am Master of the Household and sit upon the Board of Green Cloth with the other officers, the Comptroller and so on."

"An excellent post, I should imagine. Are any of our old friends with you?"

"No, none. Most of the Household officers are German. . . . Michael, we must be gone."

"Fie, you should not hurry me to the shambles; that is indecent. I do but thirst for a little news from a world we both shared when we were young. But it is a changed world now, and I have nought to do with it. Even Whitehall is gone." Then he got off the table and came up to his old friend. "Harkee, Tom, there is one favour I would ask of you."

"If it is in my power to grant it, Michael, it is yours. You know that."

"Ay, I know that. Damme, my friend, but I hope that in this whirligig of falling and rising Ministers which must come as a result of a certain imminent crash upon 'Change, you may find yourself in a better post than that of Master of the Household. If we must have Revolution principles, let us at least have men who possess principles, even though they be Revolution ones; if we must have Whigs, let us have honest, sincere Whigs like yourself, and not whiffling time-servers. You and I agreed upon that matter thirty years ago; do you remember?"

He leant back against the table once more, and sighed with fatigue.

"Concerning this favour, Tom. I know not how much you have discovered in regard to the manner of my private life since last we met, but I will tell you this upon my word of honour: the household in which I live and work as a clerk is a good, honest household, loyal to King George; it has not, and never has had, any part in my seditious work. I ask you, then, that you will protect it; that you will see to it that no member of my good master's household suffers in goods or in person as a result of my arrest. I swear to you that not one of these people is a Jack; with Michael Montague they have nothing to do, but as Michael Pennington the clerk they have protected me and harboured me and paid me and have given me more friendship and charity than ever I can describe. I swear all this before Almighty God. Moreover, you have proof there in those papers that I am guilty of the charge which shall be brought against me, nor will you find me minded to deny it; therefore there will be no occasion to call any of these people as witnesses at my trial. Will you, then, give me your word that you will use your best endeavours to prevent them being disturbed, or questioned, or otherwise inconvenienced, by reason of their having harboured me?"

"I give you my word," said Tom without hesitation, "and likewise my hand upon it."

Michael gripped the hand outstretched to him, and held it for a moment with a smile. Then, as he turned to straighten his dress and periwig, the other said to him with a certain abruptness:

"It is but right that you should know how I came to discover you. I vow I am reluctant to tell you this, for the whole affair stinks in my nostrils; yet in justice to you I must make known to you the identity of the person who informed upon you. It was a woman, Michael, a wretched drab. God knows how you came to give her your confidence; it was the worst day's work you ever did. But she was so particular in her account of you, when she laid the information this morning, that I was constrained to come hither to investigate according to her directions; and when I was come and did discover these" (he swept his hand towards the papers) "I could not doubt her story. Her name, or the name she goes by, is Moll Stephens."

The rain was streaming down upon the world in a solid blanket now, darkening the window, and he could not see the other's face. And the voice which answered him was full of some emotion equally obscure as it said quietly:

"You are mistaken, Tom. Her name is Madam Geneva. . . . Come, let us go."

Five

(i)

MICHAEL MONTAGUE (for he had no longer any need of his alias) was committed to Newgate upon Sunday, the seventh of September 1720. His arrest excited no interest in London; he had worked for thirty years in chosen obscurity, and in obscurity was his person arrested and his work suppressed. But even had he been notorious, London would have had no time to think of him at this moment, for his arrest took place on the very eve of the bursting of the great South Sea Bubble.

On Monday, September the eighth, the shares of the South Sea Company fell abruptly from one thousand to five hundred. During the week they rose again to six hundred and seventy-five; this was the result of a rumour to the effect that the Bank of England and the wealthy East India Company were coming to the aid of the tottering South Sea. But either these powerful concerns learned in time how the Company stood, or else the rumour was born of desperate optimism; at all events the stock sank and sank, first to six hundred, then plunging giddily to one hundred and seventy-five, then to one hundred and thirty-five; and still it fell and fell. The deluge was beginning; the great delusion was at an end. King George was recalled from his beloved Hanover (whither he went as regularly as King William had gone to his beloved Holland); not that he was capable of saving anybody, but the Ministry, his Whig Ministry, saw itself threatened by the failure of this vast lottery in which it had taken so dangerous and so ignoble a share, and it was hoped that His Majesty's presence might restore its credit; it failed to do so, and such a run was begun upon the Bank of England that even that solid institution staggered.

'Change Alley was as crowded as ever, but now the throng was as eager to sell as formerly it had been to buy. The hack pamphleteers and playwrights, encouraged by the Tories, who saw in this catastrophe a chance sent direct from heaven to snatch the prestige they had despaired of recovering, heaped fuel upon the flame of public panic with their caricatures, their "Merry South Sea Ballads", and their farces acidly entitled *The Broken Stock-Jobbers; as lately acted by His Majesty's Subjects in 'Change Alley,* and *South Sea; or the Biter Bit.* In the gaming clubs, when a knave was turned up in a pack of cards, it became fashionable to exclaim: "There's a South Sea director for you! " Some enterprising merchant issued a pack of "Stock-jobbing" cards, each of which was engraved with the name and project of one of the bubble companies abolished by the jealousy of the South Sea; ladies had pictures ridiculing the Company painted on their fans, and a certain Mr Hogarth launched his first political caricature on the same theme. The Tory papers were full of vicious woodcuts; there were politicians blowing bubbles, directors drawing a car of fortune whose wheels crushed the books of merchandise, an infatuated crowd hurrying from 'Change to the madhouse, and Aislabie, Scraggs, Sunderland and others in the Ministry having their pockets filled while they carefully looked the other way. But in all these caricatures, in all these sneering squibs and farces and broadsheets, the image and the name of Sir Robert Walpole were conspicuous only by their absence.

For he was a past-master in that craft of not letting his right hand know what his left hand did, of making his pile without leaving his tracks, of bluffing his fellow-plutocrats and even his enemies. He had made a fortune out of the South Sea Company, and it was a huge one; but all the public realised was that he had warned the nation from the commencement of the mania of the evils which must follow such irresponsible speculation, that he had endeavoured to get the Bank and the East India Company to engraft the South Sea stock into their own, and that, having failed, he and he alone kept his head and confidently assured the panic-stricken nation that it should be avenged if not resuscitated. In the new year of 1721, it was his influence that forced through a reluctant House of Commons a demand for the examination of the Company's books and an order to the Directors forbidding them to leave the kingdom; it was he who introduced a Bill whereby an enquiry was authorised into all stock bought or sold by or on behalf of the politicians in the Treasury and the Exchequer. The politicians, friends and foes alike, trembled in their shoes, and looked with something approaching awe upon this ill-bred, jolly Norfolk squire, who not so long ago had suffered imprisonment in the Tower for corruption, and who now, hated by the King, distrusted by all his colleagues, scarcely known to the public, played with such amazing skill that game of moderation which can so surely destroy all opponents in a time of crisis, and whose immense, ill-gotten wealth now set him above all rivals.

And all this while Michael Montague remained in Newgate, awaiting his trial. Sessions were held at the Justice Hall in the Old Bailey eight times a year, and his arrest had taken place just after the conclusion of one of these Sessions. The next one, the last of the year, would not come on until late in December, and meantime he was incarcerated in a cell called the Middle Stone Ward, on the third storey of the City gate which spanned Newgate Street, and which had been rebuilt after the Fire. This cell was eighteen feet long and ten feet broad, and he shared it with six other prisoners; its one window, heavily barred, looked westwards towards Snow Hill, with the tall spire of St Sepulchre's Church thrusting up a warning finger in the foreground.

Newgate, in common with all prisons of the period, was filthy, verminous and overcrowded, and all the officers, from the Governor downwards, demanded a bribe for the smallest favours. But on the other hand it was a human, sociable sort of place; a prisoner was liable to catch jail-fever and to be tormented by lice, but he did retain his individuality and never lacked for company. Because Michael had not the wherewithal to bribe the turnkeys he was heavily fettered at night, but during the day he was free to walk about and drink in the boozing-kens, not, indeed, in the Press Yard, for that cost money, but in the narrow yard of the Common Side where the poorer sort took their exercise. There was very little surveillance, for Newgate relied upon its high walls and strong doors for its prisoners' security; the turnkeys, though drunken and greedy, were at least human beings and not mere machines; and among his fellow-prisoners Michael found a rough sort of comradeship.

Newgate had a language all its own. Thus to "fly your kite" was to settle to an evening's drinking; "fiery" was spirits, chiefly gin; drink in general was "rum booze"; a good feed was a "double dabber"; a whore was a "hornie", a turnkey a "stag", and a pawnbroker a "rumbo ken". A man's nearest neighbour in Newgate was always his "chum"; Michael's "chum" in the Middle Stone Ward was a poor little creature known as Jen; no one, not even Jen himself, knew his real name, for he had been abandoned by his starving mother when he was an infant, and had picked up a living as best he could from the time when he could scarcely walk. But he had done well for himself, he told Michael proudly; in course of time he had risen to be a journeyman employed by a sign-painter in Hoop Alley, off Shoe Lane, but his master had taken to gin and the business had been ruined. So Jen had what he called "spoken with a famble, tattle and popps at the nest of a rumbo ken", that is, he had stolen a ring, a watch and a pair of pistols from the shop of a pawnbroker, had been caught in the act by a "cony fumble" or constable, and in due time would be tried and sentenced to death. He was a repulsive-looking creature, his face covered all over with warts, but despite the harsh treatment meted out to him by fate he had never lost an innate kindliness. He took Michael under his protection and initiated him into the mysteries of Newgate life, showing him how to lie in his fetters with the minimum of discomfort, how to drink upon score at the boozing-kens in the yard, how to get the better of the greedy turnkeys, and the correct method of killing bed-bugs. He showed a curious delicacy in refraining from asking Michael's personal history, except the story of his arrest, in which he showed an avid interest. Michael quickly conceived an affection for the poor creature; Jen was a kind of fallen Maralyn, able to "manage" in the most daunting circumstances and never without resourcefulness.

On the day of his arrest, while he was being taken to the magistrate in Tom Fields' coach, Michael had borrowed the tablets of his old friend and enemy, and had written a short note to Mr Vance, a note Tom had promised to deliver in person. In this letter Michael had explained briefly what had occurred, and had begged the brewer not to seek to communicate with him nor to ask questions about him, lest Vance should be questioned or his family otherwise inconvenienced. He had concluded by thanking his master for all past kindnesses, and by bidding him forget that ever they had met. Having discharged this duty, Michael had no occasion to avail himself of Jen's instructions as to how to get letters smuggled in and out of the prison.

But although he had no letters to write, no visitors to see, no will to make, no personal affairs to set in order, Michael knew that he should be busy during the brief remainder of his life upon earth. For the first time for thirty years he had leisure, and he knew that he ought to use it for the last time on behalf of the cause for which he had lived and for which he soon must die. He had written his pamphlets at night after the day's business of earning his bread; now he could write them all day long, for he could get pen and paper and no one cared how he employed himself here. True, he knew no way of getting such writings to Derrick without incriminating the printer, but he could circulate them among his fellow-prisoners and their friends. He had written consistently for the benefit of the common people, and here he was in the midst of such people at the nadir of their fortunes, when, no longer preoccupied with buying and selling, but desperate, ruined men, they might well listen to his message.

But he could not write, he could not preach. His mind, long trained to concentration, to an ignoring of environment, now refused to rouse itself, and his will could not master the varying moods which fell upon him. He would sit for hours in a booz-ing-ken, not drinking, not hearing the cheerful uproar which enveloped him on every hand, but hearing instead, vivid and dominant, the cawing of the rooks above the bathing-pool at his old home, the jolly clatter of the stable-yard when a hawking-party was assembling on a frosty morning. He smelt bonfire smoke and the cold cleanliness of a dairy; he saw the glint of armour upon panelled walls, the soft light of candles glimmering in silver and old glass; his nostrils would fill suddenly with the scent of gillyflowers and lime-trees; and sometimes, so vivid that he could see each detail of it, there would float before his eyes a vision of the Stone Gallery at Whitehall, with its noble pictures and its windows looking out upon the river, and its whispering courtiers clustering round the door to the privy stair as they waited for the King to come.

Then sometimes, chiefly at night when he reclined upon the lousy mattress in his cell, with the noise of restless, fettered limbs on every hand, the stink of indescribable filth permeating him, the low roof seeming to press him down, he would know stark, physical fear. Hanging, and not just hanging by the neck until he died. That was indeed a slow and painful death, but swift and merciful in comparison with the one which awaited him. To be cut down after the first dreadful choking, to lie stripped upon the scaffold in full view of the gloating crowds, and to see the hangman advance upon his defenceless body with the ripping-hook and quartering-knife. The sweat poured down his face at the mere thought; how would he react to the reality? Would he be able to prevent himself from screaming, from resisting, from altogether disgracing his manhood and the cause for which he suffered? Was he physically capable now, at fifty-six, of making a decent end of it in such circumstances?

So the tortured weeks went by, with no gleam of consolation anywhere, with his will flaccid beneath a weight of intolerable weariness, with his mind shadowed beneath the knowledge of the hideous death which awaited him, with his body fettered and fretting to be free.

(ii)

His trial took place on the second day of the Sessions.

The court-house stood upon the southern side of the prison, a large, gloomy building, set back from Great Old Bailey in a large open space. Neither Michael nor any of his fellow-prisoners was considered important enough to merit the presence of a High Court Judge, and no great official of the Crown appeared to prosecute. Upon the Bench sat the Lord Mayor and his Aldermen, the two Sheriffs and the Recorder, all very resplendent in their robes. The Lord Mayor was sniffing hard at an orange stuck with cloves, for his nervousness of jail-fever was notorious. The prosecution was in charge of three Old Bailey attorneys, who glanced at Michael in a bored sort of fashion and went on whispering among themselves about the South Sea business. The jury, too, seemed to find him quite uninteresting, and the Clerk of Arraigns read out the indictment in so hurried a manner that Michael could not catch a word of it. He pleaded Not Guilty to the charge of High Treason, and the Clerk proceeded to his task of calling the Crown witnesses. In Michael's case there was only one, and it was with infinite relief that he discovered that one to be Tom Fields, and not, as he had half feared, Moll. In a monotonous voice, and carefully keeping his eyes turned from the huge, rosemary-garnished dock, Tom described his search of the prisoner's room, his finding of the treasonable papers, which he had handed to the proper authorities, and then, very briefly, he described his early association with Michael. Having been thanked, he bowed, and withdrew. Prisoners on charges of treason were not allowed counsel and could not call witnesses, but were called upon to make their own defence, and this Michael was now ordered to do.

He started to speak with some eagerness, for he had hoped that he would have here his last opportunity for stating his convictions in public, but after the first few sentences the judges began an agitated whispering, and almost immediately the Lord Mayor ordered the prisoner to be silent because what he said was treason and insulted the Court. He was then asked whether or no the papers found in his possession had been written by him, to which he replied in the affirmative, and was told that he was a brazen, hardened criminal and could hope for no mercy. An effort was made to induce him to declare the name and whereabouts of his printer, and when he refused, point-blank, the jury were bidden to retire and consider their verdict. The foreman rose, however, and stated that they were already agreed upon a verdict, and that they found the prisoner Guilty. Michael was immediately hustled out of the dock; as he passed into the covered passage which connected the Sessions House with the prison, he heard the Clerk's voice intone the indictment of a woman accused of stealing a cotton counterpane.

On the last day of the Sessions he was led back to the Justice Hall, and placed in the dock in company with five others. The Recorder was waiting to pronounce sentence against these, the capital convicts. Each was asked in turn if he had anything to say why sentence of death should not be passed upon him; two tried to justify themselves, one poor woman sank on her knees and begged to be transported; the others, including Michael, remained silent. Sentence of death was pronounced against the five, the turnkey slipping a piece of whipcord over their thumbs and tightening it as the judge pronounced the words "Until you are dead, dead, dead"; he was about to do the same for Michael, but realising in time that this was a dis-embowelling business put the string back into his pocket, and glanced at the prisoner with an air of faint reproach.

Michael and his fellow-sufferers were led back to the prison and put into the Condemned Hold. This was a semi-dungeon beneath the gate; the entrance to it was a heavy door protected at the top by iron spikes, which served as a grate through which friends of the condemned could speak with them. This entrance was set within the Lodge, which formed the taproom of the prison and which gave on to the main door on the south side of Newgate Street. A tiny, heavily barred window, high up in the wall, looked upon the street within the archway of the gate, and the place was so dark that a candle was required at noonday. There was a fireplace, a table, some stools and an excreting-tub; for beds there were only trusses of filthy straw.

The condemned were fettered from the moment of their sentence until the morning of their execution, but they were allowed cards and dice, and if they had money they could buy as much drink as they wanted from the turnkeys; and their friends, for a "garnish" of eighteenpence, were free to visit them.

On his first evening in the Condemned Hold, Michael received a visit from the Ordinary. It transpired that this good man was anxious not only to bring the prisoner to repentance, but to induce him to write his Last Dying Speech and Confession. He assured Michael that there was no hope of a reprieve, for the Recorder's "dead warrant" had been received by Mr Pitt, the Governor, authorising the execution to take place on Monday, the seventh of January. The Ordinary then continued with admirable candour:

"You must know, sir, that it is my privilege to publish such speeches after I have trimmed them up to a tolerable decency, and indeed a great part of my income is derived from such publication. I hope, therefore, that you will oblige me in the matter, and I do assure you I will make an excellent speech for you out of anything you will scribble down for me, complete with all the best sentiments and proper expressions of penitence; and if you will be so good as to begin the business now, while you have yet some time to spend in the Stone Jug, you may read the finished article for yourself, since it is customary to have such speeches printed ready for distribution by the book-women upon the March to Tyburn."

Michael stared at him for a second. Then, to the Ordinary's indignation and astonishment, he burst into a shout of laughter. It was the first time he had laughed since he had entered Newgate, and it did him a great deal of good.

Also it gave him an idea. He would write a Last Dying Speech and Confession, but it should not be "trimmed up" by the Ordinary, nor should it enable that gentleman to make an honest penny. He, Michael Montague, would write down, for the last time, a profession of faith; he would sum up all his principles and beliefs and condense them into one last tract; and even if it should never get into print, never reach the hands

357

of those for whom he had written all his tracts and pamphlets, at least it would serve to strengthen him for the ordeal at Tyburn, clear his mind of fear and unnerving memories and a vain craving for liberty, and fix his thoughts on that for which he died. Having made this resolution, he found that Fortune had interested herself once more on his behalf. The very next morning a woman came into the Lodge, put down eighteenpence on the table, and was escorted by the turnkey to the grate. She waited until the man had gone away, and then, beckoning Michael to come close, uttered in a low voice the one word:

"Derrick."

Michael opened his lips to speak, but she gave him no time. "I am passing as your cousin, and you will refer to me as that when next we meet, for I must come again. When next I come, you must have something ready for me to carry away. A mutual acquaintance desires to have this something that he may print it. Do you understand?"

He smiled broadly upon her. (She was a plain creature with protruding teeth and a drab complexion.)

"You come in good time, Cousin. I was even now pondering upon the writing of that which you desire. I am rejoiced to learn that our mutual acquaintance continues in—good health and spirits. Pray present my service to him, and say I am infinitely obliged that he will do me this favour."

"I shall be here a week from today," said the woman shortly, "and you must be sure to have the paper ready for me."

Then, with a murmur of farewell, she turned and walked out of the Lodge.

It was too late to begin his work that night, for the candle was removed at eight o'clock when the visitors were turned out and the great gate closed; but as he lay sleepless in his straw he set upon preparing his mind for this last task which lay before him. The dreariness and dryness which had tortured him since his imprisonment was pricked now with thin shafts of light and vitality. They were killing him, they were stopping his mouth, they had not let him speak even at his trial, but he would speak after death, and he would trust in the justice of God to make men listen, if only a few, if only for a moment, if only out of curiosity. The result of their listening was not his business any longer, for when he had preached that last sermon his work on earth was done.

On the following morning, just as he was about to buy paper and ink from the turnkey, he was sent for by the Governor. Mr Pitt informed him, in a very kindly manner, that he had good news for him; an order had been sent from the Secretary of State to the Attorney-General signifying that the clemency of His Majesty had moved him to commute Michael Montague's sentence from drawing, hanging and quartering to one of plain hanging, and this order had just been handed to the Governor. William Pitt offered his congratulations with sincere heartiness; not many years before, he had been in disgrace with the authorities for allowing the escape of a Jacobite prisoner, and although at the subsequent enquiry he had been found innocent of connivance, it was suspected by all that he had a certain sympathy with the "honest party". Michael thanked him for his congratulations, and asked if he might be permitted to write a letter to Tom Fields, since he guessed that it was through the kindly efforts of the latter that this commutation had been brought about. Receiving the necessary permission, he wrote Tom a letter of gratitude; then returned to the Condemned Hold to write that which was far more important to him. Indeed, so obsessed was he now with this last task of his that he was scarcely conscious of relief from the knowledge that he need not steel himself to endure the full and awful sentence of treason.

All day and every day during the next week Michael laboured at his tract. No one interfered with him or seemed curious about what he was doing. His fellows in the Condemned Hold relieved the hideous boredom by throwing the dice or playing cards or exchanging bawdy stories or writing their Last Dying Speeches or exchanging jests with the turnkeys or baiting the Ordinary, who came daily to help them prepare their souls. The most important person among them was a highwayman, a certain "Captain" John Scott, otherwise known as Pearl Johnny because he had always shown a preference for that species of booty. It was his delight to boast that he had relieved half the ladies of London of their pearls, which at this date formed the favourite article of jewellery. One particularly large pearl ear-ring found upon his person at his arrest he claimed to have taken from the Princess of Wales at church, though nobody outside his circle of admirers really believed this story. At all events, he was notorious enough to make a certain number of the gentry brave the horrors of the Condemned Hold to gape at him, and a pupil of the great Thornhill came to paint his portrait. Pearl Johnny drove this poor artist away with threats and curses, saying that only Thornhill himself was worthy of the honour.

Forcing his senses to ignore the uproar and the filth around him, driving from his mind all thought of himself and of his personal affairs, Michael wrote doggedly, wrote and rewrote, erased, corrected, tore up, day after day. He felt no inspira-tion; emotion was still numb, and the mere writing an intoler-able effort.

(iii)

The Christmas of that year was the most melancholy London had ever known.

For the ruin which followed the pricking of the South Sea Bubble spread far and wide, and suicide, madness, penury, exile, followed in its trail. There was scarce a family in the cities of London and Westminster who had not suffered from the disaster; hundreds of little tradesmen put up their shutters, scores upon scores of the new rich saw their wealth melt away like snow, hordes of hungry men and women roamed the streets, begging and robbing, the leading goldsmiths and bankers fled the country, and the only trades which flourished were those of the pawnbroker and the retailer of spirits. Crowds mobbed the lobbies of the House of Commons demanding the persons of the Directors that they might tear them in pieces, but were given instead fervent assurances of a legal vengeance. A mood of hopeless resignation succeeded the first fury; all day long, and far into the night, Michael in the Condemned Hold heard the footsteps and the moanings of the common people, of those people whom he had never ceased to warn but who had steadily refused to listen, footsteps no longer brisk and cheerful, no longer feverishly restless, voices no longer chattering of unearned wealth or yelling for vengeance, but beaten, despairing, helpless, bewildered, anxious only for the obtaining of the next meal, for a roof to shelter them, for the bare necessities in comparison with which just government and liberty and independence can seem very little things. He raged to hear that dull defeated note, because he knew that in such a mood a nation will sell its birthright to the first man who offers it a mess of pottage.

On Saturday, two days before his execution, the strange woman came again and collected his Last Dying Speech and Confession. She brought no message from Derrick, but Michael did not doubt that the printer would keep his promise to publish it. Derrick always had kept his side of the bargain, and since he had been clever enough to prevent himself from being involved in his author's ruin, it was obvious he would find the means of distributing Michael's final tract without hazard to himself. Michael watched the woman walk away with his manuscripts secreted in her petticoat; then turned to the business of preparing his soul for death.

On Sunday morning he was taken with the other occupants of the Condemned Hold into the Chapel, which was situated in the south-east angle of the jail. They were herded into a special pew which contained the facsimile of a coffin, and which was set immediately below the pulpit. Behind were two sets of pens, those on the right for the male convicts and those on the left for the female, each pen being enclosed with partitions of wood and iron and surmounted by sharp spikes. On the day of a "Condemned Sermon" a great crowd of visitors thronged to the Chapel, and these were accommodated in galleries. After the service, the friends of the condemned were allowed to visit them for the last time at the grate in the Condemned Hold, and on this occasion the presence of Pearl Johnny attracted quite a number of the quality thither, gentlemen questioning him eagerly about his exploits, and ladies pressing gifts upon him, of fruit and sweetmeats and fine handkerchiefs. Michael was watching this scene and reflecting that the impudent rogue is always popular, let him be a politician or a tobyman, when he heard someone speak his name, and turning quickly he saw, standing at the other corner of the grate, the figure of Maralyn Moray.

The shock of seeing her in such a place and at such a moment was so great that he could scarce give her a greeting. She on the other hand looked quite composed, though perhaps a trifle pale; she was wearing her hooded cloak and had a basket upon her arm as usual. She said quietly and steadily, without forced cheerfulness:

"Good morning, Mr Pennington. I am come to bring you the things which you will need tomorrow. I thought you would not be able to come by them otherwise. My father knows and approves of my coming; and he bade me bring you his love."

He felt uncontrollable tears start to his eyes. As he did not speak, Maralyn took her basket from her arm, propped it against the grate, and uncovered it; then she produced from it a white cap with black ribbons, a prayer-book, and a little nose-gay made from artificial flowers.

"I made the cap myself," she said, still quite natural and easy; "you will find it of service at Tyburn to draw down over your eyes. And the prayer-book, of course. I——" She hesitated, and for the first time a hint of embarrassment crept into her manner. "I understand that you are a—a Papist, Mr Pennington, but I am sure you will not refuse to carry this book in your hand in the cart, for I do assure you 'tis the universal custom, and only—only decent. I am so sorry that the season of the year makes it impossible for me to bring real flowers in your nosegay, but I hope this little trifle will serve to stick in your coat. There is somewhat else which is customary since the Revolution, and that is an orange to carry in the hand, but I have not brought that for you, for you see I did not think that you would desire to carry such a thing."

He looked at her with a twisted smile, and said gently:

"No, Mistress Maralyn, I would not have desired to carry the symbol of the Glorious Revolution, for you must know that

362

I am a most hardened Jacobite. But for the rest—I do accept them with my heart's gratitude."

There was a moment's silence between them (the hum of talk went on around them, intermixed with tears and jests and laughter as the condemned bade farewell to their friends and Pearl Johnny boasted of his robberies). Then Maralyn dropped her eyes and said quickly:

"I shall be at Tyburn tomorrow, Mr Pennington, and I will try if I can get upon the wall of the Hyde Park that I may wave my hand to you before you are turned off."

He managed to say steadily:

"I thank you, mistress, from my soul I thank you, but I would prefer that you did not come. I do not think you ever relished such sights, and the crowd will be rough and troublesome."

"You have no friends in London," she said doggedly, "or so my father believes. You cannot come to Tyburn without a friend to lift a hand in farewell. I know that you are dying for something which you believe good and true, and maybe you think that your zeal will sustain you without human aid in that last dreadful moment. But you see, I have seen many folk die, Mr Pennington, some of them by violence, and always I have found that on the—the doorstep of Eternity a human being needs some human comfort. You will forgive me if I seem to presume, but I know 'tis my duty to come to Tyburn on the morrow."

It seemed to him that in those last words she summed up the *motif* of her whole life. She, like her father, was dedicated to craftsmanship, but hers was the oldest craft in the world, to minister to the sick, the dying, the insane, to make a passing easier with some friendly gesture, to bring children into the world and help old folk out of it, to make a house run smoothly, to wrestle for a sick man's life with common sense and homely remedies, to tend pots of flowers upon a window-ledge, to mend a broken toy, and to befriend a condemned criminal upon his last ignoble journey. And thinking thus he knew that while England had her Maralyns there would be craftsmanship and service, and that where there are these things there is at least a link with liberty.

363

(iv)

Michael could not sleep on this the last night of his life, though his final work was accomplished and he had conquered fear. Nor was it the filth and horror of his surroundings that kept him wakeful, for he had grown used to these. He was weary enough to have slept despite the groans and the clink of fetters, and the loud intoning of the sexton of St Sepulchre's, who, ringing a handbell, stood outside the window of the Condemned Hold and recited, in a voice made husky by a very bad cold, the customary exhortation:

> "You prisoners that are within
> After wickedness and sin,

after many mercies shown, you are now appointed to die tomorrow in the forenoon. Therefore give ear and understand that tomorrow morning the greatest bell of St Sepulchre's shall toll for you in the form and manner of a passing-bell, to the end that all good people, hearing that bell, and knowing that it is for you going to your death, may be stirred up heartily to—to—*atishoo!*— to pray to God to bestow His grace and mercy on you whilst you live. I beseech you, for Jesus Christ His sake, to keep this night in watching and prayer, to the salvation of your souls, while there is time and place for mercy. . . ."

It was his encounter with Maralyn that kept Michael from sleeping, and all the thoughts that encounter had engendered in his mind.

She had given him, quietly and unemotionally, an account of the affairs of her family. It seemed that Nat not only had been utterly ruined by the bursting of the South Sea Bubble, but had suffered during that calamity two more crushing because more intimate blows. For he had discovered that the block of shares in which he had invested everything he had, had belonged in reality to Sir Frank, and that Maynard had sold them to him just after that astute man had got wind of the coming calamity. Moreover, Susan Vance had been Maynard's accomplice in this hoax, and had deserted her husband in favour of her old lover immediately the disaster of the South Sea Company had become public. Young Alec, going early to his master's office next day, had discovered Nat's body lying across the handsome desk in the banker's private office, though whether the unfortunate man had died by his own hand, or from shock, no one could say. Alec, shaken by the tragedy, had taken over Michael's old post of clerk to his grandfather, having sickened, at least for the time, of banking. Mr Vance himself had weathered the universal storm, although many of his customers had been involved in the South Sea ruin and the bad debts upon his books must prove formidable. Maralyn had gone on to describe, simply yet graphically, how her father had raged when she had apprised him of his indebtedness to Mr Bunch, but how, next day, he had invited his old crony to dine with him, had produced a great tankard of beer which he had brewed secretly the night before, rifling Maralyn's store-cupboard for the hops, and had presented it sheepishly to Bunch. In the end, added Maralyn, both the old men were pledging each other most lovingly, Vance in beer and Bunch in ale.

There was much comfort for Michael in these things. His sturdy old master was keeping his neck above water at least; a silly feud was laid by, and henceforth ale-brewer and beer-brewer would fight shoulder to shoulder against the real alien, gin; young Alec had learnt his lesson in time; an honest citizen's household had not been involved in the disgrace of the Jacobite it had befriended; and as for the tragedy of Nat, it had been inevitable from the beginning. There was, too, a more personal comfort to be drawn from Maralyn's visit. While father and daughter did not pretend to understand the doctrine he had preached to them and their like for so many years, while they still accepted the old catchwords against it, yet they were so far from spurning the preacher that the one had sent him his love in the Condemned Hold, and the other was determined to befriend him even at the gallows' foot.

It was still dark when, on Black Monday morning, the occupants of the Condemned Hold were carried by the turnkeys to the Chapel to hear prayers and receive the Sacrament. Michael, being a Catholic, refused to receive Communion administered according to the rites of the Church of England, and so shocked was the Ordinary by such a brazen display of Popery that, after wrestling in vain for this poor wretch's soul, he drove Michael back to the Condemned Hold while he dispensed the Lord's Supper to the rest of the dismal flock. Breakfast followed, and such of the condemned who could afford it called for a last measure of gin. At nine o'clock they were taken down to the Stone Hall, where the Deputy Sheriff awaited to make a formal demand to the Governor for the persons of the condemned. After receiving the customary receipt, Mr Pitt handed his prisoners over, and they were lined up for the offices of a journeyman smith who was waiting, with block and hammer, to knock off their fetters. There were two women in the company, one of them so fuddled with gin that she had to be held up by the turnkeys, the other a respectable-looking old dame, who told Michael in an undertone, while they were waiting in the line, that she was a staymaker by trade, that she had been seduced into putting her savings into the Company for Selling Bibles to the Indians and, being reduced to penury, had taken to shoplifting. She was so thankful, she said, that she was to be hanged and not burned; it was not considered decent to hang a woman, but the authorities had decided that burnings, which attracted enormous crowds at Smithfield, must be suspended for the present in view of the unsettled state of the City. She had but two anxieties: one that the Barber-Surgeons would steal her corpse for dissection, and the other that the mob would prove troublesome. You could never tell beforehand, she explained, the temper of a Tyburn mob; sometimes it was kindly and forced the constables to cut the condemned down quickly, sometimes it was brutal and pelted them with stones. And she did so trust that Mr Banks, the hangman, knew his job; he had been at it only three years and had already bungled once.

"And you must know that I am not heavy in my person, sir, and they tell me lightweights suffer the most grievous at the hands of Jack Ketch. Darby Doll yonder has weighted her gown with stones but I had not the means to obtain any such things."

When the leg-fetters and handcuffs or "darbies" had been knocked off, an official called the Knight of the Halter stepped forward and bound around the breast of each of the condemned the rope which was to hang him, these ropes being carried hither by a Sheriff's officer in a bag. Their elbows were pinioned to their sides, but their hands left free. Such as wore a periwig had that article removed, since it would impede the final adjusting of the halter. During all these ceremonies, Pearl Johnny continued to boast and to jest and to issue his orders. He was to have a cart to himself, he said, for he was not to be demeaned by riding in the company of Jacobites and footpads; his cart was to have a space kept behind it, because he had engaged some honest men, his acquaintance, to follow after it in the capacity of mourners, all with black hat-bands and crape upon their sleeves. He was to be allowed so much time for the last recital of his exploits and the people kept quiet to hear him. Room was to be made later for his corpse to be carried, as previously arranged, in a hearse to the Barley Mow in Long Acre, where it would lie in state, with six great candles burning round it and half the quality in London coming to pay their last respects. A noted sculptor, it seemed, had begged the honour of taking an impression for a death-mask; "and by the by, Mr Ordinary," he concluded, "you may say a psalm if you please, and I will endeavour to bear a bob with you, but let it not be any of your penitential psalms." So he ran on; and his fellow-wretches, no less than the turnkeys, hung upon the words of the picturesque rogue.

When all was ready, the condemned were taken down into the Press Yard and so through the Lodge into the street. Here, in a clear space ringed by a company of Foot Guards, a procession was formed. The City Marshal rode first on his richly caparisoned horse, with his peace-officers behind him; next came the Deputy Sheriff's coach, and then, surrounded by constables, the two open tumbrils which would convey the condemned. The first was driven by one Richard Arnet, the hangman's assistant; the second, driven by Mr Banks the hangman, was reserved for Pearl Johnny and the Ordinary. In those days it was not etiquette for the hangman to enter the prison, and

Pearl Johnny, encountering Mr Banks for the first time, saluted him with all due ceremony and hoped that he would perform his function with proper decency and respect. To this Mr Banks replied that if he failed in these particulars, he trusted that Captain Scott would mention the matter afterwards, when he would have pleasure in performing the ceremony a second time to the highwayman's instructions.

Behind the second cart came Johnny's hearse and his "mourners", and bringing up the rear were some javelin-men and a posse of constables on horseback. The tumbrils had neither backs nor seats, and the condemned had either to sit down on the floor or stand up, supporting themselves by clinging to the tall sides. Michael chose the latter attitude because he desired to see London for the last time, the London whither he had come so reluctantly in early manhood, the London in which all his maturity had been spent, the London which had been his chosen sphere of work, the London which soon would see the end of him and would receive his body into a poor-hole. Looking on this London now, in the dark January morning, from the hangman's cart, on the road to death, he knew that he loved her, that, countryman though he was, he was glad to end his life in her. Perhaps he did not understand her, though he had tried to do so through thirty years. Certainly she did not understand him, and felt little interest in him, all her attention being concentrated on a picturesque highwayman. But in the smell of her, the feel of her, the sight of her, the sound of her, here at her worst, under winter skies and in her most mobbish aspect, he loved her and desired her good, and knew that if ever hereafter his spirit would yearn to roam, the place of its haunting would be London City.

This was the start of the March to Tyburn, and it was not without its spectators, who today had come to cheer themselves up from the black depression engendered by the bursting of the South Sea Bubble. The hanging-days in the calendar were holidays, and even here, so far from the gallows, the constables had to push back the crowd so that the City Marshal might lead his dismal procession across the space where Giltspur Street joined Newgate Street to the porch of St Sepulchre's, where the first halt was made. The bell in the tall tower was booming high over the heads of the concourse, and the sexton with his hand bell stood upon the wall and snuffled out his last exhortation; but his "Lord have mercy on you, Christ have mercy on you", was drowned in the shrill clamour of a bevy of young maidens who, with nosegays in their hands, assembled here by ancient custom for the macabre pleasure of bestowing a kiss on the cheeks of the condemned. There was almost a free fight on this occasion, as the eager damsels pushed and jostled for the privilege of saluting Captain John Scott.

They bore to the left down the steep slopes of Snow Hill and crossed the Fleet river. In the ascent of Holborn Hill, the constables began to press in more closely round the tumbrils, for the way was wider here and attempts at rescue were not unknown. The crowd was increasing every moment and figures even clung precariously to the chimneys of the tall houses. It was the same crowd who flocked yearly to St Bartholomew's Fair, who surged to Hockley-in-the-Hole to see a bear-baiting, who devoured the famous plum-cake at Islington Spa on Sundays, who gathered to gape at the Crown Jewels in the Tower, who lately had herded to 'Change, to buy South Sea stock in a frenzy of credulity, to sell South Sea stock in a panic of disillusionment. Mingling with the rowdy chairmen and porters and 'prentices and watermen were respectable citizens and their wives and children; the fathers wore their Sunday broadcloth, the mothers carried baskets of food and drink, the children rode hobby-horses and sucked oranges and blew penny whistles. These people looked at Michael, but their glance did not linger; he was but a poor, unknown Jacobite, and they had seen many of his kind hanged in the last twenty years. The sight of the day was Captain John Scott in his buckskin breeches and his bright green coat and his white stockings, a huge nosegay in his hand; he stood in the cart bowing from side to side in a most gracious and condescending manner, and greeting friends and calling out jests. The mob applauded him, for it adored a man who went to his death in this manner. Upon those who displayed fear or self-pity it had no mercy, and when the gin-sodden woman felon, recovering somewhat in the fresh air, began to whimper, it jeered at her and began to pelt her with refuse and dead cats.

And Michael looked upon the crowd and was tormented by a last doubt. He knew the weaknesses of these people, how slow they were to learn, how difficult to arouse, how permeated by local snobberies, how preoccupied with trade and petty feuds, how prone to disregard oppression or merely to grumble cheerfully until it was too late, how ready to accept without question the propaganda of a victorious party; he knew the depths of their credulity, the extent of their inertia, the toughness of their dangerous patience. Was it possible, then, that such a people would ever pause to think, would ever learn the lessons of history, would ever realise their own strength, would ever unite to demand just government? He did not know the answer to these vital questions, and because he did not know that answer, and was honest enough to admit his ignorance of it, he was racked by the worst mental agony of his life here, as he rode to his death. He had conquered all fears for himself; he knew now that if the friendship of Tom Fields had not rescued him from the horrors of the quartering-knife he could have faced that most dreadful sentence with equanimity. As for what remained, the choking clutch of the rope, the suffocating agony which must last, he knew, for as long as half an hour, these presented no terrors, for he had realised once and for all, during the sleepless hours of the long night which had just ended, the strength of his own convictions and the worth of that for which he died. But because, even now, his faith in the common sense and justice of the people was not absolute, he knew no peace on this his last journey.

The procession passed slowly by the New Turnstile and came to St Giles, where a second halt was made, for at a certain tavern here it was customary to present to the condemned the "hanging-cup" or "last bowl". Most of the felons called eagerly for gin, but Michael asked for a can of ale, and as he did so he heard a voice beside him make the same request. He turned quickly, and for the first time became aware that the poor little creature called Jen was riding beside him in the cart.

"No such poison as gin for me," said Jen sturdily. "Had not

the diddle-shops ruined my master I would not now be going to the Deadly Nevergreen. Here's your health, gossip, and may we meet again in the next world. I am well assured that if there be painting of signboards to be done up yonder I shall get me some honest work, for I am a skilled man at my trade, d'ye see? And I reckon the Lord, being Himself a master-craftsman, can find employment for the likes of me."

As Jen said those words, Michael saw a kind of vision.

He saw a gallery of signboards swinging in the wind, signboards innumerable for craftsmen innumerable, little craftsmen working for themselves and enjoying the fruits of their labour. He saw the red lattices of small taverns and behind those lattices the same craftsmen drinking cans of English ale and beer, and grumbling and gossiping, telling stories and singing songs. He saw old Nathaniel Vance trotting around his odorous domain, trailing an expert finger in a fermenting-vat, and bending over his mash-tun until he could see through the pungent steam a reflection of his own red face, and calling out to his journeyman to tip in another sack of malt that his customers might have good ale for their money as the old song said. He heard the cheerful clatter of pots and pans and heard a woman's frail voice singing a rousing ballad in praise of Sir John Barleycorn. He saw millions of skilful fingers making casks and watches and coats and chairs, workworn fingers proud and useful, busy at a craft learned patiently and thoroughly through many years of apprenticeship. He smelt fog and new ale and lavender and meat sizzling on a spit, he heard the splash of oars on a river and raucous voices bawling the street cries, and the rumble of iron wheels and the clatter of chairmen's feet, and the voices of London's bells.

He saw, too, the darker side to this dear picture, he saw the signboards of the pawnbroker, the goldsmith and the gin-retailer thickly interspersed among those of honest craftsmen; mingling with the scents of ale and meat he smelt the stink of spirits and the corrupt odour of gold. But he knew at last, beyond all doubting, that these latter things would pass while the others would remain or return; that the heart of England was sound; that common sense and honesty and decent living and spiritual liberty and the sacredness of property and love of independence were so strong in her that, as she had survived, though only narrowly, the ruin lately wrought in her by the rule of money, so would she survive whatever further tyranny awaited her at the hands of her new alien masters.

(v)

Maralyn sat upon the wall of the Hyde Park and stared upon the vast concourse which surged beneath her.

She was facing the great gallows, a triangular erection surmounted by three cross-bars upon each of which seven bodies could hang side by side. Upon the other side of the Triple Tree was a large grandstand, packed with the quality, whose custom it was to attend executions and give the rabble a sight of the latest fashions. The Oxford Road, up which the procession would climb to the gallows, was open upon its northern side, beyond which the pleasant country extended through Marylebone Fields to Hampstead, with the spire of Hampstead Church pricking up on the horizon. A company of Foot Guards formed a cordon round the gibbet, keeping a clear space for the carts.

Maralyn was cold and tired. She had set out from Cheapside very early, because she knew the crowd would be great. Her father had not offered to accompany her, for in the present precarious state of his business he could not afford to take a day's holiday, and she had refused the company of one of the apprentices. She felt depressed, and stared upon the mob with distaste and apprehension, though plainly it had forgotten for the moment the miseries of the South Sea disaster and was in a jolly mood. It had indulged in one of its favourite pleasantries today, that of digging holes in the ground surrounding the gallows, covering them with grass, and watching unwary folk fall into them. As usual it had come well armed with missiles, which could be used either for an unpopular victim or for the Deputy Sheriff and his men. It was busy at the moment buying itself nuts and oranges and gin from the barrows, and in mentally devouring the fraudulent Last Dying Speeches and, even more enticing, the copies of letters purported to have been written by the condemned to their wives and sweethearts upon the eve of execution.

When at last the procession came in sight, the mob forgot everything else at the sight of Captain John Scott in his green coat and buckskin breeches. But Maralyn frowned upon him. She hated the swaggering highwayman and his hired troop of mourners, his cheap bravado and the acclamations accorded him by the silly mob. He and his like were a menace to honest craftsmanship, and the applause disgraced respectable London. No one acclaimed Mr Pennington, though he had never robbed anybody and had worked hard at her father's desk for thirty years. Of course it was right that he should die, she told herself hastily; he was a Jack, a declared rebel, and a Papist to boot. He was very probably a Jesuit. In any case, he was pledged to bring in the Pretender, plunge the nation into civil war, fetch over the Irish to cut all Protestant throats, and enslave England to the Pope. It was comforting to know that he had been apprehended before he could achieve this horrible programme. But he had always been so kind, and had worked so hard, and he did believe, so sincerely, in his mistaken ideals, and he stood there so quiet and dignified in the cart, saying his prayers, she supposed, though she was sorry to see that he seemed to pay no attention to the Ordinary, who plainly was conjuring him to declare himself repentant.

She watched him steadily, forgetful of all else. The Ordinary was offering up a final benediction, and distinctly she saw Michael make the sign of the Cross. Oh, horrible! he was dying a Papist. Somehow she had hoped that in the end he would lay by such wicked superstition. Now he was putting out a hand to steady a poor female felon who was struggling with the hangman come to adjust her halter. The woman seized his hand and clung to it as though she found comfort in his grip. The Ordinary had disappeared from the cart now, and the hangman was throwing the ends of the halters to his assistant who sat astride the cross-beam above. The crowd was yelling and laughing and applauding the highwayman who was engaged in drawing over his eyes a fine cambric cap. A group was haggling with the hangman's assistant, offering him a shilling an inch for the rope which would hang Pearl Johnny, and a party of his friends was conducting a hot argument for the clothes of the highwayman with Mr Banks, whose lawful perquisites they were. Now the hangman had advanced to his horse's head and had the animal by the bridle ready to lead him forward at a sign from the Deputy Sheriff. The uproar died to utter silence as the fatal moment approached; and in that silence Maralyn heard with an indescribable thrill a familiar voice upraised for the last time on earth:

"God save King James the Third!"

The cry seemed to echo through the open country all around. Then, as the cart moved forward and six bodies danced and dangled in space, the mighty roar of the crowd, ferocious, exultant, pitiful, excited to the pitch of frenzy, drowned it and filled the world with hideous discord. She had forgotten to wave to him; tears started to her eyes at the thought. But then she saw that the hangman had neglected to draw down the cap over his eyes, and lifting her hand she waved frantically. He was alive; his slight figure turned from side to side upon the rope; there were no friends to pull at his legs in an effort to shorten his sufferings. He was at the end of the row of grotesquely dancing figures, and it seemed to her most queerly that he looked like a signpost pointing whither she did not know, but urgently, faithfully, eternally directing her upon some mysterious road. She knew that he saw her, and that in his death-agony he sent her some last wordless message. She felt it thrill across to her upon the space between them.

Years ago she had gone to comfort Nick Hammond upon the road to death, and he who had needed her all his life had felt no need of her at the end of it. But Michael Pennington needed her even while he swung upon Tyburn-tree, needed something other than the things she had to give, material comfort and womanly pity and timid friendship. What could it be, this mysterious something that only she could give him? She could do nothing for his corpse; the Barber-Surgeons would claim that for dissection, she supposed. As for his soul, it was not her business; she really could not imagine what became of the souls of hardened Papists. Certainly they could not be received into that Place of harps and white robes and endless alleluias whither all good Protestants went; but neither could she picture them in Hell, burning in slow fire, pitchforked by devils. And then, with a superstitious shudder, she had the feeling that the soul of Michael Pennington was standing by her side. So vivid was this impression that she glanced sharply over her shoulder; but she saw nothing save an eager ring of faces craning to get a good view of the end of Pearl Johnny, who, in a last gesture of bravado, was kicking off his shoes.

She got down stiffly from the wall and began to push her way through the crowd. It was high time to go home, for a free fight was developing round the gallows; the friends of Pearl Johnny, probably hoping to resuscitate the half-hanged highwayman, were threatening to burn the coach of the Deputy Sheriff because he had refused to give the signal for cutting the body down. Besides, she had done what she had set out to do, and she must hurry home to get her father's dinner. Someone thrust a paper into her hand as she squeezed her way through the crowd; she took it, because she would only be pestered if she refused, but it was rather curious, she thought, that she had been asked no money for it. She did not like to throw it down; it was possible that the hawker might pursue her for the price of it, or it might be Captain Scott's last speech, and if she threw it away the mob might round upon her, particularly as its temper was already aroused.

So she held it in her hand as she hurried towards the City, and only when she had come within those sacred liberties did she pluck up courage to glance at the mysterious paper. Then she saw that it purported to be *The Last Dying Speech and Confession of Michael Montague, Gent*. That would be Master Pennington; she remembered to have heard that his real name was Montague. The *Speech* would be fraudulent; such things nearly always were. But why had she been asked no money for it? And why had she still this curious, eerie feeling that the man she had known as Michael Pennington was at her side, trying to convey to her some last message, begging—yes, she was sure of it—begging her to read the paper in her hand? She was very tired and had not broken her fast that morning; perhaps she was light-headed. She would feel better after she had dined. And there were many homely tasks awaiting her at home; somehow it would be good to cook and wash the dishes and clean the pewter and lend a hand in the brewhouse; it was always pleasant to do these things, but today it would be especially so. The daily round, the common task, these duties prevented one from—well, from thinking about things which were not one's business. And there was Alec's coat to patch; he had ripped it on a nail yesterday, and he had no other.

During the remainder of that day she was very quiet and preoccupied, and sat sewing all the afternoon. When supper-time came, her father asked her anxiously was she ailing, but she answered No, she did very well. But after supper she said she was a little tired, and would go to bed early, and so went upstairs to her room, and for the first time in her life she locked the door as though she would hide some guilty secret. Then she lit a candle and sat down between the curtains of the bed, and drew from her bosom Michael Montague's last tract.

It would be treasonable and Jesuitical; she was prepared for that. It would tell her all kinds of things she did not want to know. It would force her to think upon "great matters" and public affairs; it would bring back uneasy memories, of Glencoe and Darien and of a peaceable English subject being arrested in the teeth of the Common Law. But in order to lay ghosts it is sometimes necessary to face them, and if you are to feel real conviction in the things you have been taught to believe in, you have just once, perhaps, to hear the other side, even if it is the side that espouses Popery and tyranny and the Pretender. Then, when you have heard it, quietly and fairly, you will find peace again, because you will see just how wicked and dangerous and false it is, and you can dismiss it from your mind for ever, and thank your God that He rescued England from slavery by giving her the Glorious Revolution.

So argued poor Maralyn Moray, sitting on her bed between the curtains, and preparing to face at last, deliberately, the lion of her secret thoughts. With fingers that shook a little, despite herself, she took up the dangerous paper and slowly, laboriously, began to spell it out.

(vi)

Nathaniel Vance awoke for a few moments in the small hours of next morning, and thought he saw candlelight stealing under his door from the room across the passage which was his daughter's, and that he heard the sound of someone sobbing. Then he told himself severely that he had imbibed too much the night before and was dreaming; and with this sensible explanation turned over and fell once more into the sleep of laborious men.

FINIS

AUTHOR'S NOTE

THE date at which this story closes was not by any means the end of the Great Gin Era. In 1721 the Government ordered the Westminster justices to investigate a disquieting rumour of certain blasphemy clubs being started in London; the justices, though they failed to unearth the clubs, took occasion to represent to the Government that the enormous increase in the number of spirit-shops was "the principal cause of the increase in our poor and of all the vice and debauchery among the inferior sort of people, as well as of the felonies and other disorders committed in and about this town" (*Order Book*, Westminster Sessions, Ap. 1721). This was the beginning of a campaign against gin, a campaign which the Government continued to ignore for as long as it dared. Fear of the Plague induced the Westminster justices to appoint a committee to consider sanitary nuisances, and the committee listed the gin-shops; a representation was made to the Secretary for War pointing out the evils of the exemption from quartering soldiers; the College of Physicians petitioned Parliament against spirituous liquors; the chairman of the Middlesex Bench inveighed against the evil in his charge to the Grand Jury: still the Government turned a deaf ear, though a report of 1725 declared that in one London parish every fifth house retailed gin. In 1728 the Grand Jury of Middlesex presented Geneva shops as a nuisance, and Parliament was compelled to take notice. Retailers were required to take out an excise licence, and a duty of two shillings a gallon was laid on compound spirits; but in 1733 the complaints of the landed interest got this Act repealed.

In January 1736 a report of a committee of the Middlesex Sessions showed that the evil had spread appallingly during the past ten years, and again a petition was presented to Parliament.

As a result, a Bill was forced through Parliament laying a duty of twenty shillings a gallon on spirits and compelling retailers to take out an annual licence of fifty pounds. The Bill was strenuously opposed, for it was pointed out that the loss to the revenue would be in the nature of seventy thousand pounds, and Pulteney prophesied that the "regulation will raise great disaffection to the present Government" (*Parliamentary History,* ix. p. 1039).

His fears were quickly justified. The common people, nurtured on gin from the beginning of the century, were not to be deprived of cheap intoxication. In seven years only three fifty-pound licences were taken out, and by 1743 the quantity of spirits sold in London had reached the astonishing figure of eight million gallons per annum (*London Life in the Eighteenth Century,* Dorothy George, p. 35). Gin was sold illicitly under cant names; riots broke out; and informers were murdered. In 1747 the compound distillers complained to Parliament of their financial hardships and were given leave to retail on taking out a five-pound licence, and the scandal became worse than ever. At last, in 1751, bombarded by petitions from the Corporation of London, the Westminster justices, and from the City Companies, Parliament was driven to pass an Act which did at least reduce the consumption of gin. The price of spirits was increased, distillers were forbidden to retail, and licences were granted only to those who had an ale-house licence.

Yet Madam Geneva was a hardy old dame, and it was not until her patrons, the landed interest, found the distilling trade less vital to them because of the high price of corn, that she showed signs of loosening the grip which she had held for so long upon the citizens of London. Even at the very end of the century, Dr Willan, in his *Reports on the Diseases in London,* wrote: "On comparing my own observations with the Bills of Mortality, I am convinced that considerably more than one-eighth of all the deaths that take place in persons above twenty years old, happen prematurely through excess in spirit-drinking."